Florence

To Dr. Singh
With Best Wishes
Mel.

I would like to thank everyone who helped and supported me during the writing of 'Florence', especially Fenney Musgrave, Nicola Whitehill and Rachel Parkinson. However my particular thanks must go to Dave Wood, without whom none of this would have been possible.

First published by NMBazaar 2009
ISBN: 978-0-9563182-3-7
www.bazaar.me.uk/NMBazaar
nmbazaar@bazaar.me.uk

Cover Illustration © Derek Colligan 2009
Book design © Dave Wood 2009
Typeset in Rockwell

Florence

J. M. Owen

Dedicated to
Moggie, Becky and Gareth

November 1918

The dayroom on Ward Four of the asylum was bathed in the spectral glow of gaslight and was relatively peaceful for once. The lunatics were always calmer towards evening. Most of them had been given their medication, which was basic, but served to calm them and they were starting to drift to the dormitories as their names were called by the warders. With a hundred distressed patients sharing the same ward there was always some disturbance, but the evenings were always the quietest time of the day.

The women lunatics were all dressed in the same shapeless blue cotton frock, which was covered by a full length white smock and they all wore the same heavy shoes that were locked onto their feet. With their hair scraped back and sewn into a severe plait they all looked identically plain and barely resembled women at all. Facially their features were alike too; they all had slack, brutalised faces and vacant eyes. Some had physical deformities as well as mental illness and very few had a full set of teeth. They seemed docile enough most of the time, but they had to be watched very carefully as their behaviour was quite unpredictable and violence could erupt without warning. They were well cared for in the asylum, but these were the women that society wanted to forget about.

However, there was one outstanding exception. Over by the fire sat a young girl. She couldn't have been more than seventeen and she was rocking gently back and forth in a large wooden rocking chair. She wore the same uniform as the other inmates, but on her it looked quite different. She was stunningly beautiful, with long ash blonde hair. Her features, unlike the others', had not yet been brutalised by the regime of the institution and the ugly uniform served rather to enhance her beauty than detract from it. She seemed unaware of her surroundings and huddled in an old shawl that the head warder had found for her, she simply rocked to and fro staring, unseeing, into the coals. She seemed to have withdrawn into herself, and set herself apart from the scene that was playing out around her. She was completely mute and during her time on the ward had never uttered a word; she lived in her own world within the nightmare of the asylum. Nothing seemed to touch her. Even when the other women fought around her, she completely ignored them and simply continued to rock backwards and forwards staring at the fire. They seemed to accept her withdrawal and rarely approached her.

However, this evening one of the lunatics shuffled over and started touching the girl's unusual blonde hair. It was tied back and sewn into a plait like the other women's hair, but the colour still intrigued them. Once, a patient attacked her and tried to rip her hair out at the roots. She said that she wanted to take it and keep it for herself. Fortunately the warders were on hand and intervened; they quickly pulled the lunatic off and disentangled the girl's hair from her fingers. Since then they had kept a close watch on her. They didn't want a repetition of the incident and the girl's hair seemed to intrigue them. However, the girl had become used to the lunatics' curiosity about her hair and hardly noticed it. Without taking her eyes off the fire, she distractedly brushed the woman's hand away. One of the warders noticed and rushed over and pulled the lunatic away.

'Aggie leave Mary alone! You've been told before not to touch her hair and if you do it again you'll be punished d'ya hear?' Aggie simply leered at the warder revealing two blackened teeth in an otherwise toothless opening, but she moved along quietly. The warder smiled her reassurance at the girl, who smiled wanly in returned and continued to rock backwards and forwards staring at the coals. The warder made sure Aggie had moved away before moving down the ward day room, she had plenty to do before lights out.

The young girl was a particular favourite with the warders. She was no trouble and had an air of vulnerability and mystery about her that intrigued them. They were also drawn to her fragile beauty. When she had been admitted to the ward she was pregnant, but the baby was subsequently still born. None of the staff knew anything about her; she was a complete mystery. On arrival on the ward she was dumb and had never uttered a word during the years that she had spent there. None of the staff knew where she came from or why she was in the asylum. However, it was quite obvious that she was unlike any of the inmates, with the possible exception of one other girl, Caroline, who was her only companion.

Chapter One

September 1976

'So,' Florence thought, 'it had come at last, as it did to everyone, the final chapter.' There was no feeling of the dramatic, in fact she felt numb and also a little grateful that she had been given a warning. She now had time to make some kind of reparation, as she had always intended she should. Inevitably the diagnosis was an ultimatum, supplying an opportunity for her to set the record straight. If it wasn't done in the next few months, then her truth would die with her.

She felt strangely self conscious, sitting in the consultant's rooms being informed that she was dying. How did one react in these circumstances? There was no prescribed code of conduct. Whilst composing herself and gathering her thoughts, she traced the outline of the gold tooled pattern on the green leather top of the consultant's desk with her finger. When she finally looked up she had to stop herself from laughing out loud. The consultant was observing her with obvious concern, his fingers forming a V on which he placed his lips in a thoughtful pose. However, someone had placed a bowl of late autumn flowers on a shelf behind his balding head, framing it like a maiden's garland crown. Florence thought he looked quite ridiculous and quickly dropped her eyes in case he saw the humour there and was offended, but then what was life if not a terrible ironic joke? When she finally dared look up again, he had moved his head slightly and no longer struck such a ridiculous pose.

'How long have I got?' she asked, 'I mean I know you can't tell me exactly, but, well there are things I want to do, things I need to clear up, you know...' She shrugged her shoulders as her sentence trailed off, unfinished.

'I know,' he smiled sympathetically, 'I can't say exactly, but at a guess a year, possibly a few months more. I would estimate that you'll have six months with a reasonable quality of life and then things will inevitably start to deteriorate. I can still offer surgery. There's a fifty-fifty chance it would be successful.'

She shook her head slowly not wanting to prolong the inevitable and strangely she felt prepared to die. Life could be such a terrible struggle and she was tired. She had felt like that since her husband Edward died. The only regret she had was leaving her children and her precious granddaughter.

'No doctor,' she replied at last, 'No, thank you, I want to enjoy the time I have left. I appreciate your frankness but I won't waste any more of your valuable time. Thank you for your kindness and for being so honest. I really do appreciate it.' With this, she bent to retrieve her handbag and gloves then rose to leave. He accompanied her to the door and opened it.

'You mustn't be afraid you know; I mean when the time comes, we will make sure that you are comfortable.'

She smiled up at him, 'I'm not afraid doctor, but thank you for your reassurance.'

Florence left the room and walked slowly along the wide Georgian corridor towards the exit. The light that filtered through the fanlight over the top of the door seemed to form a warm halo that crowned the end of the dark tunnel that was created by the hallway. As she opened the door, the warm autumn sunlight flooded in and she felt the life giving warmth of the sun on her face. It was strangely reassuring. This was to be her last autumn on this earth. How she had taken them all so much for granted. This would be a special autumn, she would make sure of that. However, she could never have imagined even in her wildest dreams just how special it was going to be.

Florence didn't feel like returning home immediately. She wanted to consider her new situation and try to accustom herself to the fact that she was dying. It wasn't news that you received every day and in spite of her outward appearance of calmness, inside she was feeling distinctly shocked. She decided to stroll through the surrounding streets and compose herself, turning out of Rodney Street she started to walk up the hill. On the opposite side of the road the magnificent Anglican Cathedral stood resplendent in the sunshine. Florence suspected that it was the last great English cathedral to be constructed in the Gothic style, the last in a long tradition of great cathedrals stretching back to the medieval period. Canterbury, Winchester, Gloucester, she had visited them all. They were quite awe inspiring and steeped in a history that seemed to have been absorbed by their very stones. Liverpool was an infant by comparison, but still an impressive infant. If it hadn't been such a beautiful day she would have been tempted to go inside and say a prayer, because she loved the calm and coolness of churches, she always had. They gave her such a feeling of relevance and joy. However, today she wanted to enjoy nature and life, so she continued up the hill.

This area of Liverpool had always intrigued her with its terraces of elegant Georgian houses. They were so graceful and well proportioned. Her mother told her that they had been built on the profits of the slave trade during the eighteenth century. As a young girl she recalled that no one had wanted these enormous houses and the area had declined into a kind of bed-sit land. Each of the huge rooms was occupied by an entire family, as often as not a black family. There seemed to be a certain irony in the fact that these great houses, which had been built with the profit from that obscene trade, were now inhabited by the possible descendants of the terrible cargo.

The area had a colourful history and it was now a kind hybrid neighbourhood of run down tenements and glorious mansions. Many of the houses had been bought by private investors, who had lovingly restored them to their former glory. Florence tried to peer in at the windows as she strolled along the street. They were set too high for her to see into the rooms, but some would frame a glorious cut glass chandelier, whilst others would have a piece of grubby net pinned across them. These signs indicated that many of the houses had been restored, but were still living cheek by jowl with their run down neighbours. She noticed with some pleasure that there were more chandeliers than grubby nets, which indicated that the area was slowly becoming gentrified. This pleased her; she had hated to see the elegant terraces decay through neglect.

Choosing the sunny side of the street, she walked along lost in her thoughts. If only Edward had been there to help her through this difficult time. They had been married for nearly forty years and sometimes she felt that he knew her better than she knew herself. Her thoughts turned to her family. They would have to be told as soon as possible. She wondered how they would take the news of her approaching death, especially her son Freddie. He always made her feel so guilty. She loved him and tried her best with him. It was hardly his fault that he was so like her father that he always brought out the worst in her. At the thought of her father she shuddered and suddenly felt cold. Her father, God forbid that she should ever have to face him again! How she hated and feared that man, however, with a supreme effort she managed to banish him from her thoughts; nonetheless, her peaceful mood was destroyed. She had enjoyed her time of quiet thought and solitude, but now it was time to return home to her family. She had to face the trauma of telling them her awful news. She would have to write to her daughter, Elizabeth, who was an ornithologist, at present working in the Orkney Islands, studying sea birds. Then there was Freddie, how would he take the news? However the one she couldn't really bear to upset was her granddaughter, Emmie. Poor Emmie, she would be so distressed, but the thought of Emmie, even a sad Emmie, always brought a smile to her lips. The thought of her granddaughter lightened her mood once more and she turned and walked towards the station.

Florence still lived in the Georgian style country residence, Chestnut Lodge, that had been built by her father in law's father at the end of the eighteenth century. It was a beautifully proportioned, light and airy house and she had always loved it. Her son Freddie was not interested in the house, his taste inclined more to the modern and he certainly didn't need the money.

Elizabeth, her daughter was childless and as an ornithologist worked away most of the time, so they had agreed amicably that the house would be left to her granddaughter, Emmie. It was not too big to live in and she would be left investments to help with the upkeep. Stupidly, in spite of the fact that she wouldn't be there to see it, Florence couldn't bear to think of the house being sold on her death. She didn't want it to go to strangers. Not yet anyway and she knew that Emmie, like her, loved the house and would try to keep it in the family.

Florence realised that she couldn't just write to her daughter with the news of her impending death, she would have to go and tell her face to face. The Orkney Islands was not Florence's first choice as a holiday destination, but she wanted to spend some time with her daughter before she died, so she would have to make the effort. Then she had to decide how she was going to tell Freddie and Emmie. Eventually she came to the conclusion that she would invite Freddie, Susan, his wife, and Emmie around to the house for a drink and tell them face to face, quickly. Then they could leave or stay, whatever suited them, and deal with their grief in their own way. The same feeling of absurdity that she had experienced in the doctor's consulting room overcame her again. Nothing in life prepared you for announcing your imminent death. Florence had always disliked scenes and overt displays of emotion; it was her Victorian upbringing she supposed. Well it couldn't be avoided; a straightforward approach was probably the best way to break her news.

Freddie, her only son, and his wife Susan were the first to arrive. She greeted them at the door and ushered them into the pale blue drawing room. Once they were settled and had been offered a drink, the doorbell rang again. Florence knew that it would be Emmie, her granddaughter and gratefully bustled off to answer the door, before Freddie started to question her. As she opened the door, Emmie greeted her with a hug and a questioning look, however, Florence took her coat and firmly ushered her into the drawing room to join her parents. She could see that they were all uneasy and rather puzzled by her summons, so she decided not to prolong their agony for one moment longer than she needed to. Once they were all settled she told them immediately what had transpired in the consultant's rooms. She explained that she was dying, that she had lung cancer and it was inoperable. A white lie perhaps, but she didn't want surgery and they would have insisted. She further explained that she had about a year to live.

She had no idea what their reactions would be, but they all reacted differently. Freddie was terribly upset and she was strangely touched. She hadn't expected such an emotional response from him and hadn't seen him cry like that since childhood. It was strange how she immediately reverted to her role as mother and comforted him as she had when he was a young boy. Susan sat quietly and respectfully, she was sorry, naturally, but not heartbroken as she had always had a slight problem with Florence. Emmie just looked pale and sad and drawn.

Eventually, Susan took Freddie home to lavish more comfort on him and Emmie stayed with her grandmother. They retired to the kitchen to prepare supper. Florence was grateful to Emmie who simply held her tight and fiercely whispered that she couldn't bear to think of life without her grandmother. Florence had hugged her back, but said nothing. She had had enough emotional upset for one day and was quite drained. Emmie instinctively knew this and nothing more was said about Florence's illness. They both moved around the kitchen, chatting about the food, which they were preparing, and occasionally touching each other affectionately as if for reassurance. Then they sat and ate their meal in companionable, yet emotionally charged, silence.

Chapter Two

Family dynamics are an inexplicable mystery. Mothers, fathers, sisters and brothers can hate each other with a blood chilling intensity, but let an outsider interfere or criticise and they will band together and attack the interloper like a pack of wolves. The dynamics in Emmie's family were no different from any other. There was no drama, no deep hatred or passionate love, just an indefinable tension that bubbled corrosively beneath the surface of their lives. Florence's relationship with her son, Freddie, had been flawed by her inability to love him unconditionally. She had a tendency to suddenly withdraw into herself, like a hermit crab taking refuge in its protective shell. Sometimes she would physically retreat into her room for days at a time; sometimes she just became silent and distracted. This retreat was accepted by her husband, Edward, without comment and he expected his family to accept it as well. However, whilst

Edward understood the reasons for her withdrawal, her children did not and in true Victorian style, he did not feel it was his place to enlighten them. Freddie suffered terribly from his mother's withdrawal and always felt that somehow it was his fault.

However, Florence's withdrawals never really affected Elizabeth, her only daughter. She asked very little of Florence emotionally. She was quite self contained and never felt that she had to win her mother's love. She accepted Florence's odd behaviour without comment, almost as if she, like Edward, understood. They were not close as mother and daughter; they almost existed as two planets with different orbits that now and then crossed. Elizabeth, however, was devoted to her father and their closeness seemed to compensate for any defect in her relationship with Florence.

Freddie grew up feeling resentful, as children do who are not loved completely. The undeserved guilt, with which he chastised himself, damaged Freddie and created an internal, emotional void that blighted his childhood and affected his relationships later in life. Susan, Freddie's wife, blamed Florence for his emotional insecurity and she tried to fill the void that existed within him, but she was largely unsuccessful.

Emmie, Freddie and Susan's only child and Florence's only grandchild, instinctively understood the complex relationship that existed between her parents and her grandmother. She learned early on in life to tip toe amongst the emotional debris that littered their lives and to recognise the signs of change or disharmony that would have been invisible to others. Like a chameleon she tailored her behaviour to suit the prevailing mood of the household. When one or other of her parents confided in her their disappointment or dislike of another family member, she learned not to comment or repeat what she had been told. She simply internalised it. This behaviour earned her the reputation of being mature and adult. She wasn't, she had simply learned a strategy for survival in the minefield that was her parent's marriage.

In her dealings with them she had learned to keep back a part of her true self, to maintain a self protective emotional distance. However, she had no such reserve in her relationship with her grandmother. Florence and Emmie had bonded almost at Emmie's birth and had always shared an easy, close, relationship. This closeness was compounded by the fact that Emmie had an almost uncanny physical resemblance to Florence. They were both small and slightly built and they were both very blonde with naturally curly hair, which they wore long. Of course, Florence's was now pure white and she wore it up in an elegant French pleat, but in her youth it had been the same colour as Emmie's. Unusually for natural blondes, they both had large, dark eyes and a rather tawny skin tone and they were physically very striking. Florence sometimes looked at Emmie and thought, rather guiltily, that she was more her daughter than Elizabeth had ever been.

Freddie and Susan's restrained relationship with her grandmother made Emmie cautious. She had always been aware of it and she never allowed her parents to realise how close she and Florence were. It was something she knew she had to do to protect her relationship with her grandmother. She knew instinctively that her father would resent their closeness, because it was something that he had craved all his life and had never achieved. Emmie could never quite put her finger on what it was that seemed to distort the relationship between her grandmother and her father. Her mother had told her about Florence's withdrawals when he was a child and how it affected him. However, Emmie knew it also had something to do with her father's tendency to control. He didn't seem to be able to stop himself interfering and trying to organise everyone's life. Her mother, Susan, had no objection to this and gave him all his own way. However, Florence was quite a different character, as was Emmie and she disliked being told what to do. Emmie noticed that when Freddie started 'suggesting', in his own dictatorial way, that Florence should do this or that, a shadow passed over her face and she seemed to shrink into herself, becoming almost immobile and completely passive until the moment passed and Freddie moved on to something else. Her father was blithely unaware of the effect that he had on his mother. He sometimes seemed a little piqued that she didn't accept his 'suggestions' with enthusiasm. He never seemed to be aware that it frightened Florence in some way.

Emmie loved her father, but it was a distant, appreciative, kind of love. She could never have flung her arms around his neck or kissed him spontaneously. She also knew instinctively that she couldn't allow him to take control of her life and she was equally aware that he fully intended that he should. As a consequence, she spent most of her adult life trying to tunnel out from under his control. Often this was to her own detriment, although she was reluctant to admit it. She often challenged his authority just for the sake of challenging it, even when she was aware that he was right. This came to a head when she started seeing boys. She had many unsuitable boyfriends, who she fully intended to stop seeing, until her father told her that she had to. This irritated her so much that she would begin to encourage the unsuitable young men and positively flaunt them in front of her father, just to make a point. This contrary behaviour often made her feel foolish and ashamed. It also had the distinct disadvantage of her having to spend unsatisfactory evenings in the company of men who she really disliked. However, she knew she had to battle for her independence and couldn't afford to give in to her father over anything. Once he perceived a chink in her armour she felt that all her hard won independence would be lost.

The only area of her life on which her father did successfully exercise his influence was that of her education. Freddie paid for his daughter to attend a prestigious private school and had plans for her professional future. He, himself, was an extremely successful barrister and he fully intended that Emmie should follow him into chambers. The fact that she showed no interest in the law did not deter him. Where her education was concerned, Emmie never tried to thwart her father. She had the good sense to take full advantage of her privileged education. She worked hard at school and was naturally bright. Unfortunately, her father was rather single minded in his determination that she should follow him to the Bar and he pushed and pushed for her to read law at university. He emphasised that it was a practical subject that would lead to a secure position as a professional woman. He took no account of what Emmie herself wanted to do, he had it all planned out. Emmie wanted to study literature and the arts and she tried to persuade her father to let her enrol on an arts degree, but he wouldn't listen. She realised that if she was not really committed to what she was studying she would lose interest and fail. Freddie pushed; Emmie resisted and then finally capitulated and accepted the place she had won at London University to read law.

Almost as soon as she had accepted, she knew she had made a terrible mistake. She didn't want to live in London. She didn't want to read law. She knew that she was doing it just to placate her father and she was resentful before she started. The whole exercise was a disaster. She did very little in the way of work because she found the law incredibly boring. Slowly she stopped attending lectures and tutorials. She fell behind with her course work and became a thorn in the side of her tutors. The result was that she failed her first year in a most spectacular style and got sent down. She wasn't proud of herself. In fact the whole experience left her feeling worthless and stupid. Her self esteem plummeted to zero and she didn't know which way to turn or what to do next.

She decided to move back to the north, but she couldn't face living with her parents again, so she rented a flat in the city, picked up with the unsuitable boyfriends and started to work in a designer dress shop. She was wounded by her failure and just wanted to find her way again. To be fair to Freddie he did help her out financially without a murmur, but both he and Susan were consumed with self pity at having produced such a stupid, selfish daughter. They seemed to think that she had failed simply to punish them in some way. On the other hand her grandmother, after the initial discussion about her future plans, just carried on as though nothing was the matter. She met the unsuitable boyfriends and made no comment. She visited the dress shop and even purchased several suits. She made Emmie feel normal, less of a failure and she succeeded in bolstering her failing self confidence. Emmie was supremely grateful.

Eventually, Emmie did find her feet, jettisoned the unsuitable boyfriends, left the dress shop and enrolled on a joint honours degree in Literature and Fine Arts at Liverpool University as a mature student. She simply blossomed, she loved the course, she worked hard, she never missed a lecture or a tutorial and she was well positioned for a first class degree at the end of her first year. Freddie and Susan were ecstatic. It wasn't a useful subject, but it was a degree and they could hold up their heads again with their friends. Florence was also secretly relieved, but acted as if it was just a natural progression. Again Emmie was profoundly grateful to her grandmother. Her kitchen had been an oasis of calm during the difficult years after the London debacle and it cemented their relationship forever.

Florence was always aware that Emmie was not as comfortable about her parent's complex relationship as they thought she was. She also realised that Emmie went to a lot of trouble to make sure that Freddie was not hurt by her close relationship with her grandmother. She was a sweet and tactful young woman and Florence did not want to add any more to her already considerable burden, however, it had to be Emmie who learned the truth about her past. Emmie would have to act as her cipher and explain what had happened to Freddie.

Florence had promised Edward that she would disclose everything to her eldest son before she died, but she knew she could never do it personally. She just couldn't face seeing his doubts. She couldn't face being judged by him. No matter how hard he tried to hide his feelings, she knew that he would be judgemental. It would be too much like facing her father again and she simply couldn't do it. Reluctantly she would have to guide Emmie to the truth and then she would have to rely on her sound judgement and sensitivity. Emmie would have to take over and decide what to do. Florence was simply too tired. She sincerely hoped that Emmie would understand and that she would not feel that Florence had given her too heavy a burden to carry, but she trusted her instincts which told her that Emmie would cope admirably with everything that she had to do. Most importantly she knew that Emmie would never judge her.

Her decision made, she sat down at her bureau, got out her writing materials and began a letter to Emmie. She would set the thing in motion. Where it would lead, she could not know, but she would have half kept her promise to Edward. Somehow she had to leave it to fate and before very long it would no longer matter to Florence. She could finally lay that burden down, or so she thought.

Chapter Three

'It's a bit of a mystery Mr. Bailey,' murmured the official whilst efficiently scrolling down the micro fiche and examining the yellowing aged documents stored on the film. 'You say you found this birth certificate amongst your late adopted mother's possessions and you have reason to believe it may be your original birth certificate?'

'Well, it certainly records the birth of someone born on my birthday, but I don't recognise the baby's name. However, if it is my original birth certificate the name would probably have been changed on adoption. Obviously I don't recognise the mother's name and there is no father recorded, so it's quite difficult to establish whether this is my birth certificate or not.'

'No, quite, mmm,' murmured the official whilst still scrutinising the micro fiche. 'Ah, just a moment, yes, here it is, the mother's file, Mary Davies, aged sixteen, address Granthall Asylum, male child, no father – but it can't be you.' She said, looking up and removing her reading glasses, 'I've found a copy of the birth certificate, but there's also a death certificate which records the baby's death. The baby was still born.'

'Oh dear, so the child named on this birth certificate died at birth?' The official nodded her assent. 'Well then it can't be mine, but why would my adopted mother have the birth certificate of a baby who was born on the same day as me, but was still born? It doesn't make any sense, yet it is too much of a coincidence for there to be no link at all between me and this child. Maybe the adoption agency gave her the wrong birth certificate?'

'It's certainly a possibility, although they are usually very thorough. There definitely wasn't another birth certificate amongst your mother's papers?'

'No, it was the only one, that's why I thought it must be mine.'

'Well there is one other explanation, there's a slight possibility that you might have been a surviving twin.'

'Well, yes that is a possibility, but then if that's so, where is the record of the other birth, the live birth and why didn't my mother have two birth certificates? No it certainly is a mystery, yet I feel instinctively that there is a link here.'

'I agree; it's quite odd. Still there's nothing more I can tell you. I'm really sorry that I can't help you any further, but these are the only records that we hold here. If I were you I would go to the social work department in the old asylum and see if they can give you any more information. It's a psychiatric hospital now, but they still hold some of the original files. They may be able to give you more details, although it's sometimes difficult to obtain information from their files as most of the children born in the asylum would have been illegitimate and the mothers often didn't want to be traced'

'What happened to this Mary Davies?'

'It says here she'd been committed to the asylum when she was pregnant. The diagnosis was moral insanity, but then she was suddenly discharged after two and a half years. There is no mention of a forwarding address.'

The gentleman looked thoughtful for a moment and then murmured, almost to himself, 'So there's no record of a death? She could still be alive?'

'Well yes,' admitted the official, 'it's certainly a

possibility; she would only be in her seventies even now. I wish you the best of luck Mr. Bailey with your search. I'm sorry that I can't be of more help.'

'On the contrary, you've been most kind. Thank you very much. I have to return to Canada in the next week, but I will certainly call in at the old asylum before I leave.' With that, Andrew Bailey smiled at the records clerk and left the office to continue his search.

As Katy swung her Mini into the driveway she was overcome as usual by the grandeur of the former asylum buildings. They had been converted into a modern psychiatric hospital now with open wards and unlocked doors. Nevertheless, they had lost none of their power to intimidate and frighten. The hospital was built on two sites which were dissected by a quiet road. Katy worked as an assistant social worker in Hampton Division. It was the oldest part of the original asylum and had been built in 1845. It was constructed of large stone blocks that had been quarried locally and with time these had acquired a blackened hue, which gave the building an even more threatening demeanour. The two side wings of this building contained the wards. Rather than prison bars, the windows of the wards were divided into small panes, which had made escape more difficult for the thousands of patients who had been contained there. The panes were like eyes, the unseeing eyes of past patients, mirroring the misery of their souls as they had looked out, yearning for freedom. They seemed to threaten and accuse Katy every time she drove up the approach to the hospital. At this time she often wondered about the patients who had been housed on those wards, imprisoned by their illness, many of them for their entire adult lives. Their misery and isolation even seemed to have been absorbed by the stones of the buildings and no matter how many attempts were made to modernise them, the past could not be eradicated and an air of sadness.

The older nurses remembered the bad old days when patients could be dangerously aggressive. Then they were locked away for their own safety and the safety and convenience of society. Thousands were certified insane and once they were admitted to the asylum, they quickly became institutionalised and very few returned to the outside world. Any kind of mental illness or physical deformity then referred to using terms such as, idiots, dwarfs, Mongols, spastics, could result in certification. Basically anyone that society found to be different could be certified insane and contained in the asylum, often for a life time. Katy had seen these terms used as diagnoses on case notes. They were terms that were now considered to be insulting and degrading, but in the late nineteenth century they were used as medical terms to diagnose various 'mental illnesses'. Inevitably the innocent were swept up with the genuinely disabled and mentally ill and the old hands told many a story of servant girls from the grand Liverpool houses getting 'into trouble' and being certified and forcibly admitted to the asylum. Neatly disposed of by their seducers their family would be paid handsomely for their silence and the girl would remain incarcerated until she died. Katy didn't know how true these stories were, for the nurses loved to shock her, but she imagined that there must be an element of truth in them. Pregnancy outside marriage, even as late as the nineteen thirties, was considered shocking and brought terrible shame on the families. Girls were often thrown out of the family home and disowned by outraged parents and had to turn to the workhouse or some other charitable institution just to survive. Katy had read about such places, how the women often had their heads shaved, were made to wear a uniform and work in the laundries and kitchens of the institutions. They were treated like fallen women, when in all probability they had only yielded to a moment's temptation with some inexperienced local boy. Usually the girls were pressured to put the baby up for adoption. Without the support of a man they had no way of keeping the child and most succumbed to the pressure. It seemed like another world to her, yet it was only forty years ago. She thanked God that attitudes had changed.

As she was thinking about these poor girls she parked her car and made her way to the social work office. It was housed in what used to be a garden store of some kind. The entrance hall was built of brick and the offices were on the first floor, which was reached by a stone staircase. Her friends wondered why she chose to work in the old asylum; the reason was quite simple the job was the only training post she could get. Granthall was now a modern psychiatric hospital, but it had lost none of the mystery and terror that surrounded it when it had been a closed asylum. Then it had been hidden behind its high stone walls, tall trees and dense foliage. For years it was a secretive and inaccessible building and it became notorious as a place of terror and intrigue in the imagination of the local population. Katy remembered her own mother warning her and her brothers that they would drive her to Granthall if they didn't behave themselves. She had no real conception what 'Granthall' was, but knew it was a terrible place where mad people were locked up. She also remembered her mother pointing out some poor unfortunate to her aunt and whispering to her that 'she's just come out of Granthall' in shocked and frightened tones. It was a place of dread and fear and was talked about in hushed tones, much like its twin the workhouse. Strangely, although both types of institutions were transformed into NHS hospitals they never lost their fearsome reputations. Some of her friends actually thought that she was in danger of being attacked or worse by 'mad' men and women! She laughed at them and invited them to visit the hospital, but few accepted her invitation.

On reflection, when she first took up her post as an assistant social worker, she had not intended to stay at Granthall, but to use it as a stepping stone to a training post at one of the major teaching hospitals in Liverpool or Manchester. However, once she started to work there, she found that she enjoyed the job and in time the old buildings had seduced her with their sense of timeless mystery. She was in the unique position of witnessing, on one hand the development of modern psychiatric medicine, and on the other the decline of the old Victorian asylum system.

As she climbed to the top of the stairs in the social work office, she was greeted by her senior, Mrs. McKendrick, who handed her a pile of files to deliver to Windsor Division or The Annexe as everyone called it. Katy's senior was a tactless, insensitive woman who had been promoted beyond her capabilities and she was not very popular with her staff. Katy took the files, but had no intention of missing her early morning cup of coffee before she set out to deliver them. Mrs. McKendrick scowled as Katy took the files into the social workers' office, but she didn't say anything.

The two definable parts of the hospital had quite different strategies and goals. The patients in Hampton Division were mainly short stay patients who were admitted for no longer than six weeks. During that time they were cared for, stabilised on their drugs and then discharged. Katy was responsible for two wards in Hampton Division and attended regular ward meetings where she was requested to help patients who were about to be discharged by finding them accommodation or employment. She also visited the discharged patients, when they were settled in their new accommodation, to make sure that they were taking their medication and coping with life outside the hospital. The patients on the Annexe, however, were approached in a completely different way. They were mainly long stay patients who had been admitted to Granthall when it was still an asylum and many had been there for decades. Some had been admitted in their twenties and were still patients there in their eighties. Katy was involved in a rehabilitation programme to try and involve the patients in life outside the hospital. At present she was trying to locate family members and persuade them to visit their long lost relatives. She loved this part of her job. The old ladies were so sweet and self effacing. Now on medication, there was no need for many of them to be in hospital, but it was the only home they had ever known. They were completely institutionalised and didn't want to leave. The National Health Service was treading a fine line between caring for these patients and transferring care to the community. Katy had her doubts about the latter, but realised that the days of the asylum were numbered. Once it was emptied it would probably be closed and the short stay patients would be treated in a unit in a general hospital.

As soon as she had finished her coffee, Katy set off for the Annexe with Mrs. McKendrick's files. It was a lovely autumn day so she decided to walk there. On the way up the drive she encountered some of the long stay patients who were taking the air. One, Bobo, was a giant of a man, at least six foot four in height. He was black, completely bald and completely toothless and spent his days wandering up and down the drive way. He waved and smiled his greeting to Katy as she passed. He was completely harmless, but she had been terrified the first time that she had encountered him. Apparently, so hospital myth had it, he had come off one of the ships that sailed into Liverpool from Africa and had become a prize fighter there. He'd lost his usefulness when he became 'punchy' and eventually ended up in Granthall sometime in the thirties. It may not have been true, but these stories were passed down until they were accepted as fact.

The drive was long and winding and Katy was enjoying the warm sunshine. She stopped at the crossing on the road that separated the two divisions of the hospital and while she was waiting for the lights to change she gazed at the porters' lodge, which was quite amazing. It looked like something out of a fairytale. The main house had a sloping roof, like a French chateau, and it had a little tower on the side with arrow slits for windows. It was a most improbable building, perhaps it was designed to look romantic so that people wouldn't suspect what lay at the end of the driveway? She didn't know, but it never failed to intrigue her. The lights changed and she walked over the crossing into the Annexe grounds. Some of the patients were out enjoying the sunshine and waved their greeting to her. As the drive veered to the right the hospital buildings came into sight. Built in 1876 to accommodate the overflow from the original asylum, they still impressed her, but they had completely overawed her the first time she saw them. The front offices seemed to resemble a French chateau and were crowned with an enormous clock tower that stretched up into the sky like Jack's beanstalk. All the dimensions of the building were enormous, with ceilings up to twenty feet high and doorways twelve or fourteen feet high and twice as wide. All the doors were fitted with massive iron locks and bolts, which were now left unlocked of course, but it was clear to anyone entering the building why they had once been necessary. The message sent out by this building was clear; the building was larger than any one individual and the building would defeat and break anyone who challenged its authority. Katy was always relieved, when she entered the building, to know that she was free to leave whenever she wished.

Behind the front offices ran a corridor which stretched for nearly a third of a mile. This was the main artery of the hospital and all the wards ran off it. Katy remembered the first time she had visited the building. Mrs. McKendrick had sent her over on her own late one November afternoon as the light was dying, to deliver a letter to the ward she was to be in charge of, Buttercup Ward. She should have known how terrifying the buildings would look to a young, inexperienced girl seeing them for the first time, but she had no imagination or sensitivity. It was tea time on the Annexe when Katy arrived and most of the staff were serving tea on the wards, so the building was deserted. Katy had entered the huge entrance hall with trepidation. The only sign of life was a lone patient mopping the floor in there and the only sound she could hear was the sound of her boot heels tapping on the tiled floor and reverberating around the hall. It was extremely eerie. She didn't know where to go so she had to ask the patient, who simply pointed to a doorway and continued with her mopping. Katy wondered why she wasn't having tea with the others and for a fleeting moment thought she might be a ghost, but she was real enough. It was so silent she was beginning to feel sick with fright. She tapped her way over to the doorway and entered a smaller hallway which led to the corridor. The massive oak doors at the head of the corridor were left permanently ajar now, their locks and bolts rusted open, but they looked as if they could clang shut at any moment and trap an unsuspecting girl forever. As she started down the corridor, Katy imagined what it must have been like to have been brought to the asylum for the first time as an inmate. The silence was oppressive, the dark domed roof loomed overhead and stretched for miles, all they would hear would be their own footsteps and the warder's keys jangling at her belt. Perhaps a lone patient would have screamed in the quiet evening gloom, while the gas jets would have cast threatening shadows on the walls. Katy shuddered. It must have been terrifying. You were alone and helpless facing who knew what? She had really frightened herself and had to keep reminding herself that she only worked there and was going home at five o'clock. Nevertheless, as she silently crept along the domed corridor she began to panic. It seemed to stretch for miles and be full of ghosts. She had to fight hard to stop herself from running down the remaining stretch to the ward. To quell her fear a little she tried to concentrate on the effort that someone had put into trying to modernise the corridor. They had decorated the walls and the ceiling with magnolia paint and placed troughs of plastic flowers and trailing ivy against the walls. Impressionist prints hung on the walls, but this attempt at modernisation had not worked. The corridor just looked grotesque, and was even more frightening in its absurdity. This corridor had been built to threaten and intimidate and no amount of modernisation was going to disguise that.

Katy could feel her heart hammering in her chest with fear and her legs were turning to jelly, but she carried on. As she passed the open ward doors she could hear the sound of jangling cutlery and the hum of conversation, which reassured her a little. After what seemed like an age she arrived at Buttercup Ward and turned into the entrance. She stood for a moment to examine the ward doors, which now stood open. They were huge oak doors with locks that would have looked at home in a castle dungeon. Why were they necessary? Suddenly a voice interrupted her thoughts.

'It's alright dear, we never lock them now! You're quite safe.'

Katy looked up to see a tall, rather handsome woman in the spotless uniform of a ward sister. Her iron grey hair was pulled back into a bun and topped with a lace trimmed cap. She was the model of efficiency and would have been quite terrifying if it hadn't been for her twinkling brown eyes.

'Oh hello sister, I'm Katy Molyneux, the new assistant social worker and Mrs. McKendrick asked me to bring this letter over.' As she held it out, Katy noticed that her hand was shaking slightly.

'On your own? At this time of night? And she didn't think to bring you over first and introduce you to me or the building or the ward? Oh, I'm Sister Parkinson by the way.' She smiled and held out her hand, Katy took it. 'No doubt the corridor scared you to death at this time of night? Yes, well you wouldn't be the first. You get used to it in time, but even then it can be daunting on a dim November evening. You look a little shaken dear. What you need is a nice hot cup of tea and a chocolate biscuit.'

Katy smiled as she remembered that first meeting with Sister Parkinson. They had become firm friends since then. She and her ladies, as she called her patients, had become favourites of Katy's. Sister Parkinson had been at the hospital for years and Katy loved listening to her stories. It was together with her that she was working on the patient's files to collect a list of possible relatives who may visit the ladies on Buttercup Ward. The corridor held no fears for her now, she was used to it, but she had never forgiven Mrs. McKendrick for what she had done that day.

Chapter Four

Emmie had been up most of the night struggling with an essay on Modernism. It was impossible, no one seemed to know what it was or what it did and apparently that was the whole point of it. It was there to confuse. It had certainly achieved its aim with Emmie. She had gone to bed confused and she had woken up confused, tired, frustrated and in need of coffee and paracetamol, but at least she'd made a start on the essay and written a few coherent pages.

She shuffled into the kitchen and put the kettle on whilst she tried to locate the cafetiere in the cupboard. Good coffee was the one thing she never stinted on, even when a she was short of money. She found it at the back of the cupboard, heaped the coffee in and drowned it in boiling water. She left it to stand for a while, popped some wholemeal bread in the toaster and shuffled off down the hall way to collect her post. There was the usual mixture of bank statements, offers to lend her huge amounts of money and charity newsletters, but in amongst them was a small brown padded envelope addressed to her in Florence's handwriting. Intrigued, Emmie shuffled back to the kitchen and placed it on the table. She buttered her toast, poured her coffee and settled down to open it. The first thing she pulled out was a handwritten letter, which was quite a treat; she didn't seem to receive letters any more everyone just telephoned. 'Bless Gran, still stuck in the nineteenth century,' she thought.

The letter was short and to the point:

My Dear Emmie,

Forgive me for sending such a formal letter. I am writing to tell you that I've abandoned you for a while, I just felt I had to go somewhere on my own and collect my thoughts. I shan't be gone long and I'll be in touch. I'm quite sure that you, of all people, will understand that my recent news has left me with very mixed emotions and I need time to adjust to my new circumstances. I will have left when you receive this letter. I didn't tell you personally, as that would have involved giving explanations, and I simply wanted to go. However, I want to reassure you that I still love you very much and value your help and support. I have also written to inform your father that I've gone away, so I'm afraid I've left you to face him and explain, sorry!

I know I'm rather taking you for granted, but would you stay at Chestnut Lodge while I'm away and take care of it for me? I would be so grateful my dear. I have left some food for you and a little money for emergencies. I realise that it may not be possible for you to stay there all the time, but if you can't, would you just call in and check that everything is alright? It would ease my mind just to know that someone is keeping an eye on the house whilst I'm away.

I have another favour to ask of you. Under the bench in the boot room is a large, tin box. It contains some confidential papers together with family documents and photographs. I really can't face going through it, but I feel it needs sorting out. Would you do that for me? It would be such a help. I've enclosed the key to the box in with this letter.

Take care of yourself,

Lots of love,

Gran.

Emmie felt a stab of pain, poor Gran, of course she

would go and take care of Chestnut Lodge and sort her old box out for her. It was probably full of boring documents, but it would be fun to look at the old photographs. She could organise them and put them into an album so her grandmother could look through them with ease. It was so hard, it seemed every day that there was some reminder that Florence was dying and wouldn't be with them for much longer. It didn't bear thinking about. She put her hand back in the padded envelope and pulled out a roll of tissue paper. The key to the box was wrapped up in it. She imagined her grandmother had done this so she would find it easily, but there wasn't much chance that she would miss it, it was huge! She unwrapped it and put it on her key rack for safety.

Actually she was delighted to have the chance to stay at Chestnut Lodge. She loved the old house and it would be peaceful and quiet. She could get a considerable amount of work done while she was there. No one had her grandmother's telephone number except her parents, so she would be left alone to get on with some work. She read through the letter again and then tucked it into her dressing gown pocket and set about clearing the table. She was about to go and dress when the telephone rang.

'Emmie this is your father,' boomed a voice at the other end. It always tickled Emmie that her father felt it necessary to identify himself in this abrupt way. Didn't he think that she would recognise his voice after all these years? She smiled to herself as she replied.

'Hi Dad, how are you?'

'How am I? Out of my mind, that's how. Your grandmother has taken off on her own without telling anyone where she has gone and she's ill, anything could happen to her. What would people think if she died and her own family didn't know where she was?'

Emmie smiled to herself. Her father was always concerned about what people would think.

'Dad, she just wants time to be by herself. She's just had some fairly shattering news and she needs to adjust to the idea that she hasn't got long to live. By the way she's asked me to look after Chestnut Lodge while she's away.'

'Did she tell you where she's gone?'

'No Dad, I just received a letter this morning.'

'Oh right, just like us. Well, I don't know.'

He sounded hurt, like a bewildered boy who'd been abandoned. She tried to comfort him.

'Don't worry, I'm sure she'll be safe and she will have made plans for us to be contacted in the event of an emergency.'

'I suppose so. Well there's nothing to be done. Anyway I'm glad you'll be looking after the house. Is there anything you need?'

'No Dad, I'm sure not, but I will let you know if there is.'

With that they said their goodbyes and Emmie put the phone down. She decided that she would move into Chestnut Lodge straight away. Having made her decision, she went to her bedroom, packed a bag, collected some books together and got ready to leave. She knew that she could always come back and collect the rest of her things later.

Emmie let herself in at Chestnut Lodge using her own key and experienced a little thrill of excitement. She loved her grandmother's house, and liked the idea of being in sole charge for a while. It was also a treat to have some time to herself, hidden away from her friends. No one knew where she was as no one knew about her grandmother's house and she had no intention of telling them. Her father would no doubt call round, but that was only to be expected. He'd be trying to find out where her grandmother was, but he would only drop in now and then so she'd have plenty of time to herself.

She returned to the car for the bags of groceries that she had brought with her and carried them through the hall to the large kitchen at the back of the house. Her grandmother had left the Aga on before she left and Emmie was greeted by a wall of pine scented warmth as she entered the kitchen. It reminded her so much of her happy childhood. Both her grandparents had resisted any attempts to modernise the kitchen. The old pine Georgian cupboards, stripped bare of paint, were still in place, lovingly waxed and cherished by Florence and an army of dailies over the years. There was a huge pine dresser on one wall covered in a collection of blue and white china and a large pine table stood in the middle of the room. It was massive and could easily accommodate twelve people. Emmie discarded her bags on this table and went back to the car for her supply of wine. This she carried through to the kitchen and then she proceeded to unpack her bags. When she opened the cupboard doors she smiled to herself, her grandmother had left the cupboards well stocked, so she needn't have bought anything. Still, whilst she appreciated her grandmother's kindness, she liked to be independent.

When she had finished unpacking the food she put a bottle of wine in the fridge to cool and carried the rest of the bottles through to the boot room. She placed the wine in the old rack and then rooted under the benches for the document box mentioned in her grandmother's letter. She found it under a bench on the back wall and pulled it out. It was quite heavy and covered in dust, flakes of whitewash and bits of cobweb. It was an old fashioned, black, tin document box, the sort that solicitors used to keep wills and contracts in and it was probably as old as the house. Emmie fished the key out of her pocket, unlocked it and peered inside. It smelt musty and damp and was full of old books, papers and photographs. No one had disturbed it for years, but no doubt Gran wanted everything put in order before... Emmie's thoughts trailed away, she couldn't bear to think about the future without her beloved grandmother. She left the box pulled out and scrambled to her feet. She would light a fire in the little sitting room, prepare a meal and then return to the box. She was curious by nature and was looking forward to delving into the past, although she doubted there was anything in the box of any real interest.

Emmie returned to the kitchen, washed the dust and cobwebs off her hands and continued on into the pretty, pink and chintz sitting room off the kitchen. Her grandmother, in her typically considerate way, had left a fire laid. Emmie lit the paper then waited to make sure that it had caught and the fire had crackled into life before she returned to the kitchen to prepare her dinner. She had brought a pasta dish with her and simply popped it into the Aga and poured herself a glass of wine. However, she was too impatient to wait and her curiosity was getting the better of her, so she returned to the boot room and the tin box. The boot room was lit by a single 60 watt light bulb so it was difficult to see properly and she couldn't make out what was inside the box. She simply took pot luck and grabbed a bunch of black books bound together by string. These she took back into the kitchen where she wiped off most of the dust and cobwebs. They smelt musty, but were not damp at all. She flicked through them to let the air get to the pages. Emmie guessed that it was some years since they had been out of the box and she looked through the books as she ate her pasta at the kitchen table. They were diaries written at the end of the nineteenth century, well journals really. They belonged to her great grandmother, Martha Clayton, her grandmother's mother.

Emmie finished her meal and left the dishes in the sink to soak. She took her wine and settled down in the little sitting room by the now roaring coal fire to examine the journals more closely. At first she just leafed through them in a random fashion. Martha wrote in a beautiful copper plate hand that was a joy to read. She meticulously dated all her entries, but tended to talk about the details of her daily life, where she had been, what she had eaten and who she had spoken to. It was all fairly mundane stuff, but an interesting insight to the life of the times. Emmie was surprised at how boring her life was. Martha lived at home with her mother and brothers. What little education she had ceased at an early age, thirteen or so and she seemed to spend most of her time with her mother, calling on friends or receiving guests. Although her brothers were involved in the family printing business, Martha took no active part in it at all.

At first the journals didn't give her much of an insight into the real woman; Martha tended not to divulge her feelings or express any strong opinions in most of the entries, which Emmie found quite frustrating, until she stumbled on a section that was quite different in tone and content. It seemed as though Martha's bottled up emotions and controlled patience had suddenly over flowed; quite unexpectedly Martha started to pour out the feelings of frustration and misery that had been masked in her usual recording of daily events. It surprised Emmie, who hadn't detected any hint of frustration or unhappiness in any of the earlier entries. The event that made Martha break her own rules and pour out her feelings on paper, was that of her younger cousin's engagement party. Martha was now nearly twenty five years old and was considered to be past marriageable age by the women in her society. Some of those women were beginning to treat her with contempt. Apparently, to be unmarried by your mid twenties was the ultimate failure. It was a social sin and unmarried women were treated with a combination of sympathy and scorn. To Emmie, who was herself only twenty five, this seemed quite ridiculous, but marriage wasn't the focus of her life. She had her education and future career to keep her satisfied and happy. Martha had nothing, other than the task of snaring a husband, to occupy her time. She was obviously feeling sensitive about her single status at her cousin's engagement party. Her language amused Emmie. It was so formal, almost pompous.

Martha's Journal 3rd November 1894

Today has been one of the most humiliating days of my life. My cousin, Elizabeth, recently announced her engagement to a young man called Reginald Stanhope. Her father decided to hold a party in her honour and I and my family were invited as guests. Elizabeth is nineteen years old and very pretty. He is twenty two and a successful solicitor. He is also boring, narrow minded and physically unattractive. But no one minds that, because he is a man and considered to be eligible. Elizabeth has succeeded in capturing a husband so she is considered to be a great success. Unfortunately, the fact that Elizabeth has become engaged whilst only nineteen years old has only served to highlight the fact that at nearly twenty five years old I have never had a serious suitor. Society, it seems, now considers that I am too old and too plain to attract one. I am deemed a failure and people are starting to treat me like an old maid. They view me with a mixture of pity and contempt. They either patronise me or look at me sadly and sigh, as though I really haven't tried hard enough.

The sideways glances and sly nudges I observed today, made me feel sick. I am well aware of the reason why I am unmarried and Elizabeth is engaged. She is pretty and I am extremely plain. However, what I find so bewildering is that they seem to hold me personally responsible for my failure to find a husband. Do they think that I enjoy being plain and unwanted? They seem think that I've remained single out of some sense of perverseness. Poor Mama suffers even more than I do. She is still beautiful in middle age and has been used to admiration all her life. I know that it mortified her today that I was being treated with scorn, yet she is so kind and sympathetic. Not once has she ever made any reference to the fact that I have failed to attract a husband and I love her for it. Nevertheless, she can't protect me from society and I still suffer from the humiliation inflicted upon me.

I often sit and look at my face in the mirror and examine it. I try to identify what it is that makes it so plain. It is quite a nice face, I think. It isn't unpleasant or ugly and it only misses being beautiful by a fraction, but it is a very important fraction. The features that on my brothers are strong and handsome, on me are large and unattractive. My nose is too long, my chin and my jaw line are too square, and my teeth are too big, too white, and too strong. I have lovely, large, brown eyes that are fringed with long, dark, lashes and I have clear skin, which is white and flawless. However, my good points are over shadowed by my defects and the overall effect is of pure plainness.

I was born plain and I will die plain. It is my lot in life and there is nothing that I can do about it. I have to accept my fate and bear it with dignity. Oh, but sometimes it is so difficult. I like my cousin Elizabeth, she is sweet and gentle, but today I hated her because her success was emphasising my failure. Our society only values women as wives and mothers, any other attributes they may have are simply discounted. It makes me feel so bitter at times. I dread the future. Will I be the maiden aunt who cares for her elderly parents and is treated with contempt by the rest of the family? When my parents die will I have sufficient means to maintain my own home, or will I have to go and live with one of my brothers as a charity case, poor old Aunt Martha? I don't know, but I dread the future and my only crime is to have been born plain, it seems so terribly unfair.

Emmie realised that Martha was extremely fed up when she wrote this entry. It was riddled with an uncharacteristic self pity, yet there was an undeniable truthfulness in what she said. Emmie remembered her own contempt for the unmarried teachers at her school. Most of them were casualties of the First World War, when insufficient numbers of marriageable men had survived. This dearth of eligible young men forced large numbers of women to live out their lives as spinsters, unfulfilled and despised by society. Their misfortune, however, didn't elicit the sympathy of their arrogant sixteen year old pupils, only their scorn. Poor Martha, it must have been a relentless struggle every day to try and show that she didn't care when others were being cruel. People could be so malicious. Probably half of the women who were being unkind to Martha were trapped in a miserable marriage anyway. They probably wanted to make quite sure that no one escaped their fate.

People's perception of how they look can be completely different from the reality. After reading Martha's last entry, Emmie was curious to find out what she actually looked like. She thought there may be some photographs in the tin box so she left the warmth of the fire to go back to the boot cupboard and have another search in the box. She had left it pulled out so she just peered inside and managed to locate some old manila envelopes lurking in one corner. These she grasped and lifted out. Her random choice was rewarded, as one of the envelopes was full of photographs. She put the other envelopes back in the box, which she carefully locked this time and stowed back under the bench. She took the photographs back to the sitting room, collecting a tea towel from the kitchen on her way.

Once back in the sitting room she laid this on the carpet and emptied the contents of the envelope onto it. It contained a wide variety of photographs, but the ones that she was particularly interested in were the nineteenth century studio photographs. They were the ones that were most likely to contain an image of Martha. Emmie picked these out and examined them one by one, whilst pushing the rest of the photographs back into the envelope.

Here was photography in its infancy! All the shots were taken in the studio and the subjects were arranged by the photographer in a series of formal poses. They were usually standing or sitting in front of a painted backdrop. The photographer usually added props, often a heavily carved oak chair or a table holding an aspidistra plant. The subjects never seemed to smile; they all looked extremely serious and were usually encouraged to look away from the camera. They amused Emmie; they were like old painted portraits, stiff and unrealistic. She shuffled through them until she came upon one that looked as though it might be Martha. It was of a young woman standing by a table with one hand resting lightly upon it. She was standing straight backed and looking slightly away from the camera. Emmie turned it over and in amongst the photographer's ornate advertising label, someone had pencilled in the name, Martha Williams. This must have been her maiden name. Anyway, Emmie felt that it was reasonable to suppose it was a photograph of her great grandmother. It showed a girl of medium height with dark hair, which she wore up. She was well dressed and had a good figure, but there was no denying that she was plain. Emmie was amused at Martha's self-evaluation, it was amazingly perceptive. She did have lovely, almost alabaster skin and beautiful eyes, but they were over shadowed by a rather long nose and oversized mouth.

She gazed at the photograph for some time then

put it to one side. She was beginning to feel as though she knew this shadowy ancestor of hers quite well, especially now she could actually picture her. Suddenly she had this urge to learn as much as she could about Martha and she started to read through the rest of the journals. She flicked through a few more pages, but they were full of the same rather tedious details of Martha's daily life and she was beginning to give up hope of finding any other revealing entries.

Martha had married, Florence was her daughter. That meant that there must have been a husband and father, but Emmie had never heard anyone mention him. She realised that she didn't even know his name. She read on, impatient to find a reference to a possible suitor. Martha was nearly twenty five when she made the last reference to her single status. It seemed from that entry that she must have been approaching her late twenties when she met her future groom, but where was he? Emmie was beginning to feel drowsy, the wine and the warmth of the coal fire were lulling her to sleep, but she was determined to find out more about Martha's future and made herself soldier on. Eventually she was rewarded with an entry that mentioned a man called Josiah Clayton. Clayton, she knew, was Florence's maiden name so this must be him, the one that Martha married. She read on with great excitement.

10th January 1896

There was quite a stir in church today. We have a new member of the congregation. He is called Josiah Clayton and he has recently purchased The Old Rectory, on Archway Road. It is a large, gloomy house, which is far too big for a bachelor to live in alone. This has given rise to speculation that he is looking for a wife! A tall man, over six feet in height, he is considered to be very handsome with his thick, dark, glossy black hair and fine moustaches. My brothers know him and they say that he is also a very successful business man. He has his own furniture manufacturing company and a series of retail outlets which sell his goods directly to the general public. They seem to think that he is on the way to making a large fortune.

The local mothers with marriageable daughters are all very excited at the prospect of securing this wealthy man as a son in law. He is invited everywhere, so I hear, and is very popular with the young ladies. My brothers don't seem to think he is actually very sociable, but rather taciturn and seriously religious. I simply watch with curiosity at the intense interest that he has aroused in the female population hereabouts. I observe the fluttering of the young ladies, when he is about, in a rather amused, detached way. I know from past experience that I am not likely to arouse his interest in any way at all. However, I shall be interested to see who is successful in capturing his attention. Up to now he has remained determinedly unattached and quite neutral in bestowing his favours. It will be interesting to see who is successful in snaring the prey!

So, thought Emmie, great grandfather was considered quite a catch was he? So how did he come to marry Martha when he so obviously had his pick of the marriageable women?

She read on:

10th March 1896

I have noticed, just recently, that Josiah Clayton keeps seeking me out after church each week. At first I thought that I was imagining things, but it has been going on for some time now and I'm convinced that it is my company that he desires. It seems to be a deliberate strategy and I am at a loss to understand why he seems so determined to speak to me almost exclusively; I mean men like Josiah don't usually even notice my existence. Initially it occurred to me that maybe he joined our family group because he was friendly with my brothers and sought their company. I thought that he was simply talking to me out of politeness; however, I noticed that once he had greeted my parents and my brothers and enquired after their health, he directed all his comments and questions to me. I find it odd and rather disturbing. I have to say though that he seems singularly lacking in humour or wit.

His conversations with me are intriguing. He seems to be trying to gauge my attitudes on moral issues and he asks my opinions on a variety of subjects. He listens carefully to my responses and seems to weigh them vigilantly, as if assessing them for substance. For instance, he always questions me in detail about the sermon. I almost feel as if he is setting me a test. I do actually attend to the sermon as our preacher is an educated and intelligent man and I find them of great interest. Josiah always questions me closely after the service, as if he is trying to establish whether I have been paying attention. He also probes to find out whether or not I have fully understood the issues being addressed. I remember particularly the week when the subject of the sermon was obedience. Well that is a subject that most women are closely familiar with! He kept questioning me to see if I thought *that obedience was a superior trait. I told him that I felt it was absolutely necessary for the smooth running of society that one section of society should be obedient to another advanced section of society. I also told him that I felt it was essential for women to be obedient to men, as they were their superiors, particularly their husbands and fathers, and for servants to be obedient to their masters and that I fully agreed with everything that the preacher had said on the subject. He seemed well pleased with my response. He completely missed the irony, but I have noticed that Josiah does not understand humour of any kind. I am much puzzled by his attentions. As, I observe somewhat wryly, are my family!*

This entry showed a wittier, more confident side of Martha. She seemed to display a quiet sense of humour. She also had the sense to hide her humour behind irony. Josiah didn't seem to be a man who would appreciate wit. Josiah's behaviour towards Martha, as a suitor, was quite conventional for the time, if not a little lacking in imagination and affection; nevertheless it certainly looked from the entry in Martha's journal as if he were starting to pay court to her with serious intent. Emmie couldn't decide why, or even how, Martha felt about this special treatment. She was obviously surprised at his attention, but she described him in a fairly objective and impersonal way. She never at any time expressed any admiration for the man, or excitement at the prospect that he may find her attractive.

What did Josiah really look like? Emmie had another search amongst the photographs to see if there were any that might possibly be him. She came across a studio photograph of a couple, which looked a possibility. The woman was obviously Martha, although she was a little older than in the first photograph and she was with a tall, stern looking man. 'Oh dear,' thought Emmie, 'he's a bit scary.' He looked like an Old Testament patriarch. He was standing behind Martha, who was seated on a heavy, oak chair. He was tall, good looking in a rather military fashion and he sported magnificent moustaches. It was his eyes though that caught Emmie's attention. He was staring straight at the camera and she thought she had never seen such hard, flinty, unforgiving eyes in all her life; they were cold and devoid of expression. Also they were almost colourless, like the eyes of an albino. 'This was certainly not a fun man,' she thought, and she felt a chill run down her spine. Whilst it had to be admitted that he was good looking in the fashion of the day, it was in an oddly sexless way. She knew that this was rather an odd assumption to draw from a photograph, but that was how he seemed to her, unyielding, cold and sexless. As she scrutinised the photograph, she noticed a distinct physical resemblance to her father, Freddie. Of course you had to discount the moustaches and she really couldn't comment on her father's sex appeal, but there was a definite similarity. Freddie was the same build and colouring as his grandfather, but he hadn't inherited those terrible eyes. She searched the journals for more information about Josiah and she was rewarded with a detailed entry in March:

17th March 1896

As usual Josiah came over to talk to my family as we left the church and assembled outside. It was becoming the accepted norm that he would join our family group in the church yard after the morning service and for the first time in my life, to my increasing amusement, I am drawing envious looks from some of the young ladies of the congregation! Today, my brother Harold, who is an old friend of Josiah's, invited him to join us at home for luncheon and he accepted with alacrity. My parents don't seem to know what to make of the situation. They can't believe that their no longer young, rather plain, daughter is being courted by one of the town's most eligible bachelors and I'm sure that they suspect underhand motives. However, my brothers, in their usual fashion, don't seem to have noticed. Where I was a little mystified before, I am now even more perplexed. I am now sure that he is actively courting me, albeit in a practical and rather unconventional manner and I haven't yet really fathomed out why he has chosen me.

My mother sat Josiah next to me at the luncheon table, which gave me the opportunity of observing him at close quarters. He is, indeed, a good looking man with dark curly hair, fresh skin and strong white teeth, however, I'm not at all sure that I like his eyes; they are a strange shade of blue, a kind of icy blue that is almost colourless. They are cold eyes that never twinkle or glow and I feel that if he wished to, he could freeze your very soul with them. There are things about him that worry me slightly and make me rather wary. I have observed a certain rigidity in his character, he is very definite in his opinions, he doesn't respond well to argument or debate and he has a harsh unbending code of morality that doesn't allow for weakness in others. However, on the other hand he is intelligent and quite well educated; he can talk with some knowledge about a wide range of subjects. I would guess that he is a sober and clean living man and I'm sure that he is not a womaniser. So on balance he seems to be a good, sensible, responsible man who *is set in his ways and lacking somewhat in humour. However, there is something in him that I fear. I can't give a logical reason for that feeling. It is just an instinct. I think that he could be ruthless and cruel and what is more worrying, I don't think that he would recognise either of those powerful emotions for what they were. He would perhaps justify them to himself. In short, I do not think that he is a man to be crossed.*

Today was a fine, if somewhat chilly day and after luncheon, when we had finished our coffee, Josiah asked if I would care to take a turn around the garden. Although the family looked knowingly at one another as we rose to collect our outdoor coats, Josiah seemed to be unaware of their significant glances. We walked in the shrubbery, where the paths are well paved. He was considerate enough to realise that my boots would have become sodden on the lawn and chose the shrubbery to avoid my discomfort. He again asked me a number of probing questions about my Christian beliefs and my opinion on the subject of the family. I felt as though he was interviewing me for a position in his firm and maybe in some oblique way he was. We stayed out for over an hour, strolling through the shrubbery and talking, but the temperature dropped towards late afternoon and the light was fading, so he suggested that we retire indoors in case I started to feel the cold. The fact that he was solicitous about my well being impressed me. I learned quite a lot about Josiah today and much of that I have already chronicled. It is my belief that he is considering making me an offer of marriage. However, it would not be an offer based on affection or love; it would be based on practical considerations. Josiah has observed me, he has spoken to me and learned my views, he has met my family and knows that I come from a good, financially sound background and he will carefully weigh up all the options. Strangely, with this particular man, I think the fact that I am plain weighs in my favour. He distrusts beauty, he allies it with sin. However, I do not think that I should accept his offer lightly, although I doubtless will, as I am sure that it will be my last chance.

We went inside and having divested myself of my outdoor clothes, I joined my parents and brothers in the drawing room. Josiah came in to pay his respects and bade them goodbye. As I sat down and took up my work, my mother looked up from hers and asked if I had enjoyed my exercise. I said that I had. She smiled and commented on what a fine man Josiah was. I just nodded in a non committal way. I love my parents, but there is a terrible desperation in their desire to marry me off.

It would give my mother such pleasure to be able to turn to all those dreadfully unkind women who have made veiled criticisms of my single status and tell them that I had become engaged. I couldn't blame her for wanting to do that. My father too, could at last be proud of me. He could boast at his club about his daughter's advantageous engagement to the town's most eligible bachelor. Their desperation to have a married daughter is stopping them from looking closely at this man. They are assuming that marriage will be the one thing that will make me happy and to a degree they are right in that assumption. I don't want to live my life out as an old maid. However, I am patently aware that marriage to Josiah will not be easy. I know that it will be a cold, business like arrangement with no sentiment, warmth or love. If he asks for my hand I will have to accept. I couldn't upset my parents by refusing, but in my own eyes I will be entering into a marriage that will be a compromise at best and a nightmare at worst. Still he hasn't asked me yet and maybe he never will and maybe that would be a huge relief to me. Maybe.

The quiet pressure that was being exerted on Martha to marry amazed Emmie. To her as an independent, educated woman of the 1970s, it was quite incredible. She was beginning to like Martha, finding her humorous, down to earth, realistic and warm. She may have had a plain face, but she had a lovely warm personality that shone through her writings and she was extremely perceptive. Josiah may have been an eligible bachelor with a fortune, but Emmie felt from what Martha had written that he didn't deserve her and wouldn't appreciate or even notice her finer qualities. There was also the fact that Martha's insight had discerned something sinister in Josiah, something that was far from obvious. But Martha's instinct had alerted her to an indefinable threat. Emmie could only know Josiah through Martha's writing, but she was troubled by his eyes. She had only seen a photograph of Josiah, but there was something almost psychotic in those dead eyes.

It seemed almost inevitable that Josiah would ask for Martha's hand, as Emmie knew that they were the parents of her grandmother. She leafed through the journal until she found the relevant entry that announced the engagement. It was dated 15th December 1896. It seemed that Josiah wanted to get engaged just before Christmas, as that would make him and Martha the focus of attention during the festivities. She wondered if that was a deliberate ploy. She wondered about Josiah's background. Was he from an ordinary working class family or was he middle class? Martha never mentioned either his background or his family so it would remain a mystery.

30th December 1896

It has been accepted since the early summer that Josiah was my official suitor, much to everybody's surprise and some people's chagrin. We have been invited to parties and balls as a couple and it was obvious that people were expecting us eventually to announce our engagement. I was gratified in one sense that I had not been imagining his interest in me during those early months. It was clear that Josiah was not trifling with my affections, but that his intentions were serious. We spent a good deal of time together, but it was usually in the company of my family and we were rarely alone. I think that it is true to say that I knew Josiah no better at the end of our courtship than I did at the beginning. He was a difficult man to understand and I found it impossible to get really close to him. He would never open up and discuss his deeper feelings. At first I did try to find more out more about the way he thought, but eventually I gave up and simply accepted him as he was.

When he decided to ask for my hand he spoke to me first, to ask me whether or not I wished to marry him, which I did appreciate. I said that I would be honoured to be his wife and once he had my decision, he asked my father for my hand in marriage and permission to announce our engagement on Christmas Eve. My mother and father were very pleased, as were my brothers and they threw a party in our honour for all their friends. Everyone was so happy for us and we received some lovely engagement presents. Naturally Josiah spent the Christmas holidays at our home.

Whilst everyone has been very kind and obviously pleased that I was at last going to be married, no one has asked if it's what I want, everyone has taken it for granted that I am happy with the way that everything has turned

*out. They think that as a plain woman in her late twenties,
I have been extremely fortunate to have captured such an
eligible man and I know that I am. However, I am not entirely
happy with the situation. I come from a warm loving family
and I am used to giving and receiving love. That will not be
the case with Josiah. My marriage will be a rather cold one.
I know now that he chose me partly because he thought that
I would be extremely grateful that he had rescued me from
spinsterhood and because I was grateful, he felt that I would
naturally be obedient to his wishes. As I have stated before
in my journals, Josiah has a deep mistrust of beauty. He feels
that plainness is synonymous with purity and goodness. He is,
I suppose, a puritan at heart.*

Poor Martha, she had to accept society's limitations
and live up to its expectations without any reference
to her personal happiness. The awful thing was Emmie
thought, that there was no way out of marriage. It was
literally for life. If things were difficult, they simply
had to be endured. How dreadful then to be unsure at
the very beginning of your life together with another
person.

February 1897

*My father is so delighted with my engagement that he has
settled a generous sum of money on me. Naturally it will be
given straight to Josiah for the benefit of our future family and
not to me, for I may spend it at my dressmakers, or so my father
thinks! Josiah already has a house, the Old Rectory, which is
where we shall live. It is an impressive house with spacious
accommodation; it has five good bedrooms, a roomy sitting
room and a fine dining room. However, it is not what I would*

have chosen. It is a gloomy house, rather dark, with lots of heavy oak panelling and carving. It has a huge stained glass window at the top of the stairs that blocks out all the light from the hall and landing and seems to give it the air of a cathedral, but I suppose that is to be expected when it was designed for a rector by ecclesiastical architects. I naturally have not let my dismay show and have been most enthusiastic about it. The problem of the interior has been compounded by the furnishings, which were all chosen by Josiah when he was a bachelor. The furniture is dark oak and it is heavily carved.The soft furnishings, carpets and curtains are also in dark colours and they simply compound the dreariness of the interior. I had always dreamed of having a light Georgian house, decorated in pastel colours and furnished with delicate Hepplewhite furniture. In my dreams it would always be full of sunshine, love and affection; however I am afraid this is not to be.

Emmie was rather puzzled by this entry. She had always assumed that Chestnut Lodge was the family home, but of course it was, but on Grandfather Edward's side. Florence had only ever referred to this house as home and Emmie had always assumed that she had grown up here as it meant so much to her. She wondered about the other house. She couldn't recall anyone mentioning it. In fact, she couldn't remember anyone talking about Josiah at all or Martha's life with him. She knew that Martha had lived with Florence in Chestnut Lodge after her marriage and somewhat ironically, it was the house that Martha had described as her ideal, so she got her dream house in the end although by default.

The wine and the fire were getting the better of Emmie

so she decided to call it a day and go to bed. She carefully collected the journals and photographs together and put them out of sight in the bottom drawer of her grandmother's bureau. It wouldn't do to have Freddie snooping. Then she wearily went up to bed with her head full of Martha and her marriage.

Chapter Five

Finally Katy had a comprehensive list of her patients' relatives so she composed a standard letter to be sent to all of the addresses which she had collected from the patients' files. It explained that the patient had been in hospital for several decades and had lost touch with their family and friends and outlined the new hospital policy, which was to try to rehabilitate these women by organising visits for them. The letter also asked for any information that the recipient of the letter may have about the patient's family or any friends of the family. Doreen, the social work secretary, typed the letter out and then sent copies to all the addresses on the list. It was a laborious job and Katy wasn't sure what the response would be, but even if they only managed to locate ten family members who were prepared to visit, it would be worth the effort. She tried to imagine the reaction of the people who received one of her letters when they realised that they had a long lost relative in a psychiatric hospital. They would either be horrified or intrigued. She hoped it would be the latter and that curiosity would prompt them to visit the patient and maybe strike up some rapport.

The weather was still fine, so she decided to walk over to the Annexe and let Sister Parkinson know that all of the letters had gone out. She also wanted to discuss with her the cases that she had extracted from the main body of files, particularly Caroline Spencer's. Her file and the others that she had put to one side didn't seem to fit the general profile, their diagnoses were, to Katy's eyes, rather vague and insubstantial and she wanted to understand the full meaning of some of the odder terms. There was one diagnosis in particular that intrigued her, 'moral insanity', what on earth was that?

It was such a glorious day that she decided to walk round the outside of the Annexe and enter the ward from the back, through the veranda. There was a paved path running between the side of the hospital and the perimeter wall, which separated it from the edge of the village. As she walked through the grounds she was struck, not for the first time, by the beauty of the gardens. The lawns were well tended and neatly mown, the evergreens were trimmed and shaped and all around there were individual beds of late autumn flowers glowing with colour. It was obvious that when the hospital had been built, great care had been taken to provide the patients with pleasant grounds to walk in. She sat down on one of the benches that had been provided for the patients to recline on and just surveyed the scene.

'What was it about autumn that gave everyone such a strong feeling of nostalgia?' Katy thought; she certainly felt it today. It was primarily a feeling of loss for the passing of summer, but autumn also promoted a sensation of anticipation, a feeling that something wonderful, but as yet unidentified, was about to begin. The air contained the smell of earth, smoking leaves and decay, yet still had the aroma of fertility. As she breathed in the heady smell, it unleashed a feeling of controlled yearning for something she passionately desired, but couldn't quite name. The radiance of the late autumn sun on her face caused a feeling of indescribable excitement to well up inside of her and she experienced the overpowering joy of simply being alive.

She sat quietly for a while longer until an uncomfortable feeling of guilt began to nag at her. She should be working not sitting there enjoying the autumn sunshine, but it was such a lovely day that she had just wanted time to take stock. At last she had discovered a line of work that would lead to a satisfying career in social work, after having drifted for so long. A sense of purpose was essential to Katy's well being. Whilst she continued to enjoy her moment of leisure, conveniently ignoring the stabs of guilt, she surveyed her surroundings and cast her eye over the still impressive asylum Annexe building. From her vantage point she could see how simply, yet cleverly, it had been designed for maximum observation. It was interesting to see the way that the wards ran off the main corridor, like veins running from a main artery. Each area fed back into that artery, no one could enter or leave the main building without using the corridor and there was nowhere in its third of a mile in which to hide.

If that building could talk, what a tale it would tell, but like the ageing monster that it was, it slumbered silently in the autumn sunlight with its secrets safe. She wondered how long it would survive. It was now 1976 and the Annexe was emptying steadily as the long stay patients died off. Soon it would be surplus to requirements as most psychiatric illnesses could now be controlled with drugs and patients no longer required long term hospitalisation. She couldn't really see how it could be adapted for any other use, especially with its disturbing history, yet it was such an extraordinary building, so majestic yet faintly unsettling. Did it suspect, lying there peacefully wallowing in the warmth of the day like an old dinosaur that its days of power were numbered and very soon it too would probably be extinct? She doubted it; the building seemed to radiate a sense of its own invincibility. A few minutes passed while Katy simply surveyed the scene and enjoyed the sunshine and then reluctantly, she stood up and continued walking to her ward.

The pathway led round the back of the ward where there was a small grassed area. As Katy approached it, she could see several of the ladies walking around aimlessly or sitting in pairs on the benches provided for them just chatting. The veranda doors were open and several more patients were enjoying the sunshine in there. She thought how strange it was that all the ladies looked vaguely alike. For instance, they all had the same standard hairstyles. If their hair was straight, it was harshly cropped to ear length and simply secured with a clip. Granted some ladies had a tightly curled home perm, whilst others simply had their hair cropped short all over, but there was little attempt at individual styling. A hairdresser came to the ward once a week. She probably had a limited number of styles that she felt were suitable for the institution and just continued to use them year after year. She had probably been coming for decades and saw no reason to alter the way she cut the ladies' hair, so there was little individuality. Katy thought that maybe it was just that when people lived together for a long time, they eventually started to resemble one another.

The same conformity that applied to the ladies' hairstyles also applied to their clothing. Although they were no longer officially dressed in a uniform, their clothes were very similar. Most of them wore shapeless crimplene dresses or skirts with a variety of nylon blouses and they all wore a formless baggy cardigan. The only part of their dress that was personal to each lady was her jewellery. They all wore totally inappropriate flashy, gaudy jewellery that looked incongruous on their everyday crimplene dresses. Massive brooches with brightly coloured stones hung loosely on nylon blouses, several ropes of showy bright beads festooned wrinkled necks, large ornate rings adorned gnarled fingers and diamante chandeliers dangled from extended ear lobes. It was so strange. The ladies tended to prefer kitsch, outlandish jewellery. However, this seemed to be the only part of their dress where they could express their individuality. Their gaudy jewellery made a statement, it said that they were not just ordinary, plain forgotten women; they too loved the beauty and glamour that had been denied them. It was odd and vaguely disturbing.

Sister Parkinson had told Katy that the hospital had always had its own dentist, but during the 1930s he had a cure all approach. He didn't bother to fill teeth, even front teeth, he just pulled them out. After 1948 and the formation of the NHS, he did actually supply some of the patients with false teeth, but before that he just left gaps. The ladies on Katy's ward had all suffered at his hand.

Very few of them had a full set of their own teeth or even false teeth and some had no teeth at all. It made Katy furious. They were women. To destroy their looks in that way was wicked. It gave all their faces a rather sunken, shrivelled look that belonged to a harsher time.

Katy walked through the patients nodding her greetings before she climbed up the few brick steps into the veranda. As she stepped out of the sunshine into the darkness of the ward, it took her a moment to adjust her eyes to the gloom. She was still dazzled by the sunshine, so she stood still and blinked until she could focus clearly, then she moved into the room. She carefully picked her way through the ward, carefully stepping over the usual jungle of chrome contraptions that littered the main day room. They were designed to help the ladies walk, but Katy viewed them more as hazards to be overcome.

Most of the ladies were sitting chatting or dozing in their chairs. After walking in the warm autumn air, the cloying smell of the institution almost choked Katy. She felt a strong desire to run back into the fresh air and sunshine and take a deep breath, but the moment soon passed. Whilst the veranda area was sunny, the day room was gloomy even on a sunny day. The main windows were set fairly high in the walls causing the light to descend in wide shafts, each one highlighted a million dust motes that danced gleefully in its rays. The shafts of light only illuminated small areas and this left the rest of the room in shadow. Attempts had been made to brighten up the ward over the years, but they were not very successful. Plant stands, colourful curtains and pleasant prints helped to cheer it up a little, but they didn't really make it look homely. Even with the luxury of a television, nothing could disguise the fact that it was a ward in an institution. Sadly, however, in most cases the ward was the only home that many of the women had ever known. Katy thought how wasteful it was that they were old now and had spent their whole adult lives in hospital. They knew little, if indeed anything at all, about the love of a man, the comfort of family life, the joy of children or the pleasure of their own homes. They had existed for decades on this single sex ward or another just like it, set apart from normal society and forgotten by the world.

Since Katy had worked her way through the files and seen photographs of the ladies as young women, she had begun to look at them more as individuals. Previously they had just been an impersonal group of old ladies sitting out their twilight years in an institution. However, the files had made her view them differently. Each one had taken on an individual identity, and they were no longer just an amorphous mass of elderly patients to her. She really cared about them. She realised that they had come in here as young women, who were mentally ill, and then lived their lives out hidden from society, forgotten and neglected. They had been robbed of a normal life. It was ironic, but they wouldn't have spent so many years locked away from society if they'd received a life sentence for murder. It seemed inhumane to Katy, yet it never ceased to amaze her that they didn't seem angry or resentful. In fact, they seemed oddly content. On reflection she thought that they had lived similar lives to those of convent nuns. Of course the difference was that a nun would have chosen her vocation and entered the convent willingly. These poor ladies, however, had had no choice, they were committed.

Nevertheless, both sets of women seemed to have an unusual calmness and peace about them.

'Penny for them.'

Katy nearly jumped out of her skin. Sister Parkinson had entered the day room by one of the side doors and she hadn't heard her approach.

'Oh, I was just observing the ladies and thinking how limited their lives have been. On the outside they could have had husbands, children, homes...'

'Ah now, you see, you are making the assumption that so many people make. You are assuming that they could live on the outside. Come on we'll go to my office. I've got some news for you.'

'What assumption?' asked Katy. As they walked along Sister Parkinson continued talking to her over her shoulder.

'You are assuming that we always had psychotropic medicines available and a complete understanding of the subconscious. You are assuming that society was educated and could cope with epileptic fits and any number of problems associated with mental illness. The reality is that there weren't and they couldn't! She paused to unlock her office door. 'Come on in and sit down. I think it's time for our tea and a chocolate biscuit.'

When the kettle had boiled, they settled down with their tea for one of the chats that Katy enjoyed so much and found so helpful. Sister Parkinson had been at the hospital for years and had watched it develop and change. Katy challenged her, 'Well it couldn't have been that bad.'

'It was that bad. People have this ridiculous assumption that thousands of innocent women were locked away when really there wasn't anything the matter with them. However, the reality was that most of them were seriously ill. There was no medication then except possibly paraldehyde and chloral hydrate. Take epilepsy for instance, nowadays people live normal, productive lives on medication that prevents them having fits. There was no treatment then that could control epileptic fits. Patients with epilepsy had to be watched very carefully as their fits could cause them to choke and die... Some patients with epilepsy were so severely ill that they had to be cared for on a special ward. Another problem was schizophrenia. There was certainly no effective treatment for schizophrenia until the discovery of Largactil in the early 1950s. Untreated it's a terrible condition and sufferers are extremely unreliable. They do hear voices and they are real to them. They torment them day and night, causing great distress. Sometimes their voices tell them to attack or even kill and they can be a very real danger to themselves and others. We had to keep a sharp eye on them I can tell you.'

'Were you ever attacked?'

'Yes! But fortunately there were no sharp instruments or tools available on the ward and there were enough staff to overpower any patient who took it into their head to attack others, but they were very unpredictable. There were also patients with severe depression who would self harm. You have no idea what it was like. For instance, you know Jane Whitlam?'

'Yes, she's lovely.'

'Well she wasn't lovely. She used to sit rocking backwards and forwards on the floor pulling her hair out until her head bled. Then she'd scratch herself and worse if she could. We used to try everything, sew her sleeve ends up, tie mittens on her, but we couldn't stop her. She was almost bald, with a head full of scabs, her face and arms were covered in scratches and in spite of our best efforts she looked dreadful. However, when we put her on the new anti-depressants she improved almost overnight, after thirty years of living misery. It was a joy to see.

Katy was thoughtful, 'I'm sorry, I didn't mean to be critical, I was just thinking it was sad.'

'Don't be sorry love, how would you know? It was sad, but it makes me cross when people insinuate that the patients didn't need to be here. They did. They needed twenty four hours observation. There were, of course, ladies who shouldn't have been here, but that was inevitable.'

'That reminds me; I wanted to ask you about some of the files. What exactly was 'moral insanity'? The other term I didn't understand was 'puerperal madness', was that what we call post-natal depression?'

'Yes post-natal depression was dreadful and it could be so serious. We had nothing to treat it with. Some mothers just seemed to regain their hormonal balance and get better, but others never recovered. As for 'moral insanity', it was nothing more than hormones,' Sister Parkinson laughed, 'any girl who seriously crossed her father or any puritanical Victorian man in charge could find herself certified. The men had all the power then and the asylum system was occasionally abused. It was true that women who were an embarrassment to powerful men could find themselves locked up in here. It was like every other system, it was open to abuse no matter how the authorities tried to stamp it out.'

'Do you think that happened in Caroline's case?' asked Katy.

Sister Parkinson smiled ruefully, 'I would think so; she'd been here some years before I started nursing. Her file doesn't make pretty reading does it? I imagine she was a rebellious teenager who was sent here and then had a complete nervous breakdown and became completely institutionalised. She never recovered poor little soul.' Sister Parkinson sipped her tea deep in thought.

'You know when I first started here as a probationer the old warders used to tell us tales about the asylum in the late nineteenth century. They said that the rich Liverpool merchants would 'have their way', with their maids. That's rape or seduction to you and I and believe me those little maids wouldn't have had much choice. Then if they became pregnant they would have them put in here and paid their families to keep quiet.'

'I've heard that before, I was never sure whether it was just a hospital myth,' replied Katy, 'it seems difficult to believe. I've often wondered about it.'

'Oh I'm fairly sure that it's true. Many women and men were put in here because they were simply a nuisance or worse, someone wanted to get rid of them. You are in the unique position of witnessing the end of the old Victorian asylum system when the only treatment for mental illness was to lock it away. They cared for the patients behind closed doors, out of the sight of society. Now, with drugs, people can live their lives outside the institution in society'

'I know,' agreed Katy, 'but I have a lurid fascination with the way the institution was. It intrigues me.'

'Well my dear, don't encourage me too much, I could go on forever telling tales about the old days! Oh I forgot to tell you I had a rather strange call from McKendrick, did she say anything to you?' Katy thought and then shook her head slowly. 'Well I don't know, she was asking some very odd questions about the hospital, arrangements for illegitimate babies, adoption that kind of thing, but she avoided telling me why. If it's to do with this ward she should pass it on to you, but she hasn't mentioned it?'

Katy shook her head again, 'No she hasn't mentioned anything.'

Sister Parkinson looked doubtful. 'That's strange. What's she up to I wonder? Keep your eye on her; she'll be up to something.'

'Trying to grab some kind of glory?'

'Quite probably and at your expense no doubt.'

Katy sipped her tea thoughtfully then remembered why she had come over to see Sister Parkinson.

'By the way all the letters have gone out now to patient's relatives and friends, so we should start to get some response in a week or two.'

Sister Parkinson beamed, 'That is wonderful; I wonder what will turn up? It'll be interesting to see. It would be lovely if some of my ladies could rediscover their families.'

Chapter Six

Emmie woke early and lay in bed for a while thinking about the information that she had retrieved from Martha's journals. It was strange that she had lived less than a hundred years ago, but the cultural differences were enormous, they made it seem like a different world. She glanced at the bedside clock and started, it was later than she thought and she had a nine o'clock lecture. She jumped out of bed and straight into the shower then dressed quickly. She didn't have time for breakfast and decided to grab a coffee at the university before her lecture started.

As she entered the refectory to buy her coffee, she was amazed to see Katy Molyneux in the queue. She and Katy had been close friends at school, but had lost touch when Emmie went to London. It was mainly Emmie's fault, she felt so embarrassed at her failure and she'd had a huge crush on Katy's older brother, Paul. When she saw Katy again, her heart jumped, she looked so like Paul. Emmie had to be honest with herself, her feelings for him had been more than a crush, she was seventeen and hopelessly in love. No one knew, not even Gran, she just loved from afar in secret. Paul was three years older than Katy. He was tall, blonde, good looking, incredibly intelligent and he saw Emmie as nothing more than one of his younger sister's little school friends. If he'd known how she felt, he would no doubt have laughed at her. She had heard that he was now a qualified doctor working for Voluntary Services Overseas in Africa. After Emmie failed her Law degree in London she didn't feel like seeing anyone, least of all

Paul, and she hadn't returned Katy's calls. Seeing her again, in the queue for coffee, the years simply melted away and Emmie felt guilty that she had allowed their friendship to founder because of her pride. At that moment Katy turned slightly and caught sight of Emmie, she let out a shriek of delight and came bounding across the refectory to gather Emmie up in a bear hug.

'Where have you been? I've phoned your house loads of times and left messages with your mother, but you never got in touch.'

Emmie felt mortified, 'I'm so sorry Katy, things just didn't work out in London and I crawled back here with my tail between my legs. I felt such a failure I just wanted to be on my own to lick my wounds.'

'You are silly; you don't really think that I'd be bothered about all that do you? Still that's all in the past, what are you doing here now?' Katy beamed.

'I might ask the same thing of you!' retorted Emmie. Katy grinned shyly, 'I'm finally making something of my life after messing about at school for all those years. I'm working at Granthall Hospital as an assistant social worker.'

'What the old lunatic asylum?' Like everyone else Emmie was amazed, little did she know how central to her own life Granthall was about to become.

Katy grinned in a resigned fashion, 'That's everyone's reaction when I tell them, but it's a major psychiatric hospital now, the biggest in the country.'

'I'm sorry,' Emmie apologised, 'that was rude of me, but I don't know anything about psychiatry.'

'Oh, don't apologise, everyone reacts in exactly the same way, but I love it there and I'm learning such a lot.'

'What are you doing here?'

'I've been for an interview for the Social Work Certificate course; I want to qualify as a social worker and make it my career. I'm really serious about it.'

'Good for you,' said Emmie, who was clearly impressed. Katy had been such a flighty soul at school and everyone had despaired of her ever doing anything useful.

'Well, now you haven't answered my question, what are you doing here?'

'Ah, well, after that fiasco in London I worked in a dress shop for a year or two and then enrolled here as a mature student to do a combined honours degree, English and Fine Art and I love it.'

Katy smiled, 'That's what you always wanted to do.'

'Yes, but Dad wouldn't hear of it, anyway he's come round to my way of thinking. Listen, I've got to dash, I've got a nine o'clock lecture, but I would love to meet up and hear about everyone. How about going to that new wine bar in town one night?'

'Love to, the sooner the better.'

'Look, I'm house sitting for Gran, here's her number, I'm in most nights trying to catch up on my back log of work! Give me a ring.'

'Sure thing! Take care.'

With that Emmie gave Katy a brief hug and then rushed off to her lecture. She was delighted to have seen her again. They had been great friends and it was silly of her to have let their friendship drift. Was it because she was afraid of seeing Paul? Maybe it was, she didn't really know. Anyway he was probably married now and living in Ethiopia with six children. Katy hadn't mentioned him. But why would she? She didn't know how

Emmie felt all those years ago.

After her lecture ended Emmie spent most of the day in the university library doing research. She had to make herself stay away from Chestnut Lodge and the tin box, or she wouldn't have got any work done at all. However, she was impatient to get back and read the rest of Martha's journals and have a look at what else was in the box.

Emmie arrived home about 5 o'clock and was followed down the drive by Freddie in his new BMW. She smiled to herself as her car drew to a halt outside the house. She had known her father wouldn't be able to stay away long. He was sure that Emmie knew more about her grandmother's whereabouts than she was admitting to. She opened the front door, left it ajar for Freddie and proceeded through to the kitchen, where she filled the kettle and placed it on the Aga. Freddie followed her through. When the kettle had boiled she made a pot of coffee and they seated themselves at the table.

Freddie launched into the conversation with no preamble, 'Emmie, where has your grandmother got to?'

'Dad, I've no more idea than you have.'

'But why would she rush off at a time like this when she knows we are worried sick about her? You'd think she would want to be with her family during these last few months...'

Freddie's voice broke as he uttered these last words and Emmie felt so sorry for him. She stretched out her hands and covered both of his with them. He smiled at her gratefully and took one of her hands in his.

'You're very upset aren't you?' Emmie asked.

Freddie still couldn't speak and simply nodded his head.

'Poor Dad, it's so hard.' As she was trying to find a way to distract him Emmie remembered the photograph of Josiah and Martha that she had tucked into the bureau drawer the previous night. Maybe her father could shed some light on the subject of his grandfather.

'Hang on here a minute Dad; I've got something to show you.'

She disappeared into the little sitting room and emerged with the photograph of Josiah and Martha. It was the one she thought had been taken on the occasion of their engagement.

'Here, I think that this is a photograph of your maternal grandparents, can you tell me anything about them?'

She thrust the photograph at Freddie. He fumbled in his top pocket for his reading glasses, perched them on the end of his nose then examined the photograph carefully. When he'd finished he peered over the top of his spectacles at Emmie, 'Where did you get this from? I've never seen it before.'

Emmie instinctively knew not to reveal the existence of the tin box so she just said she found it in the bureau.

'Who are they?' asked Freddie.

'Well, I think that they are Josiah and Martha Clayton, Gran's mother and father, your grandparents.'

'Well, well, yes strangely I can see a likeness between him and me, apart from the moustaches that is.' Freddie laughed, obviously the distraction had worked.

'What can you tell me about them?' asked Emmie.

'About him, nothing really, in fact nothing at all other than he died before I was born and nobody ever spoke about him, never. It was very odd. Nobody ever mentioned his name. What an old Victorian he was. Talk about strict and severe looking, I bet he never spared the rod and spoiled the child, so to speak. I'll tell you who would know about him and that's father's older sister, Sarah, lovely woman. She's still alive and lives in London somewhere. Your grandmother is still in touch with her, she's a bit older than Gran, but they were always great friends.'

'Do you know anything about their house, Dad? The one that Martha and Josiah lived in together after they got married?'

Freddie frowned for a moment while he thought, 'I'm not sure which one you mean. Oh I know. The mausoleum, that's how mother and my grandmother referred to it, although I think that it was actually called The Old Rectory. You know grandmother lived with us here when I was a young child? She died when I was three. Anyway she never wanted to live in her own house and it remained closed up for years. I remember it vaguely; it was next door, to the left of this house. It was by all accounts a big, rambling, gloomy old place; no one seemed to like it or want to live there. Either mother or grandmother sold it to developers after the war, the Second World War that is, and they pulled it down and built those flats. The women seemed to be glad to see the back of it. Of course, you know that the two families originally became friendly because they were next door neighbours?'

Freddie seemed lost in his thoughts of the past and then remembered Emmie who was smiling at him. 'What's brought on all this interest in the past eh?'

'Oh I don't know, Gran dying I think. I just want to enquire about the past while she's still here to ask.'

When Freddie left Emmie went into the little sitting room and lit the fire. Once it was crackling merrily she prepared herself a snack of cheese, biscuits and fruit and then returned to the sitting room and retrieved Martha's journals from the bureau drawer. She had resisted the temptation all day to return to the house and the journals. She was becoming obsessed by the need to know more about her family. She picked up the last journal that she had been reading and started to examine the entries. They became irregular after Martha's marriage. Emmie got the feeling that she didn't have the same amount of time to herself as she did when she lived with her parents.

Martha wrote about setting up home and her life with Josiah. However, there were no details about the intimate side of the marriage. Martha never wrote about her personal feelings or how she felt about her husband. The entries were business like and she referred to Josiah as she might refer to a business partner that she barely knew. There were details of dinners that she held for the family, for Josiah's business partners and for members of the church. Emmie felt that she enjoyed having her own home and entertaining. However, there was a certain barrenness about the entries and a feeling of sadness haunted the journals. Then, quite unexpectedly Emmie stumbled on an entry that almost lit up the page with joy. It seemed that the doctor had confirmed Martha's suspicion that she was pregnant and going to have a child.

15th April 1901

Oh joy of joys!!! I have just returned from the doctor's and he has confirmed that I am three months pregnant and going to have a child in October! I thought from the signs that

I was expecting, but to have it confirmed is joy indeed. It is all that I really wanted to make my life complete and I hope that it is the first of many children. I haven't told Josiah yet and I don't think he suspects a thing. In fact, I don't think that he takes very much notice of me and what is happening to me as long as his house is well run and his meals are on time and to his liking.

A little baby, my little baby, someone who is all mine to love and cherish. I can't wait, it's all so exciting. Mama will be delighted!

Emmie was so pleased for Martha; it seemed that at last she was going to have some joy in her life and an element of choice. She read on with interest:

17th April 1901

I told Josiah my good news last night after dinner. I don't know what I expected, a beaming smile, an expression of delight, congratulations, I just don't know. However I did not expect the reaction that I got. He just looked at me and nodded seriously as if I were describing some new curtains that I had ordered. Then he said that it was as it should be, hoped that I wouldn't be too much inconvenienced and then changed the subject. I was bubbling over with excitement and couldn't control myself. I asked him did he want a boy or a girl, what names did he favour, all kinds of silly, but quite normal questions. He looked at me as if I were a rather stupid child and said that we must wait and see if the child was healthy before we planned such things. It was an insult to God to take anything for granted; we must bow to his will. I couldn't have been more deflated if he had thrown a bucket of cold water over me. He is a strange man, I don't think that I will ever really understand him, but he isn't unkind and he is a good provider, so I must be thankful for small mercies.

Not for the first time was Emmie dismayed on Martha's behalf by Josiah's reactions. He seemed to be a very cold man, almost emotionally sterile. Was that just the way men were then? It was hard to tell, but she thought that he seemed unusually cold and sensed a core of ruthlessness in him. She returned to the journals and moved forward a few months. They were now full of details of the forthcoming birth. Martha seemed to use her journals to share her joy with, rather than her husband. She described the making of the baby's layette, the new crib, how she had decorated the bedroom and any number of other important details concerning the coming baby. The details were interesting in their way, but Emmie wanted to know more about Martha and Josiah's relationship. Then she came upon a distressing entry.

6th August 1901

Poor Mama is very ill. She has taken to her bed and is being attended to by Dr Kyle. She has lost a great deal of weight and is in great pain. Papa says that she cannot eat properly. It is such a worry and he looks almost as ill as she does. I have been to see her and sit with her, but I am so large and cumbersome now that I am not much help in nursing her. She looks so frail that I am afraid she won't live to see my baby and I do so want that.

Poor Martha, just when she was experiencing the joy of her pregnancy it looked as though she may lose the one person who would enjoy sharing the birth of the child with her. She had always been close to her mother. Then Emmie came upon another rather disturbing entry:

20th August 1901

Josiah has employed a nanny for our child, without consulting me!! He advertised and interviewed them and made the choice all on his own. He says that he didn't want to worry me at this difficult time, but I don't believe him. He just wants control. I don't particularly like the woman that he has chosen. She is no doubt clean and efficient, but there is no warmth about her, no love and a child needs to be surrounded by love. I don't want my child terrified by hell fire and damnation and this one talks about nothing else. Still if there's one thing I have learned about Josiah it is that you never confront him head on. If you want things changed, you have to do it without him realising.

Emmie felt sorry for Martha. Every time she thought that things were going well there were problems. First it was the worry of her mother's illness and then Josiah's interference over the nanny. Martha had married and she had her own home just as she had wanted, but it seemed to be a strange, cold, marriage. Martha was almost locked out of the relationship with Josiah. He had the wife that he wanted, who was efficient and loyal, but he didn't seem to want or need any kind of emotional relationship with her. It was hard on Martha, who Emmie sensed wanted and needed love and affection. Well obviously they slept together as Martha had conceived, but Emmie couldn't imagine it being a joyous or passionate union.

Chapter Seven

Emmie just couldn't bring herself to put Martha's journals down and read far into the night. There were no lectures or tutorials the next day, so she didn't worry too much about her lack of sleep. Martha wrote in some detail about life during her pregnancy. The actual pregnancy went well and she was in good health, the only worry she had was her mother's illness and of course her dislike of the nanny that Josiah had selected. However, the birth was complicated and problematic. Martha had a very difficult confinement. She was considered at thirty one to be quite old to be having her first child. The labour was long and painful and at one point the doctors thought that they were going to lose both mother and child. As it was they both pulled through, but at a cost. Martha was seriously ill for some months after the birth of Florence and she was told that under no circumstances was she to have another child. Emmie realised that in the early years of the century this meant that her relationship with Josiah would have to become platonic, with no sex at all, as there was no reliable birth control available. Emmie wondered how Josiah dealt with that, but Martha made no reference to anything quite so intimate. In fact, Emmie found it amusing that she never mentioned sex at all. Anything that concerned sex or child birth was couched in rather comical euphemistic terms. However, there was no hint that Josiah tried to exert his conjugal rites and thereby put Martha under pressure or place her life in danger. Emmie was sure that there were many men at that time, who would have done, despite the risk to their wife's life.

Emmie found it really difficult to build a picture of Josiah from a modern viewpoint. She knew from her general knowledge of the time that the Victorians were an emotionally and sexually repressed generation. However, Josiah seemed to be an exceptionally cold man, even by their standards. He seemed to have had little use for anything that involved emotion or pleasure and was only interested in work and duty. Yet Emmie had to admit that although he appeared to be a rather cold and aloof sort of person, he did look after his family's well being and never seemed to be actively cruel or unkind in any way. Take the fact that Martha couldn't have any more children after Florence. She didn't dwell on this cruel disappointment, but she did refer, in her journal, to the fact that Josiah had accepted that there were to be no more children and never blamed her in any way, or made her feel that she had let him down. All this was undoubtedly kind of him, but Emmie couldn't help feeling that the demonstration of emotional warmth and affection, including sex, weren't terribly important to him.

Material possessions and a lack of cruelty or direct unkindness, however, do not make a good marriage and Emmie sensed that Martha must have been very lonely with Josiah. Early on in the marriage she seemed to look to her mother for support and companionship and appeared to accept that this was how marriage was. She rarely complained in her journals, which contained quite a positive account of her married life, although Emmie sensed an underlying dissatisfaction over the personal aspect of her relationship with her husband. However, not long after Florence's birth Martha's mother succumbed to her illness and died. It wasn't clear exactly what she died of, but Emmie thought that it was probably some form of heart disease. Martha's father's health deteriorated rapidly after the death of his beloved wife and he died a year later. Martha was clearly heartbroken at the loss of her parents, particularly her mother, and her deepened ensuing loneliness shone through her journal writing.

However, her one solace was her child, Florence, Emmie's grandmother. Martha quietly dispensed with the services of the austere nanny before her confinement. She did this subtly without directly confronting Josiah's authority so that he hardly noticed that the nanny had gone. Martha then quietly employed a warm, kind woman who suited her better. This woman took good care of Florence during the post natal period of Martha's illness and relieved her of the anxiety of the day to day care of her baby. This enabled Martha to rest secure in the knowledge that Florence was being cared for and it enabled her to recover more rapidly than the doctors had anticipated.

Martha's entries about her daughter, Florence, almost glowed with happiness and Emmie felt that she had found deep fulfilment at last. It seemed that the young Florence had a loving, kind nature. She was also a breathtakingly beautiful child, with an exquisite little heart shaped face, huge dark eyes and long white blonde curls. This didn't surprise Emmie as her grandmother was still attractive in old age. Martha was delighted with her little girl and far from being jealous of Florence's looks, she revelled in them and celebrated the beauty in her daughter that she herself never had. However, Josiah was far from happy with his beautiful daughter. He ordered Martha, much against her will, to dress Florence plainly and to make sure that her hair was tied up at all times. This obviously upset Martha, who had the time and money to create a lovely wardrobe for her daughter, but she dare not cross Josiah directly. Florence was a good natured child with no vanity, so she didn't seem to mind her plain dresses and severe hairstyles. The irony was, as Martha commented, that Florence was so beautiful that her severe clothes, far from making her plain, threw her beauty into sharp relief.

Emmie couldn't understand her great grandfather at all; Josiah seemed to think that anything that brought joy or beauty into the world should be stamped out or destroyed. Emmie thought he was an appallingly joyless human being and wondered why Martha didn't become depressed, as living with him must have been a very negative experience, especially after the death of her parents when she seemed particularly isolated. However, she seemed to deal with Josiah very well. She never directly crossed him in any way and almost lived her life around him. Perhaps she was so grateful to him for marrying her that she was prepared to put up with anything. Emmie didn't know, what she did realise, however, was that these people, who she knew nothing about two days ago, were beginning to take on a life of their own. They were becoming real to her and she wanted to know more and more about them. How she wished her grandmother was there to question because she could supply the missing links for her, but she wasn't, so Emmie had to find those missing links on her own.

In the absence of her grandmother, Emmie went

back to the journals. Martha wrote prolifically during Florence's early years and then she seemed to stop for a while. The entries then began again as Florence started to grow up. It became obvious that Martha was becoming more and more distressed at Josiah's attitude towards his daughter. His relationship with her was very cold and distant and he was incredibly strict. He showed her no love or affection and was always trying to find fault with her behaviour. Whilst Martha could cope with his coldness, Florence found it bewildering and he hurt her with his rejection. He seemed to be continually waiting for her to commit an offence of some kind so he could criticise and humiliate her. He seemed to blame her for being beautiful, as though it was some fatal sinful flaw. He had the same outlook as the Puritans of the seventeenth century and it exasperated and worried Martha.

Florence strove as hard as she could to please him, but her best was never good enough. Martha did what she could to mediate between them, but she was powerless where Josiah was concerned. He was like a pillar of granite, cold, grey, hard, pitiless and immoveable. Florence was a naturally good natured young person so his attitude towards her created bewilderment but no resentment in the child, but somehow Martha feared for her. She warned Florence continually not to cross her father or argue with him in any way and Florence tried to do as she asked. However, she overflowed with a natural joy and happiness, which she found difficult to hide from her father. He disliked her exuberance and Martha feared that he would find a way to extinguish it, to crush it out of her. She saw Florence as her exotic orchid that had to be nurtured and protected from the chill, raw, wind that was her father.

Emmie was instinctively troubled when she read these entries. She knew Florence well as an adult and she realised how hard it must have been for her as a small child to crave the love and approval of a parent and have it withheld. She began to realise in some measure, why Florence had a problem with Freddie. Her son, through no fault of his own, resembled his grandfather and Josiah had not made Florence's life happy. He ruled every aspect of it absolutely. He saw no future for her other than that of a wife and mother. Florence had a talent for drawing and she desperately wanted to go to one of the new art colleges for young gentlewomen that were springing up around the country, but Josiah would hear of no such a thing. He couldn't have been more outraged if Florence had asked to join a brothel. Martha wrote in her journals that she encouraged Florence to paint in private during the day when her father was out at business. However, she warned her to hide her paintings and make no reference to them in his presence. Martha also wrote frequently about their neighbours, who Emmie now knew were her grandfather Edward's family. Martha was friendly with Edward's mother and admitted in her journal that it was their private hope that Florence and Edward might eventually marry. She was aware that Florence had always had a crush on Edward and she realised that as she grew up he had started to take particular notice of her. Both mothers could feel a fledgling love beginning to grow, which pleased them immensely.

Everything in the journals seemed to be normal and happy and they carried on in this vein for several years, then suddenly in the last one, the tone changed abruptly and after a final, distressing entry Martha simply stopped writing. This last entry was a long, confused account of Florence's health. However, Martha didn't fully explain what the problem was and she just stopped writing, almost mid flow. It was a very distressing entry and it made Emmie's blood run cold. Martha sounded in agony as she poured out her feelings on paper, but she didn't explain in any detail exactly what was going on.

February 1917

I don't know how or where I am getting the strength to write this journal. I can't understand what has changed our happy home and altered Florence so much. I am at a total loss... Last summer she suddenly changed and became very withdrawn and depressed. She lost a lot of weight and her health deteriorated, but she wouldn't talk to me. She stayed in her room and refused to eat. She became thinner and thinner and had no colour in her cheeks. She looked really ill. Inexplicably, she refused to see Dr. Pickard so his locum came to see her. He could find nothing physically wrong with her. I was distraught and didn't know what to do. I thought that maybe some sea air would help her and Mrs. Kingsley, my neighbour, suggested that I send Florence to stay with her married daughter, Sarah, in Devon. It was hard to part with my darling, but I had to do something to restore her health and normal good humour and it seemed a sensible idea. Sarah was a lovely girl and she was near Florence's age. I thought that she would cheer Florence up and restore her spirits and good health. It was hard to convince Josiah that she should go, especially with the war on, but even he could see how ill she had become. She just seemed to have collapsed physically in a very short time. Eventually he relented, but he would not let me accompany her. I sent her maid with her and waved her off with a very heavy heart.

Communication was difficult and Florence didn't write often. At first her letters were short and she still sounded depressed. Eventually though they cheered up and I thought she must be getting better. Sarah wrote as well and her letters were cheerful and optimistic, so I began to hope that Florence could come home restored to good health. I did miss her so, but Josiah wouldn't hear of me visiting her...

I left her down there for as long as she wanted to stay, because I just wanted her to get better. I wanted my happy, healthy Florence back. I never understood what changed her so suddenly. I asked Dr. Pickard, but I've never had much faith in that man and frankly have never really liked him. Josiah, for some reason, thought highly of him and insisted on keeping him as the family doctor. Dr. Pickard seemed to think that adolescent young girls often became depressed and it was nothing to worry about. He seemed uncomfortable and unwilling to talk about the subject. On one occasion he actually snapped at me, so I stopped asking him... However, I wasn't satisfied that it was to do with her age. I knew Florence and she was a steady girl, but there was little that I could do.

Suddenly after several months had passed, Charles, Sarah's husband, asked to see Josiah. They met in London and after the meeting Josiah made arrangements to bring Florence home. He wouldn't discuss his decision with me, or explain why she was coming home other than her health had deteriorated again, but that wasn't the impression I got from her letters. When she eventually arrived home from Sarah's, he took her straight up to the attics where he had prepared some rooms for her. He would not let me see her.

He told me that he had had to bring her home because she was highly infectious and dangerously ill. How did it happen? When? Where? Why did nobody write to me and explain that she was so ill. Why can't I see my child and talk to her? Why didn't Sarah tell me she was ill? Josiah has effectively banished me to my rooms and won't allow me anywhere near her. I am going out of my mind I can hear her screaming and crying, it is unbearable. I keep going over the events of the last six or seven months, over and over and I can't understand what has happened. It seemed to start that Sunday evening after Sunday School, Florence appeared to be upset and unwell when she returned and she went to bed without any supper. After that she seemed somehow to fade away and never regained her health. I put it down to her age, although I did wonder if the war was worrying her and that she was pining a little for Edward. Girls do go through a difficult time. I was pleased that the kind locum, who she saw, agreed that she should go away to the seaside for a while. Florence leapt at the idea of going away, which hurt me a little, but I could see that she was annoying Josiah and felt it best all round for her to go away. What is going on? Why won't he let me see her?

I feel as if I am in a nightmare. I am a virtual prisoner in my own house. I just pace my room in agony knowing my love is in the same house in torment and yet denied to me. What can I do? How can I help her? I am beside myself. I cannot sleep, I cannot eat. What will I do if anything happens to her?

Emmie was genuinely shocked by what she read and couldn't start to imagine what had happened to Florence. Why had she become so ill? Martha never actually said what the illness was; it was all rather vague. Emmie was outraged that this dreadful domineering man could treat his wife and his daughter in this way. He should have let Martha see Florence and comfort her. Martha's entry didn't shed any light on the matter. She just poured out her distress in page after page of ramblings and then the journals ended. There were no more left to read.

Emmie looked at the clock and was horrified to see that it was nearly four o'clock in the morning. She needed to get some sleep, but she was desperate to know what had happened to Florence. She must find out more. Maybe her great aunt Sarah would know something, grandfather Edward's sister. Freddie had said that they were still in touch, so maybe Gran would have an address or telephone number. She was too tired tonight to look so she would have a search tomorrow.

The fire had almost gone out and the dawn was starting to creep through the curtains. Emmie collected the journals together and locked them away in the bureau, when the little bunch of photographs fell out. She bent down to retrieve them. She didn't lock them away with the journals, but took them upstairs with her to examine. There was a beautiful one of Florence as a child of three or four and another one probably taken when she was in her early teens. Her hair was pulled back into a chignon and she was dressed in a severe, dark dress, but she really was breathtakingly beautiful. She looked like the fifties film star, Grace Kelly. Emmie hadn't realised just how lovely she was. As she looked at the photograph she felt the tears trickle down her face at the thought of this lovely young girl

locked up. She must have been terrified in the attics, ill
and all alone.

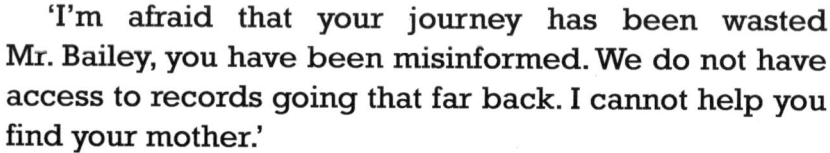

'I'm afraid that your journey has been wasted
Mr. Bailey, you have been misinformed. We do not have
access to records going that far back. I cannot help you
find your mother.'

'That can't be right, I asked at Waiston Hospital. They
hold some records on micro fiche, but they said that all
the paper records were kept here on the wards and in
the archives. The information they held was limited. They
felt sure that the paper records would tell me more and
they suggested that I ask for you. They told me that you
would help me gain access to the files.'

'As I said we do not have access to records going back
that far. They do exist, but they are covered by a privacy
ruling and we are only allowed to access them in
extreme circumstances and never allowed to disclose
their contents.'

Mrs. McKendrick sat stiff and unyielding as she lied
without conscience to this stranger. She disapproved
strongly of illegitimacy and this man had been taken
away from his misguided mother and adopted by good
Christian parents who had looked after him and given
him an education. She felt it was wrong raking up the
past and looking for mothers who were irresponsible
and immoral enough to have a child without first gaining
a husband. She wasn't going to help him. She was well
aware of the new laws involving adopted parents and
access to information, she just didn't agree with them.

'But this is an extreme circumstance, I am a son trying

to locate his birth mother and I have reason to believe that she was a patient in this hospital when she gave birth to me.'

'Believe me I would like to help you, but it is impossible. There were over three thousand patients in this hospital at the turn of the century. How do you expect to find the one that may possibly be your mother? If you want my advice you will go home and leave well alone.'

'I don't want your advice, with respect. I want to know exactly who I am. I found this birth certificate amongst my adopted mother's effects after she died. I am sure that it relates to me, but I can't find any evidence. I need your help immediately. I am flying back to Canada tomorrow.'

'Then as I say, I am sorry, but I wish you a pleasant journey.'

'Isn't there anyone else that I can talk to?'

'I'm sorry no, I am head of this department and I have the final word.'

He looked so deflated and defeated that she almost felt sorry for him, but she knew it was for the best. It didn't do for children to go raking up the past. She felt that he should have more respect for his adoptive parents. It never occurred to her for one moment that it was none of her business and that she had no right to deny him access to information that was his right by law.

The man hesitated for a moment and then seemed to accept defeat. His shoulders sagged slightly as he rose from his chair. He observed the woman sitting opposite him and thought what a mean spirited, obstructive bigot she was. However, he realised that she had no intention of helping him and he was simply wasting his time. Time that was one thing he did not have. He thought it would be much easier to locate his mother's records and he had not left himself enough time. He felt that this woman obviously had no sympathy with adopted children who wanted to locate their real mother and would be deliberately obstructive. He was going to have to return to Ottawa and try to gain the information that he needed from there, although it would be difficult given the distance. He was beginning to become dispirited, he did not have forever; time was running out, his mother would be an old woman now, if indeed she was still alive.

Chapter Eight

Sarah looked at the letter in her hand, folded it neatly and put it in her pocket. So, Florence was dying. Florence was, quite simply, her dearest friend, as well as being her sister-in-law and she would be leaving Sarah alone with her memories. When Florence went there would be no one left to share the past with her, no one to talk to about her beloved brother Edward and her husband Charles and no one to remember her youth. When she received the letter she glanced through it quickly. She absorbed the fact that Florence was terminally ill, but she could not digest the contents in full. She was deeply upset and needed time on her own to reflect. The news of Florence's death had given her a severe shock. She required time to think and digest the full implications of life without her. She had been such a large part of

Sarah's life. She looked again at the letter and felt a strong desire to get out of the house and walk by the river. She always found the water so soothing.

She went into the hall, put on her coat and left her little terraced house in Chelsea to go for a walk by the river. The lovely autumn weather was holding and the afternoon was warm and sunny. It was an appropriate season to receive the news of a death. It was the end of the summer, the leaves were dying and it reflected the end of an era for Sarah. With the passing of Florence, Sarah's own past would effectively be erased from memory, only she would be left to remember alone. There would no longer be anyone alive to reminiscence with. She suddenly felt chilled and very alone. She crossed the Kings Road and walked past one of the long terraces of elegant houses down to the river. The air was full of those wonderful autumn smells, the earthy smell of compost, the overpowering perfume of late autumn flowers and the scent of decay. Here, as all over the country, gardeners were making bonfires of the fallen leaves and the air was tinged with smoke from a thousand dead hopes. It was the wonderful smell of nostalgia and it made her heart ache with a love of life. She had always enjoyed the autumn. As her feet crunched through the piles of fallen leaves, she remembered how, as a child, she ran and kicked them in the air hoping to discover conkers, but she never did. The boys all got to them first.

Her thoughts returned once again to Florence. In her letter she had warned Sarah that she may be receiving a visit from young Emmie, her granddaughter. She asked Sarah to tell Emmie about the unfortunate and tragic events that had overshadowed her youth.

Florence begged her to do this one last thing for her, as the courage that she needed to do it herself had deserted her. She explained to Sarah that she had promised Edward that she would reveal her past to her children before she died. She particularly wanted Freddie to know her history; she felt that it would help him to understand the complexities of her relationship with him a little more easily. Sarah was touched that Florence had asked her to undertake this extremely sensitive task, touched and honoured.

When she reached the river, she strolled along the riverside path for some distance and then sat down on one of the benches that were provided at regular intervals for tired pedestrians. She had a clear view of the waterway, which was busy as usual; there was a group of rowers pulling earnestly in unison, the coxswain shouting his orders. The water glinted and sparkled on their rising oars like diamonds in the autumn sunshine which flew joyfully into the air, only to return to the predictability of the grey river.

'Bit like life,' Sarah thought, 'brief moments of ecstasy and joy, when you fly, until inevitably you return to earth with a bump to face the commonplace of everyday existence.'

'In, out, in, out,' the coxswain chanted. They rowed in unison flying deftly along the water, throwing diamonds from their oars, like profligate eastern princes, but leaving only the muddy river in their wake. Sarah turned her head, looked up the river and noticed a large white cruiser making its way stately downstream. She smiled to herself; Charles would have dismissed it out of hand as a 'gin palace'. In his opinion anything that didn't have sails wasn't fit to be on the water. She fondly remembered him splendidly decked out in his old sailing gear, how he loved his old yellow sea boots and moth eaten navy blue wool sweater. He was never happier than when he was sailing. If he and his crew didn't come back soaking wet, freezing cold and exhausted then it hadn't been a good day's sport. Serious boating required work and discomfort in his curiously male world. Sitting on board a motor boat, idly cruising along in comfort didn't qualify as boating to him. Sarah secretly loved gin palaces, all you had to do was relax in the sunshine, try to look beautiful and balance a drink. It was a wonderful way to spend a summer's day and far preferable to fighting sails in a force ten gale. However, she kept that view to herself and loyally agreed with Charles about the joys of real sailing. There were two couples on board the boat and they waved and raised their glasses to her as they glided slowly by. Sarah waved back, wishing wistfully that she could join them, but those days were long over for her.

A runner came pounding down the path, oblivious to everything but the agony of his muscles and the music blaring from the transistor radio that was clipped to the belt of his shorts. Sarah waited for him to pass then fished Florence's letter out of her pocket. She read through it carefully several times then let it fall in her lap and just gazed out over the water. It had all happened such a long time ago, in a different world, yet it was time Florence's family knew what she had endured and survived as a girl. Sarah was glad that she had finally decided to let them know the full story. It was so strange, Florence had been so completely sinned against, yet it was she who felt guilty, as though somehow everything that happened was her own fault and she had to take full responsibility. Sarah had heard of a similar condition called 'survivor's guilt', concentration camp prisoners often suffered from it. They felt guilty that they had survived when so many others had perished. Consequently they suffered from a curious feeling that everything that had happened was their own fault.

Sarah remembered so clearly when Florence had come to stay with her in Devon. It was the summer of 1916, the terrible summer of the Battle of the Somme. Sarah shivered at the memory. Charles's family had a small farm near Salcombe and at the outbreak of the hostilities he had insisted that she go to stay there for the duration of the war. She lived there alone with an old housekeeper called Dorcas and it was rather a lonely time. Apart from Charles's weekend visits she spent most of the time alone. Charles was a gifted scientist who was working on a secret project that kept him on the General Staff in London and well away from the fighting on the Western Front. He was riddled with guilt, knowing what his fellow officers and their soldiers were going through in France. As a consequence he kept volunteering for the Front. However, much to Sarah's relief he was far too valuable to the powers that be as a scientist for them to let him go to be slaughtered with the rest. It was hard enough worrying about Edward during those dark days without worrying about Charles as well. She knew how lucky she was that she had not lost either of the men that she loved most in that terrible war. There were women of her generation who had no male relatives at all left alive at the end of it. All their men folk, brothers, fathers, husbands and sweethearts had been killed. She never understood where they found the courage to carry on with life, but somehow they did. She often thought that theirs was a cursed generation.

Whilst she was living in Devon her mother had written to ask if Florence could come and visit for a while. She explained in her letter that Florence hadn't been well and that Martha was very worried about her. Sarah was delighted; she had always liked Florence and she welcomed the company. Much as she loved Devon, the farm was isolated and there wasn't much to do when Charles was up in London. Sometimes she didn't see him for weeks on end and she was overjoyed at the thought of having some company.

Florence caught the train down from Liverpool with her maid, Hettie, as chaperone, Josiah wouldn't hear of Martha accompanying her. Dorcas was as thrilled as Sarah at the thought of having another woman for company. It would mean having someone to gossip with and also someone to help around the house. The train was due to arrive at Totnes station, so Sarah took the family car to meet it. She remembered how visibly shocked she was when she saw Florence climb down from the carriage. The change in her was truly shocking. She had a deathly pallor, as though someone had sucked all the blood out of her veins and left her lifeless. Florence looked so frail and broken that Sarah knew that there was something dreadfully wrong with her. However, she quickly hid her surprise and walked over and gave her a welcoming hug, but she got another shock. Under her bulky coat, Florence was just skin and bones. She had lost a great deal of weight. She was still as lovely as ever, but there was a terrible sadness about her. Her huge dark eyes were full of pain. She greeted Sarah with a half smile, returned her embrace, politely asked after her health, then just turned obediently and walked to the car with her in silence. She was very quiet and didn't seem to care where she was or who she was with. She didn't seem to have a physical illness, but she looked as if her soul had died. Florence had always been bursting with energy and lived life to the full, dragging everyone in her wake, making them join in and enjoy every minute of every day. Sometimes she had exhausted Sarah, who was always struggling to keep up. So what on earth had happened to cause this change in her?

When they arrived at the house, Florence was obviously happy to be there, but displayed none of her usual enthusiasm. After supper they sat by the fire and talked quietly. All Florence wanted to do was talk about Edward and Sarah was quite happy to oblige her. They swapped letters and information and it was clear to Sarah that Florence was in love with Edward. Perhaps it was worry about his safety that had caused this anxious change in Florence? But no, she was the sort of person who would bravely carry on and hide her feelings. Sarah was at a loss to know just what was troubling Florence. She clearly wasn't well, but Sarah had the feeling that it wasn't a simple physical illness, but something more complex. As Florence sat silently looking into the fire, Sarah thought how beautiful she looked. Edward and Florence would make such a lovely couple if they married. But Sarah immediately put the thought out of her head. It was tempting providence to plan any future for a man who was serving on the Western Front. Not many of them would have a future at all. It was all so uncertain, Edward out there, Florence here so changed, so quiet, so still. If only she knew how to help her.

However, it was only a matter of time before Sarah realised what the problem was. If only she had known then what she knew now; she would have dealt with it all so differently. As it was she coped with it in the best way she could and did what she thought was right. It was an awful time. Sarah tried to help Florence, but she was so innocent and unworldly herself that she inadvertently did the wrong thing and ultimately caused Florence's downfall, but she had no idea what a monster Josiah really was. Sarah had tried to make Florence talk and explain how she had got into that condition, but Florence couldn't. She tried to, but the words just wouldn't come. Eventually Sarah persuaded her to write it all down, everything that was troubling her. She thought it might be easier for Florence. However, Sarah was not at all prepared for the truth. She was devastated by Florence's revelations. She still had her written testimony, which she intended to show to Emmie when she came down. But how was Sarah going make Emmie understand what happened? How could a modern young woman understand? Sarah sighed, stood up and prepared to leave the river and return home, but she was troubled. Just how was she going to tell Emmie what happened to her grandmother?

———⊂◈⊃———

The sound of the phone felt like a drill boring through Emmie's temple. She automatically reached out a hand and answered it. It was Katy. She shook her head, sat up and made an effort to sound wide awake. She failed dismally.

'Have I woken you up?' Katy asked.

'You have, but don't worry about it; I ought to be getting up. What time is it?'

'Just after mid day! Still if you can't lie is as a student, when can you?' Katy laughed.

Emmie squinted at her watch, 'Is that really the time? I suppose you are at work?'

'Of course, been here for hours and am here every day of the week, nine till five, fifty two weeks of the year, with two weeks holiday as a reprieve!' laughed Katy.

'Stop it; you're making me feel guilty. I was up until four o'clock reading. I just didn't notice the time.' pleaded Emmie

'It must have been something interesting then.' laughed Katy.

'Well it was, is. I'll tell you about it when we meet up. We are going to meet up aren't we?'

'Yes, I hope so. Are you free tonight? I could meet you at 8 o'clock in that wine bar we mentioned?'

'Great. I'll see you there.'

'Mind you don't go back to sleep and forget all about our conversation or worse still think that you dreamed it!!'

Emmie laughed, 'I won't, and it's time I got going any way. See you at eight then.' And with that she rang off.

'So Katy rang,' Emmie thought to herself as she scrambled out of bed and made for the shower. She was really pleased. She wondered if it had been left to her whether she would have made contact, she was such a bad communicator. She really would have to make more of an effort. She stepped into the shower turned it on full and gratefully let the hot water flush the cobwebs away.

As she started drying herself she started to recall what she had read the night before in Martha's journal. Why was she so distressed? She decided to look for Sarah's phone number or address as soon as she was dressed. Gran must have it somewhere in an address book and surely she wouldn't mind if Emmie looked in it for Sarah's address. She pulled on some jeans, a white shirt and a favourite pink sweater and started downstairs.

While the coffee was brewing she went into the little sitting room and pulled down the top of the bureau. There it was Gran's ancient green morocco address book. Emmie felt as though Florence had left it there for her to find, but no, that was a ridiculous thought. Now what was Sarah's surname? Her maiden name was Kingsley, like Gran's, but who did she marry? Emmie had never had a lot to do with Sarah, probably because she lived in London. She had intended to get in touch whilst she was at London University, but typically had never got round to it. She knew that she and Gran had always been close, but Gran had always rather kept Sarah to herself. Now, she married someone called Charles, it was a short name, Lowe, that was it, Lowe. She went to the 'L's and sure enough there was Sarah's address in Chelsea and a telephone number. She suddenly felt very nervous. Would Sarah mind her contacting her? Here she went again; prevaricating, delaying contacting someone until she never contacted them at all. She decided to have some coffee and then ring.

She finished her coffee, and then rang Sarah from the kitchen phone. The voice at the other end of the phone was crystal clear and sounded very young. Sarah didn't express any surprise at hearing from Emmie, but sounded delighted and immediately invited her down to stay. They arranged that Emmie should travel down by train on Friday morning, that was the day after tomorrow and stay at least until Sunday. Emmie was pathetically relieved that she had made contact and the visit was organised, but she did wonder exactly what she was going to find, or, in fact, just what she was doing. She roamed aimlessly back into the sitting room. The journals were still on the sofa. She gathered them together and put them with Gran's morocco address book in the top of the bureau. She then locked it and pocketed the key. She didn't want her father snooping. Her father, heavens, she had to tell him that she was going to London, but not why she was going. She would invent an old university friend. That would satisfy him.

She needed to have another look in the tin box and see what other treasures it held. She had thought about searching the box for clues before contacting Sarah, but she felt the need to talk to someone who had known the people in the journal. She wanted to ask questions that couldn't be answered by pieces of inanimate paper. She returned to the boot room and turned on the 60 watt bulb and pulled the box out again. She peered into the gloom, but couldn't see clearly what was in there. She rifled around. There were a large number of official looking documents in the bottom; they looked like birth certificates, death certificates, old passports, that kind of thing. There were a number of large brown manilla envelopes containing a variety of letters, photographs, ration coupons, and identity cards and all kinds of invoices. She decided to see Sarah and learn more about her family before she started to sort through this huge pile of paper. So she closed the box, locked it and pushed it back under the bench. She would come back to it at a later date, when she had learned more about the people that it concerned.

———◆———

Katy put the phone down after calling Emmie. She was so pleased to have seen her old friend; she thought that she would never meet up with her again and was looking forward to seeing her that evening. When she returned to her desk she saw that Doreen had brought in the post and there were a pile of letters sitting on her desk. They were probably replies to the ones she had sent out about the ladies on Buttercup Ward. There were about twenty in all, not a bad response and it was early days yet. She was really excited as she sat down at her desk and started to open them. There were a mixed bunch of responses. Some kind souls had taken the trouble to write and say that they didn't know anyone of the patient's name and had lived at the property for several years but had no knowledge of the previous occupants. Katy put these on one pile. She would have to see if she could organise visitors for those ladies if she couldn't locate a relative. She felt in dire need of coffee so she wandered over to the corner where the kettle stood on the coffee stained tray that celebrated the Queen's coronation in 1953. It lived amongst an assortment of mugs with witty logos, an array of tea stained spoons, a fairly new looking bottle of milk and some powdered coffee additive. She shook the kettle to see if there was any water in it before she switched it on and then sniffed the milk to see if it was fresh. For once it was. Whilst waiting for the kettle to boil, she gazed out of the window. Her office looked out onto the fire station. Bill, the fireman, was polishing the antique fire engine, the love of his life. She wondered idly if it would be any actual use if there ever was a fire. It must have been there since the hospital was built. It was probably worth a small fortune as an antique, much like the hospital itself. Once again Katy found herself wondering how long it would stay open. The government would be only too delighted to unload this expensive and unpopular white elephant. It would be so much cheaper, although totally ineffective, to replace it with care in the community.

The kettle boiled so she turned away from the window, made her coffee and wandered back to her desk. Everyone was out on the wards or the district, so Mrs McKendrick had instructed Katy to stay in the office until someone returned. The peace and quiet meant she could get on with her correspondence without any interruptions. Some of the letters held lovely surprises. Several grand children had replied to Katy's enquiries. Apparently many of them occupied their grandmother's old houses and in many cases had no idea that their grandmothers were still alive in the hospital. They certainly had no idea that they were allowed to visit relatives on the wards. Some had no knowledge that they had ever had a relative in an institution. However, most of them wanted to come and see the long lost relative, even if it was just out of curiosity. Some were a little afraid and were concerned that the patient might be dangerous. These letters made Katy laugh a little. Most people's perception of madness was so out of date and misconceived. She put those letters in a pile so that she could draft individual replies. Some of them had given a contact telephone number so Katy made a note of these, with the intention of phoning at a later date. Some people wrote to say that they didn't know the patient themselves, but knew someone who did and supplied an address. Again she made a note of these. Sorting the letters took most of the morning, but she was delighted with the response. She had at least twelve contacts that seemed willing to visit. Sister Parkinson would be thrilled and this was only the first batch of replies. How would they feel these old ladies to suddenly be confronted by a long lost grandson or granddaughter? Would they be able to understand who they were? She did hope so.

Chapter Eight

The dinner with Katy had been a great success. Emmie wondered, not for the first time, why she had allowed the friendship to drift. They had talked for hours about their various professions and Katy had even asked Emmie if she would like to 'adopt' one of her old ladies, one of the long stay patients on the Annexe. Emmie didn't say no, although she was a little apprehensive. She did, however, agree to go to the hospital and visit the ward, little did she realise at this stage how important that visit would be to her after her London trip.

She had time to ponder as she sat on the Liverpool, Lime Street to London, Euston train. Katy had mentioned Paul without any prompting from Emmie, who just hoped that Katy didn't notice the flush that rose from her neck at the mention of his name. He had indeed qualified as a doctor, but to Emmie's relief he wasn't married. He was no longer working in Africa; however, he was in Canada, in Ottawa to be precise, doing some recruitment work for VSO. Emmie didn't know whether to be relieved or disappointed. However, Katy told her that Paul was coming home shortly on leave and his sabbatical in Canada was coming to an end, so there was a possibility that she might meet up with him again. She really was pathetic, but every time she remembered him her heart seemed to melt. She had met so many men since those long ago teenage years, but none of them had affected her like Paul. It wasn't just that he was tall, blonde and good looking, although those three points were not entirely irrelevant, he was also clever and witty. He made her laugh. She smiled to herself as she thought about him, her head leaning against the train window watching her reflection appear to fly over fields and towns as the train sped down to London. She had spent many evenings after school at Katy's house where Paul would regale them with stories about college that had amused him. They would laugh until they cried as he told his stories, mimicking tutors and students alike. He never showed any interest in her or gave her the slightest encouragement. She was sure that she was no more than Katy's school friend to him, just another silly teenager. However, she couldn't help wondering if she would meet him again after all these years, especially now that she was in touch with Katy again. Life was strange and full of coincidences; she was still surprised that she had bumped into Katy in the refectory at university. Of all the places she ever expected to see

Katy, this was the most unlikely and she thought that may be it was just fate dictating that she would meet up with Paul again, but then she put that thought out of her head as absurd. He probably had a steady girlfriend and would still think of her as nothing more than Katy's school friend who had grown up a little.

Her thoughts moved from Paul to her father, Freddie, he had visited her again at her grandmother's and spent the afternoon with her. He seemed lost, like a little boy, since he had learned of Florence's imminent death. Emmie too was heartbroken at the thought of life without her grandmother, but her love had never been dependent like her father's. She sat and chatted with him and tried to comfort him. In order to distract him from dwelling on the subject of her grandmother's illness, once again she used the tactic of trying to extract more information from him about his ancestors. However, he wasn't much use to her. He didn't actually seem to know as much as she did, but it took his mind off his own unhappiness. On reflection, Emmie did think it was odd that Freddie didn't know anything about his grandfather. It seemed that Josiah's name was never mentioned, that he was never talked about at all. In a normal family, a dead husband wasn't usually banished from memory. He was often referred to, even if it was in a negative way. But it seemed as though Martha and Florence had never mentioned Josiah and acted as if he had never existed at all. It was strange, but she knew enough about family politics not to be too surprised.

Emmie knew that her mother, Susan, had little patience when it came to Freddie's complex relationship with Florence. She felt strongly that he had only come round that afternoon in order to seek comfort and to create an opportunity to talk about his mother. She felt sorry for him so she was patient and listened carefully. She hadn't the heart to shoo him out like she normally would have done, but it meant that by the time he had gone she didn't have much time to pack and get ready to meet Katy. She hadn't really considered what she was going to ask Sarah, or indeed how she could really explain why she felt the overwhelming need, quite suddenly, to know about her family history. She just hoped that Sarah had a sympathetic and understanding nature.

As the journey to London continued Emmie became more and more excited. She was extremely curious to find out if Sarah could tell her more about her family history. She realised that Florence's illness had caused Martha terrible anxiety, but her journals had stopped so abruptly that Emmie felt an overwhelming curiosity to find out why it seemed to have caused such a drama in Martha's life. Emmie knew enough to realise that Florence must have recovered from her illness and gone on to marry and have children. She hadn't died, so why did Martha's journals stop so unexpectedly? Emmie instinctively felt that there was more she should know and that was why she needed to see Sarah.

As Emmie had never visited her before, Sarah wanted to meet her at Euston, but knowing what the London traffic was like, Emmie wouldn't hear of it. She was quite capable of finding her way to Chelsea on the underground. She got the Northern line to Victoria and then the District Line to Sloane Square and then it was only a few hundred yards along the Kings Road to Sarah's delightful little Chelsea house. Having arrived a little early, just after lunch, and feeling slightly apprehensive, she hesitated a little before ringing the door bell. She wasn't sure what to expect, although she had been reassured by the sympathetic phone conversation that she had had with Sarah, who seemed warm and caring. Eventually she rang the bell, waited for a while and in due course heard a noise from deep within the bowels of the house.

The door was opened by a smart elderly woman, who was obviously Sarah. She was very like her brother, Edward, Emmie's grandfather. She had the same dark brown, deep set eyes and high cheek bones; although her dark hair was now snowy white and she wore it swept up into an elegant chignon. She looked at Emmie for what seemed like an age before she said anything. She seemed to be struggling with her emotions and Emmie wasn't quite sure what to do. Eventually Sarah spoke.

'Oh my dear, I am so sorry but I am lost for words. It's just that you are so like your grandmother.' Then she stepped forward and embraced Emmie, who was also feeling quite emotional. Stepping back, Sarah held Emmie at arms length whilst she collected herself, then realised that they were still standing on the doorstep and she hadn't even invited Emmie in. 'My dear, what must you think of me! Do come in, just follow me, and leave your case in the porch for now.'

Emmie followed her down the narrow hall way into a bright, modern kitchen which had been extended sideways into a conservatory. The doors from the conservatory opened onto a small garden, which held a decorative wrought iron table and four chairs.

When Sarah reached the kitchen she turned and looked at Emmie again, tears shining in her eyes. 'I'm sorry my dear, it's just that you are so like your dear grandmother and I am still a little upset at the news that she is so seriously ill.'

Emmie stepped forward and embraced Sarah without saying anything. It was Sarah who spoke first. 'Well come along, I think she'd be laughing at us if she could see us getting so upset on her account. I've just opened a bottle of Chardonnay and it's nice and cold. Shall we make the most of the lovely weather and drink it outside?'

'That sounds lovely. Can I take anything out?'

'No, my dear, thank you it's all ready outside waiting for you.'

With that Emmie followed Sarah into the delightful little garden where they sat in the warm autumn sunshine enjoying the wine, whilst Sarah asked Emmie about herself. Previously, although the two women had known of each other's existence, they hadn't met very often. Florence seemed to keep Sarah to herself somehow, it was hard to know whether it was a deliberate ploy, or just a simple matter of convenience. Sometimes it just wasn't possible for the family and Sarah to meet. Emmie obligingly ran through her brief history, her time at school, the disastrous decision to read Law at London University, her return home in disgrace and her subsequent, more successful, decision to return to university to study subjects that she was interested in, English and Art. Sarah listened attentively and only made an occasional, relevant, comment. Eventually Emmie told her about the old, tin deed box in her grandmother's house. She explained to Sarah that Florence had asked her to sort through it and catalogue the photographs and papers that were inside. Naturally, Emmie had started to read through some of the papers and amongst them were Martha's journals. It was the contents of the journals that had caused her to contact Sarah to find out more about her family's history. The journals had awakened a strong desire in her to talk to someone who had actually known her grandparents. Following a short pause Sarah nodded knowingly, but she didn't comment on the subject of the box immediately.

Emmie found herself warming to the older woman and she was almost as comfortable in her company as she was in her grandmother's. They chatted companionably in the garden for what was left of the afternoon. The constant background hum of the traffic was the only thing that reminded Emmie that she was in the centre of a major city. Sarah had cleverly placed latticed trelliswork on top of the rustic Victorian walls that enclosed the little garden and grown numerous trailing plants over them. It gave the effect of being in a secluded corner of a large country garden. She had created sloping beds which were full of flowers and in each corner there was a large earthenware pot overflowing with colourful autumn flowers and herbs. The warmth of the late afternoon had brought out the heady scent of the honeysuckle and the bees droned lazily in and out of the late summer blooms. Sarah and Emmie enjoyed getting to know one another over the bottle of wine. Eventually the garden fell into shadow, the air became cooler and both women started to feel the chill. Before they went inside, Sarah outlined her plans for the evening and it soon became obvious that she knew exactly why Emmie had decided to visit her when she told her about her grandmother's letter.

'Emmie, I have a confession to make. I was rather

expecting you to contact me; I had a letter from your grandmother warning me that you might get in touch at some stage.

'How did she know that I'd contact you?'

'Oh I think she guided you here by letting you have an insight into some of the past without knowing the full story. She knew that the contents of the tin deed box that you mentioned wouldn't tell you everything. I think she hoped they would whet your appetite and make you curious to know more about the past. I am the only person alive who remembers what happened, so I was the next logical step. I think she knows you pretty well.'

Emmie felt herself smile in the shadow of the garden. 'I think that she does, she certainly knows how curious I am.'

'Well thank goodness you are. Your grandmother wants me to tell you the story of her youth, to explain to you sympathetically just what happened, and to fill in the parts of the story that are missing. I am only too willing to do so, but if you hadn't had a curious nature it would have made my task very difficult! Now, I thought we would go out tonight and I will then attempt to tell you all that I know. I've booked a table at a small, quiet Italian restaurant round the corner. We can talk privately there. Would that suit you?'

'Yes, that sounds lovely.'

'I don't know about you, but I am beginning to get a little chilly. Shall we go inside and I'll show you to your room? I'm sure you would like a rest before dinner. Shall I see you down here about half past seven and we'll have a drink before we go over?'

'I would like that, I'm starting to feel chilly myself and I would appreciate a bath and a lie down before we go out.'

'Good, that's settled then. Come on we'll go in and I'll show you to your room and you can have some peace before we go out!'

Emmie hadn't realised how tired she was and welcomed the chance for a rest. She lay on the bed and dozed for a while and when she woke up the bedroom clock told her that it was half past six and there was barely enough time to get ready. She grabbed her dressing gown, clambered off the bed and rushed over the landing to the little bathroom, where she began to run a hot bath. She left that running whilst she returned to her room and unpacked her things. She chose a simple, but elegant, white linen dress and jacket to wear that night, together with a pair of black high heeled shoes. She then tidied the rest of her things away. She returned to the bathroom to check on the bath, which was full, poured in some scented lotion and had a very welcome long, hot, soothing soak before putting on her makeup and getting dressed. When she was quite ready she went downstairs where Sarah was waiting for her with a bottle of champagne. Dressed in an elegant claret coloured trouser suit she looked twenty years younger than her eighty years. 'Well you look lovely,' she said as Emmie entered the room.

'So do you,' rejoined Emmie and they both laughed as they were absurdly pleased with the mutual approval.

'I thought we'd have a bottle of champagne to start our evening and to celebrate Florence's life. I shall miss her so much you know, as I'm sure you and your family will.'

Emmie smiled and accepted the proffered glass with pleasure. Sarah lifted hers and pointed it towards Emmie.

'A toast to Florence.'

They touched glasses as Emmie replied, 'To Florence, and may I say how kind it is of you to see me at such short notice and to put me up like this.'

'I assure you it is my pleasure. I have no family of my own, Charles and I couldn't have children, so it's a pleasure to spend some time in the company of a young person. I rarely have the chance.'

They had two glasses of champagne at the house and then walked through the cool autumn evening to the little Italian restaurant where Sarah had booked a table. Even though it was a Saturday night and all the tables were taken, there was only a gentle hum of conversation. Sarah had reserved a secluded corner table where they settled down, selected their meal and chose the wine. Only when they were settled did Sarah broach the subject that had been on both their minds since Emmie's arrival.

'Your grandmother has quite a story you know, she finds it impossible to talk about the events that scarred her early life and it's not very surprising. However, as I told you earlier, she wants you and the family to know what happened to her before she dies and she has chosen me to tell you and I am honoured that she would trust me with such an important mission. In turn she has also chosen you to tell your parents.'

Emmie grimaced, 'I know and I'm not looking forward to it. By the way do you know where Gran has gone?'

'No, although I suspect that she has gone to see your Aunt Elizabeth, to say her goodbyes and make her peace before she dies. Elizabeth is so wrapped up in her bird project that I very much doubt if she wanted to come down to Liverpool, or in fact whether she could actually have left it as she is in sole charge. It's a shame really, but your Aunt Elizabeth and your grandmother were never very close.'

'Do you think that she will tell Aunt Elizabeth her story?'

Sarah shook her head, 'No, I don't think Florence can tell her own story. I think it will be left to you or possibly your father, once he knows the full story, to explain everything to Elizabeth.'

'Well I just hope that I can do her justice.'

'I'm sure you will.'

'Sarah, I can't tell you how grateful I am to you for seeing me. Ever since I read Martha's journals, which were in Gran's tin box, I have wanted to know more about my family, but not just from papers. I also wanted someone to talk to about them, someone who knew the people concerned and could flesh them out for me. I have drawn some of my own conclusions from what I have read, but then I could be completely wrong in those conclusions couldn't I? I could have completely misinterpreted what Martha was trying to say.'

'Well how much do you know? What did Martha's journals tell you?'

'I don't actually know very much really. Martha wrote about herself. She seemed to be obsessed with the fact that she was so plain that she would never attract a husband. She dreaded being an old maid and living on charity.'

Sarah laughed, 'Oh Martha! Well I suppose she could have been described as plain, facially that is, but she was such a lovely person that once you knew her she became beautiful. She didn't have a suitor not because she was plain, but because she was so limited in her choice and was far too intelligent for most of the local men. She terrified them. What else did she say?'

'Well she describes Josiah's arrival in town and his courtship of her, which sounded very formal and rather loveless, but then I don't know if that's the way people were then. She also discusses the circumstances of her marriage to Josiah. She seemed to have deep reservations about him. Instinctively he troubled her. She had no real reason to fear or doubt him, but he made her feel uneasy. Nevertheless, he was considered to be such an eligible gentleman that she knew if he proposed to her she had no option but to marry him.'

At the mention of Josiah Sarah's face darkened. 'She was right to be troubled by Josiah. It's strange the way that Martha always thought that she was plain. She did herself such an injustice. As I've already said, she wasn't conventionally pretty, but was such a sweet, kind, gentle and very intelligent woman, that you soon forgot her looks. Anyway, she wasn't that unattractive. I think it was more that men were shallower in those days and liked pretty, empty headed girls, particularly in the provinces. But to marry Josiah, my God, no wonder she had reservations. My family also had reservations, which we kept to ourselves. Everyone seemed to think that he was wonderful. Emmie dear, he was quite awful. How can I describe him? He was humourless, cold, lacking in emotion and sexually repressed. In many ways she would have been better off staying single, except of course that she would never have had Florence and her family were so thrilled that she had attracted such an 'eligible' suitor that I don't think she had any choice other than to marry him.'

'I can see you had a high opinion of him!' Emmie joked, 'But just from Martha's description of him and the way he looked on their engagement photograph he frightened me. It was his eyes that worried me, they were so cold. Here, I have it with me,' Emmie took the photograph of Martha and Josiah out of her bag and handed it to Sarah.

'Good Lord, I've never seen this before. When was it taken?'

'Well I can't be sure, but I suspect it was taken when they announced their engagement.'

'You're so right about those eyes. They are as cold as ice, just as they were in real life, ice cold blue. It's strange though, even I have to admit that he was a conventionally good looking man. You can understand why he was considered a catch and the family were so pleased when he started courting Martha. He was financially sound, as well. They didn't really look any further than that in those days.'

'From the journals it seems that Martha was lonely in her marriage, yet she seemed relieved to have her own home and the status of a married woman. She never seemed to be defeated by him and she was obviously delighted to have Florence.'

Sarah's face darkened again. 'Oh she most certainly was defeated by him in the end, but I'll tell you about that later. Martha certainly adored your grandmother; Florence was all that she lived for and she made everything worthwhile. They were very close.'

'She was obviously very happy when Florence was born, but later Martha started to make references to Josiah's attitude to Florence. It seemed to trouble her. From what I could gather from the journals, he seemed to almost resent Florence's beauty, her joy of life, and her loving nature. Martha seemed to be afraid that one day he would destroy Florence, crush the life out of her in some way. He was always criticising her, but I suppose she stood for all he disapproved of in life.'

'Indeed she did and Martha had just cause to be concerned. But let's keep first things first.'

'Well I'm willing to be patient. It was Martha's last journal entry that bothered me and prompted me to contact you. It was heartbreaking. Florence was locked in the attic and Martha was confined to her rooms. She knew Florence was terribly ill, but Josiah wouldn't let her see her. Something dreadful had happened, I know, but her journals just stop abruptly. She simply stops writing and there is no explanation about what had happened.'

Sarah seemed to have paled slightly and Emmie hardly heard her as she almost whispered, 'That was my fault.'

'What was your fault and why was it your fault?'

'Because I underestimated Josiah and I handed him the weapon he had been waiting for. I think underneath the Christian exterior there lurked a refined sadist.'

At this point the waiter approached with their meal and Emmie waited until he had finished serving them before she replied, 'How could Florence's illness and Martha's distress be your fault?'

'Well, I'll tell you the whole story and then you can make up your own mind.' Sarah took a deep breath and had a long drink of her wine before she continued. 'It started in the summer of 1916. It was a terrible summer indeed, the Battle of the Somme had been raging since July 1st. The war, which was supposed to have lasted until Christmas 1914 was far from over, in fact, it was gathering momentum by the day and taking a terrible toll. I think that it was just beginning to occur to people that they were witnessing something very close to Armageddon. I was living in Salcombe then, in Devon. My husband Charles's parents had an old farmhouse down there, which they used for holidays before the war. They both died in 1912 so it was unused and empty apart from the old housekeeper, Dorcas. Charles wanted me away from London and the threat of Zeppelin raids, so he persuaded me to move to Devon for the duration of the war. I was lucky, as he was a scientist involved in war work; he was kept in London, in spite of continually volunteering for active duty. They wouldn't let him go, his work was too important, so at least I knew that he was fairly safe. The downside was that it was rather lonely down there with only Dorcas for company.

In the August of 1916, I received a letter from my mother telling me that Martha had asked if Florence could to come and stay with me. Mother said that Martha had been very worried about Florence for some weeks, she had been quite ill it seemed, although Martha was very vague about the details of the illness. Anyway, she felt that it would do Florence good to spend some time by the sea and get some fresh air. I replied immediately saying that I would love to have Florence to stay and that she should come at once. I was delighted at the thought of having some company whilst Charles was in London.

My mother and Martha arranged for Florence to travel down by train with her maid, Hettie, as a chaperone. Josiah would never have consented to Martha coming as well and a young woman couldn't travel alone in those days. I think he only allowed Florence to come because even he was concerned about her health.

Oh Emmie, I will never forget seeing her for the first time. We had a car at the farm, so I arranged to drive over and meet the train at Totnes station as it was only a few miles away. I got there early and I was waiting on the platform as the train drew in. When Florence stepped down onto the platform I hardly recognised her. She was always a wisp of a thing, much like you, but she had lost so much weight. She looked like a scarecrow and her clothes just hung on her. It wasn't just the weight though, it was her face. I can see it now. She was so pale with dark rings under her eyes and oh those eyes, they looked haunted. I couldn't start to imagine what had wrought this change in her, but I was fairly sure that it was more than an illness. Today we would recognise that she was traumatised, only then doctors tended to look for physical reasons for their patient's ill health. Martha hadn't actually explained what was wrong with Florence, though looking back now I don't think she actually knew. I quickly smiled to hide the shock of seeing her, but I think she had seen my initial reaction and she just smiled ruefully at me. It wasn't just her appearance that had changed though, it was everything. She didn't seem to have any life left in her. Florence had always been so joyful and full of verve. Well, it was that part of her that Josiah strongly objected to, but now she was quiet and cowed. It was as if someone had given her a good beating and she was afraid of earning another one, almost like a brutally, broken horse. This Florence looked as though all the life had been sucked out of her. I greeted her and gave her a big hug and I could feel that she was just skin and bone under her bulky coat.

We loaded up the car and started back to the farmhouse. It was Hettie, her maid, who kept the conversation going. She never stopped exclaiming with delight about the scenery, the little thatched cottages, the rivers and anything you would care to mention. I could have kissed her because she broke what would have been a very awkward silence. Normally Florence too would be chattering away and commenting on what she saw with delight, but Florence hardly uttered a word all the way home. When we got to the farmhouse, Dorcas unloaded the car, took Florence's luggage to her room and then whisked Hettie off to the kitchen. Dorcas was as thrilled to have Hettie for company, as I was to have Florence. It was so lonely during the war with all the men at the Front and all normal social life at a halt.

Once she was settled in, I took Florence out into the garden and we sat and chatted, mainly about Edward, who of course was serving on the Western Front. At the mention of his name Florence started weeping. She said that she'd seen him on his last leave and he looked well, but slightly haunted. I thought quietly to myself then that that made two of them and I did wonder if that's what could be the matter with Florence. Was she pining for him? Was the worry that he may never return making her ill? Goodness knows I understood how she felt. The thought of Edward being wounded, maimed or killed made me feel ill. She was very much in love with him that much was obvious and we talked about him for hours. I showed her my letters and she let me read hers. We exchanged what few photographs we had and indulged ourselves in nostalgia. Suddenly she stopped, pushed the photographs and letters away from her saying, 'It's no good. He's lost to me forever.' Then she burst into a frantic sobbing that wracked her little body. I didn't know what she meant until later. I'm not sure that she knew exactly what she meant; she just knew that something was lost to her. I still thought that she was referring to the danger he was in at the Front. It wasn't until later that I found out what she really meant. I didn't know what to do so I comforted her and sent for Dorcas. She went off and prepared some hot milk and brandy and we got Florence to bed. I was so worried about her.

It really is difficult for your generation to realise just how naïve we were about sex. We knew virtually nothing and there was no way for us to learn anything about it. Our mothers were too repressed and embarrassed to talk about it, other than to explain the necessary rudiments when you were about to get married and some mothers didn't even do that. I knew girls who got married and still didn't know on their wedding nights what was expected of them. It was left to the poor husbands to explain to their horrified wives just what was normal in these circumstances. There were no books on the subject, no sex education at school and no radio or television. You just had to pick up what you could. This lack of education, of knowledge, was ridiculous I know and it could also be dangerous. If you didn't know what sex was, how could you safeguard against the danger that it presented in an unscrupulous man? Do you follow my meaning?'

Emmie said she did, but she really couldn't begin to comprehend a world where you grew up knowing nothing about sex.

'Well I hoped that Florence's health might improve, whilst she was staying with me. I took her for long walks and we chatted all day long. Dorcas cooked all her specialities for her and she soon began to put on weight. A little too much weight as it happened. I realised though that she was ill and I did wonder about calling the doctor. She was terribly sick all the time, especially in the mornings. I mentioned this to Dorcas, who eyed me like a duellist.

'Madam,' she stated firmly, 'That girl is not ill, she's pregnant, nearly four month gone if I'm any judge.'

Chapter Nine

Emmie felt as though Sarah had poured a bucket of ice cold water over her head. She simply couldn't comprehend what she had just heard and sat for several minutes just looking at Sarah, unable to speak. Sarah smiled at her knowingly. 'It's alright, I quite understand Emmie that was my reaction all those years ago. I thought that maybe Dorcas had got it wrong, but I knew in my heart that an old country woman like her would know when someone was expecting a baby.'

Emmie finally found her voice, 'But Gran, pregnant at fifteen, how? Who? Where?'

'Those are all the questions I asked myself at the time. I spent a while talking to Dorcas and asking her advice, I mean I was hardly more than a girl myself with absolutely no experience in these matters. Dorcas was fairly sure that Florence hadn't a clue that she was pregnant, if she understood the concept of pregnancy at all. Obviously Florence was aware that there was something wrong, she kept being sick and felt generally ill, but Dorcas was sure that she had no idea that she could be expecting a baby. She told me that Hettie had suspected for some time and obviously thought that was why Florence had been sent to the country. Hettie thought that my mother had arranged with Martha and Josiah that Charles and I should look after Florence quietly, here in the country, until she had the baby, then arrange for the poor little soul to be adopted. Apparently, we were then to send Florence home and pretend that nothing had happened. That way the Claytons would avoid a scandal. Dorcas assured me that lots of families did it. I was stunned, as you can imagine, because nothing could have been further from the truth.

Obviously neither my mother nor Martha had the slightest idea that Florence was pregnant. If they had they would have explained the situation to me, not just sent Florence to Devon without telling me what was going on. I mean preparations had to be made, there was the child to consider, who would arrange the adoption? Florence herself would have needed maternity clothes and medical care. No, there were so many things to consider that I knew for sure that my mother would never have left me to sort it all out alone.

I asked Dorcas if Hettie had any idea who the father was, but she hadn't. Apparently, Hettie told her that all the servants knew that Miss Florence was sweet on Mr Edward, but they felt he was an honourable young man and as Miss Florence was only fifteen and a moral girl, Hettie didn't think it was likely to be him.

She just couldn't see a man like Mr. Edward taking advantage of Miss Florence and leaving her to take the consequences alone. He knew he had to go back to the Western Front and that there was every chance he wouldn't return. He would never have risked leaving her in this condition. Anyway, she thought that with Miss Florence being under age, he would have been committing a criminal offence and he'd never have done that. I fully agreed with Hettie, I knew Edward well. He would never have considered making love to Florence before they were married. He wouldn't compromise her like that. No, I was sure it wasn't Edward's child, but I couldn't start to think who the father could be.

Dorcas became quite conspiratorial, and told me that she and Hettie had been discussing the situation. Hettie was sure that there had been foul play. I just looked at her uncomprehendingly and she enlightened me, by saying that Hettie thought someone had forced themselves on Miss Florence. I asked did she mean that Florence had been raped, which was a mistake because Dorcas looked shocked to the core when I used that word. When she recovered from the shock, she admitted that she thought someone had forced her. Apparently Hettie had told Dorcas that about twelve weeks before Miss Florence had gone off to teach at the Sunday School, which she hated, but Mr. Josiah insisted that she went every week. Anyway, when she came back she was all dishevelled and really upset. Hettie said she seemed to be strung up and silent. After that she started to go into herself and Hettie said she hadn't been the same since. She also told Dorcas that she had found some stained underclothing stuffed into the back of her wardrobe. It's amazing, Emmie, how much servants knew. We, the employers, thought we were being really discreet, but they knew everything, and usually before we did.

I was sceptical. I couldn't think who would attack Florence like that and get away with it. I said to Dorcas she would have told her mother. She wouldn't have kept quiet about it. Dorcas just put her head on one side and looked at me as if I was simple. She said obviously Miss Florence wouldn't have told anyone. I asked her why and she, who knew so much more than me about the world than I did, said it stood to reason; the woman always gets the blame. Well Emmie I wasn't sure about that, but she was probably right. I knew nothing about such things. I was out of my depth. I just didn't know where to go and what to do next. I had to decide what was best for Florence. I was shocked and insufficiently experienced to deal with such things. My first instinct was to ask Charles what to do, but he wasn't there. You girls nowadays, I mean you would just find help or go to the police, but people had such an odd attitude to sex in those days. I decided the only thing that I could do was talk to Florence and see what she could tell me. I thought that there was something really strange about the whole affair. It appeared to me that Florence didn't seem to understand what had happened to her and she certainly had no idea that there could be consequences. As it happened, I was right.

I told Dorcas of my intention to tackle Florence and find out what could have happened. She warned me to be careful with Florence and to approach her carefully. She got upset, she said she liked Miss Florence and 'it weren't right.' I agreed fully with her. I mean to have no idea, well about anything actually and then to be told that you're expecting a child. That was enough to send any young woman over the edge and Florence was already in a fragile state, both mentally and physically. But I had to find out what had happened and I had to explain to her that she was expecting a baby, no matter how unlikely that may seem to her. Apart from any other consideration, she needed medical help.'

Emmie had listened in horrified silence to Sarah's account. It seemed inconceivable to her that you could be pregnant and not know, but then she realised that she lived in a far more enlightened society than that which had existed at the end of the nineteenth century, 'How on earth did you approach Florence,' Emmie asked Sarah, 'I mean how do you tell someone that they are pregnant when they've no idea even that they might be? Did young girls understand about pregnancy? Did you have anything to do with pregnant women, was their condition discussed?'

'No, not really, the older women would whisper about it and talk in the usual euphemisms, but after the first few months a pregnant woman would wear smocks and retire from society. She would naturally see close friends and family, but I can't remember seeing many pregnant women. I vaguely knew about it, but I'm not sure how. What a stupid way to carry on really. Anyway I watched Florence carefully for a day or two just to make sure that she was pregnant and that she really didn't know about the child. Then I broached the subject. I had to; she was beginning to show and kept making jokes about Dorcas's wonderful cooking and the weight that she was gaining.

Anyway, we were having our coffee after lunch in the little sitting room one or two days later and I spied my chance. Terrified, I broached the subject carefully, I began by telling her about a neighbour of ours who had just found out that she was pregnant and was going to have a baby. I watched carefully to see if this news provoked any kind of a reaction, but it didn't. She just showed a polite interest, as if she were not terribly sure why I had told her. I soon realised that Florence was a complete innocent and had only a sketchy idea about what I was telling her. She did ask a few vague questions, but was obviously a little embarrassed by the subject and didn't show any further interest, in fact she changed the subject completely.

I was at a loss what to do next; so I decided to try the direct approach. I sat on the sofa with her and held her hands and told her as gently as I could that I suspected that she was expecting a baby, like my neighbour. She looked at me as if I had gone mad. The idea had never entered her head and she just couldn't understand why I had suggested such a thing. She really had no idea at all that she might be pregnant and simply looked at me in horrified silence for several minutes. Then suddenly her face relaxed and she started to smile. She obviously thought that I needed enlightening about the facts of life and informed me, quite seriously, that you had to be married to have a baby and she wasn't married. I was beginning to become exasperated, so I asked if she knew how babies were made. She said yes, of course, you got married and if you were good, God gave you a baby. She only had the vaguest idea how this might happen. I don't think she'd given it much consideration actually, which made me wonder how she'd got into her present predicament. I tried again, but I was finding it quite hard to talk about such things, even with a friend. In those days newly married young women just didn't talk about sex and babies, unless it was to an older and more experienced female.

I decided to try a different approach and find out how she had got herself pregnant and who the father was. I asked if she'd ever been alone with a man. Again she just looked at me as if I were talking nonsense and said of course she had, lots of times, with her father and her uncles and neighbours. This was getting me nowhere. I asked if she had ever been alone with a young man and again she said of course she had, she'd told me herself that she'd walked to Sunday School with Edward and they were alone. I took a very deep breath and asked her if Edward had tried to touch her. She was becoming quite annoyed by now with what she thought were rather pointless and stupid questions, mainly, I suspect because she couldn't understand exactly what I was trying to imply. She asked quite archly just what did I mean by 'touched'. Oh Emmie I was getting very embarrassed by this time, I asked her had Edward tried to kiss her and she said he certainly had not, he was a gentleman.

I have to admit that I was really quite puzzled by now, but I had one last attempt and asked her if a man had hurt her or…, but before I could finish my question, quite suddenly, she turned ashen and became quite immobile. At last I had struck a chord. I repeated my question, but she didn't answer, she just sat very still, but began to tremble. She just kept whispering that it couldn't be; she wouldn't believe it. Then she asked me if you could get pregnant if someone hurt you in a private place. I was horrified. I just couldn't imagine what she was talking about, but I nodded slowly and said that you could. She started weeping and then she flung herself into my arms sobbing, she sobbed and sobbed. I just sat and held her till she calmed down. I asked if she could tell me what had happened, but she just shook her head. I was so worried I wanted to send Dorcas for the doctor, but this seemed to terrify her more and she begged me not to. She said doctors were evil, they hurt and punished you. I couldn't understand why she seemed so afraid of doctors, but tried to calm her down and reassure her that our doctor was a good man and I promised he wouldn't hurt her.

I put Florence to bed and stayed with her, whilst Dorcas fetched the doctor. I was so worried and confused. I just couldn't start to imagine what had happened to her, but something surely had and I felt so inadequate to deal with it. Eventually the doctor came and I explained the unusual circumstances of her pregnancy. Florence was adamant that she wouldn't see him, she seemed petrified. I know why now, but then I just couldn't understand why anyone would be scared of our doctor, he was a lovely man, very sympathetic and kind. Eventually, after much reassurance, Florence agreed to see him. He just chatted to her and calmed her down a little. When he came out of her room he spoke to me and told me that he didn't think it was wise to even suggest an examination of her in this state and he prescribed a mild sedative. He said that he would keep calling in to see Florence, until he gained her confidence, then perhaps she would consent to an examination. He asked where she was sleeping and I told him she was in the spare room. He suggested that I move her in with me; he didn't want her to spend more time alone than was absolutely necessary. I asked if he was worried about her and he said he was, very worried, he thought she looked very strained and shocked. After he left, Florence took the sedative and calmed down a little and eventually she fell asleep.

The next morning she came down to breakfast and behaved more or less as though nothing had happened, although she was very quiet. I tried to talk to her about her condition after the meal, but she refused to accept that she was pregnant and certainly didn't want to discuss it with me. She just didn't want to admit what was happening. I tried and tried to make her talk to me, but she either clammed up, changed the subject or left the room. She was getting very angry and I was getting nowhere. Suddenly I hit upon an idea. It was something that I had seen in a magazine, an article about shell shocked men who had witnessed and experienced the horrors of the trenches. It affected their nervous systems in various ways and they were so deeply scarred that they couldn't talk about their experiences. The doctors hit upon the idea of encouraging them to write down what they couldn't speak about. They found it easier somehow to write about their appalling experiences. I suppose that is where the word unspeakable comes from. Some things are so awful, that you cannot talk about them at all. I think this is now an accepted therapy, but then it was quite revolutionary. Anyway I decided to try this approach with Florence. I simply said to her that if she found it impossible to tell me what had happened to her, maybe she could just write it down.

At first she refused, but it was a passive, stubborn resistance, so I just kept on asking her and prompting her. I showed her where all the writing materials were kept in the little study and then I avoided the subject of pregnancy and chatted about generalities, desperately hoping that she would eventually find the courage to tell me what had happened. I found it difficult to be patient and talk about trivial matters when I was so worried about her well being, but eventually my patience was rewarded. One day Florence quietly slipped into the study, she didn't say anything; she just went in there and closed the door behind her. She stayed in the study for several hours and I can tell you it took all my self control to leave her in there alone, but I did. I also instructed Dorcas and Hettie to stay away from the study until she came out. Eventually she emerged. She looked very pale and quite shaken. She handed me two pages of hand written script and then went straight up to her room.

I took the pages into the little sitting room and sat and read them on my own. What she produced in those hours shocked me to the core. Even now it makes me sick when I think about what happened to her, but to the protected and innocent little soul that I was then, it was horrifying. I still have those handwritten pages and when we get home I want you to read them. You can take them to bed with you. I think that you should be on your own when you look at them. Afterwards, I will answer any questions that you might have.

'What happened when you had finished reading the account that Gran had written?'

'Oh, I went straight up to her room. She was lying fully clothed on the bed just staring at the ceiling, her hands on her stomach. I climbed onto the bed beside her and hugged her to me. We didn't say anything; in fact we never really discussed what happened. I just accepted her written version of events; I think it would have been too painful for her to discuss it any further. However, she did finally accept that she was expecting a baby, so we focused on that and tried to make it as joyous as we could. She decided to see the doctor as long as I didn't tell him what had happened and I agreed to that. I would have agreed to anything that persuaded her to have medical help. We also started knitting little coats and sewing cot sheets and generally preparing a layette, but it wasn't an easy time.

Emmie was very thoughtful at the end of Sarah's story. She could hardly believe that it was her grandmother's story that she had been listening to. It was like hearing about a complete stranger.

'What did she say happened to her?' Emmie finally asked.

'I want you to read her account, let her tell you in her own words. I couldn't explain it half so well or as realistically as she did. I really wouldn't know where to start. What I will say though, is that that Josiah had a lot to answer for. Now my dear have you enjoyed your meal?'

'Oh yes I have, but I was so interested in your story I hardly noticed what I was eating!'

'Would you like anything else, another drink or a second cup of coffee?'

'No thank you, I am full,' replied Emmie smiling, 'Thank you so much for a lovely dinner and for taking the time to tell me about Gran.'

'My dear the pleasure has all been mine, however I have by no means finished yet, but that's for tomorrow. Shall we wander back to the house now? If you don't mind I'll have an early night, all this reminiscing is tiring.'

When they got back to the house, Sarah was as good as her word. She made some cocoa for herself and Emmie and then went up to bed, but before she retired she handed Emmie some yellowing handwritten pages saying,

'If I were you I would get into bed before you start reading this or you'll never settle.'

Chapter Ten

Florence's Story

Oh Sarah please forgive me, if I have seemed difficult, but I just couldn't tell you or, in fact, anyone else, what had happened to me. I'm not even sure that I can write it down, but I will try. My head is in such a muddle. There is so much that I don't understand. I know that I love Edward and I thought it was good to love someone. But I now know that it isn't. It is sinful to love a man, Dr. Pickard told me. He said I had evil thoughts then he hurt me to punish me. He hurt me to stop me having such thoughts. He said he was God's instrument come to drive the demons from my soul. He told me that it was my fault that I was being punished. He said I had brought this on my own head, because I was really a seductress... I don't know how loving someone is sinful. I don't know how to be a seductress; I don't really know what it means. Then you told me here in Devon that God had punished me for loving Edward, just like that foul man told me he would. God has shamed me by giving me a child, so all the world will know my wicked thoughts. But I don't think that loving Edward is wicked, it's a lovely thing to me, if it is so wicked that God has punished me, I must be the most sinful girl in the world. I don't understand anything, just that I feel strange and sick all the time. My head aches until I want to scream. I just don't understand what I've done wrong, why everything is such a muddle.

This nightmare started some months ago. I think it was in June, nearly four months ago? I don't know everything is in a jumble. It was on a Sunday. My father insisted that I taught at the local Sunday School every Sunday afternoon, even though I hated it. I tried everything in my power to get out of it, but he wouldn't let me. It wasn't the teaching that I minded, in fact I loved the village children, they were so bright and funny, no it wasn't them. It was the superintendent, Dr. Pickard. He frightened me. No, that is not quite the right word, it was a funny feeling that I didn't understand, he repulsed me and he was always fussing round me. His manner was inappropriate; he was always touching my arm or flinging his arm around my shoulders or cracking pathetic jokes and laughing close to my face with his yellow teeth and foul breath knocking me sick. He was an elder of the church with my father, so I had to be polite to him, but I hated him being anywhere near me. He pretended to be so pious, but believe me there was nothing Christian about that man. His wife was disabled and he made such a fuss over looking after her, always playing the uncomplaining, devoted, husband. Watching him you would have thought that he was a saint, but privately he was unkind to her and shouted at her and called her a stupid cripple. Their maid Annie told Hettie. Everyone except my father could see through him, but my father thought that he was a devout, committed Christian and perfect husband and he held him in high regard.

That particular Sunday was just like all the others. I used all kinds of excuses to try to get out of going to Sunday School, but my father wouldn't accept any of them, so after lunch I went to get ready. I wore my new red dress which had a beautiful white lace collar and a matching hat and jacket. It was a present from mother's brother. Father hated it, but he couldn't really stop me wearing it as he didn't want to upset Uncle Harold. He was right, though, I should have worn my plain, black, dress then maybe I wouldn't have been punished. Father always said that vanity led to sin, but I wanted to look my best, because Edward was home on leave. I thought I may catch a glimpse of him as I walked to Sunday School. I knew that my red dress suited me. I particularly loved the lace collar because I wasn't normally allowed to wear pretty things and I wanted to look grown up and attractive. Father usually made me wear my hair in a bun, but that day I brushed it hard, twisted it up and hid it under my hat so that I could let it down when I was out of sight of the house.

When I was ready I went downstairs. Father was waiting in the hall, as usual, with my Bible. He frowned when he saw what I was wearing, but for once he didn't say anything. He just told me to hurry up and handed me my Bible. It was a joy to be out of the house and alone for once. It was the only time I was allowed to do anything on my own. I suppose that Father thought that if I was going to church the Lord would protect me on the way. I set off down the drive happily humming a tune to the beat of my feet crunching on the gravel. It was one of those glorious June days when all the new buds have opened and the leaves are that wonderful shade of green that is so fresh and full of hope. The rhododendron bushes were in full bloom on either side of the drive and their perfume made me dizzy. Once out of sight of the house, I tore off my hat, shook my hair free and skipped down the drive. The sun shone down and I thought how wonderful it was to be fifteen and alive. I swung out of the drive and bumped straight into Edward, who was calmly smoking a cigarette whilst leaning against our gatepost. He looked so handsome and grown up in his officer's uniform that my heart skipped a beat. I felt so embarrassed. I know I must have blushed to the roots of my hair and I felt like a silly child beside this worldly-wise soldier. It never occurred to me then that he was waiting for me. He said he had come out to smoke a cigarette, because his mother didn't approve of him smoking in the house. I thought, well I don't know what I thought, perhaps that it was my good fortune to have bumped into him so casually. I didn't really care because I was so thrilled to have him all to myself for once. He fell in alongside me as I turned out of the drive and he asked me where I was going. I told him to the Sunday School, to take my class. He teased me about being a school teacher and asked if he could walk me to the church hall. Obviously I said he could. Sarah, I was so happy that I was almost floating on air. I asked him about France and the trenches. He was quiet for a moment, but he made light of it all. He said it was mainly cold, uncomfortable and very boring. However he did say that he felt there was going to be a big 'push' soon. That meant a direct assault on the German lines, which we now know was the terrible Battle of the Somme. He seemed so grown up and clever. He asked what I wanted to do with my life and I told him about my paintings and how I wanted to go to an art academy but father wouldn't let me. My life seemed so trivial compared to his. He was putting his life in danger for his country almost every day. I thought then that if this war lasted as soon as I was old enough I would apply to be a volunteer nurse. I suddenly felt that I had to support what he was doing in some way.

I'm repeating myself Sarah, I know. I've already told you all about this meeting and how happy I was to see Edward, but I didn't tell you what happened later and I have to remember how wonderfully the afternoon started out before I can bear to write about the nightmare that was to follow. We laughed and joked all the way to the church hall, but as we reached the gateway to the entrance, we could see Dr. Pickard standing on the steps, scowling at his pocket watch, which he held in his hand. I whispered to Edward and told him how much I hated Dr. Pickard, how he made me feel sick because he smelt like an old goat. Edward, who disliked him as much as I did, roared with laughter and I joined in. This was how we approached the hall, arm in arm and shaking with mirth. Pickard must have heard us because he looked up from his watch and caught sight of us. He gave us such a terrible look that it froze the smile on my face. It was indescribably vicious and Edward felt me stiffen. He smiled at me and patted my arm for reassurance.

More than ever that day I was reluctant to go into the Sunday School. I had a sudden, horrible, premonition that something awful was going to happen and a wave of absolute terror swept over me. I just wanted to hold on to Edward and beg him to come into the hall with me, to protect me, but I knew that I was being ridiculous. Edward had also seen the look on Dr. Pickard's face and realised he was very angry with me for some reason. He knew how strict father was and he didn't want to get me into any trouble so he just squeezed my hand and whispered goodbye. He told me he valued my letters and asked me to continue writing and asked me to send a photograph if I had one. I just smiled at him, held on to his hand and promised that I would. I couldn't bear to let him go, but he had to.

I felt so confused and as I watched him walk away, I felt as though my heart would break. I had enjoyed the stroll to Sunday School so much. I had so little time with him and who knew what dangers he would face before I saw him again? Only God knew. I prayed that He would keep him safe. I felt a sudden fury at all the old men who had such enormous power over our young lives, the generals, the politicians, even my father. They controlled us so completely, so ruthlessly. Stupid, outdated, convention would not allow us to spend any time alone with the boy we loved, yet that same convention allowed those loved ones to be carelessly sacrificed in defence of their country. What was it all for? It was too cruel to bear.

I reluctantly turned into the Sunday school gateway with my heart full of loathing for old men generally and for Pickard in particular. I remember him looking at his watch as I approached the steps saying, in a sarcastic tone of voice, 'When you're quite ready Miss Clayton.'

I hesitantly started to walk up the steps whilst he

glared down at me, his face red with fury, then two little village boys tried to creep past him unseen. They drew his attention from me as he turned and clipped them both round the ear. They unfortunately bore the brunt of a fury that was really directed at me, however I gratefully took advantage of the diversion and whilst his attention was elsewhere I slipped quickly past him and into the entrance lobby.

The main church hall was dark, dingy and incredibly dusty. There were eight classes held in there every week, four down either side of the room. Each class was set out with a full sized chair for the teacher which was surrounded by miniature chairs for the children. I always kept paper and coloured pencils in the hall desk which I handed out to the children, together with a church Bible, at the beginning of each lesson. This was so that they could illustrate the Bible story that I was reading to them. That day it was the story of Jonah and the whale and I thought that would produce some interesting drawings. The children raised my downcast spirits, they were a lively lot and they thought the idea of a man living inside a fish was extremely funny. They kept interrupting my reading and laughing and joking. We were really enjoying ourselves, when suddenly I looked up and there was Dr. Pickard glaring down at us. His face was suffused with purple; he was livid and he bellowed at them to be quiet. They immediately stopped laughing and applied themselves to their drawings, not even daring to look up. He then told me that he wanted to see me in his office at the end of the lesson. My heart sank. Not again, he found some excuse to keep me behind every week and I hated being alone with him in that suffocating, claustrophobic, little room. The children were no longer enjoying the lesson, they were afraid of attracting his anger again. The happy mood had been lost and the lesson simply limped to the end. With relief I told the children that they were dismissed. They fled out of the hall and I envied their freedom. With a heavy heart, I collected up the Bibles and coloured pencils and placed them back in the desk. Then I placed the chairs against the wall and collected up any stray paper that was left lying around. I would have done anything to delay going to Pickard's office. It did occur to me to ignore him and just go home, but he would have told father and I would have been in more trouble.

Sarah I don't know if I can go on. I don't know if I can even write down what happened after that. I have kept to the details of the day, because I knew that I would reach this point eventually and I don't know if I can even write down what happened it that terrible room. I must try; I will try to explain... I picked up my jacket and hat, smoothed down my skirts, took a deep breath, walked over to the office and knocked on the door. Most of the other teachers had left the building by then.

Dr. Pickard shouted for me to enter, which I did. The small, claustrophobic, room was at the rear of the hall and was cast into deep shadow by the large overhanging trees that surrounded the back of the building. It was almost dark in there and the air was full of his stale smell, which was a mixture of musty Palma violets, cough medicine and tobacco. It made me feel sick. I could only just make out his silhouette in the shadow, he was standing behind the desk and what light there was came from the window behind him. He was completely still and silent and poised like a lion or a tiger that was waiting to pounce. I stood on the other side of the desk looking at the floor; I couldn't bear to look at him. He left me standing there for some moments in silence and then he seemed to explode into a fury of life. He hissed at me across the desk, asking me just what I thought I was doing displaying myself like a street woman, throwing herself at a common soldier on the way to the Lord's house. That's how he talked to me, as though I was a servant. I objected strongly and tried to tell him that it wasn't a common soldier it was our neighbour, Edward, but he interrupted me and thundered at me to be quiet. I was too shocked and terrified to argue. He walked round the desk and round the back of me. He put his cheek close to mine; I could smell his foul breath. He picked up a strand of my hair and I felt him wind it round his finger. I was rigid with disgust and terror. Oh, how I wished I'd scraped it into a bun out of harms way. I had left it loose to please Edward, not him. He whispered in my ear something about wearing my hair loose to tempt men, like a whore. I was sick with fright. I thought if I kept still and quiet that he would stop, but he didn't. His foul breath seemed to be everywhere and he was whispering strange strangled things in my ear about lust and whores. His face was coming closer and closer to mine. I shook my head and tried to move away from him, but I was trapped between him and the desk. He then started to stroke my hair and nuzzle his face into it. I was horrified and tried again to shake him off again, but he persisted.

He'd never been this forward before; never behaved in this strange way. All the time he was moaning and muttering in my ear that he knew my thoughts, knew what I really wanted, how I'd rot in hell, but he'd save me. He kept on and on whispering nonsense. I was petrified and rooted to the spot. He continued to stroke my hair and I tried and tried to shake him off and I asked him to stop, but he didn't seem to hear me. Then horrors, he began to nuzzle my neck. I couldn't bear that so I tried to turn and push him off. I told him that I was going home and would tell my father, but when I twisted my head round to look at him, his eyes were glazed. He looked strange as if he couldn't hear me. He started kissing my neck. No. I tried to push him off. He hit me hard across the head. I struggled and he hit me again hard; I was dazed for a second and then quite suddenly he forced me forward onto the desk and pinned me down while he leaned on top of me. I started to struggle. I kicked him. He had his arm round my neck and was pressed up against me. I couldn't breath. Then he pushed me hard, face down on the desk and held me there with one hand. He jammed his body up against mine. I was terrified. Then he kicked my legs apart, I stumbled, nearly fell and tried scream. He put his hand over my mouth and muffled it, but there was no one to hear anyway... I was abandoned. He started muttering obscene words in my ear; words I had never heard before, but knew were wrong. I had tempted him and he was going to hurt me, but it was to save me from myself. I bit into his hand. It was scaly and covered in ginger hairs. He swore and gripped me tighter. Then I felt him fumbling with my underclothes, pulling and ripping frantically. What was he doing? This was a nightmare. Then I felt his fingers on my flesh, fumbling. I was too dazed to react, but I couldn't move anyway. Then the disgusting fumbling stopped and he seemed to be fiddling elsewhere. Suddenly he thrust himself at me. Again and again until suddenly I felt the most dreadful searing pain, still the thrusting went on, wave after wave of pain; it was agony, awful, over and over. I think I may have passed out, I can't remember. Then I felt him shudder and moan and it was over. He seemed to collapse on top of me and the pain stopped, it finally stopped. I lay there sobbing. He lifted himself off me without saying a word and I heard him go out and lock the door. Where had he gone? How would I get out?

My whole body was afire with pain and something horrible was trickling down my legs. I reached down and wiped them with my ripped undergarments and tried to clean myself up. I just lay there sobbing; I didn't know what to do. It was late, I would be in trouble. There was a jug and basin in the room. I poured some water from the jug and splashed my face with cold water and dried it on a piece of towelling that was hanging there. I retched and dropped it, it smelt of him. I gathered my hair up and twisted it back under my hat. I was in so much pain I thought that I would faint. I sat on a chair for a moment and noticed that there was a piece of cracked mirror on top of the book case. I stood up, wandered over and looked at my face. The crack ran down through my reflection and my face appeared all jagged and distorted. I was scarred for life. I was looking at the face of a stranger.

I heard his footsteps walking back across the wooden floor of the hall and I froze. He unlocked the door and walked in. He acted as though nothing had happened, he told me that our little talk was over and I mustn't dally with the village boys and must hurry on home. Little talk, dally, village boys? What was he talking about? Had I imagined the torture of the last hour? Was I going mad? I didn't know, but I fled out of that room. In spite of the pain I ran as if the hounds of hell were after me.

I don't really know how I got home that night, but somehow I did. I knew, instinctively, that I must not let my father know what had happened. I must have looked terrible when I got home, but I just went straight up to my mother's sewing room and thank God she was in there. I told her I was unwell, the monthly thing. She never could bear to talk about that, and I was going to bed. I struggled to my room and ran a bath. My clothes were covered in blood, so I stripped them off and pushed them to the back of the wardrobe. I never saw them again. I had a bath and washed my hair. I scrubbed my skin until it was raw, until every trace of him was removed. I knew something very strange had happened to me. I knew it was secret and wrong and it hurt, but I didn't understand the consequences. I didn't get out of bed again for weeks. I couldn't face anything or anyone. I just lay there in silence until I came to you.

Sarah, I am so ashamed of what happened. I tried to fight him off but he was too strong. He said I made him do it that I was a woman who made men do things like that and if I told anybody no one would believe me. He said God would punish me. I know I felt that God and all earthly beings had deserted me anyway at that moment. No one in all my life had ever treated me like that; certainly no one had ever hurt me or caused me such pain. It was unimaginable. Oh Sarah, why did it happen? What had I done? I am afraid even to write this down, afraid that you will reject me. That you will think I am a terrible being to allow this to happen to me. But he was right; God has punished me anyway, so I may as well break my silence. I can't eat, I can't sleep and I haven't smiled since. Help me Sarah, please help me.

Chapter Eleven

Emmie just couldn't believe what she had read: she couldn't believe that her grandmother, her lovely, sweet, loving grandmother, had suffered this appalling abuse. It was no wonder that Florence couldn't talk about what had happened to her, it was incredible. It defied belief. She wondered how any man could treat a woman in that way. She couldn't understand what terrible bitterness and hatred caused that man to ruin the life of an innocent young girl for no apparent reason other than the fact that he wanted to and he could. He was an elder of the church, a man entrusted with the responsibility of looking after the well being of young people. He repaid that trust by brutally raping a fifteen year old virgin, with no sexual experience at all.

She wondered if men like that ever considered the consequences of what they did or were they so driven by their sexual needs that they were past caring. The sexual violence of inadequate men, the rapists, paedophiles, wife beaters and others, was something that the world would never fully come to terms with or understand. These men seemed to step outside the boundaries of civilised behaviour and consider it was their right to satisfy their needs. They seemed somehow unaware of the heartbreak and chaos that they left in their wake. Instead of using sex to demonstrate their love for a woman, they twisted it into a weapon of revenge and destruction. What was more terrifying was the fact that they somehow managed to justify their behaviour to themselves.

Emmie could understand why Sarah had given her Florence's testimony to read whilst she was on her own. It aroused such a fury of mixed emotions that she needed time to control them. She was outraged, but within that feeling of outrage was mixed a deep sorrow. Tragedy struck her grandmother whilst she was still young and innocent. Her first experience of sex was unwanted and violent. It was forced upon her before she was even sexually aware and she was an unwilling victim rather than a loving participant. All the dreams that young girls have of their first sexual experience had been ripped out by the roots in Florence's case. It was unthinkable, and she was so young that it could have ruined any chance of her having a normal relationship with a man as an adult. Nevertheless, Emmie knew that Florence did have a good marriage eventually, but that was because she was loved by an exceptional man. The saddest thing of all, though, was that Florence felt ashamed. All her life she had carried the guilt and shame of that one act, when she was completely guiltless. It was a life sentence.

Emmie wondered about the resulting pregnancy. How did her grandmother cope with that and what happened to the child? These and many other chaotic thoughts tumbled around in Emmie's mind and it took her some time to settle down and go to sleep. However, in spite of her anger and confusion, she did eventually fall into a fitful sleep, but throughout the night her sleep was broken by dreams of her grandmother.

For one brief moment when she woke up, she didn't know where she was then it all came back to her, the Italian restaurant, Sarah's revelations and her grandmother's shocking testament. She felt a strong need to talk to Sarah so she jumped out of bed and had a quick shower. She pulled on her jeans and T shirt and collecting Florence's testament on the way, she hurried downstairs to another lovely misty autumn morning and the smell of percolating coffee.

Sarah had prepared breakfast and was waiting for her in the little garden. She rose to greet Emmie as she entered the kitchen. 'Good morning, Emmie. How are you this morning?''

'Shocked, shocked beyond belief. I couldn't believe what I was reading. I couldn't believe that my lovely grandmother had been abused like that.'

'I'm so sorry Emmie; will you forgive me for leaving you to read such a shocking document alone?'

'Of course, I think that was the only way to read it. Firstly I needed time to digest what was written there, I couldn't believe what I was reading and I had a struggle to control my fury. When I did calm down again I needed time to explore my reactions. Does that make any sense?'

'Oh yes indeed. I know how appalled and confused I felt the first time I read it. It took some time for me to control my own feelings. That's why I left you to read it alone, but not without some reservation I have to say.'

Emmie just walked over to Sarah and gave her a hug. 'I'm very grateful to you for your time. It can't be easy for you going over old ground like this, raking up unpleasant memories.'

'I don't mind, my dear, I love Florence and I want

to help her 'put the record straight', as it were, before she dies and I dearly want to help you to understand. Everything else is irrelevant.'

Emmie gave Sarah a rueful grin and Sarah took her arm and guided her into the garden.

'Come on and sit down, I'll get you some breakfast, as a way of atonement. Coffee and croissants ok?

'Thank you Sarah and yes please I'd love coffee and croissants'

Sarah returned with Emmie's breakfast and when she had settled back into her chair she turned and looked at her. 'So,' is all she said.

'I was frankly horrified, I just couldn't believe what I was reading, but then I started to make connections.' responded Emmie, 'it certainly explains why Florence looked so ill when she came to stay with you. She must have been completely traumatised by the attack. Well, not only the physical attacked, but the brutal rape. I think the worst aspect of it all is that she didn't actually fully understand what had happened to her and she didn't dare to tell anyone. I just can't find the words to describe how angry that makes me feel.'

'I know; I agree that the worst thing of all is that Florence knew nothing about the sex act and I mean nothing. She knew that she'd been attacked and humiliated. She thought that she'd been punished for, what, for loving my brother Edward? But she had no idea of the significance of that punishment. I have no idea exactly what went through that innocent little head of hers. She must have half believed that she was to blame for what had happened; you see Dr. Pickard was a respected elder of Josiah's church. She had been taught to trust those men and if he told her that she had sinned and he was saving her, she would have considered that there was justification in what he did. I don't mean logically, but then is it logical for a senior church elder to have enforced sex with a fifteen year old child in the church hall after Sunday School? That is the one place where she should have been safe.'

'What did you do after you read her testament? How did you react? Did you talk to her about what had happened?'

'Well yes, it was difficult as you can imagine. I had to approach the subject very carefully. I had to convince Florence that she was pregnant and she had slowly begun to accept that, so I then progressed to teaching her the basic facts about sex and believe you me Emmie, my own knowledge was pretty sketchy so I wasn't the best teacher. However, Florence had no knowledge at all; she didn't even fully understand the differences, anatomically, between a man and a woman. She had never even seen a naked man, so I slowly explained, as best as I could and in the simplest terms, the physical differences between men and women and what happens when they have sex. The poor little soul was horrified, as I'm sure we all were when we first learned about sex. I think that I actually made things worse at first. When she realised that it wasn't God who had made her pregnant, but Pickard, she vomited all over my best rug. It was a terrible shock to her, just terrible. But slowly she accepted what had happened and began to realise that he was not a man of God who was trying to save her, but an evil bastard. Sorry to swear Emmie, but he was, he really was. I explained to her that the abuser always blames the abused. He relies on their sense of guilt and fear to keep them quiet. I also explained to her that she was extremely beautiful and that now she was older, men would start to desire her in that way and that she must be on her guard. Rather like shutting the stable door after the horse has bolted, but I wanted her to feel that she was in control and every man couldn't or wouldn't think of doing what Pickard had done. He was obviously an extremely sadistic, immoral old man who probably blamed his disabled wife for his lack of a sex life. Well, he would blame anyone but himself. Probably felt he had been cheated out of a married life and thought that somehow that justified his actions. The sad thing is that one bad apple like him can give other, wonderfully committed church elders a bad reputation. I wondered if he'd got away with it before, the old sod, probably because he was in a position of trust. Still I think it helped her greatly to talk about what had happened and once she started it just poured out of her, like the poison out of a lanced boil. It seemed to release a bottled up pressure within her. It also helped her that there was someone who believed her story and didn't hold her responsible. She began to improve visibly after that. She started to eat and sleep properly and she lost that dreadful haunted look. I had to play it by ear and she did have setbacks. But I think just by explaining fully what had happened and by listening and believing her that I helped her recover to some extent. After that I started to see a slow return of the old Florence.

I have to admit that I was initially annoyed with Martha that she hadn't explained the facts of life to Florence and put her on her guard, but I imagine that she intended to. I mean Florence was only fifteen and Martha was the victim of her suppressed Victorian upbringing. I suppose that she left it as long as she could. There was no reason to think that Florence needed to know before she was sixteen anyway. It was just a dreadful tragedy that events overtook Martha. I know she would never have done anything to hurt Florence.

After we had sorted everything out, I thought the best thing would be for Florence to stay in Devon, have the child and arrange for an adoption. Eventually she could return home as though nothing had happened. Well, that's how it would appear to the outside world at any rate. What could be simpler? No one beyond the immediate family need know anything about it. There would be no scandal and your grandmother's reputation, which was so important then, would be unscathed. I became very close to her during that time and grew to love her very much; she became, I suppose, the sister that I never had. That's what makes the thought of losing her now so very hard to bear.'

'I suppose,' proffered Emmie, 'that's what happened is it? She had the baby in secrecy and then went home and married Edward, but no, Martha's journals. She writes about Florence being locked in the attic. Was that after she'd had the baby?'

Sarah went very quiet and then sighed, 'Don't, please don't. If I had my way again I would have kept Florence out of sight of Charles and told no one about the pregnancy. I'd have let her have the baby in private. However, I was young and in love and thought my husband knew everything about life. Eventually I told him what had happened to Florence. Of course, he was outraged and thought that Pickard should be charged and punished. He naturally had sympathy for Florence, but I noticed that it was tinged with that, 'she must have done something to encourage him', man attitude to rape, which rather troubled me. Anyway, he insisted that Josiah be informed at once. He pointed out that Josiah was her legal guardian and only he could decide what to do for the best. Although I loved Charles, I wasn't sure that he was right, but I realised that what he said was true. Josiah was her legal guardian and she couldn't have a child and have it adopted without his knowledge. Well legally she couldn't, but if I'd known then what I know now I'd have taken that risk.'

By now Emmie knew not to push Sarah when she lapsed into one of her silences, she realised that Sarah would tell her everything in her own time, but that she needed to be patient, so she just sat quietly eating her croissants while Sarah looked into the middle distance, lost in her memories. Eventually Emmie could wait no longer and she prompted her, 'What happened then?'

'What? Oh well Charles wrote to Josiah and told him that he wanted to see him. He felt it was better to tell Josiah man to man, as it were, rather than to commit anything to paper. It could fall into the wrong hands, you see, everything took so long then, remember it was still wartime. There were a few telephones, but not on a farm in Devon, and travel was also difficult due to the war and troop movements. Anyway, it was some time before we received a reply. In it Josiah outlined his intention of seeing Charles. He felt that it would be more convenient for both of them if Josiah went to Charles's office in London, rather than coming all the way to Devon to see us.

I didn't know Josiah very well in those days; to me he was just a rather cold and intimidating man who lived next door to my parents. I had very little contact with him. Anyway it took some time for him to make arrangements to visit London. It meant leaving his business and he had to make sure that it was being properly managed. Then we had to make sure that Charles was actually in London to meet him, but eventually the arrangements were settled and the two of them met alone in London. Meanwhile back in Devon, we happily and innocently got on with our quiet life, totally unaware that Florence's fate was hanging in the balance.

Charles came down the following weekend, after the meeting, to tell me what had taken place. It seemed that Josiah doubted Florence's story was true. He knew Dr. Pickard to be a man of the highest moral integrity and felt that Florence was flighty and was probably using this story to hide the truth. He thought it was more likely that she had been with one of the village boys and was scared. I was outraged. I knew she was telling the truth, they hadn't seen how ill she had been and how frightened she was. I raged at Charles, who just stood and listened. Then, quite reasonably, he asked me what I wanted him to do. Josiah was her father and her legal guardian and she was a minor, he couldn't interfere. Anyway, Josiah wouldn't hear of her skulking in the country, as he called it and hiding her condition, she would have to face the music. I was horrified; did Josiah want her to go home to have the baby? Charles said he did. He thought that she should be with her mother. That calmed me a little because it made sense, but wouldn't it have been better for Martha to have come to us? Charles said Josiah wouldn't hear of it. He said he couldn't do without her for any length of time.

Eventually I calmed down a little and reluctantly agreed for her to go home. It did make some sense, but I still thought it would have been better for her to have had the baby whilst she was in Devon with me. It was now January. Florence had been with us since August and by this time was nearly seven months pregnant. It would be obvious to anyone who saw her at home that she was expecting a baby. I could see no advantage in her returning to Liverpool. Everyone would know and her reputation would be in shreds. I felt so helpless, trapped by all these oh so reasonable men, but I had no power. I had to tell Florence that she was returning home. I dreaded it.

Eventually I plucked up the courage and told her that Josiah knew about her condition and had requested that she return home to Martha. She was terrified of her father and didn't want to see him at all, but she loved her mother dearly. I think she really wanted to be with Martha when the baby was born. If only I had known. I was such a naïve fool, but with very mixed feelings I agreed that she and Hettie should return home. I was terribly upset. I had enjoyed having Florence to stay and I felt as if she were part of my family. It was so hard to part with her. If only I had known what was going to happen. I would never have allowed her to return to that monster.

I still feel responsible because Florence trusted me implicitly to do the right thing, to help and protect her and I let her down so badly. I didn't mean to, but I did. I even helped her pack her clothes.'

Sarah fell into a deep silence and Emmie quietly finished her breakfast.

Chapter Twelve

Eventually after being lost in her thoughts for some time Sarah began her story again.

'I will never forget the day I took Florence, together with Hettie, to the station at Totnes and waved her goodbye. We were all devastated at being parted. Hettie and Dorcas had become such good friends and I knew that I would miss Florence's company terribly. She was sad at leaving Devon, but I know that she was looking forward to seeing her mother. She felt safe in the knowledge that Martha knew her story and its terrible consequences and had accepted it. Her nightmare seemed to be coming to an end at last. It is as well that we didn't know that it was just beginning in earnest. We embraced at the station and she promised to write and let me know how she was as soon as she settled in at home. We parted tearfully as the train drew into the station. Heavily pregnant she struggled aboard, assisted by Hettie, then as the train moved out of the station she leaned out of the window and waved until it turned a corner and she disappeared out of sight.

Little did I know then that for nearly three years Florence would effectively be dead to me. I had no premonition at all. Yet I heard nothing from her, except for one garbled message, which I didn't understand. She just went home to Josiah and it was three years before I learned what had happened to her. I couldn't understand why she didn't write to me. It was such an upsetting time.'

'What?' asked an unbelieving Emmie, 'three years? What happened to her?'

'You might well ask. After Florence returned home, it was just as if she had disappeared into the abyss. We heard nothing at all for over two months. I wrote to my mother asking if she'd seen her, although I didn't tell her that Florence was pregnant. I felt that Martha must decide whether people should be told. It was a terrible scandal in those days to have a child before you were married. I simply wrote to Mother to see if she had any news of Florence, but Mother hadn't seen either Martha or Florence since Florence's return. I was frantic. I pestered Charles to write to Josiah and ask what had happened. He was reluctant to do so at first, but after several weeks had passed and we'd heard nothing, even he became concerned and he did as I asked. There was no reply. I wrote continually to both Florence and Martha, but my letters were never answered. Then I received a letter from my mother containing news from an unexpected quarter, Hettie. She was friendly with my mother's maid, Mabel, and she had called to see her. Through Hettie we gleaned what little information we had.

Apparently when Florence returned to Liverpool, both she and Hettie were met at the station by an extremely grim and silent Josiah. He hardly spoke to either of them on the journey from the station to the house. Hettie told Mabel that Florence, almost immediately, began to gain that haunted look again. After what seemed to be an endless journey, which passed in total silence, they reached the house. Hettie said she almost sighed with relief. She thought that Florence would be reunited with Martha and that there would be a return to some semblance of normality. However, that was not to be. As soon as they arrived at the house Josiah ordered the carriage to stop at the servant's entrance. He took Florence by the arm and guided her into the house and up the back stairs. These were normally only ever used by the servants. Hettie heard later in the kitchen that he had ordered a room in the attics to be prepared for Florence. It was a little used room, which was situated at the far end of the house, away from the servant's quarters. Hettie never saw Florence alone again.

'So,' deduced a shocked Emmie, 'this was the point that I had reached in Martha's journals, it makes sense now, Florence must have been screaming for her mother from her attic room and Martha was told to stay in her rooms and keep away from Florence and of course she wouldn't dare disobey. Didn't Martha see Florence at all then after her return? Josiah must have told her about the rape and Florence's condition?'

Sarah slowly and silently shook her head. It was a few moments before she responded.

'Martha, like me, didn't see or speak to Florence for nearly three years.'

It was Emmie's turn to be silent; she was more shocked than she had been when she read about the rape. Eventually she found her voice,

'But Josiah did go to the police about Pickard and have him charged with rape?'

Again Sarah silently shook her head.

'But he was eventually arrested wasn't he? I mean Josiah wouldn't let him get away with such a terrible crime?'

This time Sarah didn't, in fact couldn't reply. Instead she recounted Hettie's version of events.

'Florence was hysterical when she realised

that she had to stay in the attic room and couldn't see Martha. She screamed and shouted for her mother, but nothing happened, eventually she calmed down and accepted her enforced imprisonment, because effectively that is what it was. She didn't have any real choice. That evening Josiah went up to see her. Hettie only heard what happened from a 'tweenie', a little kitchen maid called Jane, who had been instructed to look after Florence and told not to discuss her or her condition with anyone. She was apparently sleeping in a small box room next to Florence's room, so that Florence could summon her easily if she needed her. She had been threatened with dismissal and no reference if she discussed what was happening with anyone. Even during the First World War, with alternate employment possible in the munitions factories, that was a fate worse than death for domestic staff. I think it was a relief for her to discover that Hettie was also aware of the fact that Florence was pregnant and she could at least confide in her. Hettie herself had been cautioned by Josiah to keep quiet or face the same fate as Jane, dismissal and no reference. Hettie had no intention of telling anyone that Florence was pregnant. She thought the world of your grandmother and didn't want to harm her reputation.

Well it transpired that Jane could hear what was happening in Florence's room through the dividing wall. She told Hettie everything that she heard. When Josiah confronted Florence about her pregnancy, he didn't offer her any words of comfort or reassurance, he was cold and hard. He humiliated her as much as he possibly could. Jane told Hettie that he was horrible, cruel and sadistic. He asked Florence to tell him, in her own words, just how many men she had been with and just how long it had been going on. She naturally protested. She had assumed that everyone would be like me and believe her story, but Josiah was having none of it. Oh no, not him. Jane told Hettie that he didn't raise his voice, but was calm and steely. She said that she felt he was enjoying himself. He was doing what Martha had instinctively dreaded, crushing Florence and wringing all the joy of life out of her. It had irritated him for so long and now he had the power to do it. '

'That's monstrous, couldn't Martha intervene?'

'Martha didn't really know what was happening. It was worse than you could ever imagine. I think he was totally perverted, I'm no psychiatrist, but he seemed to be afraid of women's sexuality. It was odd the way he tried to stifle Florence's beauty, you know, making Martha dress her severely and keep her hair tied up, very strange, and the fact that Martha felt that it was her very plainness that attracted him. Anyway, initially Florence stayed calm and stuck to her story that she had been raped by Dr. Pickard. Josiah did not believe her and worse still he had tackled Pickard who had denied that he'd ever touched Florence. In fact, he told Josiah that she flirted with the older boys, the village boys, at the Sunday School and led them on. It was absolute nonsense, of course, but Josiah believed him. Pickard told him that she met them after class; he said he was sure that's when it must have happened.

'Surely he didn't believe him, didn't he realise that Pickard would be panic stricken about being discovered and would make up any story to direct suspicion from himself?'

'No. He believed Pickard and thought that it was Florence who was lying or rather that's what he wanted to believe. He said that it was inevitable that such beauty would be accompanied by great wickedness; you only had to read about the temptresses in the Bible. He said that he always knew that Florence would get up to no good. They talked quietly like this for some time. Florence repeated her story over and over again which must have been nightmare for her. I think it is one of the reasons that she can't talk about it even today. To keep telling that nightmare story over and over again and not be believed must have been torture. However Josiah was unbending; he would not believe her story.

Eventually it all became too much for Florence, she lost her cool control and started to shout at him and demand to see her mother. He stayed coldly calm. She cried and sobbed and begged to see her mother, but he wouldn't allow it. Eventually, Florence became hysterical and do you know what he did?'

'I can't begin to imagine.'

'No you couldn't really. He called for a doctor.'

Emmie was ahead of her,

'No, no he wouldn't, not even Josiah could be that cruel'

'Oh he could be just that cruel, he called for Dr. Pickard to come and see her. Jane said she was completely hysterical when she saw him. She was absolutely terrified and refused to allow him anywhere near her. The three of them had a mammoth struggle and eventually Pickard and Josiah managed to get her under control and give her an injection of something which completely knocked her out. According to Jane, he kept coming back periodically to give her more injections, always accompanied by Josiah. Jane said that Florence was in a kind of trance after that. The injections made her very docile. She stopped protesting and just submitted to them, but Jane said they made her very odd. She became incoherent and she dropped things, she spilled her food and dribbled.

'What was he injecting her with? It's a wonder that she didn't miscarry.'

'It is indeed. Well whilst this was going on upstairs, Martha was downstairs in a terrible state. She begged Josiah to be allowed to see Florence, but he wouldn't hear of it. He told her that Florence had contracted a virulently infectious disease and had to be isolated for her own good and the good of the household, that Dr Pickard was caring for her. He also persuaded Dr. Pickard to give Martha a sedative. It was outrageous that men had that kind of power in their own households, but they did.'

'How did he expect to get away with that when you knew the truth about Florence's pregnancy?'

'Well remember I hadn't told my mother and I lived in Devon, which in those days may as well have been on the other side of the moon. None of my letters reached Martha or Florence. He gambled on my silence and he got it. I wasn't going to besmirch Florence's memory, I loved her too much for that and I certainly wasn't going to upset Martha. Anyway, if I had told the truth he would just have dismissed it as a lie. No one would dare to cross him, least of all Martha.'

'You said memory? Why Florence's memory?'

'Martha accepted what Josiah told her, that Florence had caught a disease. He and Pickard concocted some story about her having to stay in quarantine. Martha wasn't even aware that Josiah had seen Florence. During this time Florence did manage to smuggle one note out with Jane that somehow she managed to post to us, but it didn't make any sense. The writing was all over the place and it was difficult to follow. Here, like everything else I kept the note.' Sarah handed Emmie an old yellowing piece of paper which had been torn out of a book. It was covered with uneven, spidery writing and was very strange.

> *Sarah, Help, please Josiah tell him make him believe. Cant think it's all confused help me please help me I'm afraid.*
> *Florence*

Maybe if I'd taken some action then I could have helped Florence, but I didn't understand it. I thought it was a joke or a forgery. Why would Florence write such a peculiar and badly spelt note? I did write to my mother and ask if anything was the matter, but she didn't know anything either.

It was agony for me to read it. If it was from Florence she was asking me for help and I was helpless to do anything. Anyway, one night Florence simply disappeared. Josiah told Martha that she'd become so ill that they had to take her to the infirmary. She believed him. My mother believed him. I couldn't tell them the truth.

Then he informed her that Florence had died, in the infirmary, from her infectious disease. I received this letter from Martha telling me. I naturally assumed that Florence had died in childbirth and I didn't want to upset Martha by telling her the truth. So I kept my own counsel. I thought that Josiah had done it for the best intending to have the child adopted and so keeping Florence's condition a secret. I just thought that Florence and the child must have died during the confinement and death in childbirth was extremely common then. I was so naïve it doesn't bear thinking about.'

'So, let me get this straight,' Emmie interrupted, 'For three years you and Martha thought that Florence was dead? Where was she then?'

Sarah didn't answer Emmie, but handed her another piece of old yellowed paper, this time it was conventional writing paper.

'Here read this and tell me what conclusions you would have drawn. Remember I didn't know then that Florence hadn't died.' Emmie looked closely at the paper. She immediately recognised the copper plate handwriting. It was a letter from Martha:

My Dear Sarah,

It is very difficult for me to write to you under such trying circumstances. The death of my darling Florence has hit me very hard. I can hardly believe that it has happened. Yet I know I must be brave. We live at a time of great suffering and loss and all around me mothers and fathers are having to come to terms with the deaths of their beloved sons. I must try to be brave like them, but it is so hard. She was my life.

I would like to thank you for taking care of Florence when I asked you to. She was very ill when I sent her to Devon and perhaps it wasn't fair of me to ask you to take on the responsibility, but you took great care of her and I know she was happy with you. I'm sure that you made Florence's time with you a memorable one. The only reproach I have is self reproach, if I'd realised how close to death Florence really was I don't think that I would have parted with her. I would have nursed her here at home, but I sent her to you because

I thought that the sea air and change of surroundings would help her to recover her health. I feel very resentful towards Josiah that he wouldn't let me accompany her for her last journey. I know a good wife should not speak ill of her husband, but my feelings towards him at present are not kindly.

I'm sure that it must have been difficult for you to nurse Florence on your own without the support of Charles or your mother and you never said a word to us. You just sent positive, cheery letters that gave us hope for Florence's full recovery and you never complained about the onerous task of caring for her. You were very brave and self sacrificing, Sarah, and I thank you. I know that my little Florence spent her last days in an atmosphere of kindness and love.

When Charles wrote and asked Josiah to meet him, we both feared the worst. It took Josiah some time to arrange the meeting, which as you know took place in London. I think that Florence must have deteriorated in that short time for when he returned Josiah told me to prepare myself for bad news. He said Charles had told him that Florence's health was failing and she was now very ill. He told me that he was making arrangements for her to return home in the charge of her maid, Hettie. He explained that her disease had entered its final stage, which was very infectious. He reassured me that you would have been safe while you were nursing her; it was only in the last stages that she could infect others. Thankfully you and Charles are well, so he must have been well informed.

Josiah also insisted that I must leave him to make all the decisions about Florence's treatment and care. He stressed that these final days were crucially important and promised me that he would see that she got the best nursing possible. I was demented with grief, but so grateful that he was doing all that he possibly could. However, it seems that even the best care and nursing couldn't save my little girl. I don't know how I am going to go on without her, I really don't.

When she arrived home, Josiah prepared a sick room for Florence upstairs and arranged for one of the maids, Jane, to look after her, together with Dr. Pickard. I wanted to nurse her myself, but Josiah wouldn't hear of it. He wouldn't even let me see her in case she infected me. He told me that the doctors said that her disease was very contagious and he was afraid that I may catch it and become ill myself. I didn't make a fuss as I was sure that Florence would recover and we would be together again.

To hear her crying out and screaming alone upstairs, nearly broke my heart in two. I so wanted to go to her and I thought that Josiah was being very harsh when he forbade me to see her, but I knew he was only being sensible and I had to obey him. Eventually, Florence became too ill to be nursed at home, so one night Dr. Pickard and Josiah had her admitted to the infirmary. She was very ill then and within the week she was dead. Because her illness was so contagious the infirmary insisted in taking charge of the burial. The service took place in the chapel there and only Josiah was permitted to attend.

I arranged a small memorial service here in St James. It was only for the family, Sarah and hastily organised, so please don't feel that we were excluding you. Unfortunately, funerals for young people are far too common at present and draw very little comment. It was a lovely service. I decorated the church with lilies, which were Florence's favourite flowers and we sang the hymns that she loved most. I felt as though I was living through a dream. Florence couldn't be dead, but she was and is and I must adjust to the fact. Josiah arranged for a small white marble plaque to be put in the garden of remembrance and I go every day and put flowers in the little urn. It is some small comfort, but the strange thing is that I don't feel that she is there. I know I'm not making sense, but when my mother died I felt her spirit all around me, especially when I visited her grave. I don't feel that with Florence and it disturbs me a little.

I am trying to pull myself together for I know that I must go on, but sometimes it is so hard. I would love to see you dear Sarah, but I fear it will be after this terrible war has ended. Please write to me and tell me all about my daughter's stay in Devon. What you did, what you talked about, how she bore her illness. I want to glean as much information about those last few months as I can.

I pray for you and your family, especially your brother Edward, who is still facing daily danger on the Western Front. I realise that so many families have to bear the brunt of losing a much loved child and this helps me to stay strong in the face of my tragic loss. Pray for me dear Sarah, God bless you.

With deep affection
Martha Clayton

Emmie was so choked after she had read the letter that she couldn't speak for several moments, 'How many more shocks am I going to have to endure?' Emmie asked, looking at Sarah over the top of the letter, 'How could he? How could he keep Martha away from her own daughter and deny her the truth? How could he lie to her and watch her grieve, knowing that Florence was still alive. It's inhuman, but what had happened to her? Where was she? And what happened to the baby?'

Sarah smiled back at her philosophically, 'One thing at a time! I was terribly shocked when I read the letter and truly heartbroken to think that poor Florence had gone into labour afraid, alone and obviously in great pain and distress. As far as I knew she died alone too. I didn't feel confident enough to talk to Martha about her stay here in case I let something slip. I didn't want to say anything that would spoil her memories of Florence. I wrote to her naturally, but it would have helped me if I could have talked to her, truthfully, but it wasn't to be. Florence's death broke my heart and the last years of the war were dark years for me. The loss of Florence and the daily death toll in France depressed me beyond belief, especially after the massacre on the Somme in 1916. Then I feared that I would lose Edward as well. I wrote to tell him of Florence's death. He was devastated, even though he was witnessing death on a daily basis. After the bitter fighting on the Somme he was exhausted. He had been at the front for three years and his nerves had got the better of him, then he got a flesh wound, a 'Blighty' as it was called, so in September 1917 he was sent home suffering from wounds and shell shock and was admitted to Granthall Hospital, the local lunatic asylum, which had been partly converted into a military hospital for the duration of the war. Whilst he was in there something happened which made sense later, but at the time made Edward doubt his sanity. Remind me later to show you the letter that I received from him whilst he was a patient there, I really think it is important that you read it before I continue with the next stage of my story.

Anyway, to get back to Martha's letter, after I read it I suppose I thought that Josiah was acting for the best. I thought he kept Florence's condition from Martha to save her any embarrassment and he kept Florence isolated so that no one would suspect that she was expecting a baby and she could go into hospital, quietly, have the baby and have it adopted without anyone knowing. I thought that I had misjudged him. I hadn't.

'One thing I don't understand,' commented Emmie who was reeling the shock of Josiah's deception, 'is how he expected to get away with such an outrageous lie.'

'Oh, quite easily, Dr. Pickard was superintendent of the infirmary and no one was going to contradict his version of events or if they did they knew that they would face the sack and no one ever dared challenged Josiah, so it was so easy for him. Now my dear, I have a lot more to tell you, as you probably realise. Martha, Edward, my Mother, even me, we all thought that Florence was dead and lost to us forever, but you know differently so you will realise that something had happened to her during those three years. However, if you don't mind I think that I will finish the story tonight. You look tired out Emmie, these revelations have been a terrible shock for you. A break from Florence's story will do you good, even though I know you're bursting to know what happened. We'll get ready and go out now and do some shopping on the Kings Road. Perhaps we could then take a walk up to Harrods and Harvey Nichols and have some lunch in one of the little wine bars on the way? I think you need a break while you absorb everything that I have told you so far. I warn you Emmie there are more shocking revelations to come and I don't want you to go home emotionally exhausted. You realise that you are going to have to tell your father all this when you return home? It won't be easy for you, so I think a break this afternoon will do you good.' Emmie agreed. Although she was incredibly curious to know where Florence had disappeared to for three years she was physically weary and emotionally exhausted. She welcomed a little light relief before returning to Florence's story. She also realised that Sarah needed a break. She was an old lady and it couldn't have been easy to revisit the past, especially such a traumatic past, without it stirring up deep emotions.

'I'm not going to argue Sarah, I need a break and a shopping trip would be most welcome.'

Sarah smiled at her, 'I think it's wise, obviously I'm not going to ban all mention of Florence, but I think you need some distraction and a break. When we get back I'll give you Edward's letter to read while I prepare supper. It tells of an incredible coincidence, which meant nothing at the time, but helped us locate Florence later. Come on now before I start talking again, let's go and get ready.'

Chapter Thirteen

When Emmie and Sarah returned from their very successful shopping trip, Sarah gave her Edward's letter to read while she prepared supper for them both:

November 1917

My Dear Sarah

You will see from the address that I am now back in old Blighty. I'm suffering from a small flesh wound and, I'm rather ashamed to say, a mild case of the shakes or shell shock as the military call it. It is a relief to be away from the front for a while. However, I shall be going back as soon as I'm rested and my wound has healed, but that should take several months.

There are nearly fifty of us on this ward and we're a rum lot! We're mainly officers who've served in France and are suffering with our nerves. Most of us also have a minor wound. It is good to be safe, warm and well fed for once. Who would have thought that I would be grateful to have been admitted to a lunatic asylum? But I am, very grateful; I'd forgotten what it was like to be clean, sleep in a bed with fresh, white, linen sheets and to be free of my friendly lice! Conditions in France are bad at the best of times, but we all dread the approach of winter. Standing in a trench in the rain with no shelter and the east wind knifing into your back is no fun and I can't remember when we last had regular hot meals served at a table. We are all grateful that we can shelter in here hopefully until the spring.

We are on an old male ward in the lunatic asylum. Most of it still operates as an asylum, but part of it has been converted into a military hospital for the duration of the war. We're all suffering from various shakes, ticks and all manner of nervous jerks! Some poor chaps have been rendered dumb by all the horror that they have had to witness, but in the main we're a cheery lot, if not a little jumpy. The warder, Alf, is a good sort. He lost his only son at Mons and he does all he can to make us comfortable, but this is a grim place. I find it quite unnerving. At night, when it is quiet you can hear moans and screams from the lunatics who are all locked into their part of the hospital. Some of them are allowed off the ward to work, the non refractory ones, that is. The men work on the farm, whilst the women work in the sewing room or the laundry. We occasionally meet them when we are allowed out for exercise, but they tend to ignore us and look straight through us. I find them quite unnerving.

We are quite a depressing lot, although there are some

moments of grim humour to keep us going. For instance yesterday after lunch Alf went out and left the ward in charge of a hapless young assistant called Tom. He was carrying an empty tin tray back from one of the tables to the sideboard and he tripped. The tray shot out of his hands and flew through the air like a bird on the wing, glinting and flashing in the beams of sunlight that streamed down from the high windows. Up and up it went, and then down and down it swooped. All eyes were glued to it and as it hit the ground with a resounding crash, there wasn't a man left sitting at the table!! We had all taken cover! It was chaos! Chairs, benches and tables were up ended, men cowered behind them shaking and moaning with their arms wrapped around their heads for protection. In one minute that crash had them all back at the front and their reactions were purely instinctive. Alf was furious when he came back. The one thing that is impressed on the warders in charge of a shell shock ward is not to make any sudden loud noise. Our nerves are so attuned to listening for shells that the slightest bang sends us running for cover! Still Alf quickly restored order and some of us managed to laugh about what happened. Sadly though, there are those amongst us who are still too terrified to find anything funny in any situation. I wonder if they will ever recover.

Mother and Father have visited me. I think they were upset to see me in a place like this. It's understandable, but I assured them that we are well looked after. It was so good to see them. They brought me a parcel of warm clothes for when I return to France and one of cook's walnut cakes. That was a treat indeed! Mother mentioned Martha, I think that she is worried about her. She hasn't really been herself since she lost Florence. This is the first time that I've really had the peace and the privacy to write to you at any length about Florence. Her death has had a profound effect on me. I was devastated when I received your letter telling me that she had died. Lovely, young, vibrant Florence, I just couldn't take it in. It was such a terrible shock. The last time I saw her was when I waited for her outside her house and walked her to Sunday School. Sarah, she looked so beautiful that day, so young, fresh and above all so innocent. Since being in France I had forgotten what innocence was. She made me feel alive, she made me want to live and I was secretly hoping that she would one day share that life with me when she was older.

In France I managed to push Florence's death to the back of my mind, but here, where I have time to think, thoughts of her have dominated my every waking moment. So much so that two days ago when I was out walking in the grounds, I had the most peculiar experience. I thought I saw Florence, here, coming out of the laundry with a warder! I was so sure it was her! I tried to shout her name, but no sound would come out of my mouth and I was rooted to the spot with the shock. She didn't see me as she crossed from the laundry, then the warder unlocked the door to the main asylum and she disappeared inside. Of course it couldn't have been her, dressed in a lunatic's smock, but someone who resembled her. Oh Sarah, I was in a dreadful state, the shock brought on a terrible attack of the shakes and it was all I could do to return to the ward. Once I was back there I told Alf what had happened. He said it was common symptom for shell shock patients to hallucinate. He said that she was the main thing on my mind and I had made her appear. But Sarah, she was so real to me, so very real. Anyway I made Alf check that there wasn't anyone in the hospital by the name of Florence Clayton. He laughed at me, but nevertheless he checked. Of course there was no one in here by that name. Naturally! However I think that little episode demonstrates what a state I'm still in over her death.

I know you won't be able to get to see me here as Devon is so far away, but you are always in my thoughts. I long to sit by the nursery fire with you and have a good talk about everything, like we used to as children! After all the horror and death I've experienced during my time in France, I can hardly believe that such a time of peace and innocence ever existed. It is such a relief that I can write the truth to you and I don't have to pretend that everything is fine, when it's hellish. Maybe one day when this war is finally over, if I'm still alive, we can sit and talk like we used to?

Do take care Sarah and keep writing to me. I sometimes think your letters are the only things that keep me sane, or as sane as I'll ever be after this lot!

With love,

Your dear brother,

Edward.

After she had read the letter, Emmie wandered into the kitchen where Sarah was preparing their evening meal,' What a terrible time your generation had. That war, how did you all survive it? How could you accept the terrible loss of life, all those men maimed, mentally destroyed and slaughtered? With both your brother and your husband involved in it, I don't know how you stood the strain.'

'We stood it because we had to. There was nothing we could do to stop it. We didn't want to be ruled by militaristic Germans, so we had to beat them. There was no media coverage, no television to record the conditions in the trenches and raise public awareness and generate objection. The generals justified the loss of life somehow and we had to believe it was worthwhile or we would have gone mad. I was lucky Emmie, my brother and my husband survived it. Some women lost everyone they loved, brothers, husbands, lovers, fathers and friends and they had to carry that loss through sixty lonely years until they died themselves. In most cases all the men that would have normally replaced their loved ones were dead too. We were, quite simply, a forgotten generation of women.'

'I feel awful that I never understood. You know so many of my teachers were in their sixties and unmarried. They had probably lost loved ones in the war, but rather than admiring them, we made fun of them and called them old maids; we didn't know what they had been through. One day my housemistress heard me talking about her, I was being rude, making suggestions that she couldn't get a man, arrogant, you know.' Sarah smiled quietly, 'Well anyway she took me into her study and on the mantelpiece she had three beautiful silver photo frames, two contained photographs of men in uniform, First World War uniform. They were both tall and handsome, one was blonde, she told me that he was her fiancé, and the other was dark, he was her brother. They had both been killed, one on the Somme and the other at Passchandaele. She then showed me the third frame, which contained a photograph of a beautiful young woman in a white evening dress. It was her. She then produced an old ring box and inside was a beautiful ring; it had three diamonds side by side. It was her engagement ring and her fiancée had been killed three weeks before she was due to marry him. She told me to remember the handsome young man, the beautiful young woman and the hope of the future represented by the ring every time I looked at an elderly unmarried woman, because that was probably their story too. They had their lives taken from them by that war and should be admired not despised. I felt so embarrassed, but I never forgot and I told my friends the story. We all had a different attitude to the older, unmarried teachers after that. We also noticed that many of them wore a diamond ring on their engagement finger.'

'It was a dreadful time Emmie, a terrible time when life was cheap and death plentiful. I am sure it was because of the drama of the war that Josiah managed to get away with his treatment of Florence. What was the disappearance and death of one more young person amongst the wholesale slaughter of an entire generation? We were almost numb to suffering.'

Emmie thought for a moment, 'I know, I can understand that it wouldn't have had the impact that it would have done in peacetime, but did no one question what he did?. It is simply criminal that Josiah let so many people suffer so much grief. He must have known that Martha and Edward, in particular, would have been torn apart by the death of Florence, who they loved so much. Yet he kept quiet. I mean I am assuming that Josiah did know that Florence was alive all this time?'

Sarah was bent double putting a dish in the oven. She straightened up stiffly, rubbing the small of her back, 'Oh yes he knew she was alive all right, but he made quite sure that no one would find her. As soon as we sit down to eat I will finish the story. Why don't you go upstairs and freshen up and put on those lovely black trousers you've just purchased while I finish preparing the meal and I will complete Florence's story.'

Emmie kissed her on the cheek, she smiled and Emmie departed upstairs.

Chapter Fourteen

Sarah and Emmie sat down to eat in the companionably small conservatory off the kitchen and Sarah poured two large glasses of wine for them both, 'Drink up; you're going to need it.'

Emmie looked at her sharply, 'There can't be worse to come, surely?'

'Oh yes there can. What I am about to tell you is going to be very hard to accept and it will take me some time to tell the whole story. Eat your dinner and help yourself to wine; when you have everything you need, I will begin. Ok? Well, Josiah and Martha lived quietly after the 'death' of Florence. Martha never recovered from her loss and I don't think that there was any meaning left in her life. Josiah carried on as though nothing had happened. If he mourned Florence he never showed it and he never spoke her name. In fact, he would not have her name mentioned in front of him. This made life even harder for Martha, because she had no one to talk to about her daughter. She wrote to me, of course, and she came to see me in Devon, just after the war ended. During that visit I told her as much as I dared about Florence's stay in 1916 and certainly didn't mention the fact that she was pregnant. Martha had been told that Florence's health had deteriorated during her stay, so I had to exaggerate a little, tell Martha that she had been very fragile and weak whilst she had been staying with us. It was so difficult withholding the truth from Martha, but I genuinely felt that telling her about Florence's pregnancy would only cause her pain and present her with a lot of unanswered questions. What good would it have done to reveal to her that her lovely young daughter had been brutally raped? I would just have sullied Florence's memory. So I kept up the pretence, but I wasn't fully comfortable with my decision to conceal the truth from Martha.

After the war I returned to live in London with Charles. We bought this house and set up home together for the first time. Charles was offered a chair at London University and we settled down to a fairly uneventful, but pleasant, academic life. When Edward was finally demobbed, he came to stay with me here. We spent hours talking, just as we had done in front of the nursery fire as children. At least he had that one wish fulfilled, because life generally was pretty bleak for him. I like to think that I helped him in some way to make the difficult adjustment back into civilian life. I got a shock when he first arrived here; he hardly resembled the optimistic young man who had left to join the army in 1914. He was a terrible colour and awfully thin. I thought he looked broken. Like many of the young men returning from a long spell of duty on the Western Front, his nerves were bad and he suffered terribly from nightmares. He would wake up screaming and when I went into him he would be lying in bed shaking, drenched in sweat, too terrified to go back to sleep. It was awful. During the day he wore a haunted look, similar to the one that Florence had when she arrived at Totnes station. He sat around the house chatting with me or we went for long walks down by the river and slowly he started to improve and settle a little.

He stayed with me for about a month and then returned home to mother. He went to work in father's practice, took his articles and qualified as a solicitor. He never showed any interest in women, although I believe he often visited Martha, in spite of Josiah's disapproval. I like to think at least she was able to talk to him about Florence. I never told Edward, either, about Florence's predicament. I couldn't see what good it would have done to tell him the truth any more than I felt it was wise to tell Martha.

Dr. Pickard was never charged with rape and I hate to admit it, but he got away with his crime, unless God saw fit to punish him. Josiah remained on good terms with him until his sudden and unexpected death in May 1919, just after the end of the war. Officially Josiah died of a heart attack, but I like to think that it was his conscience that killed him. He left everything to Martha, the house, the business, a large amount of capital and his share portfolio. She was a wealthy, if somewhat lonely, widow and had full control of his affairs. Naturally they took some time to sort out. Father had been Josiah's solicitor, but he was now retired so Edward did most of the work for probate. However, there were a number of private papers of Josiah's that Martha had to sort through before she could pass them on to Edward.

Josiah always kept his private papers under lock and key in his desk. During his life time he had always kept the desk securely locked and the keys were always attached to his watch chain. During their marriage the locked desk had become a symbol of Josiah's autonomy and was an area of his life to which Martha was denied access. At certain stages during their married life she had an overwhelming desire to break into it and see what it contained. But she would never have dared. And anyway she never had the opportunity as the key never left his watch chain and he always wore his watch. However, once Josiah was dead, she had the keys and no one could stop her. It was with great delight that she was able finally to enter his study, quite freely, to unlock the desk and find out exactly what Josiah had hidden in there. As it had once been a symbol of Josiah's power, Martha felt it had now become a symbol of her newly found independence.

The desk, like all of Josiah's furniture, was made of solid oak, which was stained a dark colour. It was heavy and singularly masculine and it had a roll top which could be pulled down to cover the writing area then locked into place. Once the roll top was opened it revealed a tooled leather desk top, and a complicated system of drawers and pigeon holes, which contained a variety of papers and stationery items. Below the desk top was a band of ornate, heavy carving, which was several inches deep. It ran around the entire desk. Below that there were three deep drawers, all with their own individual locks.

Martha observed this symbol of masculine power with something akin to triumph. She felt like a child who had broken into a sweet shop and was about to raid all the glass jars. The feeling that she experienced was a mixture of excitement, daring, fear and anticipation. She could hardly wait to see what surprises Josiah's desk would hold, but she was still afraid that he may walk into the room and discover her rifling through his papers. It was a completely illogical feeling, she knew Josiah was dead and could no longer exert any power over her, but she couldn't shake off the sensation that he was watching her. This sense of being observed made her feel unaccountably guilty, as though she were about to steal from him. In some ways she was.

She approached the desk slowly, slipped the key into the lock and turned it. She heard it click open and pushed the roll top up. It slid back surprisingly easily and there were all Josiah's secrets just waiting for her to unlock them. She pulled the leather chair back, sat down in his place and with a childish delight started to sort through the papers. During the following days she systematically worked her way through the contents of the desk. She was rather disappointed. All it contained were bank statements, cheque book stubs, household accounts and receipts. She sorted them into the various categories and threw out anything that was of no use. Although she found nothing exciting in the desk, she still enjoyed the fact that she had the power to look through Josiah's private correspondence. She had to admit to herself that it gave her a certain sense of grim satisfaction. D'you know Emmie, I don't think she ever really mourned him at all.

Anyway, it was on the second day that she was sorting through his desk that Martha made her terrible discovery. She was clearing out the last of the papers in the pigeon holes. Some of the papers had become stuck at the back of one of the large central alcoves and she had to stand and push her hand right in to try to release them. They seemed to be caught somehow. She gave a huge tug, heard a loud click and suddenly the papers were free. However, she realised that in pulling at them she must have triggered a catch of some kind, because when she looked down a secret drawer had sprung open. It was concealed in the decorative carving above the drawers and was the same depth and half the width of the carving. She couldn't believe her eyes. She eased it open. It was quite stiff and obviously hadn't been opened for some time. A musty smell rose from the drawer and she could see that it contained a set of papers which were held together with a rusted paper clip. She reached down, lifted them out and spread them on the desk top so that she could have a closer look at them.

When she examined them, she found she had discovered a sheaf of grey-blue, official looking forms. They had obviously been lying there undisturbed for years. She was dumfounded. What on earth was Josiah doing hiding forms in a secret drawer? She assumed they were his papers as he had owned the desk from new. On closer inspection the papers appeared to be medical forms of some kind. They were filled out in the name of a 'Mary Davies.' She wondered what they could be and who this 'Mary Davies' was. She put on her glasses and started to read through them.

It took her a while to realise that they were medical documents from the local lunatic asylum. They were certifying that 'Mary Davies' was insane and should be committed to the asylum for her own safety and the safety of others. The official diagnosis was 'morally insane.' They stated that this unknown woman was morally insane and should be committed to Granthall Asylum 'in perpetuity' for her own safety and the safety of others. The forms were signed by Josiah, Dr. Pickard, another doctor whose name meant nothing to her and Mr. Turnbull, who was a local Justice of the Peace during the First World War. She was stunned. She had so many unanswered questions. Why did Josiah have forms relating to someone called Mary Davies? She had never heard of such a person. Was she a distant relative of Josiah's? Why did he have these forms locked away in a secret drawer and why had he never mentioned it to her? None of it made any sense at all. What did 'morally insane' mean? She unpinned the papers and very carefully unfolded them in order to examine them more closely. They were complex and detailed and she found them quite puzzling.

Eventually she came to a page which contained the personal details of 'Mary Davies', her age, weight, hair colour that kind of thing. But it was the accompanying sepia photograph that held Martha's attention. It was stuck in the box provided on the form. She couldn't take her eyes off it; she couldn't make any sense of it. And then suddenly with a terrible clarity she realised what it meant. She sat immobile looking at the photograph for several minutes then went into the dining room and poured herself a large brandy and drank it in one. She normally never touched alcohol, but she needed courage to continue reading through the papers. Fortified, she returned to the desk and read through the forms again very carefully.

There could be no mistake. It said that this young woman, Mary Davies, was sixteen years old. The forms stated that she had such loose morals that she couldn't be trusted with young men. She had seduced a number of the underage village boys and had relations with them. As a result she had become pregnant. She had then started hallucinating and accusing the Sunday School superintendent, who was a medical practitioner and a church elder, of raping her. She named him as the father of her child. This accusation, of course, proved that she was obviously delusional and needed to be committed before she caused trouble for decent men. But the girl in the photograph was not this fictitious Mary Davies; it was her fifteen year old daughter, Florence Clayton.

The horrible realisation flooded in on Martha and in spite of the brandy she felt very faint. She put her head between her knees to recover a little, then went into the downstairs cloakroom and vomited. Once she had her emotions under control and was sufficiently calm, she went to the newly installed telephone in the sitting room and put a call through to me, here in London. I remember taking it quite clearly. Without any preamble she just said, 'Sarah, it's me Martha. I have something to ask you and something to tell you.'

'Hello Martha, how are you?'

'I'm alright Sarah, well no I'm not. I need you to answer some questions for me, important questions.'

I had a premonition and a chill ran down my spine. 'Alright Martha, this is a little unusual, but I am listening.'

'Before Florence died, was she,' she hesitated, 'was she pregnant?'

I was so shocked I couldn't reply. Why had she asked me? Who could have told her? Why did she want to know?

'It's alright Sarah; I understand fully why you have never told me and I don't blame you in any way. But she was pregnant wasn't she?'

'Yes Martha, she was pregnant and she died in childbirth, she didn't have an infectious disease, but I didn't want to upset you any further.'

'Oh no Sarah she didn't die.'

'I know it's difficult to accept, Martha dear, but I know the full story and she did die in childbirth.'

'You don't understand Sarah, she didn't die in childbirth, I know she didn't, because she didn't die at all.'

My immediate thought was that Martha had gone mad that Josiah's death, together with the loss of Florence, had driven her over the edge. She seemed to read my thoughts.

'I'm not mad, Sarah. I'm quite sane, but I have just made an awful discovery and I am going to need all the support I can get, my dear. I think Josiah lied about Florence's death; I think that he had her committed to a lunatic asylum and I need to know everything that you can tell me about her pregnancy. It is just possible that she is still alive.'

With that she put the phone down. I was stunned. I couldn't take in what she had told me, but I knew that I must get to Liverpool as soon as possible and find out what was going on. I too had a brandy to steady me. I rang Edward and told him that I was coming up to Liverpool and asked him to meet me at the station. I then went straight upstairs and packed. I left it to Edward to tell Martha that I was on my way. Whatever had happened I knew that I must get to Martha as quickly as possible. Together with Charles, I was the only living person who knew what had really happened and Martha was going to need me. I left him a note and caught a taxi to Euston.

Later Martha told me that after she had spoken to me she rang Edward. She asked him to go over to the house immediately, which he did. She then told him to sit down and offered him a brandy too, which he took. Then she just told him, bluntly what she had found out, 'Florence is still alive.'

'What?'

'Well I think that she's still alive, what I am trying to say is that she didn't die in 1917 of an infectious disease Josiah told us. She was pregnant Edward, and Josiah, had her committed to Granthall Asylum. If she's survived, she will still be an inmate there.'

Edward just looked at Martha; he could hardly believe what he was hearing, 'How do you know this Martha? Are you absolutely sure?'

'Oh yes, as sure as I can be.'

Edward swallowed his brandy. It seemed to put some life back into him, 'Have you got any proof of what you say?' Martha started to sob, long, silent, shuddering, sobs, terrible to hear.

'Oh yes, I'm sure, she was pregnant and that bully, Josiah, had her committed as a lunatic. Oh Edward, how could he do that to his own daughter? How? How could that sadistic bigot watch us, knowing we were breaking up inside and never tell us the truth? Here read these forms and look at the identifying photograph. This is how I know; I found them in a secret drawer in his desk. I must have hit the catch my mistake. He never intended me to know. He must have been so sure that I would never find that drawer. He must have been confident that it was so well concealed it would never be discovered. And of course, he always kept it locked and carried the key on his watch chain. He intended that my daughter would rot in that place until she died. However, he didn't take into consideration the fact that he might die suddenly, without warning and I might gain access to his desk.'

Edward read through the forms and suddenly he too was looking at an old sepia photograph of Florence. A shock ran through his body; at first he couldn't understand what he was reading. The name on the form was Mary Davies, but the photograph was definitely Florence. Slowly the meaning became clear to him also. Josiah must have forged her name in order to have her committed at fifteen and to make quite sure that she would never be traced. He would be afraid of being incriminated if anyone ever found her. The bastard, the evil bastard! He ran his hand through his hair then handed them back to Florence.

'You are quite right, they are genuine enough and I can only draw one conclusion. He intended to put Florence away for life. I can't believe it; he made sure that she could never be traced. What was the matter with the man? She was his only daughter; how could he?'

Martha said that the shock was almost too much for Edward to bear. He could hardly cope with the barrage of feelings that it released. Firstly, it was so difficult to cope with the fact that Florence was pregnant. It provoked a rush of jealousy so strong that he felt dizzy. This was followed by a second feeling, this time of joy at the thought that she may still be alive and he may see her again and then the full horror of Josiah's actions flooded in. How could anyone be so cruel? Sweet, cherished Florence exposed to the brutal regime of the asylum, suddenly he was ashamed at his reaction to the news that she was pregnant. He was overcome with remorse at his own selfishness, when all he should have been concerned about was Florence. How would a delicate person like Florence, who had only known love and kindness all her life, survive in such a place? He immediately banished the thought. He dare not even consider that she hadn't survived, having just found out that she may still be alive.

Suddenly something came to him in a flash, a half forgotten memory, 'Martha, do you remember when I was a patient in Granthall myself, when I was suffering from shell shock?

'I'd forgotten about that Edward.' The two of them were sitting quietly in the sitting room surrounded by the wreckage of their appalling discovery. They had been lost in their individual thoughts until Edward spoke, 'I was walking in the grounds one day when I thought I saw Florence dressed in a lunatic's smock coming out of the laundry with a warder. She crossed the grounds and the warder unlocked a door into the main hospital and she was gone. It happened in a few seconds. I tried to call out to her, but I couldn't speak and I couldn't move. It was such a shock. I wasn't very steady myself then and of course I thought Florence was dead so everyone thought that I had imagined it. I was so convinced I made Alf, the warder, check the records and of course there was no Florence Clayton, but there was a Mary Davies. Do you realise Martha that it must have been Florence. If only she'd seen me, if only I could have called out.'

'I remember some story at the time, but we thought it was just your nerves playing tricks. Good Lord, it probably was her. This is so hard to accept. Edward, we have to get her out. How are we going to get her out?'

He looked at her determinedly. 'If she is still alive, we will get her out Martha, of that I am quite sure.'

Chapter Fifteen

A palpable, deafening silence lay between Emmie and Sarah. Neither was capable of speech for several minutes, Sarah, because she was struggling with the emotions that retelling the story had unearthed and Emmie because she was shocked rigid. All the colour had drained from her face and she sat stock still. She just looked at Sarah in silence. Her revelations were so devastating that no words could express Emmie's feelings. She simply willed Sarah to continue. When she had recovered sufficiently she carried on with her story,

'The journey to Liverpool seemed to be endless, which was difficult for me as I was in a state of feverish excitement. It finally pulled into Lime Street in the early evening, about five o'clock. Edward met me at the station. It was good to see him, but he looked nervy again and preoccupied. During the journey we spoke of generalities. He enquired after Charles and hoped he was enjoying his new post at the university. I asked about his work as a solicitor and enquired how it was going. He explained to me that he and mother had arranged for me to stay with Martha as they felt that she needed someone with her, under the circumstances, which would be revealed to me presently. It was the sort of conversation only the British could have when their emotions are surging like a river in full flood. The French or Italians would have fallen on each other's shoulders sobbing and wailing and revealed all in a minute, but we are so controlled. I think that's what I like about us really.

Anyway, when we arrived at Martha's she showed me to my room, where I quickly freshened up before I went downstairs for a pre dinner drink. I was hoping that when I went downstairs I would discover what had happened, exactly what had prompted Martha to telephone me. At that stage I was completely baffled. I wondered how Martha had found out that Florence was pregnant. I thought that perhaps one of the servants had broken their silence. I couldn't for the life of me imagine where Florence could have been for three years if she was, in fact, still alive which is what Martha had maintained when she rang me in London. The reality never crossed my mind.

Martha and Edward were waiting for me in the drawing room. As soon as Edward had given me my drink and we had all settled down, Martha silently handed me some grey, musty smelling forms, 'I think the easiest way to explain what has happened is for you to read these papers. They are self explanatory and they contain all the information that we've got at present. Both Edward and I have seen them, have worked out their significance and have drawn the same conclusions. We would be interested to see what you think and we felt that you could also probably fill in some gaps for us. We think that these papers explain what happened to Florence when she returned here from Devon.

I took the papers and looked questioningly at both of them but they merely returned my look in silence. Then I started to examine the papers. I was as perplexed as they were when I started to read about this unknown 'Mary Davies'. I wondered what her significance was, then like them I came upon the old sepia photograph and everything fell into place. I can't explain how I felt when I saw that old sepia photograph of the young Florence looking back at me. I thought I was going to choke. I realised almost at once what Josiah had done; he had taken Florence to the local lunatic asylum and had her committed under a false name. He had left her there to have her baby alone and abandoned and intended that she should stay there as a punishment for the rest of her life. It was beyond belief. It all rushed in on me and quite literally took my breath away. It was beyond my comprehension that anyone could have done that to a lovely person like Florence and the awful thing was that if I had acted differently I could have prevented it. I could hardly breathe, let alone speak, so I sat quietly and tried to control myself.

Eventually, when I finally felt that I had my emotions sufficiently under control to enable me to talk, I looked up and spoke to them, 'He had her committed,' was all I could utter and they nodded silently in agreement. I asked if they knew whether or not she was still alive, but they knew no more than me. We all thought that it was possible that she was and that Josiah had invented the story of her death to prevent us looking for her. However, she may have died in childbirth in the asylum. But that was simply too awful to contemplate.

Obviously I immediately confessed to them that I had known all along that Florence was pregnant. I told them that I felt that I could have prevented this happening to her if I'd followed my instincts and kept her in Devon until she had had her baby. But at the time I was young and inexperienced. I told them that I did what society expected me to do and asked my husband's advice and Charles, like most men, advised that her father should be told. In agreeing to this I delivered an innocent, trusting, young girl into the hands of a sadist. Thankfully Martha and Edward were sympathetic and agreed that in my position that they would have done the same thing.

I told them everything that I've told you during this weekend. I explained to them that initially I had no idea that Florence was pregnant, but I thought that she looked very ill and drawn when she arrived in Devon. I told them that it was Dorcas, the housekeeper there, who alerted me to the fact that Florence was expecting a baby. I explained that I had to approach Florence with care as Dorcas was sure that she didn't know that she was pregnant. In fact, I only realised when I asked her about the baby that she knew nothing of sexual matters at all and didn't actually fully comprehend what pregnancy really meant.

I took Florence's written version of how she was raped with me and Edward and Martha both read it, like you did, with horror. It was obvious to them that Florence was telling the truth. She was far too naïve to have made up such a story. However, they couldn't believe that Josiah had chosen to believe her abuser and had disbelieved her. I explained that I wanted Florence to stay with me in Devon and have her baby. I thought that Martha could have come to stay for the confinement and then we could have had the baby adopted by a local family and no one would have been any the wiser, except poor Florence herself. But I couldn't contact Martha directly as there were no phones at the farm and I didn't want to just write to her. However, Charles was adamant that Josiah should be told, as her legal guardian, because a crime had been committed. He felt that it was up to him, as Florence's father, to contact the police. I suppose to some extent that he was right, it wasn't as though she had just had an affair with a local boy, she had been raped. Reluctantly I agreed that Josiah should be told and then he could make any decisions about the baby. I thought that he would want Florence to stay in Devon, as I had intended she should, and have the baby there. I never thought for one minute that he would doubt Florence's story and accept Dr. Pickard's version of events. I was stunned when I heard that he wanted Florence to return home, but then I thought it was because he wanted her to be with her mother. I confessed to them how terrible I felt that I had betrayed Florence. She had confided in me because she trusted me to keep her safe and I had delivered her into the hands of a devil, and Emmie, I did. It was because I was innocent myself, but I did betray her trust.

Whilst I was telling my story I hadn't realised that I was crying. Martha came over and sat on the sofa and held my hands while she spoke reassuringly to me, 'Sarah, dear Sarah, you mustn't blame yourself, we are all impotent in the face of evil. I am her mother I am riddled with guilt that I allowed her to remain ignorant about sexual matters long enough for this man to take advantage of her innocence. I didn't even know her well enough to realise that something traumatic had happened to her that afternoon to cause her to become so withdrawn and ill. Don't you think that I have asked myself over and over again why I didn't insist upon seeing her when Josiah brought her here on her return from Devon? I was too afraid of him and I let her down. Edward is also guilty by default; he escorted her to the Sunday School that fateful day and handed her over to Pickard. He could have insisted on waiting for her, or gone in with her, but he too was afraid of Josiah. He thought that he would get

Florence into trouble if Josiah knew that he'd been with her that afternoon. A few years later he thought that he saw Florence in the asylum, but at the time thought that it was his nerves playing tricks and that he was imagining things. How could he see her when she was dead? We all let her down, but that is because we are normal people who could not imagine evil on this scale. Why should we?

We both understand why you decided not to tell us what had happened to Florence and that she had become pregnant as the result of a rape. You thought that she was dead and you would just have destroyed the memory we had of her as an innocent. You did it out of kindness, not malice, we fully understand that. This has been a terrible shock for all of us. Josiah was mentally ill, I think. He had an unnatural fear of beauty, especially in women. He seemed to want to punish Florence for the fact that she was beautiful, because she affected his feelings and made him want to love her. He thought love was synonymous with weakness and had to be controlled. How could any normal person start to understand what was going on in his mind? He was determined not to love her as everyone else did. I was always afraid for her, I felt that given the opportunity that he would try crush the spirit out of her, but I thought that I would always be there to stand between them. I thought that I would always be there to protect her. That devil Pickard must have picked up on Josiah's suspicion of Florence and calculated that if she did tell her father he could talk his way out of it, which he did. He probably realised that Josiah would be all too willing to believe the worst about Florence. Village boys indeed, the only boy she ever had eyes for was Edward.' I noticed that Edward threw her a grateful look at her parting comment.

Oh Emmie, I was so relieved to be able to tell the truth at last. I had carried that knowledge around with me for nearly three years and I hated withholding the truth from Martha and Edward, but they were very understanding. I think all three of us felt guilty of letting Florence down. But there was truth in what Martha said. If you are not evil yourself, how can you anticipate what evil will do?

We talked about Florence all through dinner and made our plans. Edward told us his impressions of Granthall from when he was a patient there. It sounded grim, but he was well cared for. We were all extremely worried about the effect imprisonment in a place like that would have had on Florence. We didn't even know if she was still alive. We discussed what our next move should be. Firstly we had to establish that she was indeed in Granthall and still alive, up to that point we only had our fairly well founded suspicions. We then needed to establish her state of mind and try to get her out. We were very concerned that we may not be able to secure her discharge. Firstly, we had to prove that she was Martha's daughter, Florence Clayton, and not Mary Davies, then we had to find out where 'Mary' was being held, then have her diagnosis reversed. It was not going to be easy.

One of our main worries was that her state of mind might have been permanently damaged. If Florence had been sane when she entered the asylum would she still be sane? The shock of finding herself in there alone and helpless would have been terrible and the sense of abandonment could have completely overwhelmed her and easily have turned her mind. Martha said that didn't matter, she was a wealthy woman and would have Florence cared for at home no matter what her state of mind was. We talked on and on through the night trying to work out a strategy.

Edward felt that the legalities were a nightmare to unravel, but the one advantage that we did have was the fact that he had been a patient there during the war and he had contacts in the hospital. His warder, Alf, had been a good, honest man and he thought that the best thing he could do was to contact him. Edward was fairly sure that he was still working there and he could help us to establish whether Florence was in the hospital, alive and well Perhaps Alf would see Florence, anonymously, on our behalf, and assess her state of mind. That was of the utmost importance, we had to face the fact that she may not be well enough to be discharged. We would have to be very careful no matter how much we felt like simply storming the place and bringing her home. It was going to be difficult to get her discharged even if we found her. We knew we were going to have to tread very carefully.

I rang Charles that night to tell him what had happened. He was as distressed as I was and felt equally, if not more, guilty than I did. I told him not to be silly, but I explained that I was going to stay with Martha until we could establish exactly what had happened and had located Florence. He was fully supportive and said he would come up at the weekends and help as much as he was able to. However, for now we had to be patient and leave things to Edward.

Chapter Sixteen

Edward still had an old contact address for Alf. From the beginning of his stay on the ward he realised that Alf derived some comfort from looking after the men in his charge. It was as if he felt that he was doing something for his dead son, David, who was now beyond his help. It seemed to help him deal with his deep sorrow at the loss of his son. Alf, for his part, realised that Edward's grief at the loss of Florence had sharpened the normal feelings of despair that the war had spawned and nearly sent him over the edge. So it was that they had developed a special empathy, each in his way replacing something of what the other had lost. They were brought together in their mutual grief. It wasn't exactly friendship, but there was an unspoken bond of affection between them. So when Edward was discharged they exchanged addresses and kept in touch, mainly through the annual tradition of Christmas cards. They exchanged one every year almost as a continuing coded message of support.

At this stage in the proceedings Alf was really the only hope Edward had. He couldn't think of anyone else who could prepare the ground for him before he approached the authorities regarding the situation with Florence. He realised that one wrong move now could bring down an impenetrable wall of silence, which would effectively prevent him from ever being able to obtain Florence's discharge. I know he felt awkward at just turning up at Alf's house without any warning. He felt it was a gross intrusion of his privacy and probably stretching the limits of their unusual relationship, but he was sure that once Alf realised how desperate the situation was he would be only too pleased to help.

Edward only had a vague idea where Alf lived and it took him a little time to find the house. As he expected, it was a simple stone cottage in a terrace and it overlooked farm land near the hospital. These were the days before cars were fashionable, remember, and his arrival in one, and rather a smart Bentley roadster at that, caused quite a stir in the modest terrace. After he'd visited Alf, Edward told us what had happened.

'It was early summer and the days were long and warm. It was still light as I pulled into Alf's cobbled street of terraced cottages. As was their custom in the warm weather, the women were taking a rest from their relentless housework and were sitting on wooden stools and kitchen chairs outside their respective terraced houses and enjoying a gossip. The children, thrilled that no one had yet called them to bed, played barefoot in the street between them. As I pulled up they stopped their games and swarmed all around and all over my car, with undisguised curiosity. I identified the leader and gave him a shilling to 'guard' my car. I knew he would take his position seriously and that way I made sure that no little souvenirs, such as badges, were pocketed. Feeling anything but confident I smiled at the curious neighbours. It was a beautiful, warm evening and the air was tinged with the freshness of the wild flowers in the field beyond the terraced row, but all I could think about was Florence languishing in the asylum across the same field behind the perimeter wall. As I approached Alf's house, I just wished that I was free of this worry and had Florence safe at home. I knocked on the door, which was standing ajar on this warm summer's evening. I could see that there was no lobby or hallway; you stepped straight into the front room from the street. I didn't want to look intrusive or nosy so I stepped back after knocking at the door. Eventually I heard movement within and a dishevelled Alf appeared in shirt sleeves and braces carrying a white enamel pail. I remembered from my days in the hospital that he was something of a pigeon fancier; he'd probably been seeing to them in the back yard. He was astonished when he answered the door and saw me standing there. He thought it was kids playing knock and run and was about to go out and shout at them for disturbing him. He was touchingly pleased to see me and was delighted that I was looking so well and in such good health. He was so genuinely delighted to see me that I immediately relaxed. He shook my hand in greeting and quickly ushered me into the privacy of his front room away from prying eyes.

He realised straight away that I wasn't just making a social call and he asked me, in his comfortably blunt way exactly what the problem was.

'Well lad,' he said, 'what brings you here this fine night? You'll have to excuse my shirt sleeves, I'm just seeing to the pigeons. You look a sight better that last time I saw you, but I'm betting that this isn't just a social call eh?' He was nothing if not shrewd. I just stuttered out my apologies at having barged in on him unannounced, but explained that I really needed to see him. In his usual friendly manner he told me to think nothing of it and told me to sit myself down while he put the kettle on. Apparently his wife was at her mother's, she'd been taken ill and so there were just the two of us. I knew better than to start my story until Alf had made the tea, so I just waited while he wandered off into the back kitchen. I remained quietly in the front room, the best parlour and listened to the sounds of Alf making the tea in the back kitchen. I heard the sound of rushing cold water hitting the base of an enamel kettle, the hiss of gas and the striking of a match followed by a clunk when Alf put the kettle on the hob to boil. They were sounds that were all too familiar to me. As the comforting hiss of the steam gathered enough strength to blow the kettle's whistle, I was taken back to the long nights at the hospital when I had awoken from my nightmares and gone in search of Alf and comfort. In his little office I had looked for and found the tea and company that helped to drive away my demons.

I looked around the little living room whilst I waited. It was spotlessly clean and in it the elderly couple had created an intimate little shrine to their dead son, David. It really choked me to see the photograph of him in uniform mounted on the wall next to a wooden glass fronted case containing his medals. They were all lovingly polished and mounted with their campaign ribbons on black velvet. There was a photograph of him in his cricket whites, with what I assumed to be the village team, and what must have been his prized cricket bat stood in the corner. I wondered how many millions of families had created a similar shrine in their front parlours to a cherished son that they had lost in the war. It was cold comfort, but it at least kept alive their memories.

Alf came back properly dressed in a summer jacket and tie and carrying a tray covered by a paper doily containing a china tea pot, milk jug and two matching cups, all prettily decorated with red climbing roses.

It was a beautifully presented cup of tea. He informed me, laughing fondly, that the wife would have killed him if he had not laid the tea tray properly for company. He was afraid she might come back unexpectedly and he was taking no risks. He said he preferred a white mug, but he knew she would expect the best china to be used for such a distinguished visitor and he did as he was told. I smiled and then asked him about the photographs of his son, his lad, David. His eyes filled up, in spite of himself. He was so proud of him, proud that he had played cricket for the village team and proud that he had died for his country. It was touching how much he had loved his only son.

To hide his emotion Alf busied himself pouring the tea and then asked me directly how he could help me. I didn't have to start at the beginning as Alf already knew about the supposed 'death' of Florence. He listened quietly as I told him of Martha's unexpected discovery and then I handed him the papers that she'd found. He recognised them at once as the hospital's committal forms and was shocked at our discovery. However, he admitted that he had heard rumours of it happening before, an inconveniently pregnant young woman being quietly hidden away in the asylum. I went on to explain that I was concerned about alerting the authorities until I was certain that Florence was an actually an inmate in the hospital. I told him that I was fairly certain we'd have a problem asking for information because we couldn't actually prove that this 'Mary Davies' was, in fact, Florence and therefore related to us. Alf listened grimly. He didn't make any comment, he was a man of few words, but his expression showed his dismay. He realised at once what

I required of him and was more than glad to help. He realised that I'd need his help to find 'my lass.' He always referred to Florence as 'that lass of yours'. I told him that I'd feel more confident if I knew for sure that she was an inmate, although I hated to say it, I actually needed to establish that she was, in fact, still alive. We didn't know anything for sure. I didn't really have to go into detail, Alf understood. He realised that I was concerned about her state of mind after three years in the asylum. He was very angry, on my behalf, that I'd been led to believe that she was dead for all those years, especially when I was trying to cope with conditions on the Western Front. Bless him, he didn't hesitate to offer his help. I did get a bit angry about Josiah, but he settled me down in his usual philosophical way and I knew he was right.

He commented that it seemed likely that it was Florence who I had seen leaving the laundry in 1917 when he was so sure that I was hallucinating. He was very apologetic about that, but how was he to know? Anyway, he agreed to try and locate 'Mary Davies' and then go to see her in person to establish whether or not she was Florence. If she was, he could then assess her state of mind. He was a very experienced warder, so I knew that he would weigh up her condition accurately. He was very kind and reassuring and we agreed that he would contact me at my office when he had some news for me and I could come back to the privacy of his home to discuss it. I was so very grateful to him. I don't know how I would have approached the problem without his help. Our business completed, I stood and took my leave of him. He escorted me to his front door and gave me a reassuring, almost fatherly, pat on the back as I left.

When I stepped out onto the street, my young guard had done his job well, as promised and my car seemed to be intact so I threw the delighted lad another shilling and then got in and drove home.'

Emmie those three days of waiting after Edward returned from Alf's were a nightmare. Martha wrote letters to everyone she could think of to pass the time, but she didn't post any of them. I just sat around and tried to comfort her. Eventually Alf sent word to Edward, who arranged to call and see him again. After his visit he came straight round to Martha's to tell us what had happened. It was raining when he went back to Alf's so the women were inside with most of the children, thank goodness, and it spared him having to undergo their scrutiny this time. Some young lads, too big to be cooped up in a small terraced house, were sheltering from the rain in a shop doorway. They included his 'guard' of the previous visit, so he recruited him to watch over his car again, then knocked at Alf's door feeling fairly confident about the car's survival. He loved that car almost as much as he loved his family. Anyway Alf answered the door as before and led Edward into the front room. His wife was round at her mother's again, so they were free to talk. After Alf had made him a cup of tea they settled down to talk and Edward was quite pleased with the progress that he'd made. Alf had managed to have a look at the hospital records and he found a Mary Davies on Ward Four. She was the only one listed so he'd been fairly hopeful that it was Florence listed by her alias. He knew the warder in charge of Ward Four; she was an old timer by the name of Jane Worthington. He told Edward that he was bothered about how to approach the problem and then decided just to go over there unannounced for a social visit. It wouldn't be that unusual, he often went walk about when he wasn't working. All the warders enjoyed exchanging gossip and examining the progress on other wards. Sometimes they called in on him and he was usually glad of the company, especially on the night shift, so he didn't think it would look that odd.

When he'd finished his day shift he just strolled down the corridor until he came to Ward Four and simply rang the bell. He heard footsteps approaching the doors and then the cover of the spy hole slid to one side, whilst an unidentified eye surveyed him. They obviously recognised him because he heard the key turn in the lock and the door swung open to reveal one of the assistants on the other side. He asked if Jane was on duty and they took him to her office. He found her sitting in there doing her paper work. She seemed pleased to see him and have the opportunity to stop work and have a cup of tea and a gossip. She sent down to the kitchen for two cups of tea and some biscuits and they settled down to chat. Alf had a good sense of humour and he made her laugh with some of his tales about the staff and patients, eventually he casually broached the subject of 'Mary Davies'. The first thing that he needed to do was to establish that she was still actually on Jane's ward.

Jane immediately knew who he was talking about. Those warders knew every one of their hundred or so patients personally; they were a special breed Edward said. Jane told Alf that 'Mary' had been on her ward for a number of years. She was very curious about why he wanted to know. Alf didn't tell any lies but didn't reveal the full story of why he was interested in her, just said a friend had asked him to enquire how she was. Jane admitted that she was an intriguing case, most unusual. She'd been admitted some years ago, heavily pregnant. It was immediately obvious to Jane that she was, as she put it, 'a cut above' her usual patients. You could tell by her clothes and her hair that she had been well looked after. Many of Jane's patients were paupers and in poor physical health as well as having psychiatric illnesses. She told Alf that 'Mary' was never any trouble. When she was first admitted she was drugged to the eyeballs with chloral hydrate and a heavy dose had been prescribed for her once she was in there. Both Alf and Jane knew that an overdose of chloral hydrate induced a state that resembled insanity. It caused disorientation, clumsiness, slurred speech and a general impression of confusion. Alf said Jane looked knowingly at him and he put into words what she'd been thinking; that someone wanted 'Mary' to look more out of control than she actually was Jane said she ignored the prescription and stopped administering the chloral hydrate and 'Mary's' condition improved at once. Besides she didn't think it was wise for a pregnant girl to take strong drugs like that.

She told Alf that 'Mary' was obviously deeply distressed to find herself in there, but she never uttered a word. She was completely dumb from the day that she entered the ward. They tried everything to make her talk, but she simply couldn't or wouldn't speak. They thought it was probably the shock. The staff warmed to her and protected her from some of the more troublesome patients. She was a beautiful girl, kind and gentle. She was obviously terrified to find herself in an asylum, but nothing could induce her to speak, she never uttered a single word, so they never found out any more about her. Another comment Jane made was that she never smiled.

Jane told him that 'Mary's' waters broke while she was on the ward so they took her to the hospital infirmary to give birth. She heard from one of the infirmary staff that she'd had a terribly hard confinement, first baby you see. She was gone for quite a long while. She was ill after the birth and ran a fever so they kept her in the infirmary until she was better. She looked terrible when she eventually returned to the ward, although Jane commented that she seemed a little calmer, less agitated, but deeply depressed and she still didn't speak. They sent 'Mary's' medical report down from the infirmary to the ward to be put in her file. It simply stated that she had had a male child who was still born, which was probably as well under the circumstances, and was being kept in the infirmary until her temperature dropped as she was running a post natal fever.

She told Alf that they reckoned 'Mary' was from a good background; you could tell by the way that she carried herself and the way that she behaved. But they were all surprised that no one ever enquired after her or wrote to her. She never received a parcel or a birthday card. It was doubly strange because better off families usually kept in touch with relatives in the hope that the patient may be improving, but there was nothing. The staff always felt that someone had wanted 'Mary' to disappear because she was an embarrassment, as sometimes happened. However, that was none of Jane's business. Alf asked her what the diagnosis had been. She nodded at his papers, and said it was just as the papers stated, morally insane. But they hadn't seen any sign of insanity whilst she'd been on the ward.

Alf said Jane wasn't daft and he caught her looking at him questioningly, one eyebrow raised and he knew that he'd been found out. She told him that he was not fooling her for a moment just turning up with a vague enquiry about a patient he just happened to be acquainted with. She wanted to know what the real story was so he told her. He knew realistically that he couldn't get much past an old timer like Jane. She was the salt of the earth, had been at the asylum for decades and Alf trusted her, so he told her Florence's story. Jane took it in her stride, nothing much shocked her. She'd seen it all before. She thought it was particularly cruel to have her admitted under a false name so she couldn't be traced and simply appalling that Josiah let the family think she was dead. She wanted to know how the family had found her, in spite of the father's best efforts to cover his tracks. Alf told her that Josiah had died suddenly last month and the mother found the committal papers whilst she was rummaging through his desk trying to sort everything out for probate. He said it was a miracle that she unwittingly hit a spring that opened a secret drawer. The papers were hidden in there. They were never meant to be found.

Jane laughed at Alf and called him an 'an old fox', sneaking onto her ward and playing detective, but she wasn't unsympathetic. She liked 'Mary' or Florence, as she now knew her and she was willing to help all she could to get her discharged into the care of her family. She thought that basically Florence was alright but the shock of finding herself in the asylum had triggered a kind of defence mechanism. She said she'd seen it before and thought that with care she would recover and start to react and eventually speak again. She couldn't guarantee mind, but Alf said she knew her stuff and he respected her opinion.

Edward and Alf talked for a long time about getting Florence discharged. They both realised that there was going to be a problem establishing her identity. However, as a solicitor, Edward thought that he could overcome that, especially now that he knew for sure that she was in the asylum. Jane had told Alf that if they applied through the normal channels the committee would ask for a doctor's report. However, the doctors never got to know the patients as well as the warders and they usually asked for Jane's opinion. Alf explained to Edward that there were so many patients that the doctors found it hard to know each one individually, whereas the warders lived with them day in day out. Jane said if she was asked for an opinion about Florence's discharge, she'd definitely recommend discharge into the care of her family under the supervision of a medical doctor.

Alf said she knew he was dying of curiosity so eventually she asked if him if he would like to see Mary. He eagerly accepted. They left her office, which she locked and walked through the gas lit refectory into the day room where a number of the patients were sitting around after their evening meal. It was far from peaceful in the day room. There were women in tears, women walking up and down muttering to themselves, some were singing, others just staring into space and rocking back and forth moaning quietly. Many women ignored the bedlam around them and seemed fairly quiet and were just sitting in corners sewing or knitting. It was a scene that was quite familiar to Alf, one that was repeated throughout the hospital on all but the worst wards. Two attendants were on duty in the day room and they were just beginning to round the women up and get them ready for bed.

He told Edward that he recognised Florence immediately from her photograph. She stood out somehow. She was sitting in a wooden rocking chair by the side of the fire and was wrapped in an old shawl. She ignored everyone and everything around her and just sat rocking gently to and fro, staring at the fire. She was exquisitely beautiful, even dressed in the asylum smock and pinafore. Alf's heart went out to her. She looked painfully young and so vulnerable. She was a tiny little thing and looked like a little bird with broken wings, trapped in a cage. She looked up at them as they approached but she didn't give any indication that she recognised them. When they reached her Jane put her hand on her shoulder and bent down to look into her eyes, Florence avoided eye contact, she spoke to her gently calling her 'Mary' but she didn't react, so Jane just stroked her hair affectionately and straightened up. Alf asked if he could try and Jane nodded. He tried the same approach as Jane and again Florence avoided eye contact, but this time he spoke gently to her and called her Florence and he swore to Edward that he saw a flicker of life in those dead eyes. He tried to talk to her, to tell her about Edward, but she soon lost interest in him and returned her gaze to the fire. Jane shook her head at Alf and took him to one side.

'She won't react; I'm sure that she can hear, she reacts sometimes to sound, but she never speaks, not a sound, well not during the day anyway. She has terrible nightmares at night when she screams out, but otherwise nothing. That is a good sign as it means the dumbness is self inflicted, not a physical defect.'

Alf nodded in agreement. Out of interest he asked if she had ever worked in the laundry. Jane confirmed that she had, in the sewing room, in fact, she still did. Alf looked knowingly at Edward in a regretful way. It seemed that it was Florence that Edward had seen that fateful day during the war. It seemed inconceivable. Yet, as Edward commented, if she had been admitted under her own name, Alf would have found her then when he made enquiries. It was just the sadistic cunning of Josiah's twisted mind that made him change her name and keep her buried for life. Then Alf explained to Edward that he had gone one step further and asked if Jane, once Edward had confirmed her identity, thought it would be wise to visit Florence. She felt it would be good for her as long as it was one trusted person who came regularly. It didn't matter if she brought a friend, but if a number of different people suddenly took an interest in Florence and started visiting her it would only confuse her, which would not be helpful in Jane's opinion.

Edward told us that he just sat quietly when Alf had finished his story and Alf respected his silence and just sat lighting his pipe. All Edward could think about, as Alf's story sank in, was the realisation that Florence was actually alive, she was alive and seemed to have survived the horrors, well almost. He realised that he had a momentous task ahead of him. Firstly establishing her identity and then persuading the authorities to discharge her into Martha's care. But she was alive. And where there was life there was hope. An overused cliché, but it was true. Once he had his emotions back under control he discussed with Alf what they should do next. They decided that the obvious course was to establish Florence's true identity somehow, then ask for visiting rights, then approach the subject of her discharge. Alf felt that now contact had been made there wouldn't be too much trouble. They would be aware that they had allowed an innocent girl from a good family to have been admitted under a false name. The fact that they hadn't checked her identity was inexcusable. They obviously accepted what Josiah told them without question because of Josiah's standing in the community at the time. But that was really no excuse and they wouldn't want any scandal. Alf said he would call in regularly to make sure that she was alright, but he was confident that Jane would continue to look after her, as she had always done, with care.

Oh Emmie, we were all so relieved when Edward retuned to tell us that Florence was still alive and relatively sane. We were obviously distressed that she couldn't or wouldn't talk, as that gave us some measure of the effect the trauma had had on her. But she was no longer dead to us. It was a miracle. We decided, amongst ourselves, that Martha should be the one to visit her and if they allowed it, I would go with her. It was hard on Edward, but he agreed that it should be her mother who initially made contact. We were, quite simply ecstatic with happiness, but it was tinged with a controlled fury at Josiah and not a little guilt that we hadn't managed to protect her in the first place.'

Chapter Seventeen

Emmie couldn't quite take in all that Sarah had told her. It seemed unbelievable to her, a young woman living in the 1970s, that a woman could simply disappear. If she disappeared her mother and father would look for her. Her grandmother would make enquiries and so would her friends. But Florence was locked away for life on the word of her father, because he wished it and everyone believed him when he said she was dead. He had the power to do that and no one dared question him.

Florence would never have been found if Martha hadn't accidentally pressed the release catch on the desk and discovered the hidden committal papers. If they hadn't been found, Florence would have stayed in the asylum for the rest of her adult life. She would never have married and had children, Freddy would not have existed and neither would Emmie herself. Emmie's very existence had all depended on the discovery of those papers. It was all down to fate and was almost too incredible to contemplate. Emmie explained to Sarah how difficult it was for her to accept that men, fathers in particular, had such power then. Sarah merely smiled. She understood that Emmie would find it strange. Things had changed such a lot, but during the nineteenth century, when she was a girl, her father had to be obeyed. She smiled and added that her mother knew how to get round him so he didn't always win, but he always thought he had. Sarah patted Emmie's hand reassuringly and told her it wasn't as bad as it sounded. However, there were certain men, like Josiah, who abused their power and needed to control everything.

That was why there had to be more equality in society and slowly women had gained their independence. After their discussion, Sarah continued with her story:

'Edward worked with the asylum authorities to secure Florence's discharge. Firstly he had to establish her identity. He had to prove that it was Florence in the asylum and not this fictitious 'Mary Davies'. It took weeks of correspondence and meetings with the asylum board. He had to use all his legal skills to convince the authorities that Florence was indeed Martha and Josiah's daughter and had been committed using a false name. They were incredibly reluctant at first to admit that a mistake had been made. Eventually, however, they realised that it could cause them more trouble if Edward were to expose them. It was when he threatened to do this that they backed down.

During this difficult time I stayed up in Liverpool with Martha. It was a most dreadfully trying time for her. I don't know that I was really any help to her. I was more anxious than she was, but I was a familiar face to have around and someone to talk to. Charles came up to see us as often as he could and gave us all much needed support. He also talked things over with Edward, which helped him enormously. We willed Edward to success. We simply couldn't contemplate defeat. I think if that had happened, if they hadn't accepted that 'Mary Davies' was Florence Clayton we would have broken in and helped her escape, but that is the stuff of melodrama; it doesn't really happen in real life. Once I'd seen inside that place, the asylum I mean, I realised just how impossible it would have been to spirit her out. It was like a fortress with all its locks and bolts and vigilant warders.

Anyway, as it happened, we didn't need to stage a

dramatic escape. After an almost unbearable wait, Edward eventually received the papers acknowledging that Florence was indeed Martha and Josiah's only daughter and not this fictitious Mary Davies. The papers also appointed Martha as Florence's legal guardian. Remember Florence was still only eighteen and had been certified insane. She was not considered to be fit enough to take responsibility for herself. Once her identity had been established, however, Edward applied for visiting rights for Martha. This was far more difficult to achieve. They came up with all kinds of excuses and reasons why we shouldn't be allowed to visit. However, Edward persevered and eventually they gave permission for Martha to visit her daughter under strict supervision. I'm sure it was only because of the unusual nature of Florence's committal under a false name that persuaded them to cooperate.

They had been negligent in not checking her identity, but in their defence they had thousands of inmates and many of them had identities that were in doubt. Also, Josiah had misused his influence and power to ensure that the authorities wouldn't question the legality of the papers and Pickard made doubly sure that they didn't. His professional life, reputation and freedom were hanging in the balance. If anyone had ever believed Florence, Pickard would have been finished as a doctor. He may not have been charged with a crime, but it would have been the end of his professional career.

Anyway, I don't suppose that the reasons why they allowed the visits matter anymore. Martha did eventually receive official permission to visit Florence together with an official pass. This allowed her to take one person with her for support. We discussed at length which one of us she should take. We knew that Edward was desperate to see Florence again, but we thought it would be wiser for Martha to take me. We pointed out that she had lived amongst women for several years and may be distressed to see a man. We felt that it would be less upsetting for her if she was visited by two females who were familiar to her. Edward didn't argue. He saw the sense in what we said. All he wanted was for Florence to be discharged into our care. He would know then that she was safe.

We were terribly excited at the thought that finally we would see our little Florence again, but we were also extremely nervous. I lost a stone in weight during this time and Martha was disappearing before my very eyes. It was a very difficult and anxious time, Emmie. Eventually we were given a date for the visit. We were told to present ourselves at the gate house of somewhere called the Annexe and we were given a time when we could attend. Apparently we would be met at the gatehouse and then we would be taken to the main hospital. Here we would be met by a different warder in the main reception area, she would then escort us to the ward. At no time would we be unaccompanied. This was to ensure our safety and make us feel secure at all times. The fact that Edward had been a patient in the hospital was a great help. He was able to give us a sketchy outline of the layout and brief description of the actual building. It made it less threatening somehow. Also my parents had visited Edward during the war in the hospital, so they were able to confirm what Edward told us and put us at our ease a little.

Apparently we were to see Florence in a private room, possibly the warder's office. For reasons of privacy and safety, they wouldn't allow us on the main ward, which was understandable. We didn't really care about that, except that we would have liked to have seen what Florence's living conditions were like. You know, where she slept and ate that kind of thing. We felt it may help us to understand what she had been through, but, oh Emmie, nothing prepared us for the real thing. I have never been to such a place before and I never want to go again. It was so large and threatening. I can still almost taste the sour, stale smell of disinfectant mixed with stale food and urine that permeated every corner of the place. It made me retch every time we visited. It was such an ugly place. It was painted in dark, depressing tones. There was no colour anywhere. All the inmates and the staff were dressed in uniform. There was no beauty anywhere. I don't know how Florence survived it.

The day of our visit finally arrived. Martha and I were very nervous, as you can imagine. It was now November and winter had set in. It was nearly five months since Martha had first discovered Florence's committal forms in the secret drawer. We were almost beginning to despair of ever seeing her again. Edward arranged to drive us to the asylum on the assigned day. It was a typical November morning cold, dark and dank. It was one of those winter days when it never seems to get light. A damp fog hung over everything and refused to move. As we left the house a mist wreathed itself around the shrubs that bordered the driveway. They looked like spectres forming a guard of honour to escort us to our fate. Obviously we were thrilled at the thought of seeing Florence, but we wished we could avoid having to go to that place to see her. I think Martha and I felt that once we got inside we would be kept there with Florence and never be seen again. The asylum had such a power to frighten. It was such a place of secrecy and mystery. Everyone was afraid that they may one day end up there and I felt that Josiah's malign force might exercise its power from beyond the grave and trap us. We were very silly I know, but we were very scared.

We drove to the asylum in silence. Martha and I sat in the back of the car, hands clasped tightly together. Edward just kept his eyes on the road until eventually out of the gloom the outline of the hospital tower appeared. He turned off the main road and pulled up at some large wrought iron gates that were closed. Martha looked out and beckoned me to do the same. She pointed to a strange little red brick house which could only have been the gatehouse, it was built like a normal house but had a sharply inclined roof, rather like that of a French chateau. There was an extraordinary miniature turret on the side of the little house, with six small windows round the top of the tower, like arrow slits, Martha muttered to me that she wouldn't have been surprised if Rapunzel had appeared at one of the upper windows of the tower and thrown her plait out. It made me smile and it broke the awful tension that was beginning to build in the car. Edward had rung the bell on the side door of this little house and a porter came out. They talked for a while then the porter took a huge key out of his pocket and walked over to the gates, which he unlocked. He then swung each one open in turn in order for Edward to pass through. They were very heavy and he had to work hard to move them. I noticed that he carefully locked them again once we were safely inside.

He proceeded down the drive. Edward told us over his shoulder that he had permission to drive us to the front entrance and he was going to be allowed to wait for us in the reception area. That made Martha and I feel more secure.

We drove slowly down a winding drive bordered by huge rhododendron bushes. Like the bushes at home these were wreathed in a swirling mist and seemed to be watching our progress like silent spectres. Suddenly the asylum was before us. I just wasn't prepared for such a forbidding building. It was built of red brick and was enormous. Edward handed us out of the car with reassuring words and smiles. I can't remember exactly what he said, I was so agitated. I know that I wished he were coming in with us.

While Edward locked the car, Martha and I looked up at the clock tower, which fronted the massive square building and we almost got a crick in our necks trying to see the clock at the top. Edward joined us and we walked up to the enormous double front door. We felt so small and vulnerable standing there in front of this huge door. Edward rang the bell and we could hear it echoing hollowly inside. Then we heard a grinding sound as a bolt was withdrawn and the rattle of keys. Another porter opened the door and beckoned us in. We found ourselves in a cavernous room, tiled with white brick-shaped tiles, you know like the ones you find in public lavatories. He asked us our names and then checked them off against a list, which he held. Once he was satisfied that we were expected, he beckoned to Edward to take a seat and told us that someone would collect us presently. He then returned to a booth in the centre front of the hall, from where he continued to keep a strict eye on us.

We stood huddled together whispering until we heard a door open at the far end of the room. A woman appeared holding an oil lamp. There were some fairly ineffective lamps in the entrance hall. I think they were gas lamps, only they weren't very strong and the overall effect was gloomy. The lamp helped to cheer it a bit. The porter took us over to the lady, who was dressed in a dark blue ankle length dress. She wore a crisp white apron over the dress, which covered it from her neck to the hem of her dress. She had a cap on her head, like a nurse. The attendants weren't called nurses though they were called warders. Anyway, she smiled and asked us to follow her. We obliged and after nervously saying goodbye to Edward, we followed her across the rest of the hall. Our footsteps echoed around the room and it was the only sound we could hear. We left the hall through a large wooden door, which the warder opened with a key that was hanging from her belt. Once we were through she locked it again. Then she allowed the key to fall and join the others hanging from her belt. She chatted to us quite pleasantly on the way to the ward, but I hardly heard a word she said. I felt so numb, so dwarfed and so insignificant. Everything was so dour, there was no colour anywhere, but as I've already told you Emmie, the worst thing of all was the smell. It was a strong combination of carbolic scrubbing soap, stale food and uric acid. To my horror I found myself retching, but no one seemed to notice.

With our footsteps echoing, we crossed another hall until we reached some large solid oak double doors. The lady, whose name was Lily, selected another large key from those on her belt and opened one of these doors, again once we were through she turned and locked it. The asylum was just like a prison with its keys, bolts and locks.

Once we were through the doors we were at the head of the long corridor that ran the full length of the asylum. Edward had told us about the corridor, but it still took my breath away. Emmie, it seemed to go on for miles, I could hardly believe my eyes when I stood looking down it. My knees were knocking when we started walking. Martha had her arm through mine and was grimly hanging on to me. It took us what seemed like an age to get to the ward. It was lit by gas mainly, but there had been some electrification, nevertheless it was a gloomy, forbidding cavern and the oil lamp made it more eerie by casting long shadows, which seemed to dance all over the walls and laugh at us. It was awful. Our progress was slow and we seemed to be in the corridor for a long time.

I noticed that there were doors set into the wall at intervals. I asked Lily, the warder, what they were and she told me that they led to the wards. All of them were shut and locked. All I could think of was Florence. What on earth went through her mind when she walked down here for the first time? She must have thought she was in prison. She must have been terrified. Did they warn her? Did they tell her where she was going? I doubt it. Eventually Lily beckoned us to stop outside one of the doors. They were huge double doors, at least eight feet tall and five feet wide. I suppose they opened them to get furniture in and trolleys. I don't know, but they were, like everything else in the building, overwhelming. We had arrived at Florence's ward.

Lily unlocked the door and beckoned us in. We found

ourselves in a corridor. One wall of this corridor was made up of small square paned windows, which looked into a large dormitory. I glanced in as we passed. It had rows and rows of beds in it. They were wrought iron beds, black, each one covered with an identical green counterpane. There were three rows of about fifteen beds, one row stood against the wall on either side of the huge dormitory and one ran down the middle. Martha and I exchanged glances. We had never seen so many beds in one place. There was no privacy and there must have been at least fifty beds in there. We walked a little way and were ushered into an office. Lily put her lamp down on the table and told us to sit down. She then offered us a cup of tea and told us she would go to find the warder in charge. She told us that under no circumstances were we to leave the room. She left and locked the door after her leaving us alone and not a little frightened. We didn't speak we just held hands and stared at one another. Eventually Lily came back with the tea, accompanied by an elderly lady who introduced herself as Mrs Worthington. This was the woman Alf had told Edward about and she was obviously the head warder. She sat down with us and talked to us about Florence. She explained that she was completely dumb and in a semi-catatonic state. She didn't think that she would recognise us or react when she saw us. She told us that we mustn't be upset, but must talk quietly to her and explain who we were. She said no one knew just how much Florence had buried away in her mind and tried to forget. We did ask if there was any chance that Florence would be discharged in the near future. She said she didn't really know, but that she thought that now that they had located her family, who obviously cared for her, then it was more likely and it would be a good thing. She then went to fetch Florence.

I have to say Emmie, I would have given anything to have had a look on that ward, you know having come so far I was really curious, but they wouldn't allow it. We could hear things, muffled voices, the odd shriek and moan and the clanking of pans in the kitchen. It was now about 11.30 am and they were obviously cooking lunch, because there was a strong smell of cabbage. We waited patiently, whispering the odd comment to each other and trying to keep our spirits up. Eventually we heard a key grating in the lock, the door opened and they ushered Florence in. My heart lurched then went out to her. I have never seen such a change in anyone. Even when she came down to Devon and looked so ill and haunted, at least she seemed alive, but this Florence looked like the walking dead. Her skin was so pale, almost alabaster, from lack of sunshine I imagined. Her hair was pulled back into a severe plait and secured with what looked like cotton and she was so thin. She was wearing the asylum uniform blue dress with tie fastenings. It was loose fitting and hung on her like a sack, over it she had on a grey tabard pinafore, which was also too big for her and on her feet she had a pair of heavy shoes which seemed to be locked in place.

She looked just like a little broken bird. But it was her blank expression, Emmie, that tore at my heart. She looked at us, but saw nothing. She didn't give any sign of recognition at all, which was heartbreaking. We were seated on a hard, high backed wooden bench of some kind behind a table. Florence was placed in front the table on a wooden chair. It was a bit like an interview situation, which wasn't terribly helpful. I don't know about Martha, but I just wanted to fling my arms round her and sob, but Mrs. Worthington had said we mustn't do that under any circumstances, because we may startle or frighten her. Florence just sat looking at her hands which were clasped in her lap and never said a word. We did as Mrs. Worthington had told us and just talked to her quietly. We told her who we were, why we were there and what had happened. There was no reaction from her at all, absolutely none. It was heartrending. We felt she was rejecting us, holding us responsible, but Mrs. Worthington said that wasn't so, she had just blotted everything out in order that she could survive.

After a while, Martha stood and put her hand on Florence's shoulder and bent to look into her eyes, trying to establish some kind of eye contact. Initially she looked away, but Martha persisted. I don't think that Martha realised that there were tears running down her face, I am sure she was totally unaware of them. She just talked quietly and lovingly to Florence. I couldn't hear exactly what she was saying, but suddenly Florence turned her head and looked at Martha for a split second, just a moment and then looked away again. You know Emmie it was hardly anything at all. You couldn't call it recognition, but it was something and it made my heart soar. Martha looked back at me with a significant glance and then briefly stroked Florence's cheek before sitting down.

We continued to talk quietly to Florence until Mrs. Worthington came in to take her back to the ward, but there was no further reaction. She obediently stood up when asked and left the room with the warder to return to the ward. Mrs. Worthington came back and asked how it had gone. She shrugged her shoulders when Martha told her about the glance and said it was so hard to tell, but she was confident that Florence could be reached. She did say that we must be prepared for pain and anger if we were going to persevere with helping her. She would have to let out all the feelings that she had buried during her years in the asylum before she could start to heal. I look back to that woman now and realise how lucky we were that Florence was on her ward. She had an innate intelligence and years of experience. These were the years before the warders were trained in any area of psychology and Freud's teachings were only just being taken seriously. There were many warders who would not have understood Florence's condition at all.

When it was time to leave we were escorted back down the forbidding corridor, again it was Lily who guided us. We didn't speak. I think we were both trying to deal with our turbulent emotions in our own way. We passed through the double doors into the inner hall, which didn't look quite so oppressive now. It's amazing how you can accustom yourself to the strangest surroundings. Then before we knew it we were back in the enormous reception room where Edward was waiting. He leapt to his feet when he saw us and rushed over. I let Martha speak. She just gave him the bare outlines of what had taken place and said she would give him the details at home. She just couldn't talk about it straight away. We left the asylum to the sound of the harsh mechanism of the lock securing the door against intruders, the jangle of keys and the sound of the bolts sliding into place.

As soon as I stepped outside, I took a deep breath of clean, fresh, free air. I have never been so grateful to be out of anywhere in my life. I think I know now how prisoners feel on release from prison and I'd been in there less than an hour. We climbed back into the car and drove back up the drive to the fairytale gatehouse. The porter saw us arriving and stepped out to open the gates and then we were out on the road again. We felt liberated.

When we got back home I left Martha to talk quietly to Edward and explain exactly what had happened during our meeting with Florence. I went to my room. I was exhausted. I just lay there looking at the faint water marks and cracks on the ceiling until the light died. As the afternoon progressed, I slipped into the blessed relief of sleep, but I dreamed about the asylum and my dreams were far from peaceful.

Chapter Eighteen

'How long was it before you managed to get Florence discharged?' asked Emmie, who continued to sit quietly listening to Sarah's story. She was still finding it difficult to accept that she was listening to her grandmother's story. Florence was such a calm, sensible, balanced woman. How could she have survived all that and remained sane? Emmie asked Sarah how was it possible and she said, 'It was love that healed her, just love. Edward was deeply in love with Florence, her mother adored her and so did I. We simply loved her better, but, she added, it did take the expertise of a professional as well. Emmie, Edward worked night and day to get Florence released. He used all his tact, diplomacy, knowledge, contacts and energy and he was eventually rewarded. We received a letter some two weeks after our first visit to say that Florence's case was going to be re-examined in the light of recent developments. She was going to be reassessed by a doctor and they would let us know their findings in due course. If they felt that she was well enough, then she would eventually be discharged into our care. However, she would be under the supervision of our GP, Dr. Kyle. He would monitor her progress and would be required to report back to the hospital on a regular basis until they felt Florence was completely well. Dr. Kyle had been the family doctor for years so we were quite confident that he would have Florence's best interests at heart.

As to the assessment of Florence's mental health, well, we felt cautiously optimistic. We were fairly sure that they would refer to Jane Worthington, you know the warder of Florence's ward? We felt fairly confident that she would recommend Florence's discharge into our care. However, it still depended on what the doctors thought. We were fortunate that Dr. Pickard was no longer involved in the hospital. Without any clear explanation he had resigned his position, sold his practice and retired at the end of the war.

The decision to discharge Florence took a considerable time coming through. However, the authorities continued to allow us to visit Florence once a week while they assessed her case. Each visit was very like the first one. We went through the same process each time. Florence didn't seem to improve. She did make some small advancements, for instance she would occasionally make eye contact. Otherwise she just sat and listened silently, while we talked to her. However, there was one small incident of interest; we got to know Jane Worthington quite well during this time. One day, against all the rules, she took us on a tour of the ward. I'm so glad she did Emmie, it gave me a greater insight into what Florence had to put up with and it made it easier for me to empathise with her when she came home.

It was a huge ward, very grey and functional. But it was clean and warm. It held over a hundred women and some of them were very ill. Some were sitting on chairs talking furiously to themselves. Lots of them just paced up and down or followed a favourite warder around. Many of the patients were sitting on the floor in corners just rocking back and forth and moaning. All of them wore the uniform of the asylum, the shapeless blue dress and pinafore and the heavy, locked on shoes. Most of the women had their hair scraped back, plaited and tied. One or two patients had only tufts of hair and their heads were covered with scabs. Jane explained that no matter what the warders did, they kept trying to pull it out. There was no privacy on the ward. There seemed to be people everywhere and the noise level was quite high. There were no quiet places to escape to. Jane told us to be careful with certain patients; they looked mild enough, but could change suddenly and become violent. There were one or two scuffles between patients and warders whilst we were touring the ward. It was certainly an eye opener. I don't think I could have spent any time on that ward as a patient and retained my sanity. I have no idea how the staff did their job. They worked long hours for low wages and seemed totally committed to me. One thing that struck me quite forcibly, Emmie, was that whilst the women were cared for and fed, they had all lost their identity as women. There was no sense of individuality or, and I know this sounds silly, but their sexuality was erased. They couldn't express their individual preferences, do their hair, and make themselves pretty. You know the things all women do. Even Florence looked plain in the hospital clothes. I'm not criticising the warders or even the system. They did their best in very difficult circumstances, but it just struck me as very sad that because they were mentally ill they had to be stripped of all vestiges of their femininity. Anyway they were my thoughts at the time.

Seeing the ward, the place where Florence had lived for over two years helped me understand what Florence had had to endure. I think it also helped Martha, you know, later, to understand Florence. After knowing what Josiah did to Florence and seeing the ward, I began to understand why she had almost disappeared into herself and ceased to communicate with the world. It was the only way she could survive in that place. It was the only way you could achieve any peace or privacy. I'm just glad that we found her when we did or I think she would have disappeared so far into herself that we may never have reached her at all. But thankfully we did. Eventually Edward received notification of Florence's imminent discharge. They informed us that we could collect her on the 20th December 1919, just in time for Christmas. We were ecstatic at the thought of having her home. We continued to visit her every week until the date of her discharge. During our final visit Jane Worthington came into the little 'interview room', as we'd come to call it, to give us our final instructions. She asked us to bring in some suitable clothing for Florence to wear to go home in as she was required to leave her uniform at the asylum. We stifled a smile as we couldn't imagine anyone wanting to go home in such awful garments. But Jane was quite serious; she told us that she had to account for all of the patient's clothing. Apparently, in the past, some patients tried to take them home.

Jane still had a bundle of the clothing that Florence was wearing on admission, which still officially belonged to her, but we told her to give it to charity. We all felt that Florence wouldn't want to see anything that reminded her of that awful time. Jane then gave us the hospital's standard list of basic clothes to bring in for the patient when they were discharged into the community. It included items such as underwear, stockings, boots, a warm dress, a coat or shawl and a hat. We took the list and thanked her for all she had done for Florence during her stay on the ward. She was an intrinsically good woman and I liked her. Then she brought Florence in to see us and we explained to her that we were taking her home when we next came to visit. I have no idea whether or not she understood what we were saying. If she did, she gave no sign. It was so strange when we left knowing that next time we visited, we would be taking Florence home for good. The challenge that taking her home presented was daunting, but we were very optimistic. I don't think we had any idea how much time and patience her recovery was going to take.

On the morning of 20th December we arrived at the hospital with a suitcase containing Florence's new clothes. As usual Edward waited in the entrance hall, but this time with the knowledge that his patience would soon be rewarded. He was going to see Florence at last. He had been so tolerant over the weeks, bringing us to see her and waiting quietly until we came out. Lily came to escort us holding her oil lamp and, as usual, she guided us to the ward. We had got to know her quite well during our visits and she was a pleasant, well meaning girl, who was obviously fond of Florence. I found it strange, the way that the asylum ceased to intimidate me on that last visit. It had ceased to be unpleasant and had become quite familiar to me. It had lost its power to frighten me. I am not suggesting it had become a pleasant place, it was still an institution, but it wasn't as terrifying somehow.

We walked down the long corridor to Ward Four for the last time in complete silence. Lily unlocked the ward door, ushered us in and guided us to the little room where we normally saw Florence. We handed her the suitcase with Florence's clothes in and sat down to wait. After a while Jane Worthington appeared, accompanied by a new Florence, who was dressed in the black coat and fur hat that we had brought for her. I nearly cried when I saw her dressed in normal clothes again. We had only seen her in that dreadful blue dress and grey pinafore. She looked very frail, and her expression was still completely blank, but she looked so beautiful and so like our Florence again that it was hard not to embrace her. We said goodbye to the warders and thanked them. Martha gave them a small gift each, a little gold cross on a chain, to thank them for taking care of Florence and then we left. As this was our last visit, Jane herself was escorting us off the premises. She wasn't sure how Florence would react to leaving the ward without a warder. She may have become anxious and she wanted to be there to reassure her. As it was she threw Jane a frightened glance as we stepped out into the long corridor, but once we left the ward she just walked docilely between us, seemingly unconcerned about where she was going. It was only when we reached the entrance hall that she looked a little perturbed, but she quickly calmed down. Edward was waiting in his customary chair, when we walked into the main reception hall. As soon as he saw us he stood up and rushed over, his eyes glistening with joy at actually seeing Florence at last.

However, he was very controlled when he greeted her. He moved slowly and spoke to her gently. She just looked at him as blankly as ever. Fleetingly he looked a little hurt, but he simply turned to Jane, shook her hand and thanked her for all that she had done. I think she was quite upset at losing Florence. We wrote to her till her death, you know, and when Florence had quite recovered she wrote to Jane and asked if she could visit her at home, with Edward. She wanted to see her because she remembered her kindness whilst she was in the hospital. Jane was delighted to see her looking so healthy and happy. Florence managed the visit very well. She didn't seem to regress into the past as we thought that she may have done. Anyway, I digress.

Eventually when all the niceties had been completed, we stepped into the fresh, frosty, morning and guided Florence to the car. Apart from briefly glancing at the clear blue sky, she didn't react; she just did as we told her to and climbed into the back of the car. As we approached the gates the porter rushed out as usual and unlocked them. As I heard them clank shut behind us I felt as though chains had fallen from my heart and

I thanked God. Until that moment I don't think that I really thought we would ever get Florence out of that dreadful place alive.

We had put a lot of thought into Florence's convalescence and we didn't really feel that it was sensible to take her back to a house where she would be reminded of Josiah's cruelty and those years of unhappiness. We wanted her to feel at home in familiar surroundings though, so we decided that she should be taken to Chestnut Lodge. She had spent many years there as a child and it was next door to her own home, but had no unhappy memories. My parents were going on a lengthy European trip and thought it was a good idea. I think Mother was pleased that there would be someone to look after the house and Edward whilst she was away!

Mother had prepared a room for Martha at Chestnut Lodge and I returned to my own childhood room. We more or less closed up Martha's house. I don't think she ever returned there again to live. I don't think she could face it. Sadly both my parents died a year later, whilst they were still abroad and Martha, Edward and Florence settled in Chestnut Lodge as a family.

Before we collected Florence from the asylum we prepared the little sitting room off the kitchen for her. We put a bed in there and an upholstered rocking chair and sofa and had it redecorated in pink with floral chintz curtains and matching chair covers. It was a lovely room, always full of sunshine and it had French windows that opened up onto the garden. We felt that in the spring Florence could walk in the garden and sit in the sunshine. Another reason why we chose the sitting room is that it had an adjoining door to the kitchen, which was always full of people. Florence wouldn't have spent one minute alone for two and a half years so we felt that she would be reassured by the nearness of people, whilst she still had her own privacy.

It took a long, long time for Florence to recover. I think at times we almost gave up completely. Hettie had left Martha's employ after Florence was taken away to the asylum and we never saw her again. I often wondered what became of her. Anyway we trained one of mother's maids to look after Florence. She needed to be reminded to dress and bathe and even to eat. Otherwise she would just have stayed in bed all day. Molly, the maid, was very good, she wasn't just a maid, she was more a carer for Florence. Once Molly had got Florence up and dressed, she would just sit in her rocking chair, rocking back and forth gazing into the fire. She remained just as Alf had described her that first evening when he saw her on the ward. We would all take it in turns to sit with her reading or sewing. She did start to make a little eye contact, but not much and her eyes remained dead.

After six months there was little improvement and Edward started to despair a little. She still hadn't recognised any of us, or spoken. Then we had a break through. Edward went to a regimental dinner, a reunion with the comrades he had fought alongside on the Western Front. There he met one of his old fellow officers, a close friend who had suffered badly with shell shock during and after the war. His name was Harold Williams and he was now much recovered. He felt that it was because he had been referred to a doctor in London. He was a psychiatrist, a disciple of the famous Dr. Rivers of Craiglockhart, the one who did so much for shell shocked officers during the war. Harold recommended the doctor to Edward and gave him his name and London address. Edward told us about it on his return. He wanted our advice as he was considering asking him to see Florence. He felt that there was a parallel between her experiences and those of his officer friend. Not gunfire and trench warfare, obviously, but they had both been severely traumatised. Anyway Martha and I thought it was an excellent idea. We had begun to realise that we needed expert help that our love and care alone weren't enough to break through to Florence's subconscious.

Edward contacted the doctor, whose name was Felix Cripps, and he agreed to come and see Florence at the house. We all felt that she wasn't well enough to undertake the journey to London. He was a charming man, very young and very enthusiastic. He spent some time talking to us and asking questions about Florence's background and the reasons why she had been put into the asylum. He dwelt quite a long time on her childhood and asked Martha a number of in depth questions about the kind of child that she had been. He was particularly interested in her relationship with her father. He questioned us closely about Josiah. He even asked Martha if Josiah, himself, had abused Florence. She was very shocked, but she was fairly sure that he hadn't actually physically abused Florence. She felt that the abuse was more subtle than that. She told Dr. Cripps that she thought that Josiah withheld his love from Florence deliberately. Because she was such a beautiful and charming child she troubled Josiah's emotions and it was precisely because of this that he was so cold towards her. He avoided anything that affected him emotionally. Dr. Cripps was very interested in Josiah's attitude to Florence as a child.

You must understand Emmie that Martha, Edward and I had only vaguely heard of Freud and his theories of the subconscious. Martha's observations were based on common sense and what she had witnessed with her own eyes. She had no knowledge of psychiatry. Dr. Cripps told us that he thought that Josiah had spent most of his life subduing his natural sexual desires and impulses. He thought it probable that at some point in his childhood he had been taught that such desires were dirty and sinful. This, he told us, was quite common during the Victorian era. He said that he felt Josiah had spent his entire life avoiding any woman who affected his senses or who aroused him sexually. He apologised to Martha at this point, but she was very open and honest with him and told him bluntly that she had always thought that Josiah had married her precisely because she was plain. He politely contradicted her on this point, but said that it was not because she was plain, but because she was not overtly sexual. She didn't arouse Josiah sexually. However, the one person that he had no control over, the one person he couldn't choose was his daughter and she had been born beautiful to his horror. Dr. Cripps felt that subconsciously Josiah must have desired her physically. However he was too honourable a man to do anything about it. When Pickard raped her Dr. Cripps thought that Josiah recognised that it could have been him. That was his great fear that he would lose control and his feelings for Florence would overwhelm him. He couldn't see that they were just the normal feelings of a man for his only daughter.

Anyway, he began to see Florence as some kind of evil temptress and he decided that she had to be put beyond his reach; hence he had her committed to the asylum. He did this with no conscience as he blamed Florence. He saw her as a wicked seducer of men, not an innocent young girl who had been attacked and raped. He told us that Josiah had spent his whole miserable life as a man in denial. He also commented that he was probably relieved when he found out that Martha shouldn't have any more children. It meant that he could avoid having sexual relations completely. He felt that it was very sad that his thinking had been so distorted. We found all this very difficult to absorb, but we had complete faith in him. He was the only doctor who seemed to understand Josiah's motives at all. I will never know if his theories were correct, but they made some sense to us and he certainly helped Florence.

He went in to see Florence alone. When he came out he sat and talked to us again for some time. He was sure that he could help her, but there were one or two problems. He didn't think that she should be taken from her home again and put into a clinic and he was based in London. He felt that although she wasn't showing any sign of it to us, she felt safe and secure at Chestnut Lodge. If we tried to move her she would think that the whole nightmare was beginning again and that would be counter-productive. He said he would be prepared to come and see Florence, but it would be expensive for us. We didn't care; we would have spent our last penny getting her cured. Eventually we came to an arrangement where he would come up once a week and stay overnight with us whilst he was treating her. As we got to know him better, he told us a little about his work with traumatised patients from the trenches. He explained to us that when a situation is too horrific for a person's nervous system to accept it rebels. This rebellion, as he called it simplistically, for our sakes, could take many forms. Sometimes the body just shut down and refused to accept the situation. This could result in what they called hysterical symptoms, deafness, blindness, paralysis and significantly to us, loss of speech. They were protective measures that prevented the patient having to accept what was too much for them to cope with. He felt that was what had happened in Florence's case that she had simply closed her mind to a reality that she couldn't cope with and didn't want to talk about.

He came to see Florence every week for over six months. We never really knew what went on during the time he was with her. He just spent time talking to her. Then he asked our permission to hypnotise her. We, or rather Martha, gave her permission. The next time he came up he brought his nurse with him to assist. He made Florence re-visit the painful time of her committal to the asylum. Under hypnosis she screamed and cried and spoke out. He hypnotised her a few times and then continued to talk to her. We just watched, waited and prayed, but it was hard and at times we thought that she would never recover.

Some time towards late summer Edward was reading to Florence when he looked up. To his surprise, he saw that she was crying, silent tears were just pouring down her face. He put his book down and quietly moved over and put his arms around her. To his surprise she reacted and buried her head in his shoulder. She sobbed and sobbed and he just held her tightly. It seemed as though the flood gates had opened at last and the damn of misery had started to break down. It was only the beginning, but Dr. Cripps, when he was told, felt that we had finally reached Florence and we could now help her to talk and heal herself.'

Emmie began to realise that it was incredibly late, Sarah had been talking for so long that darkness had fallen and Emmie had simply switched on a small table lamp to give them some light. She just wanted Sarah to talk, to finish Florence's story. She needed to have Florence back in the real world, away from the asylum. She needed to know that she was safe before she allowed Sarah to stop talking. Now that she seemed to be secure, Emmie felt that it was safe to interrupt Sarah at last.

'Did she talk much about what had happened to her? Did you ever find out what she was really thinking?''

'Little by little her story started to unravel, we didn't press her, but she would suddenly start to tell a little anecdote about a badly behaved patient or a funny incident in the dormitory. It was a long time before she spoke about the death of her baby and even longer before she mentioned Josiah and Dr. Pickard, but we were patient and waited. We never pressed her for any information. Dr. Cripps continued to see her, but he left a longer gap between his visits and only came once a month until he felt that Florence could cope without his support. We were so very grateful to him. You can't imagine. It was a strange time. Because of the war there were hundreds of thousands of damaged men and women walking around destroyed psychologically. Yet some good came of it. It helped the medical profession to take psychiatric medicine seriously for the first time ever.

Anyway Emmie, it was time for me to leave Chestnut Lodge and return home. I had been with Martha for a year then and Charles had been wonderfully patient, but I couldn't leave him forever. And anyway I was missing him. He travelled up to Liverpool nearly every weekend during that year because I think, like me, he felt partly responsible for what had happened to Florence. By alerting Josiah, we both put Florence at risk, unbeknown to ourselves. But it wasn't the same as living together and I felt that it was time for me to return home. I knew that Florence was in safe hands and Martha no longer needed my support.

Edward wrote to me often once I returned to our little house in Chelsea and he kept me informed of Florence's progress.' Sarah suddenly stopped talking and stretched and yawned, ' Emmie my dear, I must go to bed. I think dawn is breaking and I'm far too old to be up so late. I was so engrossed in the past that I hadn't realised that I had been talking for so long.'

'Oh Sarah, I'm sorry to have kept you up so late, but I needed to know what happened to Gran. I couldn't let you stop until I knew that she was safe.'

Sarah smiled at Emmie and squeezed her hand that was lying on the table between them.

'You love her very much my dear don't you?'

Emmie nodded, holding back the tears. It had been an emotional evening for her.

'She's very lucky to have you and I'm sure you've brought her great joy. I don't mind staying up, but unfortunately this old body of mine does. I must go to bed.'

Impulsively Emmie said, 'Sarah, will you come

back with me tomorrow? Help me tell Father. I don't know if I can.'

'I don't think that's possible my dear, not just yet. Reliving the past like this has quite exhausted me and I need time to recover. But I will give you Edward's letters to read on your journey home. They will tell you the final part of the story and I would like you to have them. I won't live much longer now, and I would like to think that they were in safe hands. When I have a little time alone to recover I will come up to Liverpool. I want to see Florence when she returns. I would love to see her again, amongst her family, at peace, with the past laid to rest.'

'Well that would be lovely. I feel guilty that I have worn you out by asking you to re-live the past for my benefit, but I am very grateful.'

'It has been wonderful having you here to stay Emmie and I'm glad I could tell you firsthand about what happened to your grandmother, but I am eighty two years old and I normally lead a quiet life. You have quite worn me out! Nevertheless, I've enjoyed telling you what happened. When I've rested I'll ring you and we will arrange for me to visit you in Liverpool.'

'That would be lovely. Thank you for all you've told me. I know the effort it cost and I am so grateful. I would love to take you back now, but I quite understand that you need time to yourself. You have been kindness itself to me.' With that Emmie stood and the two women embraced. Emmie then kissed Sarah on the cheek before going up to bed, quite exhausted.

Chapter Nineteen

On the train home Emmie sat by the window watching the changing countryside flash by. The weather still hadn't broken and the leaves on the trees were a wonderful patchwork of gold and bronze that gleamed and glinted richly in the mellow sunlight. The newly harvested fields wore their golden stubble self consciously, like a newly shaven youth. Everything in sight seemed to be bathed in the late autumn sunlight and only the red of the combine harvesters added a dash of colour as they ploughed through the sea of shimmering gold. They silently cut a swathe through the remaining unharvested fields like invading troops as they rolled on and on, taking what they needed and laying waste anything that was of no use to them. The whole landscape was as vivid, brightly coloured and disquieting as a Van Gogh painting.

What a glorious exciting autumn it had been though. Emmie couldn't believe that it was only two days since she left Chestnut Lodge and started on her journey of exploration. She had never expected to uncover such a terrible story, but it had given her a much deeper understanding and appreciation of her wonderful grandmother. As she looked through the window at the lovely autumn scene that was flashing by she felt pensive. How had she missed getting to know Sarah? Had Gran kept them apart to protect her well guarded secret, or had it just been a matter of fate? She didn't really know, but she was grateful to have come to know her, even at this late stage. She was such a wonderful, intelligent woman. Emmie felt that she was lucky that she had learned about her grandmother's history from Sarah. She had revealed it with tact and sensitivity and had made it acceptable for Emmie.

Before she left for the station at lunch time, Sarah had given her an old leather writing case which contained Edward's letters. She had given them all to Emmie, even the ones that were sent from the Western Front during the First World War. Sarah felt that as she and Charles had no children they should go to Emmie as she was his granddaughter. When the journey was underway, Emmie pulled the writing case out of her bag, extracted the letters and put them on the table in front of her. Before she started reading them she looked out at the autumn landscape and thought how strange it was that she had suddenly become so enmeshed in the world of her grandparents. She looked again at the letters. They were organised in date order and the earlier ones had been sent from the Front. Some were still smeared with mud and candle grease. They conjured up images of her grandfather crouching over a make do table in a dug out, scribbling to his sister whilst shells were bursting all around him. He had opened up his heart to her in his letters. Yet Emmie was amazed at how casually he spoke about the extreme conditions that he had to endure. He would talk about the appalling injuries inflicted on friends, the unsanitary conditions in the trenches and the death of comrades with such a calm, detached tone that he could have been describing every day events. But the unacceptable was normality to them and she supposed they had to be matter of fact about it to survive at all. They were quite exceptional men.

Regardless of her grandfather's casual style, Emmie

could detect the controlled pain that seemed to lie just beneath the surface. It seemed to escape from the pages and engulf her, in spite of his heroic efforts to stifle it. This was particularly noticeable after the Battle of the Somme in July 1916. He had lost both of his closest friends. One died on the battlefield and his body was never recovered, the other died of wounds at a casualty clearing station. At this stage he had lost most of his close comrades from the beginning of the war. It was clear that he was appalled at the sacrifice his generation was making. Yet what choice did they have? They had no option but to follow where the politicians and generals led them. Emmie read the letters carefully and was touched. They helped her to understand the young man who she had only known in later years as an old man and grandfather. She put them to one side to study later. The letters that now interested her were the ones written after Florence's supposed death.

It was a year later, 1917, that Edward was informed of the 'death' of Florence. It was not long after that he returned to England with a 'blighty' and nerves shattered beyond repair. It occurred to Emmie that it was probably because of his painful war experiences that her grandfather was able to empathise so easily with Florence's suffering and ease her back to normality. It was a path he himself had already trodden and he was familiar with every step of the way. From what Sarah had told her he seemed to have had terrific patience with Florence and he was so kind. Perhaps, because of his experiences in France, he had learned to value love and life above all else.

The letters written to Sarah just after he had been told that Florence was dead were harrowing. He didn't seem to be able to accept that someone who was supposed to be safe in England, away from the war, had died, especially someone so young and beautiful. He sounded as though he was reaching the limit of his endurance. They were tragic, heart rending letters. His attempts at courage were so transparently forced that it must have been very difficult for Sarah to read them, knowing that she was helpless to do anything to help him, even years later Emmie found them difficult to read.

The later letters, the ones about Florence's recovery, were far more optimistic and hopeful. Edward wrote regularly to Sarah and kept her well informed about Florence's progress. Emmie continued to be impressed with her grandfather's tremendous patience and she remembered how protective he was of her grandmother in later life. There were times, as she got older, when Florence seemed overwhelmed by life and retreated into her shell of silence, like a little hermit crab. Edward understood and accepted these withdrawals, but it was her father, Freddie, who seemed to suffer most from what he considered to be his mother's rejection at these times. However, Emmie realised now that her grandmother's withdrawal from the world was a legacy from those terrible years in the asylum. Every now and then she needed to retreat and draw on an unseen store of energy before she could emerge again to carry on in the real world.

There was one letter in particular that caught her attention, it was dated January 1922, over twelve months after her grandmother had been discharged from the asylum and almost six years after she had been raped. In all that time she had not spoken to anyone about the terrible events of that afternoon. Dr. Cripps and

Edward had apparently spoken to each other about the significance of that event. They both felt that it was necessary for Florence to talk about what had happened. Even under hypnosis, Dr. Cripps had not been able to reach the depths of her subconscious where she had buried that traumatic memory. He felt that it was crucial to her recovery that she talked about it. He believed that she could not fully recover until she faced up to what had happened and gave voice to all her anger and outrage. As he pointed out to Emmie's grandfather, she had not even spoken about it to Sarah. Florence had written down the details of what happened in the Sunday School that afternoon, but had never actually spoken about what had happened to her except to Josiah and he had not believed her. Dr. Cripps felt that fundamentally that inability to make herself be believed may have planted the seeds of Florence's subsequent refusal to talk. On the one occasion that she did talk about something that was so painful to her, she was not believed. By preventing her from talking about her ordeal, her subconscious was protecting her. If she remained silent on the subject, no one could reject her truth again.

'Even to this day,' thought Emmie, she can't talk about it. She can't tell her nearest and dearest, who love her dearly, her story.' Her grandmother had felt it necessary to lay a paper trail for Emmie to follow in order to discover the truth and then it would be Emmie's voice that she would use to tell her children. What a strange and complex thing the human mind was, so complex that her grandmother, who loved her and knew that she was loved in return, could not overcome the obstacle put there all those years ago by her subconscious and talk about her experiences.

In spite of the fact that Dr. Cripps felt strongly that Florence should talk about what happened to her in Pickard's office, he felt equally as strongly that she must not be coerced or forced into talking about the horror of that afternoon. It had to come from her voluntarily. She had to feel secure enough to know that when she did talk about it, there would be no doubt that she would be believed and there was no possibility that she would be punished again. Sarah had told Emmie that Florence had slowly started to communicate in the months after she left the asylum. First she started to smile, then she tried a few faltering words, then graduated to fairly normal conversations. However, Dr. Cripps felt that they would not make a major breakthrough until she felt she could talk about her ordeal at the hands of Dr. Pickard. With a feeling of triumph Emmie found the letter that informed Sarah that Florence had finally felt sufficiently secure to talk to Edward about what had happened.

22nd January 1923

My Dear Sarah,

I have so much to tell you. We have had quite a difficult time during the last few days. It started really on Saturday evening. I was sitting with Florence in her little sitting room and she asked me to read to her. It was a cold, dark, winter's evening and I was thinking how lucky we were to be safe and warm in front of a roaring fire. You know I have never really got over the horror of standing in a freezing trench. I seemed to spend the whole war standing up to my knees in icy water. I don't think I will ever recover from my dread of being cold!

Anyway, Florence was lying on her little sofa listening whilst I was reading and she fell asleep. I realised that she was no longer paying attention and I stopped and just watched her. She looked so peaceful Sarah, so innocent, like she did before the war. It was difficult to believe that she had endured so much since then. However, she started to become restless and she began to mutter under her breath. I could only catch parts of what she said, odd phrases such as: 'No, please no father. I won't. He'll make me.'

They were just odd disconnected phrases at first so they didn't worry me. It wasn't unusual for Florence to have nightmares, although they were becoming less and less frequent as time passed. But I knew instinctively that this not one of her normal nightmares. I watched her carefully and she began to become more and more agitated. She seemed to be very distressed so I tried to wake her gently, but I couldn't rouse her at all. She just muttered and started to toss and turn. She was very pale and she was perspiring so I put a cool, damp cloth on her forehead and held her hand and talked to her as soothingly as I could. I kept trying to rouse her, but she seemed to be in a trance. Then I heard his name 'Pickard'. I tell you Sarah my blood ran cold! She was reliving the rape, I was sure of it. I didn't know what to do and Martha was out visiting friends. I knelt down by the sofa and held Florence's hand. She was having a terrible struggle somewhere. I felt so helpless. It seemed to go on for ages. I kept trying to wake her, but there was no response. Suddenly she screamed loudly and it seemed to rouse her. She looked at me wildly, she didn't know who I was at first and then she recognised me and flung her arms about me. For a moment I think she thought she was back outside the Sunday School. She kept saying, 'You waited, you waited.'

She was disorientated for a moment then realised where

she was. She looked at me and then said, 'I was having the most terrible nightmare, I was reliving the afternoon when Dr. Pickard raped me.'

She said it Sarah; she said it! She had never referred to it before. I just held her and asked her if she wanted to talk about it and she nodded. Her story was pitiful, I could barely listen. She was fifteen years old and didn't even know what was happening to her. Well, I don't need to tell you, you know how inexperienced and ill informed she was. She told me that she was angry with me because I just handed her over to him and walked away. She said she knew that it was illogical, but she felt that I should have protected her. I told her that I had felt guilty ever since. I knew that I could have prevented it. But we were young and obedient. Oh how obedient we were! Thousands walked under orders into a hail of murderous bullets and I handed over the girl I loved to a rapist. I handed her over simply because I was afraid she would get into trouble with her father.

She seemed touched that I felt guilty. We talked about her father, his attitude to her, everything. The most awful thing was that she thought that I no longer wanted her because she wasn't a virgin. She thought I blamed her. That was because Josiah had cruelly told her that no one would want her. I just asked her to marry me there and then. Of course I told her it would only be when she was ready and only if she loved me enough. She accepted me, but she couldn't believe that I still wanted her. Sarah, what had that monster of a father done?

Anyway my dear Martha was thrilled and I'm sure you will be happy for us when I tell you that we are engaged to be married. Once we cleared the air and talked about what had happened all the boundaries that separated us disappeared and anything became possible. We will probably marry next year, but there is no rush, it is up to Florence to decide. I am

so happy I could die and I am pleased to say Florence is too.
I think I am the luckiest man in the world. I hope, dear sister
that you and Charles will visit us soon to celebrate.

Your most affectionate brother,
Edward.

Intrigued Emmie read some more of the letters, but they took a disturbing turn as she read on:

1st February 1923

My Dear Sarah

I am afraid. Florence, who is gaining in strength every day, has asked me about Pickard, whether anything had been done about the fact that he raped her. I told her that since Martha discovered the letters of commitment and we found out Florence was in the asylum we used all our strength to get her home and make her well. We really hadn't given him any thought at all.

However, Sarah, I know he is still alive, I know that for a fact. He no longer practices, he retired at the end of the war; he'll be in his mid sixties now and lives alone out at Hever Manor. His wife died just before he retired. Florence wanted to know all about him. I told her what little I knew; she listened quietly and then wandered off into the garden. I was very concerned.

I thought that was an end of the matter, but she brought the subject up a few days later. She has decided that she wants to meet him face to face. I am horrified and have done everything I can to dissuade her, but she is adamant. I rang Felix Cripps to ask his advice. He said to make sure that she does nothing until he has seen her. He said if he feels that Florence is strong enough mentally it may do her good to confront him. However, I am afraid that she isn't and that it could send her over the edge again back into that silent world where we couldn't reach her.

I asked her if she wanted to press charges, go to the police, let them deal with him, but she said no, that wasn't her aim. She had been terribly young and at his mercy when he raped her. Later, when she discovered she was pregnant she felt that she was totally at the mercy of him again. But this time it was worse because he had the support of her father and between them they had the power to banish her from the world. She wants to see him now as she is, a woman with a family who will protect her. She wants to take revenge as it were, for the vulnerable little girl that he hurt and to see him to conquer her fear. She wants to confront him from a position of strength and know that he can never hurt her again.

I can understand that it is helpful to face your fears and overcome them, but she was so very ill and I love her so much that I am afraid that it will plunge her into despair. Let me know what you think Sarah, please. You are very level headed and probably understand Florence's motives better than I do.

Your affectionate brother,
Edward.

Emmie was stunned. She hadn't really thought about Pickard at all. She had assumed, because Josiah was dead that he was too. However Josiah had been relatively young when he had his heart attack, so it was feasible that Pickard would still be alive. It was so like her grandmother to confront her demons and destroy them, thought Emmie, although this was a fairly gigantic demon. Emmie thought about what she would do. She thought that she too would want to see him. She would want to prove to him that he hadn't won that he hadn't ruined her life and silenced her forever, as he intended to. She looked for the next letter, which contained another development.

3rd March 1923

My Dear Sarah

Well what can I say? Felix decided that Florence was strong enough to face up to her past and he felt that she could deal with confronting Pickard. He was of the opinion that for someone like Florence it would be a positive therapy. I still had my doubts and if it had been up to me I would have dissuaded her. Anyway it wasn't up to me so we planned our attack. Sarah, you would hardly recognise the Florence we collected from the asylum in my Florence today. She is like she used to be, lively and funny and a joy to be with. She had a very spirited and confident approach to meeting Pickard. She wanted to simply turn up at the Manor and confront him. If he wasn't there, she said we would simply go again.

We drove out last Sunday, just the two of us. Felix was staying at the house as backup in case it was too much for Florence and she regressed. I was a nervous wreck, Sarah, although I had to hide it. I would rather have faced the trenches again. Anyway, we drove out to Hever Manor, which as you know is out towards the coast near Formby. Florence was quiet during the journey and I left her to her thoughts. Eventually we arrived and turned into a much neglected driveway. The gates were rusted and hanging off their hinges and the roadway was pitted and choked with weeds. It was a mess. The house looked no better when we pulled up outside. It was in need of decorating and it looked dirty and neglected.

We climbed out of the car and I accompanied Florence to the door. She rang the bell which we heard echoing somewhere inside the house. Eventually the door opened and there he stood, Pickard. He looked old and seedy. He never was a prepossessing character, but standing there in his threadbare cardigan and stained trousers he looked like something quite degenerate. He disgusted me and I had to control a strong urge to hit him.

Oh, but Sarah his face, it was something to behold! He couldn't believe his eyes. So many emotions were mirrored there, disbelief, horror, terror, it is hard to list them all. I think he thought that Florence was a ghost. He eventually managed to choke out some words:

'It can't be you, you're...'

'Buried alive Dr. Pickard so that I could never bother you again and your obscene secret would die with you? Is that what you were going to say? Well it is me, my family did not desert me and they found out the truth and had me discharged. I am not the raving lunatic you intended I should become. I am not locked away from the world. I am fit, free, strong and sane.

I swear he started to lift his hand to hit her, but thought better of it with me standing by her. He just snarled at us to get off his property, to go. At no time did he express any regret or remorse for what he'd done, but he was terrified. I could see that. Absolutely terrified at what she might do or say.

Florence just looked him in the eye and said, 'I didn't know how I would feel when I saw you, but do you know something, I pity you. I am no longer afraid of you.'

With that she turned on her heel and made for the car, with me rushing behind her, really rather surplus to requirements. She was magnificent. She didn't speak when she got in the car. I think it was harder for her than I had imagined, she was very pale and I noticed that she was shaking, but she had won. I glanced in the mirror as we drove away and he was still standing there watching us go. I don't think he could quite believe what had happened. We had not told anyone, other than the immediate family, about Florence's discharge from the asylum. It was not public knowledge, so he would never have expected to see Florence again. He certainly would never have voluntarily told us where she was. He would have left her there to rot and taken his secret to the grave. Nevertheless, I like to think that his conscience had troubled him over the years. He was reduced to a wreck of man when we saw him.

About a week later I read in the local newspaper that Pickard had been found dead at Hever Manor. It appeared that he had been drinking heavily and had tripped and fallen down the stairs. His neck was broken. I like to think that his demons chased him along the landing and pushed him, or that he was so afraid that Florence would go to the police and denounce him that he threw himself down those stairs. We will never know the truth, but I'm glad that he's dead and can never hurt Florence again. I read the article out loud to her over breakfast, but she didn't make any comment. He had ceased to matter to her even before he died.

We talked about the visit on our return home to Dr. Cripps, but we have never referred to him since, except very briefly when we saw the announcement of his death in the newspaper. She did talk to Felix in depth about the visit and I think he analysed her feelings. He told me that he was satisfied that she had buried her ghosts, as it were. He felt that the visit had been a useful exercise.

Florence will never completely recover from her ordeal, much as I will never fully recover from my years on the Western Front. There are times when life seems to overwhelm her and she retreats into her shell and needs to be alone, but those periods don't last long and I feel that we can limp along together quite successfully from now on.

What a time we've had my dear, but perhaps now we can look forward to our wedding and our future together. I hope you and Charles are well and preparing to come up to see us soon. We will need all the support that you can give us for the wedding. That translated means that I am extremely nervous and need the support of my big sister!! So come and see us soon. Florence asked me to say she wants to come to London to buy her dress. Will you help her and can she stay with you? I am sure you will be delighted at the thought of a shopping trip. Take great care of yourself my dear.

Your affectionate brother,

Edward

After she had read her grandfather's letters, Emmie carefully folded them up and returned them to the leather case that Sarah had given her. She spent the rest of the journey just thinking over all that she had learned about her family, especially her grandparents, over the last few days. She had come to the conclusion that life was simply a lottery. Fate dictated what was going to happen to you and all you could do was play the hand that she dealt. Take her grandmother's case. She would have stayed locked away in that asylum for ever if Martha hadn't put her hand into that pigeon hole to retrieve those invoices and hit the mechanism that released the secret drawer. She could have pulled the papers out, she may not have pushed her hand in far enough or hard enough or the mechanism may have jammed. There were so many things that could have happened differently and Florence would have rotted in the asylum until she was an old woman. Martha would probably have died of a broken heart, Elizabeth and Freddie would never have been born and she herself would never have existed. All their fates had rested on the mechanism of a secret desk drawer. It was terrifying really.

Chapter Twenty

Emmie was emotionally drained after her visit to Sarah, but at the same time she was exhilarated. What an experience it had been. It had changed her life completely. Up until a week ago she had no knowledge of her family background, no idea of Martha and Josiah's existence or her grandmother's tragedy. It had been upsetting, yet at the same time, enriching for her. She only hoped that her father would react in the same way. She didn't know how she was going to tell him. How could she approach the subject? She would have to think carefully. Sarah thought that her grandmother had gone to Aunt Elizabeth's to stay after her sudden disappearance, but when was she coming home? How long had Emmie got? How would Gran know that Emmie had completed her task? She supposed that she would just have to leave it to fate, yet again, and tell Freddie as soon as she was able to. These questions and more went round and round in her head until she reached Lime Street Station. She was so tired when she arrived at the station that she treated herself to a taxi. When it pulled up she just collapsed thankfully into the back. She sat in silence and simply watched the world pass by on her journey from the station. It was early evening when she reached Chestnut Lodge. She had been travelling for over four hours. She was glad to be back and relieved that nothing dreadful had happened in her absence.

On her arrival, Emmie had a snack and a medicinal whisky in the kitchen and then went straight up to her room. She must have fallen asleep on the bed without getting undressed and hadn't even closed the curtains so the morning light woke her early. She had been so exhausted that she didn't even have the strength to dream. She felt refreshed after her early night, but she was stiff from sleeping so soundly in one position. She gently pulled herself up and off the bed. She felt extremely grimy after her long journey so she ran a hot shower, peeled off her clothes and gratefully climbed under the steaming deluge. The shower washed away her cobwebs and refreshed her. She put on her warm bathrobe and towelling her hair walked back into the bedroom. The weather had broken at last and it was raining hard and was quite cold. She dried her hair, pulled on an old pair of jeans and a warm sweater and then ran downstairs and lit the fire in the little sitting room. She let it catch whilst she had her breakfast in the Aga-warmed kitchen. After breakfast she returned to her bedroom, emptied her case, hung up her clean clothes and brought her washing down to the kitchen. She popped it into the washing machine then made another cup of coffee and took it into the little sitting room.

Emmie was feeling a little guilty about all the work that she had intended to do whilst staying at Chestnut Lodge. But Florence's story had completely dominated her life. Her work would have to wait. She could catch up with it later. She never let too much work build up so it wouldn't take long to clear the backlog. This morning, however, she had other, more pressing matters to attend to. She sat down by the fire and looked around the room. This was Florence's sitting room, the place where she had hidden until she was prepared to enter the land of the living again. Her rocking chair was still there, but it was banished to a corner now. Emmie pulled it forward and placed it in front of the fire. She then sat in it and rocked to and fro looking at the flames, just as her grandmother had during those months after her discharge from the asylum. What went through her head during that time? Emmie couldn't start to imagine. How did she feel when she suddenly found herself out in the world again? Had she expected to be released? Emmie thought not. After the death of her baby, as the months passed and she heard nothing from her family, she must have reconciled herself to living the rest of her life locked away from the world. She must have been desperate and wondered what had become of her mother and her friends. She knew Josiah had committed her under a false name and the chances of her family finding her were nearly impossible. Why did she never communicate with the warders? Write down who she was? It was impossible to understand the working of someone's mind when they had been so traumatised.

Mulling things over, Emmie sat for a while alone with her thoughts. She decided that she wanted to spend the morning alone. That she wasn't ready yet to discuss what she had learned with anyone else. After a while she made a decision and stood up and went upstairs where she retrieved a dust sheet from the airing cupboard. She brought it down and spread it on the floor of the sitting room. Then she went to the boot room and dragged the tin box out from under the bench. Using the key, which she had taken with her, she opened the tin box. It was impossible to see exactly what was in there by the light of the 60 watt bulb, so she gathered all the papers together and stuffed then into a supermarket carrier bag that she found in there. As she did so she made a mental note to persuade her grandmother to install a more modern light fitting in the boot room.

There were too many papers to fit into one bag, so she returned to the kitchen for two more. When she had emptied the box she carefully locked it and pushed it back under the bench. She then returned to the sitting room and began her task. She emptied the first carrier bag onto the dust sheet and started to sort through the papers. It was much easier in there, she had room to sort the papers and good light so she could see what she was doing. She sorted the papers into different piles. There were official forms, birth certificates, death certificates, marriage lines and old, out of date passports. There were bundles of photographs, invoices and bills, old theatre programmes and tickets, hat badges and insignia from Edward's army uniform and bits of paper that had no significance whatsoever.

For years Florence must have just thrown odd bits of trivia into the box. Emmie didn't see any evidence that she'd ever tried to sort it out. Everything smelt very musty and old, but as she had observed when she removed Martha's journals, they were all dry and in fairly good condition. The contents desperately needed sorting and filing in some way. Emmie thought for a moment and then remembered that she had some coloured envelope files outside in the car. She always had a good supply because she used them to keep her university notes in. She struggled stiffly to her feet, left her piles of forms and photographs and went outside to collect a bundle of empty files from her car. She had decided to use them to classify the different categories of papers. The photographs she put to one side, together with Edward's army memorabilia. She then set about putting the papers into some kind of order. The official documents, share certificates, bank statements, house deeds and such things she separated from the private papers. She organised them into coloured envelope files which she labelled and placed in a drawer in the desk that she had cleared for the purpose. The private papers she put to one side. She wanted to spend more time reading through them to see if she could extract any more information about the family. She emptied the second carrier bag onto the dust sheet and organised the contents in much the same way as those of the first bag, then she started on the third bag and came to a full stop. As soon as she emptied the contents onto the dust sheet she saw them. They lay there, blatant, accusing and obscene in their ordinariness; the grey committal forms in the name of Mary Davies. They had been locked away in the dark for the second time in their lives, but they had surfaced again. They lay there, an accusing testimony to the cruelty human beings exacted on one another. Emmie picked them up gingerly; somehow she had never expected to find them here. She didn't know what she thought. She imagined that Martha or Florence would probably have disposed of them in some way. Stumbling on them in this unexpected way shocked her, but when she thought about it, she realised that no one could dispose of documents that had such significance.

Emmie unfolded them carefully; they were nearly sixty years old and were very fragile. As she read them, she realised that they were exactly as Sarah had described them. She carefully read the diagnosis and examined the signatures of her great grandfather and Dr. Pickard. The proof of the brutal reality of the crime committed against her grandmother hit her hard. Then, as if to emphasise that brutality, Emmie, like Martha before her, stumbled on the small sepia photograph of her grandmother in the guise of Mary Davies. She looked so young, so fragile and above all, so afraid. Emmie was profoundly shocked and deeply moved. The forms brought home the stark reality of what Sarah had revealed to her. She struggled to her feet and placed the forms on the top of the bureau. She was aware that they were a vital piece of evidence and must be kept safe. She realised that she would need them to show to her father when she told him what had happened to her grandmother. She had also borrowed Florence's written 'rape' testimony from Sarah for the very same reason. She needed verification. She knew her father would need convincing that the story was true. He would need evidence and she was quietly preparing a case to present to him.

She spent the rest of the morning sorting through the papers and photographs, putting them in some kind of order. She needed to be kept busy to keep her emotions under control. It was almost as if by organising the contents of the box, she could erase the committal forms from her conscious mind and re-order her grandmother's life. If she put the contents into neat little boxes, she could somehow remove the chaos and tragedy and her grandmother could die peacefully. It made no sense of course, but it comforted Emmie somehow. It was therapeutic and it helped her to absorb and digest all that she had learned from Sarah. As she sorted the papers, she felt the approving spiritual presence of the young Florence. She seemed to watch the re-ordering of her life with calm eyes as she rocked gently in her chair.

Katy was extremely pleased with the outcome of her search for relatives and friends of her patients. It was amazing how many people still lived in the same house as their grandparents, or if not in the same house then in the same street or neighbourhood. Most of those who received a letter that was not meant for them had at least made an effort to find the people who the letter was addressed to, so there were a large number of replies.

One of Katy's fears had been the thought that young people would have no interest in an unknown elderly relative. Especially one who had been locked away in a lunatic asylum for sixty years, but she couldn't have been more wrong. She managed to locate a relative or friend for at least seventy five per cent of the ladies on Buttercup Ward and she was absolutely thrilled, as was Sister Parkinson. They were overwhelmed by the kindness and compassion shown by these long lost relatives and friends. Many came initially from a sense of curiosity. They wanted to see the inside of a real asylum. Some visitors came because they were intrigued to find that they had a living relative who they knew nothing about. Most were more enlightened than their parents and grandparents. They were embarrassed at discovering an elderly relative who had been locked away for years and conveniently erased from family memory. However, once they had visited their lost relative, most of them continued to keep in touch. Katy wondered if it was because they felt the collective guilt of a society that had allowed innocent patients to be locked away for and forgotten. They were the only section of the population who could be imprisoned without trial. She didn't know why they came and she didn't care. It was lovely to see the joy on the ladies' faces when they realised that they had, at last, been remembered.

The whole experiment was of great interest to Katy and Sister Parkinson as they watched it unfold. It was, in the main, a great success, but it was not without its more amusing moments. Some of the old ladies were quite frankly bemused when they started receiving visits from a family that they hadn't seen or heard from for decades. Some of them had simply forgotten that they ever had a family. Nevertheless, it was touching when they realised that they had grandchildren or even great grand children who wanted to see them. They couldn't believe that they were not ashamed of being associated with 'a lunatic'. It was so satisfying to see that these young people had no fear of mental illness. They had a far more relaxed attitude than their parents. It gave many of the old ladies a new lease of life and on the whole it was a very successful experiment. There were mothers and daughters who were reunited, brothers and sisters who discovered each other and even old friends came together again.

Of course, some of Katy's letters went unanswered and she was unable to locate relatives or old friends for some of the ladies. However, she never gave up trying and followed up even the most unlikely connections. In the cases where she couldn't locate anyone, she arranged for the patients to be visited by a member of the hospital's League of Friends or she tried to recruit a visitor from among her close friends. One of those friends was Emmie Clayton. Katy had promised to contact her so she decided to give her a ring and remind her that she had promised to help. Also she didn't want to lose touch with Emmie again and was determined to make an effort to make sure that she didn't. She picked up her office phone and rang the number that Emmie had given her. She knew she had been to London for a few days visiting friends, but thought it was worth trying to contact her.

Emmie was delighted that Katy had phoned her. She was the one person in the world that she needed to speak to. Katy would understand all that had happened to her grandmother and she wouldn't be prejudiced in any way. They arranged to meet up for a pizza that evening. During the conversation Katy mentioned the hospital visiting and was surprised at Emmie's enthusiastic response. She told Katy that since her visit to London she had a very special interest in visiting the hospital and befriending a patient. She added mysteriously that she would explain later in detail when she met up with Katy. As she put the phone down from Emmie, Katy's phone immediately rang again and this time it was her brother, Paul.

Paul was a qualified doctor who was completing a sabbatical year in a hospital in Ottawa, Canada. He was home for a short visit before his contract finished and he was making enquiries about other employment opportunities for when he returned to Britain. However, as he was only home on a short visit he was having difficulty in fitting in his job search with visits to all of his very demanding family. He had phoned to ask Katy if he could see her that night as he had a free space. She realised how precious his time was and didn't want to disappoint him, but she also wanted to have a gossip with Emmie as she was intrigued to hear her news. Not wanting to disappoint either her brother or her friend, she compromised and asked him to join them at the pizzeria after they had eaten. She arranged for him to come about 9.30 pm. She was meeting Emmie at 7.30 pm so that would give them time to chat before he arrived. She didn't have time to consult Emmie, but she just hoped that she would understand the situation. Little did she know that she couldn't have planned it better if she'd tried!

Chapter Twenty One

Emmie had been genuinely pleased to hear from Katy. She was the only person, besides her father, who she wanted to discuss her grandmother's history with. She knew that Katy, of all people, would understand. She felt it would be a pleasure to spend some time in the present. During the last few days she had been completely absorbed in revisiting the past, to the extent that she almost felt a part of it. As a result she took extra care when she got ready to meet Katy. She wore the expensive black trousers that she had bought in London and teamed them with a white silk shirt and black suede jacket and boots.

She walked to the pizzeria where Katy was already

waiting for her. She sat down and while they ordered she started to tell Katy what she had learned, firstly from the journals, and then from Sarah. She told Katy the full story from beginning to end, with all the details. Katy was enthralled, yet horrified at the same time. Emmie had even taken the precious committal papers containing her grandmother's photograph to show to Katy. Naturally they looked quite familiar to her as she had just ploughed her way through a hundred similar case files. But these were special because they belonged to someone she knew well, the relative of a close friend. When she was researching the files of the ladies on Buttercup Ward and looking for lost relatives she read all the patients' files. She learned all about their backgrounds and the reasons that they had been committed. She suspected then that some of them had been certified and admitted to the asylum because they were an embarrassment or an inconvenience to someone. It was really interesting to have access to a case where she had all the background information. She wanted to know more though and asked Emmie's permission to look for Florence's, alias 'Mary Davies's', file. It hadn't occurred to Emmie that Katy could do that, but she readily gave her consent, although she wasn't entirely sure that it was hers to give.

Whilst Katy had a professional fascination with Florence's case, she also had an enormous amount of sympathy for Emmie. She knew that it must have been very difficult to uncover such a traumatic history. Emmie and Katy had been very close friends during their school years and Katy knew how much she loved and admired her grandmother. To discover that she had been abused and mistreated in her youth must have upset Emmie more than she was willing to admit. It must have been especially hard as it closely followed the news of Florence's imminent death. Her heart went out to her old friend and she wished she could do something to ease her pain.

One thing Katy hadn't realised was how alike physically Emmie and Florence were. She had only ever known Florence as an old lady, as Emmie's grandma. It was a failing of youth that they often didn't see beyond the fact that people were old. As far as she knew she had never seen a photograph before of Florence as a young girl and she couldn't get over the similarity between Florence and her granddaughter. Emmie was one of those rare women who were totally unaware of the fact that they were beautiful; it was one of the endearing things about her.

Katy told Emmie about her exercise to find visitors for her ladies, as she now called them, and how pleased she had been at the success. She thought it would be good for Emmie to visit the hospital as it would give her an insight into the years that her grandmother had spent there and it would possibly help her to lay a few ghosts. Katy realised now why Emmie's interest in her project had risen from mild inquisitiveness to extreme concern and they made arrangements for her to visit the ward towards the end of the week. Katy asked to have another look at the committal papers, especially the page with the photograph of Florence on, just out of interest and then Emmie carefully stowed it away in her bag.

Once Emmie had completed her story and they had arranged her visit to the hospital, the two old friends just chattered away about their lives. Emmie told Katy about her abortive years in London and apologised again for losing touch, just because she was embarrassed about her failure. Katy told Emmie of a failed relationship that had left her heartbroken and directionless. One minute she thought that she was getting married and the next minute she was single. At that point she felt that her life was completely pointless again. That's when she decided to take up social work and the job at the hospital had quite literally changed her life. They talked about school friends and what had become of them. They had both kept in touch with different girls and were able to provide news of them. They were giggling away about the exploits of one particularly outrageous friend, when Emmie looked up and saw Paul walking over to their table. She couldn't believe her eyes; she thought that he was still in Canada. Katy had completely forgotten to tell her that he was joining them. Her face must have registered shock because her expression prompted Katy to turn and investigate. She swivelled around in her chair to see what had upset Emmie and saw her brother approaching the table. She waved and then turned to apologise to Emmie, who had by this time recovered some of her composure.

'Oh I'm so sorry Emmie; I forgot to tell you that I asked Paul to join us. I hope you don't mind, but he's only home for a week's visit so I'm trying to see as much of him as I can.'

Emmie was delighted, but was immediately transformed into the love sick teenager she had been last time she saw him. She told herself that it was ridiculous to feel like that at her age. She tried hard to pull herself together, but every time he addressed her she felt as though she was blushing and stuttering and making an idiot of herself. Strangely, Katy and Paul didn't seem to notice. They had fallen into the natural banter of a brother and sister who were very close. They were so happy to see one another, fencing gentle insults and expressing their closeness by arguing about everything, that they didn't seem aware of Emmie's discomfort. She, however, was in mental turmoil. Paul looked as gorgeous as ever. He was taller, his naturally blonde hair had been bleached white and his face was tanned to a deep mahogany from the warm Canadian sun. He had also developed a gentle Canadian drawl and had started to call English objects by their Canadian names, which was rather endearing. He referred to the chemists as the drugstore and taps as faucets. Katy had great fun mimicking him and he took it in good spirit, but Emmie was transfixed and simply looked on in silent homage, cursing herself throughout for being so immature.

They had been chatting for a while when Katy asked Emmie's permission to repeat Florence's story to Paul. He was now a doctor and was interested in Katy's work. He was also as relieved as everyone else that she had finally settled down to a serious career, although he would never show it and continually pulled her leg about her job. He was quite visibly shocked when Katy related Emmie's story. He seemed very concerned for her and was worried that the revelations about her grandmother's past may really have upset her, especially as she had only recently learned about her grandmother's terminal cancer. She was touched by his concern, but reassured him that it had been a positive experience, which had helped her understand her grandmother better. She also had the added bonus of getting to know Sarah, who she knew would be a comfort when her grandmother finally passed away. Paul seemed very impressed with her attitude and she was flattered. During the years since she left school she had met many men. There were, of course the unsuitable 'Freddie baiters', but there had also been some very attractive and intelligent men. However, none of them had made her feel like Paul did and sitting in the pizzeria listening to his tales of life in Africa and Canada, she realised that nothing had changed. She wasn't a silly teenager now, she was a grown woman and she realised with a lurch of her stomach that she was in love with a man who had never given her a second glance.

All too soon the evening ended. Katy and Paul dropped Emmie off at Chestnut Lodge. She asked them in for a coffee, but Katy declined as she had to be up early for work. They arranged for Emmie to visit the hospital towards the end of the week and to her surprise Paul asked if he could come along as well. He said it was probably the last chance he would get to visit a working Victorian asylum. Katy corrected him by insisting it be called a hospital. He apologised, but said he still wanted to come and see it. Katy agreed, although she thought Sister Parkinson might think he was a doubtful candidate to become a visitor and they all laughed and then parted company. As Emmie scrambled out, she heard Paul say that he would ring her and arrange to pick her up and take her to the hospital. She was delighted at the prospect of seeing him again and found herself humming one of her favourite love songs as she opened the front door and let herself in. She gave herself another firm talking to, but couldn't stop the warm glow of excitement that she felt at spending some more time in his company.

Chapter Twenty Two

The lovely Indian summer had finally ended with a vengeance. It seemed to Katy, as she prepared for work the following day, that the seasons had changed overnight. The gales that morning were relentless, the dark skies swirled with stormy rain clouds and the temperature had plummeted. Leaving for work, Katy donned boots and a coat for the first time in months, a sure sign that winter was setting in. All the way to the hospital the wind buffeted Katy's little car as it roared through the tree branches in a determined effort to tear the last ragged leaves from the knarled twigs before winter set in. Nature, like a tardy housewife, had suddenly woken up to the fact that autumn was nearly over and she hadn't put her house in order. Driven by the wind, the rain lashed down in torrents, gleefully bouncing off the pavements like a chorus of dancing fairies. Down and down it poured; it streamed along the gutters, poured over the top of downspouts clogged by leaves and collected into deep puddles ready to drench the unsuspecting pedestrian.

It hammered down on the top of Katy's little car as it struggled valiantly through the deluge. Her wipers were barely managing to clear the windscreen and visibility was down to a few metres. The halcyon days of summer were certainly over. Watching unsuspecting pedestrians try to avoid a drenching as cars ploughed through the puddles, Katy thanked God for her little car. The thought of struggling to work on public transport surrounded by a forest of damp, steaming commuters did not appeal to her in the least.

As she turned into the hospital driveway, Katy caught

site of the hospital building as it lay black and brooding, its shoulders hunched against the driving rain. It was a daunting sight. She had never felt less like working and she pulled into the car park with a heavy heart. Having found a space, she swiftly locked her car and skipped through the pouring rain to the entrance of her office. Rather than fight with her umbrella she sheltered her head with her newspaper and it was drenched by the time she reached the office doorway.

She stamped up the stairs, but once she reached her cheerful office, her heart lifted. At least the heating was on so it was warm and the lights were bright: it made a comforting contrast to the grey scene outside. The weather was so bad that she decided to stay in the office all morning and catch up with her long neglected paper work. She felt no inclination to move unless she absolutely had to. Philip, her fellow social worker, had the same idea and they worked quietly at their desks until 11.00 am, which heralded coffee time. Philip offered to make it and he stood up and loped across to the corner table that served as a coffee bar. He collected the kettle and took it down the corridor to fill it from the washbasin in the gents. Meanwhile, Katy nipped downstairs to collect the daily pint of milk that was left on the step by the hospital milk man. Having made the coffee Philip carried the two mugs over to Katy's desk. They took a well earned break and sat on her desk exchanging gossip.

Philip was an unusual young man. He had studied for the priesthood then had a crisis of faith and decided to take a year out to examine his conscience. He had decided to stay at the hospital until he either found his faith again or abandoned it forever. Katy wasn't at all sure where he was up to in his struggle with God. It was a subject that she studiously avoided, as it led to long agonising discussions on the subject with Philip. However, he was a hive of gossip and knew everything that was going on in the hospital. He told her over coffee that there had been an American snooping around looking for information about a long lost relative. Unfortunately, he had fallen into Mrs. McKendrick's hands and she had been less than helpful. During his visit, Philip had been listening at the partition between the two offices. Katy laughed, if Mrs. McKendrick had had any idea how easy it was to overhear her conversations she would have had a soun proof barrier erected. Philip didn't know who the man was, but apparently he had found some old papers in his mother's house and wanted to trace a relative or something. He had heard the man ask if he could access the hospital archives. Apparently Mrs. McKendrick was outraged and told him in no uncertain terms that he certainly could not. She told him that they were confidential and could only be examined by staff. Both social workers knew that this was nonsense. The whole philosophy of the hospital was now openness and freedom of information. They were both of the opinion that she was a menace and was going to make a serious fundamental mistake one day. Both of them silently hoped that they wouldn't get the blame for one of her blunders. As Katy well knew, she would have no compunction in letting them take the blame, as long as she avoided suspicion.

As they sat peacefully sipping their coffee, Katy started to tell Philip about the partial success of her attempts to find visitors for her ladies on the Annexe.

It was, as she told him, all part of the rehabilitation programme, an effort to make them less institutionalised. He just laughed.

'What after sixty odd years, some hopes,' Katy just smiled at him and said it was worth a try and it had made some of them very happy. Philip had an aversion to the Annexe; it seemed to depress him somehow. He worked mainly with the short stay patients in the main hospital building. He empathised well with them and enjoyed seeing them go back into the community. He left the long stay wards to the female members of the department, which suited everyone well.

Whilst they were chatting Katy was thinking about Emmie's grandmother, Florence. If the rain stopped she had intended to go over to the Annexe and see if she could locate the archives. There was a slim possibility that she may find more information that may help Emmie understand what had happened all those years ago. She knew that the basic details of patients had been transferred onto micro fiche and were readily available, but the detailed paper notes were still kept on the ward or filed away. She wasn't sure what happened to the files of discharged patients. They could have been kept at the hospital or transferred to a central archive. She thought Philip would probably know, he was the sort of person who was a fund of useful information. She asked him if he thought the hospital would have kept the files of a woman who had been discharged over fifty years ago. She knew the live files were kept, but she had never looked for the file of someone who had died or been discharged.

He laughed when she asked him, because he was of the opinion that they never threw anything away in the hospital. Philip had no romantic feelings about the old buildings and their history. He would have demolished the ancient hospital in an instance, but he knew everything about it. Of course that included knowing where Florence's file would be kept. Apparently all the old records were still stored at the hospital, nobody had attempted to move them, because there was plenty of room at the hospital. He was surprised that Katy had never been to the huge archive room, which was housed in the Annexe basement. It was a massive library containing all the details of everyone who had ever been a patient in the hospital. They were stored on rows and rows of metal shelves and were cared for and guarded by a former patient called Stan. Philip warned Katy that if she was thinking of going over there that he was a complete obsessive with a photographic memory. He guarded the files with his life and had been known to hound to death members of staff who hadn't returned files on time. Katy was intrigued to know how Philip, who never visited the Annexe, knew all about the archive room and its guardian. He started chuckling. Apparently Mrs. Morgan, who was one of the senior social workers, had endured a running feud with Stan because she had once forgotten to return a file. He had to come looking for it and never quite trusted her since. Katy knew Mrs. Morgan was one of the most sensible and reliable members of staff, so Stan must be a problem. Ever astute, Philip asked her why she wanted to go looking for dead files of discharged patients. She didn't really want to discuss Emmie's business with him so she vaguely referred to one of the ladies on her ward. He accepted her story quite readily so she didn't elaborate.

Now that she knew where the files were kept, she

thought that she would go over to the Annexe that afternoon. Philip said that it was warm and dry in the Archive room so it was a good place to be on a wild autumn afternoon and Katy relished her visit. There was nothing more that she loved than poking about in old files. The rain had eased off a little so she decided to go into the village and buy a sandwich and then go to the Archive room and see if she could locate anything on 'Mary Davies.' It would be interesting to research a case where she had a personal interest. She hoped to shed some light on what happened to Florence whilst she was staying in the hospital because she wanted to be able to tell Emmie something that might comfort her as she knew that it had been quite a shock for her finding out about her grandmother's past history.

After she had eaten her lunch in the car she drove to the Annexe in order to locate the archive room that Philip had described. She wouldn't have been a bit surprised if he had been teasing her. As soon as she arrived she went to look for Charlie, the head porter. He lived in a little office just off the main entrance hall, where she caught him having a quick cup of tea. Having explained that she wanted to root around in the archives, he laughingly directed her to the old stone staircase, which led down to the basement. As she was about to descend, she heard Charlie shout to her telling her to look out for the man eating cockroaches. She laughed. He also shouted to her to beware of Stan and joked that young girls had gone down there in search of files and never been seen again. She just smiled to herself and started to descend the staircase into the basement. All the porters teased the young nurses and secretaries and they all took it in good part.

It was very warm at the bottom of the staircase. Katy thought that she was probably near the central hospital boiler room. The light was also dim down there. There was only a sparse supply of natural light from the windows, which were covered with old gratings and years of grime. It was quite eerie, very silent and there was no one about. However, once she got onto the central corridor, there was plenty of electric light, so it was easy to see where she was going. She felt more confident here. The usual green hospital signs directed her along the corridor to the archive room at the end. They gave the basement a feeling of normality, of belonging. Katy noted that this must have been the only part of the hospital that had ceilings that were placed at a normal height and didn't dwarf the average human being.

Eventually she found a door marked 'Archives' and gingerly opened it. She was astounded at the size of the room. It was enormous. It must have covered half the area of the hospital. There was a wooden counter in front of her as she entered the room and acres of shelving stretched for what seemed miles behind it. A small room to the right contained some long reading tables. A tall thin man in a stiff, brown, cotton coat was standing behind the counter. This, she thought, must be Stan. He was exceptionally tall and exceptionally thin, with tufts of grey hair which grew in isolated clumps out of his otherwise bald head. He wore a pair of very small, round, thick, spectacles, which he peered over as she entered the room. Katy thought that he looked like one of those plants that they grew in the school labs to see what happened if they had no access to sunlight. They grew too tall, with no substance and were all pale, thin and weedy just like Stan. It was probably because he had been locked away for years in the basement of the hospital.

He saw her come in, but he didn't speak, just stared at her over the top of his spectacles. She was a little intimidated, but then she was used to meeting odd and eccentric people in the hospital. She just went up to him and asked for Mary Davies' file. Without uttering a word he turned round and disappeared into the forest of shelves and files, where he appeared to have been swallowed up. However, this was not the case as he emerged again a few moments later holding two files which he silently handed to Katy. She was surprised to receive two and glanced at them quickly, but there was no mistake. They both belonged to Mary Davies. She jumped as Stan suddenly spoke to her, or rather barked, 'They're not to be taken out of here, you can look at them over there.' He nodded to the reading area to the right of the counter. Having uttered his instructions he handed the files to a bemused Katy, who simply thanked him and took them to one of the tables to read.

The first file was just like all the other files that she had sorted through on the ward. She turned the pages slowly. It was quite detailed and Katy found it strange to be reading about the grandmother of a friend of hers, rather than a patient who was really a stranger. The file made interesting reading. Josiah and his fellow conspirators had not only given Florence a false name, they had also found her a fictitious address. It was one that Katy didn't recognise and was probably the address of a solicitor or maybe another doctor, she didn't know. All the other information was much the same as it had been on the committal forms. There was a report on

her progress and it stated, quite simply that she had
been a well behaved patient and caused no trouble,
but that she was completely dumb. It mentioned her
nightmares, but otherwise it was fairly straightforward
until she came to the birth of the baby. It described her
waters breaking on the ward, but nothing more, she
was sent straight to the infirmary. The infirmary sent
a report to the ward after her confinement and it
contained the birth certificate and death certificate
of a still born male child. This brought a lump to
Katy's throat the poor little mite had no life at all.
Mary's notes finished with her discharge. They were
fairly straightforward and didn't contain any additional
information that she could pass on to Emmie, which
was slightly disappointing.

Katy then turned her attention to the second file,
which had come as a surprise to her. It was a report from
the infirmary reporting on Florence's confinement.
It was written on yellowing vellum in a copperplate
hand. Katy had never seen one before. Most of the
patients on Buttercup Ward had their hospital notes
pinned to the back of their case notes. The report
contained far more details about the progress of the
labour than the one sent to the ward and Katy read
through it with fervour. Poor little Florence, she didn't
seem to have been given any pain relief and there
was only a midwife in attendance together with a
patient orderly, but no doctor. The labour was long and
painful. Reading on Katy felt quite upset at the thought
of Emmie's grandmother, alone in that old infirmary.
She would have been terrified.

In the middle of the report, Katy came across two
forms folded up and just tucked into the page. Carefully

she removed and unfolded them. She was astounded by what she read. She had been led to believe that Florence had given birth to one male child, who was, tragically, still born. However, she had in her hand two birth certificates, one for the still born child, and one for another live male infant. Katy was astounded. It looked as though Florence had been pregnant with twins. As she had never had any ante natal care, no one had realised that she was expecting two babies. They were very small and they were both male. Looking around furtively she saw that Stan was bending down behind the counter. Having briefly scanned the birth certificates she quickly stuffed both of them into her bag. She then carried on reading the rest of the report, convinced that at any minute she would feel Stan's hand fingering her collar as she was sure he had seen what she had done. What if he would came over and demanded that the birth certificates be put back in the file? He would then, no doubt throw her out and report her. She forced herself to remain calm and read on, however Stan hadn't noticed her take the birth certificates so she was safe.

The first baby was stillborn; he weighed barely 4lbs at birth. However the second baby was a live birth, a little boy who weighed less than 6 lbs. Katy read on avidly. Florence was very ill for some time after the birth. She had a fever, ran a high temperature and was often delirious. They kept her in the infirmary for several weeks, until she was fully recovered and then sent her back to the ward. It seemed that she had no knowledge that she had given birth to a live child and she never saw her son. Katy again cross checked with the case notes that had been held on the ward, but there was no mention of a live birth, or twins. Only a note was sent up to the ward stating quite simply that her baby was still born. It wasn't clear to Katy whether that was a simple mistake, or whether it was deliberate concealment. However, she was sure that Florence thought that she had given birth to only one still born child and there was no mention of a surviving baby.

The second child was looked after in the infirmary nursery for the first few weeks and then he was sent to Canada for adoption under a scheme that was fashionable after the First World War. There was a drive to populate the colonies and war widows, young women with no one to marry and unemployed males were persuaded to emigrate to the colonies on assisted passages. Under this scheme, illegitimate babies were sent to childless couples for adoption and children from orphanages were also shipped out to Australia, New Zealand and Canada. It seemed that the hospital had an arrangement with the Canadian authorities that unwanted illegitimate babies born in the hospital were sent to Canada for adoption. This included Florence's son. There they were adopted by childless Canadian couples. It must have been felt that they would have the opportunity of a better life in Canada.

Katy was astounded. She took out a pad and made a note of the address of the Canadian adoption society and then neatened the papers and closed the file. She slipped on her coat, picked up the files and took them over to the counter to hand them back to Stan. She was extremely nervous as he pointedly peered at her over his glasses, looking for signs of guilt. He flicked carefully through the files, but seemed satisfied that all was in order and he let her go. She smiled her thanks and strolled out of the archive room, into the corridor and then ran up the stone staircase. Charlie, the porter was still there. She called out to him that she had managed to fight off the man eating cockroaches and survived the day. He just roared with laughter and added that it was more unusual that she had survived Stan. She laughed back and then headed for her car. She hurriedly opened it and then scrambled in. She was sure that Stan was going to come after her, having discovered the removal of the two birth certificates and demand their return. Before returning to her office she drove into a quiet street in the village and parked up. She took the two birth certificates out of her bag and examined them closely. There was no mistake. Two boys, both born on the same day, within minutes of each other, same mother, same location, they had to be twins. Katy was stunned. She placed the precious forms in a plastic bag and slipped them under the carpet of the car. She then drove back to her office to finish her day's work.

On the way home her head was reeling with different thoughts. She didn't know what to do with this new discovery. How was Emmie going to take this news? It was quite neat and tidy when they believed that the child, one child, was still born, but this was a different set up altogether. She had arranged for Emmie and Paul to visit the hospital in two days time. That was on Wednesday. She pondered on it all the way home. Then she made a decision. She would discuss it with Paul. He was a doctor, he was intelligent and he was older than she was. He would know what to do. She would take him out for a drink when she got home and ask his advice.

Chapter Twenty Three

That evening after dinner Katy persuaded Paul to go out to the local pub for a drink. There she presented him with the evidence of her day's research. Her brother examined both the birth certificates carefully and then looked up at Katy.

'Well, this is a turn up. There seems little doubt that Florence gave birth to twins and one of them survived. How on earth could the authorities keep that from her? It was a dreadful thing to do. To let her think she had given birth to one child, who had died and not even tell her about the live birth. Then to have the other child adopted, without her consent. Can you imagine that happening today? But then I suppose if you were certified in those days you lost all your legal rights, in fact, all your rights as a human being altogether. It's incredible. Are you quite sure that he was adopted and sent to Canada?'

'Well, I'm as sure as I can be. I couldn't remove the file from the Archive room, but obviously it's still there for someone else to examine. It was fairly clear to me that the surviving male child was going to be sent to Canada for adoption. I managed to scribble down the name and address of the adoption agency here in England and the corresponding office in Canada.'

'You've done well Katie. We've got enough information to begin looking for this surprise child. Isn't it handy that I'm going back there at the end of the week?' Paul said smiling knowingly. 'It's such a coincidence that if I didn't know better I would think that you'd planned this!'

'Well I didn't plan it, but you will help me to discover

what happened to him won't you? I mean help me to find him?'

'Of course I will. I'll follow up any leads over there that I can find. Of course I'll help you and Emmie, anyway that I can.'

'But Paul, Emmie, I mean what are we going to do?'

'I don't follow you, what do you mean by 'do'?'

'Well, are we going to tell Emmie about this latest development? I mean it seems so cruel to add more complications to an already difficult situation. It is already hard for her to take in what she has learned over the last few weeks.'

'I know what you're saying, Katy love, but we must tell her. Of course we must. This is a serious situation. If this baby did survive and was adopted, he will be a man now. He is Florence's son, Emmie's uncle, a blood relative, she has to be informed. She has to make any decisions about contacting him or even telling Florence. It wouldn't be fair not to tell her. She's old enough and sensible enough to deal with the consequences. We also have to consider the situation of the man, the adopted child. He has a right to know about his family. He may even have been trying to trace them. The days when these things were kept secret, when only the adoptive parents had any rights, are over. The mother and child have rights now, thank goodness.'

Katy was surprised that her brother felt so strongly about human rights. She wasn't as sure as her brother that Emmie should be told, but she felt that he was probably right. He usually was.

'I can see what you mean. I suppose she will have to be told, poor Emmie. But when shall we tell her?'

As usual Katy's older brother took charge and she

was grateful.

'Leave it to me. We're visiting the hospital tomorrow aren't we?' Katy nodded. 'Well I've arranged to pick Emmie up so we could come together. I'll just pick her up earlier and take her out for lunch first then I can break the news to her in private and we can come on to the hospital later.'

Katy was a little surprised at this turn in events. She wondered if her brother might have a hidden agenda when he suggested taking Emmie out for lunch. However she kept those thoughts to herself. She knew Paul was sensible and would break the news to Emmie sensitively. Katy didn't want the difficult job of telling Emmie and she knew that Paul would handle it well. She had to leave things in his capable hands. It was all she could do. In a way she wished that she hadn't looked for the records and then no one would have been any the wiser. But no, it was wrong that this crime had been hidden. And it was a crime to rob a mother of her son and hide his very existence from her. Florence had a right to know that she had a son and he had a right to know who his mother was. What happened after that was up to them.

'Bless you and thank you for offering. I know you will be kind and you are right. Florence and her family should be told. There is just one more thing that needs consideration. This son, can we give him a name? Let's call him Tom for now. We can't keep referring to him as 'the child' or 'the son'. Right, this Tom, he was the product of Florence's rape. I mean how will she feel? Will she really want to meet him? What if he looks like Dr. Pickard and just gives her nightmares?'

'I don't know Katy, but remember he was Florence's child, she carried him for nine months and gave birth to him. No matter who the father was, or the circumstances of his conception, he was half her child. Anyway, these are not our decisions to make, they are Emmie's and they need to be thought through. All we can do is talk about what needs to be done and help Emmie in any way we know how. I suppose we could even trace Tom and if he did look just like his 'father' we could explain the problem to him. Emmie might want to ask her grandmother what she wants to do. They have to make the decisions Katy, not you or I. One thing I do know is that we can't be responsible for withholding the truth from them. Now drink up and we'll start back. Mum is starting to miss me even before I return to Canada, so I think I better devote some time to her before I leave, or I'll be up for adoption!'

Katy smiled, she knew that Paul would know what to do and she felt less anxious now that she had shared her discovery with someone else. Their decisions made, the brother and sister quickly finished their drinks and left the pub. Katy felt as though a weight had been lifted from her shoulders and she was very grateful that Paul had been there to ask for advice.

———⬤———

It was late evening and Emmie was still in the little sitting room sorting through the photographs and papers when the phone suddenly rang. She jumped. As she went to answer it she hoped it wasn't her father. She had spoken to him since her return and arranged for him to come to supper on Friday night. That is when she intended to tell him all that she had learned about Florence's past, but before she saw him she wanted to organise some photographs and papers to show him whilst she was relaying her story. Her father was a barrister and always required written evidence. She was relieved to hear it was not her father on the phone and was even more delighted when she recognised Paul's voice. She thought he was ringing to make arrangements to collect her the following day before they visited the hospital. She was absolutely delighted when he asked her out to lunch prior to that visit. She agreed readily and put the phone down in a haze of happiness before she returned to her task in the little sitting room.

She had worked hard and had managed to organise the contents of the tin trunk. She now had all the birth certificates in date order, followed by the death certificates and finally the marriage certificates and old passports. Many of the share certificates and business letters looked out of date, but she had dutifully arranged them in date order and put them in a file for Florence to go through and identify. She was sure that most of her financial papers were with her solicitor or the bank so these probably weren't that important, but she didn't know so it was better to be safe than sorry. The photographs she had put into an album and she had named each of the people in them so that future generations could identify them. There seemed to be at least one photograph of each member of the family and it was lovely to be able see what they looked like. They then became real people instead of just names.

Whilst sorting through the photographs she had found the one of Florence and Edward on their wedding day. Florence looked lovely in her wedding gown. She really was beautiful. She wore a veil close to her head, in the style of the cloche hats of the 1920s and a calf length, low waisted dress in chiffon and lace. You could just see her white high heeled shoes, with their wide ankle straps, peeping out from under her dress. A show of shoe and stocking must have been quite daring then. She looked glowing with health and happiness and Emmie could only marvel when she thought of what she had endured in the asylum just a few years previously. Edward also looked very handsome in his morning suit, with his white tie and spats. They made a lovely couple and looked so happy that Emmie had bought a lovely silver frame and put the photograph on display. She hoped her grandmother wouldn't mind too much.

There were also photographs of her father and Aunt Elizabeth as babies and then toddlers. Martha, now grey, featured on some of them, but they all had one thing in common, everyone was smiling and everyone looked happy. They were quite unlike the stiff Victorian photographs of Martha and Josiah. She had arranged Martha's journals in date order and tied them together in groups of four. There were also odd books, lists of furniture, household accounts and other trivia. None of it meant anything to Emmie, but her grandmother may want them, so she just tied them together in some kind of sequence. The letters she had just put in an old shoe box that she found in her grandmother's room. She intended to read through them when she had a bit more time. She had glanced at them and there didn't seem to be anything significant amongst them, they were mainly personal letters between Florence and her husband and mother.

When she had finished sorting everything she

went back into the boot room and pulled the tin box out from under the bench. She turned it upside down to clear out the dust and to make sure that she had removed everything. To her surprise there was one other rather curious item still in there. It was a small leather pouch, which had got stuck in a corner of the box. Emmie lifted it out and looked through it. She was surprised to find that it contained jewellery. She took it back into the sitting room. The jewellery looked quite old fashioned to her eyes. There were two pairs of gold earrings, a cameo brooch, a locket with the photograph of a little girl in it, a small diamond pendant and matching ring and a wedding ring. Emmie separated them and wrapped each item separately in tissue paper then she wrapped all of them in an old piece of soft cloth that she found in the kitchen and placed them in a drawer in the bureau. She then locked it for safe keeping. She had no idea whether they were valuable or not so she felt that it was better to be cautious.

She went back to the tin box and wiped it out with a damp cloth and detergent and dried it. She then placed the envelope files and bundles back in the box and locked it. She kept the photograph album, the committal forms and Florence's 'rape' testament out to show to her father. Her task more or less completed she gently collected the dust sheet up and took it to the back door where she shook it out. She then put it in the washing machine as it was very dirty. She was pleased that she had completed her task and had a curiously satisfying feeling of putting the past to rights. She was covered in dust and bits of cobwebs so she went upstairs to shower and wash her hair. All she had to do now was tell her father about his mother's past, or so she thought.

Chapter Twenty Four

Emmie had a nice, long lie in. She hadn't realised how tired she really was. She rose about 11 o'clock and prepared carefully for her lunch date with Paul. She was extremely nervous and tried on at least six outfits before she settled for a smart blue trouser suit, pale blue cashmere polo neck sweater and black boots. He had arranged to collect her at 12 o'clock and arrived promptly. They went to a local French restaurant where he had booked a table. She found Paul's physical attractiveness overwhelming and felt as though she was behaving like a silly girl, blushing, giggling and stuttering. She was appalled at herself. However once Emmie had settled in the restaurant and finished her first glass of wine, she began to relax and chatted quite easily with Paul. He told her all about his experiences in Africa. He had some narrow escapes from both wild animals and rebel troops, but had done some useful and satisfying work and enjoyed his time there. He then went on to explain what his job in Canada entailed. He obviously loved both countries and had enjoyed travelling. She in turn filled him in on her life since she last saw him. She told him about her initial failure at London University and the subsequent feeling of worthlessness. He agreed with her that had she been allowed to do what she had wanted to do initially, which was to study the arts, her time in London would probably have been a success.

Paul was very interested in her recent revelations about her family's past and wanted to hear all about them. She told him exactly what Sarah had told her and how she felt about that. He told her that he admired her realistic approach to the shocking events that she had discovered and felt it demonstrated a maturity beyond her years.

Towards the end of the meal, as the coffee was being served, Paul leaned over the table and took one of her hands in his. She was quite taken aback, 'Emmie, I have to reveal something to you. It will shock you, but I feel the only way to tell you is to come straight to the point. I don't know what else to do. Is that alright?'

Emmie was absolutely stunned; she had no idea what Paul was going to say. She thought perhaps that he was going to confess to a wife and children, but she just kept silent and nodded her head and Paul continued, 'Yesterday Katy went down to the Archive department of the hospital to locate your grandmother's file. I think that she had asked your permission?' Katy simply nodded overwhelmingly conscious of the fact that Paul still had hold of her hand.

'Well she did locate the file, in fact there were two files, one was her normal hospital file and the other was a report about your grandmother's confinement in the asylum infirmary. It was whilst reading this that Katy made a surprising discovery. When your grandmother was pregnant, she was expecting twins. She had no idea, as she hadn't really seen a doctor during her pregnancy, apart from a brief consultation in Devon. Probably if she'd had proper ante natal care the doctor would have realised that she was expecting twins, but no one knew and your grandmother was just too naive to understand the signs that might have alerted a more experienced woman. Naturally, when she went into labour it was difficult, as it often is with twins, and there was no doctor to hand, only a midwife. The first baby was small and underdeveloped and he was still born... However, the second baby... Emmie had gone very pale and had caught her breath; Paul held her hand more tightly and continued, 'The second baby was quite a good weight and he was born healthy and survived.'

Emmie was stunned; she didn't know what to say. She couldn't quite take in what Paul was telling her. 'Are you saying that my grandmother had a son who died and a son who lived? Twin boys and one of them lived and she knows nothing about him? The asylum hid his existence from her? Is that what you're telling me?'

'I'm afraid that's the way it seems.'

'I can't believe it. Where is this son? Is he still alive?'

'I know it's hard to believe, but it's the way things were done then. It was thought that it was better for illegitimate children to know nothing about their 'shameful' mothers. It was felt that they were better off with an adopted family.'

Emmie made a kind of choking sound so Paul quickly continued, 'We don't know where he is now or even whether he is still alive. Katy and I felt that you should be told. We felt it was up to you to make any decisions about what we should do next. Katy doesn't think that your grandmother ever saw the surviving twin or held him. In fact, as far as anyone knows she has no idea of his existence to this day. He was sent to Canada to be adopted and we can only assume that he is still there.'

Emmie was stunned into silence. When Paul began to tell her what had happened she felt incredibly relieved that he was telling her something that would affect her grandmother and not her directly. Initially she thought he was going to tell her that he was in a committed relationship and was very thankful when she realised that was not the case. When she grasped the full significance of what he was telling her though, she felt terribly guilty. How could she be so selfish that she didn't immediately think about the impact that this news would have on her grandmother? Hadn't she already had enough to cope with?

Emmie realised at once that she would have to make all the decisions. How were they going to deal with this new development? How could they ensure that her grandmother wasn't hurt as a result? She was finding it hard to absorb Paul's news. She couldn't think clearly. Possible scenarios were rushing through her head and she felt out of control. She tried hard to think clearly and Paul just sat patiently holding her hand while she tried to sort herself out. He was so kind. After a while he spoke soothingly to her.

'You've had too much to cope with my love. You don't have to make any decisions about anything at this very moment.' All Emmie heard was, 'my love' and suddenly she felt calmer. She smiled back at him.

'My grandmother is such a lovely woman, she's so good. It just isn't fair that she had to suffer such an injustice when she was so young. It has had a negative impact on her whole life. One thing I am fairly sure about is that if she had brought a child into the world, she would want to know about it. She would want to make some reparations, get to know him. I mean, it wasn't his fault that he was born into such deprived circumstances. Then the poor little mite was shipped off to another continent never knowing his real mother. Was he even told he was adopted? However, there is one aspect of all this that troubles me. What if this son looks just like his father, Pickard, you know the chap who raped my grandmother? She would find it hard to warm to him under those circumstances.'

'We have a lot to think about, Emmie, but no decisions have to be made immediately. I'm due to go back to Canada at the end of this week and with your permission I will try to find the adoption agency over there. It may no longer exist, but even so I will try and locate the records. I think under the law they are duty bound to keep them for a certain number of years. Then maybe I could find this chap and see what he's like and report back to you. There are so many things to consider. We have to think about how this will affect your grandmother as well as the way it will affect her newly discovered son. Incidentally, we have christened him 'Tom' for now; we felt that he did at least deserve a name!'

Emmie smiled, she was delighted that Paul wanted to help her and wanted to be involved. She was so grateful that she had the support of both Paul and Katy. Events were moving too fast for her to cope. She needed some steady, sensible help. Lost in her own thoughts, she suddenly realised that Paul was still speaking.

'Tom has rights as well, you know. We need to consider them.' Emmie nodded in agreement. 'Then we have to think about your father and his sister, it is quite difficult, I imagine, having a brother suddenly thrust upon you in middle age. But Emmie whatever happens I want you to know that you are not alone in this anymore, you've got me and I'm not going away, alright?' Emmie nodded dumbly, 'I'll write as soon as I get to Canada. Ok?'

Emmie simply gulped and nodded, but she wasn't at all sure what he meant. Did he mean that he would be there to support her over finding this man or did he mean a little more than that? She couldn't be sure. Anyway they finished their meal deep in conversation. As they left, Paul paid the bill and they walked to the car. He opened the door for her and helped her in then leaned in and kissed her, saying:

'I've wanted to do that all the way through lunch.'

Florence 1916

'Oh I wish that I could think my head is so jumbled. They've told me I'm ill, my father and that terrible man. They say that I've imagined all that has happened to me. They keep telling me that Dr. Pickard is a good, religious, man. But I know differently, he's evil, he's the devil. He's cast a spell over Father. I'm the only one who knows he's the devil. He punished me. I know he did, but I can't think, I can't think what I did wrong. They won't believe me. They say I've been wicked with the village boys, but I don't know any village boys. I wish my head would stop aching.

I keep stumbling. I keep dropping things as well. I can't see clearly, everything is blurred. I want to sleep all the time and I spill my food down my clothes. That terrible man keeps injecting me with medicine to make me better, but it makes me worse. I am so afraid of him, I want Mama. They say I'll kill her if I see her that I will give her my disease. I don't want to kill Mama, I love her. Where is Sarah? Oh my head aches so.'

Emmie 1976

Paul and Emmie chatted easily on the short journey to the hospital. She was glad of the diversion. Talking to Paul calmed her. She was extremely nervous about actually seeing the hospital that she had only heard or read about until now. She was especially nervous since she learned of the existence of her grandmother's son. What kind of an impact was that going to have on the family? Oh well she would have to take it all one day at a time.

As Paul slowed down and indicated, she realised that they were approaching the entrance to the hospital. They pulled off the road and Emmie looked out at what appeared to be the old hospital gatehouse. It was a most peculiar little building with its chateau style roof and turret tower on the side. Sarah had mentioned seeing it when she and Martha visited Florence for the first time. Martha said it looked like Rapunzel's tower and Sarah did think that it had a fairy tale quality about it that was rather odd in this setting. Emmie pointed it out to Paul, who laughed and said the architect must have had a warped sense of humour. He drove slowly through the open gates. They were neglected now through lack of use; they hung oddly on their hinges and were starting to rust in places, as they hadn't been painted for some time. Weeds and wild flowers choked their base. It seemed a sad ending. They were once powerful prison gates and marked the boundary between those who were judged to be fit to mix in normal society and those who weren't. Paul drove carefully down the winding hospital drive. Large rhododendron bushes obscured the view and there were patients wandering about.

Florence 1916

It is night time. They have told me that they are taking me to the infirmary, a strange man and woman. We are in a horse drawn carriage; it rocks about so I feel sick and we seem to have driven for miles. They won't talk to me. Suddenly we are slowing down and stopping, he is getting out. There is a moon so I can see a strange little house like a castle. Maybe I am ill and imagining everything. The gates are creaking open and suddenly we are driving through. They clang shut behind us. Why are there gates? Does the infirmary have gates? Suddenly a large building looms up; I can't see it all from the carriage. I am afraid, where am I? I wish Mama were here. We've stopped again at the front of the enormous building. The man has jumped out and rung a bell, I can hear it echoing, inside the building. Keys jangle and scrape in a lock and suddenly the large door is opened by a woman in a uniform. She is holding a lamp. The woman in the carriage tells me to stand up, but I don't think I can. I feel so sick. He comes back to the carriage, they tell me again to stand, I can't so they help me, but they are rough.

I stumble up the steps to the door, supported by the man and the woman. We step into a huge cave. It is dark. Gas lamps make our long thin shadows dance all over the walls and ceiling; they dance and dance like spectres at the feast. The door shuts with a clang. I hear the jangle of keys again as they turn in the lock. We move forwards and walk across the wide expanse of floor. The woman with the lamp leads, our footsteps echo and our shadows dance. They look so funny, I laugh and the man tells me to be quiet. I stumble and the woman grabs my arm and holds it tight. I want to laugh out loud and scream, because I am so afraid, but I know I shouldn't so I laugh quietly to myself; it stops me *being so frightened.*

Perhaps I'm dreaming and am really still in bed at home. I don't know. Is this the infirmary? I can't tell. The four of us, with our shadows as partners, dance into the smaller room, but the shadows do not dance in here, they shrink to nothing. The woman in the uniform takes another key from her belt and opens a huge door. The other woman still has hold of me. We pass through the door and there it is the corridor of fate; it stretches before me like the River Styx. I feel like one of the dead as they enter the darkness of Hades. That's it, of course, Hades, hell, the man is Charon, the ferryman and the women are the Furies and I am the walking dead. The corridor river stretches for miles; it is dark and cold. We glide along with the ferryman. A foul stench assails my nostrils, of stale food, unwashed bodies, urine and carbolic soap. I retch and vomit. The Fury is angry and shakes me. We glide on down the corridor. The shadows are back, but they don't dance. They pour themselves all over the walls and ceiling. Like ghouls, slithering and sliding and occasionally disappearing into doorways set into the walls, then slithering out again to enclose us. They are our escort down the corridor. I hear screams and shouts from behind the doors. Are they lost souls shouting for redemption? The sound is terrible and it makes me shake, but we mustn't stop, not yet. On and on we glide, the shadows wreathing around us, on and on. Where will we stop?

Emmie 1976

Paul pulled up outside the main building of the hospital and walked around to the passenger side of the car to open Emmie's door. He helped her out then locked the car. As she climbed out, Emmie examined the building. She was totally overwhelmed and so was Paul. They stood in front of an enormous red brick building topped with a massive chateau-style tower. Sarah had described it to her, but no words were really adequate to describe this outlandish building with its huge proportions and mix of styles. She realised that her reaction to the building echoed Sarah and Martha's reaction and even Katy's, when they first saw it. The only difference was that Sarah was afraid of entering the building in case they never let her out again. She was imbued with the Victorian's deep seated terror of being confined in the asylum. She was also afraid of seeing how the years in the asylum had affected Florence. Emmie had nothing to fear, she was merely curious, but it still made her feel anxious.

The massive oak door was now kept permanently open and a user friendly glass entrance had been fitted into the doorway. This was now the entrance to the building and Paul pulled the heavy glass door open and stepped aside to allow Emmie to enter first. She walked into a large entrance hall that looked like an enormous public convenience. Emmie couldn't work out immediately why it looked like a lavatory, then she realised that it was the tiles. They were white, glazed, brick shaped tiles that were used in all public lavatories before the Second World War. To break the monotony of the wall of surgical white, the designer had placed a raised tile with a green stripe half way up each wall. Emmie breathed in the familiar smell of disinfectant and stale cooking, the standard smell of all Victorian institutions. It was a cloying smell that mingled with a musty smell of dampness and it reminded her of her school days.

Katy had arranged to meet them in the entrance hall, but she was nowhere to be seen so they simply sat on an old wooden bench set into the wall for visitors and waited. It wasn't long before Katy appeared in the doorway, red in the face and very out of breath. She had been working at her desk and forgotten the time. She was most apologetic. They chatted for a little while and Paul informed Katy that he had told Emmie all about Florence's living son. Katy put her hand on Emmie's sleeve as a gesture of sympathy and Emmie managed a wan smile. She arranged to see Emmie after the hospital visit to talk over the various options that they had open to them. Paul told her that he had already offered to try and locate the adoption agency in Ottawa and she threw him a grateful smile. She then had to hurry them to the wards as they needed to have had their tour before tea was served at four o'clock and it was getting late.

Katy guided them across the large entrance hall into a smaller hallway and then onto the long corridor. The whole place was overwhelming. Emmie found it hard to imagine any government department funding a building on this scale in the late twentieth century; it must have cost a fortune. The corridor was reputedly the longest in Europe, it was a third of a mile long, or so Katy had told Emmie. She could well believe it. She asked Paul and Katy to stop at the top of the corridor while she looked down towards the end. She just wanted to try and imagine what her grandmother must have felt when she looked down that awesome corridor. She had so many unanswered questions, yet she knew that she could never ask her grandmother how she felt as she entered the asylum. That was something that she had to try and imagine herself. Sarah had said she had been drugged with something called chloral hydrate so her senses would not have been as sharp as normal. Nevertheless, she must have been terrified and fully aware that she was beyond the help of anyone, including her mother and Sarah. She was completely at the mercy of those two perverted men. It was hard to imagine being a woman in a world where you had no voice, no legal power and no status. The powerlessness that Florence felt must have been echoed in the inability of Martha and Sarah to do anything to help her. Emmie thanked God that times had changed for women.

Emmie looked at the huge oak doors with their massive locks. They were wedged permanently open now and the corridor had been brightened up. Emmie shut her eyes and used all her powers of imagination to try and envisage it as it must have been. She wanted to put herself in her grandmother's skin, to try and imagine how she felt as she gazed down that never ending corridor. It was strange really, but the corridor wasn't improved by the user-friendly pastel colours and plastic flowers that had been used to soften its image. It was easier to imagine it dark and threatening. Katy and Paul seemed to know instinctively what was going through Emmie's head, so they waited while she tried to imagine how it had been, then walked beside her in silence. Emmie drank in every detail. The height of the corridor, the smells, the way the light slanted across the top of the corridor, so it always seemed quite dark. The massive oak double doors to the wards were wedged open now, like the doors at the head of the corridors. Nevertheless, she couldn't avoid seeing the large bolts and locks. When they were locked shut, the corridor must have seemed like an endless tunnel. It was a chastening experience for her.

Emmie was also trying to cope with the not altogether welcome news that one of her grandmother's sons had survived in this place. She was reassured by Paul's earlier offers of help, but she was still finding it hard to deal with all the emotions that the discovery of this son had dredged up. She decided that she had to forget about the problems that lay ahead for the time being. This afternoon belonged to her grandmother and the time spent in this institution. As far as it was possible, Emmie wanted to retrace her grandmother's steps and try to imagine how she had felt.

As she walked down the corridor she wondered if anyone explained to her grandmother what was going on. Did she know where she was or why she was there? She doubted it. Only one week had passed since she received the letter from her grandmother asking her to house sit Chestnut Lodge. It was only a week since she had read Martha's journals and started on her journey of discovery and she felt as if she had lived another lifetime. She had moved from the world of a girl to the world of a woman. She had seen, for the first time, how really tragic life can be. Wars and hatred, imprisonment and death, these were daily occurrences for her grandmother's generation. She thanked God that she had never had to survive a world war or an abusive parent.

Suddenly, Katy's voice woke Emmie from her reverie. They had reached their destination.

'Here we are, Buttercup Ward, or Ward Four as it used to be.'

Paul looked at his sister in amazement, 'Buttercup

Ward? Whoever thought that one up? They must have had a warped sense of humour.' All three of them smiled as they entered the ward through the large open double doors. Emmie felt quite sick with apprehension. She was now going to see the ward where her grandmother lived during her years in the asylum. It was going to be quite a journey of discovery and she hoped that it would help her to have a deeper understanding of what her grandmother had suffered.

Florence 1916

Charon and the Furies have stopped. She's taken a key from her belt and is now opening another door. She turns and takes my arm and we enter a narrow corridor. The smell of carbolic soap and humanity is strong in here and it is much warmer than in the corridor. We walk down and down. Women seem to materialise from everywhere to stare at me. They are very odd looking, some have open, slack, mouths, and some have no teeth. They try to touch my dress. They are not normal; they are mad women; lunatics; Am I to be locked away with lunatics? Is this my father's plan? Did he really hate me so deeply? I want to scream and scream but when I open my mouth no sound will come. The Fury in the uniform pushes them away. Another woman comes out of a side room. She smiles and calls me Mary. Who is Mary? I am Florence, but I won't tell them. I won't tell them anything because I refuse to be here. I won't play their little game. Mary may be here, whoever she is and she can have my body, but I will never be here. From this moment I shall inhabit a silent universe. I can't exist here so I shan't.

Emmie 1976

They walked down the corridor past the enormous dormitory towards Sister Parkinson's office. Some of the ladies were lying on their beds, probably having an afternoon nap. Sister Parkinson came out to meet them. She was a striking woman and Emmie liked her straight away. Katy had told her about Florence's experience, so she knew who Emmie was and she realised that it must be quite an ordeal for the girl to visit the ward where her grandmother was kept. She would do her best to make the visit as easy as possible. After Katy had introduced her to Emmie and Paul, she told them that she would show them around the ward first and then they could have a cup of tea and a chat in her office. She took them through the refectory and into the day room. There seemed to be hundreds of elderly ladies in there. Most of them were sitting in high backed, green plastic, institutional chairs, which were lined against the walls, They were surrounded by a forest of chrome contraptions, Zimmer frames, walking sticks and other complex aids to walking. All the women seemed to know Katy. Some smiled and waved and others stopped her to talk. Emmie was very impressed with her calm response to all of them. She seemed to have great patience and empathy.

Emmie tried to see the ward as it had been in her grandmother's time. It wouldn't have been as pleasant with pretty curtains and paintings. It would have been far more functional with dark paint and heavy fabrics. The patients would have been a mixture of young and middle aged women then; they wouldn't have had time to grow old. The fireplace was still there, but it was no longer in use. The gaping hole where the grate was now held an arrangement of dusty looking dry flowers. The ward was now heated from a central system, which was very effective. Emmie tried to picture Florence sitting there in front of the fire, wrapped in her shawl. She tried to see her isolated little figure rocking to and fro and suddenly it came to her in a flash. Florence had never really been there. She had retreated into a parallel universe and she had survived there until she was discharged. The thought gave Emmie a great deal of comfort. Up to this point she had imagined that her grandmother had spent her years in the hospital in a state of hopeless despair, but she had tempered that hopelessness with a sense of denial.

As Emmie observed the ward, locked in her own thoughts she felt someone pull at her jacket, quite urgently. She turned around to find it was a patient. She was very old, but she still had the remnants of great beauty. She had large dark eyes, wonderful bone structure and a halo of pure white, naturally curly hair. She was looking up at Emmie with wonderment, her eyes filled with unshed tears. She said something that Emmie couldn't quite hear, so she knelt down. In a cracked elderly voice she heard her saying; 'Mary, is it you Mary? Have you come back to see me?' Emmie was stunned and not a little confused. She couldn't answer the lady, who just stared at her and held out her hand. As she realised what had happened Emmie grasped it.

Katy and Sister Parkinson had noted the look of confusion on Emmie's face as she took the old lady's hand and knelt by her chair so they wandered over to that part of the ward. Katy knelt opposite Emmie on the other side of her chair and Sister Parkinson just stood watching. The old lady was Caroline one of Katy's favourites, so she asked gently, 'What was that Caroline, what did you say to the lady?'

'It's Mary, Katy, Mary come back to see me. They took her away you see, we didn't know where. She was dumb, she never spoke, but she was kind and we were friends. She was the only friend I had here and they took her away last year.'

Sister Parkinson immediately realised what had happened. It was unbelievable really. Caroline had been on the ward for so long that she would have actually been a patient in the hospital with Florence, or Mary as she had been known then. They would have been young women in those days and probably befriended each other. Because of Emmie's uncanny resemblance to her grandmother, Caroline thought she was actually seeing her friend Mary. She thought that she had come back to visit her. Caroline was nearly ninety and had a touch of dementure. She had simply regressed when she saw Emmie; she thought that she was seeing her friend, Mary, Emmie's grandmother. Sister Parkinson took Katy's place by Caroline's side and spoke to her gently, 'This is Mary's granddaughter, Caroline, not Mary herself.' But she wasn't listening. She was just gazing at Emmie through her tears and grasping her hand tightly. Emmie hadn't said a word, she was too choked.

'You came, I knew you'd come, I'm so glad. I needed to tell you, I found something out. After they took you away I was sent to work in the infirmary. The orderly who nursed you after your confinement was still working there. She remembered you quite clearly and she knew that you were my friend. She told me. It lived, Mary. I know they didn't tell you. It lived, a boy. The orderly nursed it till they sent it away.'

Emmie leant forward and hugged the old lady, 'I know, I found out,' was all she said and Caroline looked at her in wonderment.

'You can speak, when did you start to speak?'

Emmie was so choked herself that she couldn't say any more. She just held Caroline whose birdlike little face was alight with joy. Emmie sat with her for a while, but eventually Caroline seemed to forget she was there and sank back into her own world. At this point, Sister Parkinson signalled a retreat to her office for tea. She had not anticipated that anything as dramatic as this would happen. It never occurred to her that there would be patients on the ward who still remembered Florence and that Emmie might be mistaken for her grandmother by one of them. However, with the benefit of hindsight it made sense as the physical resemblance between the grandmother and granddaughter was quite striking. Once Caroline had mistaken Emmie for her grandmother there was little that Sister Parkinson could do. She was afraid that the shock of meeting one of her grandmother's contemporaries might be too great a shock for Emmie and she felt responsible. She certainly looked drained. She was so pale that Sister Parkinson gave her a small medicinal brandy when they got back to the office.

'What happened then?' asked Katy. 'I've never seen anything like that before.'

'I've seen something similar, but not quite the same.' responded Sister Parkinson.

'All I can think is that Caroline must have known Florence as Mary when she was a patient here. They would both have been young girls and naturally drawn to one another. And Katy as you have pointed out so many times my dear, Caroline should never have been put in here in the first place. They were probably the only two sane teenagers on the ward and befriended each other. Florence must have been Caroline's only point of contact during those years. Seeing Emmie here, who you tell me is very like her grandmother, simply triggered her long term memory. It is quite amazing. Are you terribly upset my dear? I am really sorry that this had to happen.'

'Being mistaken for my grandmother you mean? Well I must admit to being rather shaken at first, but when I got over the shock I found that it was comforting to think that she had someone in here that cared about her, a friend of her own age. I just wish that Caroline's family had cared enough to have her discharged.'

'Extraordinary, amazing,' was all Sister Parkinson could say, 'All that nonsense she spoke about someone being alive in the infirmary did that make any sense to any of you?'

'Oh indeed, it made very great deal of sense,' responded Katy and she proceeded to tell Sister Parkinson about her discovery in the archives the day before, tactfully omitting to mention that she had 'borrowed' the birth certificates.

'You know this kind of thing has happened a few times since the asylum became a hospital and was opened to the public. As you know many women were put in here for someone else's convenience and simply left to rot, forgotten about by friends and family alike. No one dare talk about them at home and they existed here in a twilight world. Then suddenly in the last few years, as the hospital has actively encouraged visitors for long term patients, long lost relatives have suddenly turned up. I remember on one of the male wards, a charge nurse discovered that one of the old men he was nursing was his grandfather! The family told him that the old man had died of wounds in the First World War, but he had been locked away, suffering from shell shock. They were ashamed. It was such a terrible stigma to have a relative in here. People immediately thought that insanity ran in the family so rather than admit that they were in here they simply 'killed them off.' It was very sad really. That charge nurse was furious with his family and had his grandfather discharged into his care. Well, what an afternoon we've had. I don't suppose either of you'll be volunteering to visit any of my ladies after this.'

'Oh on the contrary,' retorted Emmie, 'I am going to adopt Caroline. If it gives her any pleasure to think that her old friend Mary is coming to visit her after all these years, then I intend to give her that pleasure. I think she deserves that at the very least. Just look at what has happened to her, the half life that she has led.' Sister Parkinson beamed.

'That's very kind of you, though I am surprised. I would have thought that you would want to put any memory of your grandmother's time here behind you. I think that you're quite a remarkable young woman Miss Clayton. Katy and Paul smiled their agreement and Emmie, thoroughly embarrassed, blushed furiously.

After all the excitement, the four of them sat chatting for a while in the office. Emmie, Katy and Paul wanted Sister Parkinson's advice about what to do about Florence's surviving son. She was in agreement with Paul. She felt that they should try to find him first and talk to him. He had a right to know who his mother was and they should be aware that he may be trying to trace her. It would be awful if he succeeded and just turned up one day and they hadn't even told her of his existence. None of them had even thought of that possibility, but it had to be taken into consideration.

Eventually, they took their leave of Sister Parkinson and wandered back up the long corridor. When they got back to the entrance hall, they said goodbye to Katy, who returned to her office. Paul then ran Emmie back to Chestnut Lodge. She invited him in, but he declined. He was flying back to Canada the following evening and he was trying to see as much of his parents as he could. He intended to start looking for 'Tom' as soon as he returned to Canada and he promised to keep in close touch with Emmie. He got out of the car and walked round to help her out then gave her long hug and a swift kiss on the lips before climbing back into his car and disappearing down the drive.

Emmie felt curiously flat when she entered the house. She was drained and confused. Her time with Paul had been fleeting and she wanted to believe that he cared about her, but she wasn't sure whether he was just being kind and sympathetic. She wandered into the little sitting room and started to light the fire and suddenly found herself in floods of tears. She sobbed and sobbed, for herself, for her grandmother, for Martha and Sarah and all the family members that had been affected by Josiah's cruelty. She cried until she couldn't cry any more, then she stood up, walked into the kitchen, splashed her face with cold water and patted it dry on a towel. Afterwards she felt better; it was as if all the lurid discoveries about her grandmother's past had been bottled up inside and needed to be released. Then on top of that she was trying to cope with her mixed feelings for Paul. She was terrified that she had misunderstood his kindness as something more. If he was just behaving as the brother of a close friend then she needed to be careful not to read more into it, but how she hoped that there was more. Well there was no point in dwelling on it, only time would tell and she had other problems to face. She still had to tell her father what she had found out. They had made arrangements to meet the day after tomorrow and she really wasn't looking forward to it.

Chapter Twenty Five

Paul was glad to be back in Ottawa in many ways. He never ceased to be amazed by the sheer size of Canada. In this huge country with its small population there was enough space for everyone to have their own place in the universe. Life was far less stressful, travel was easy, the freeways were nearly empty and traffic was light. There was room to breathe and develop without being closeted with your neighbour. The sky seemed larger than in Britain and it covered the land like a protective blue umbrella, under which the light was somehow clearer and seemed to sharpen one's perceptions. Even when the vicious Canadian winter set in, it didn't seem to be as grey and depressing as a British winter. It had a harsh brightness about it. Paul loved it.

With its European influence, Ottawa was a particularly

beautiful city. The parliament buildings betrayed the French influence that had dominated Canada in the past. They were designed to look like a large French chateau and they dominated the skyline of the capital giving a feeling of age and maturity. The Rivers Ontario and Rideau met at and flowed through the city giving it a feeling of being in perpetual motion. Britain was home and would remain so, but this magnificent country would always hold a special place in his heart.

Once away from Liverpool he had time to think, especially about Emmie. From the past, he remembered her as a rather striking looking school friend of his sister's, but no more than that. However, when he met her again during his visit home she made a deep and lasting impression upon him. He realised that he hadn't spent very much time with her and he had no idea whether she returned his feelings, but he found that she was on his mind more than he would have liked. He had only been home for one short week and it would be foolish to try to build an entire future on that, but he was allowing things to move on in his mind. He hoped that their relationship would develop. However, he realised that what she needed from him at the present time was practical help and support in tracing Florence's son.

The first thing he did, once he had settled back into his work, was to locate the address of the adoption society that Katie had given him. He drew a complete blank there. He found the location of the society, but the building had been completely demolished during the 1960s. However, he was sure that the records would have been stored somewhere and preserved. He asked the records clerks at the hospital if they had any idea where they might be stored, but no one could help him.

That was as far as he got initially, unfortunately once he was back at work he was kept busy. During the first week he had to catch up on his case load and there wasn't really time to concentrate on anything else. Then quite unexpectedly, in the middle of the second week, he received a phone call from Mavis. She was the chief records clerk at the hospital and she had been on holiday when he made his original enquiries in the department. On her return one of the other clerks mentioned that Paul had been down to the department asking questions. When she realised that he wanted to locate old adoption records she thought she may possibly be able to help him. Before she came to work at the hospital, she'd worked for an adoption society and knew of a large central archive that held all the old records of adoption agencies that had closed. That is where she thought Paul might locate the original records that he was searching for. She rang him and gave him the name and address of the archive, together with a current telephone number. He was extremely grateful and his enthusiastic thank you obviously embarrassed Mavis, who was a middle aged spinster. He could almost feel her blushing down the phone. He made a mental note to buy her some flowers.

He finished his shift at the hospital on Friday lunchtime that week and decided to go straight over to the address that Mavis had given him. There was still a possibility that the archive had some trace of Florence's records. He took a taxi as he knew that the taxi driver had a far better chance of finding the address than he had. The taxi driver dropped him outside a modern looking building downtown. He walked into the building and looked around for some directions then he noticed that there were a number of business plaques at the side of the lift, or elevator as the Canadians called them. He smiled as he recalled how Katy had pulled his leg at his use of Canadian terms. Looking through them he soon located the archive on the fifth floor. He climbed into the lift, pressed the appropriate button and was soon gliding skywards. He felt strangely excited, a bit like a knight errant. If he helped his lady in her quest maybe she would bestow her favours on him? He would have to wait and see, but first he had to succeed.

Eventually, the lift glided to a halt and Paul stepped out a into a very modern reception area. He walked over to the desk and waited while the efficient looking secretary finished typing the document before her. When she had completed it she looked up and asked if she could help him. He explained, as well as he could, exactly what he was looking for. She asked him to wait a moment and then disappeared into an internal office. She came out some minutes later followed by an elderly lady with grey hair and a kindly smile. She knew exactly what Paul was looking for. She explained that when an adoption agency closed, for whatever reason, the records were automatically transferred to them. This created a central archive that made it easier for children to locate their birth parents should they wish to. She realised at once that he was English and assumed that he was trying to trace his natural parents or a long lost relative that had been adopted by a Canadian couple. He thought it would be easier to let her think that it was his relative that he was trying to trace so he played along. The lady, whose name was Miss March, explained that although the adoption agency he was searching for had ceased operating, its records had been preserved on micro fiche, so that they were still accessible to anyone trying to trace a relative. Paul felt a surge of hope when he heard this and asked if it would be possible for him to look through the records. She said indeed he could and asked him to follow her. She took him down a corridor and they entered a room that was obviously a library or archive room. It occurred to him that they must have thousands of adoptions on file and wondered how difficult it was going to be to trace Florence's son. She left him in the hands of a very capable librarian who efficiently found the relevant micro fiche film and set it up for him. He settled down to trawl through the hundreds of entries. He was almost cross eyed with peering at the screen. It was a difficult task as all he had to go on were the dates that Katy had given him. The records gave the name of the mother of the adopted child and the name of the adoptive parents, together with an address. They were organised in date order, not alphabetically and there were hundreds of them. All Paul could do was scan down the relevant lists and look for Mary Davies's name. He was afraid that he would miss it as it was so difficult to focus and concentrate. He felt as though he was developing word blindness when suddenly, there it was, 'Mary Davies, Granthall Asylum, Lancashire, England. Male Child.' He sighed with relief. The entry contained the name of the adoptive parents, which was Bailey, together with an address in Ottawa. He was elated and made a careful note of it. He asked the librarian if there was any more information available and she said unfortunately not. All the information that had been recorded by the adoption society had all been transferred onto micro fiche. He thanked her, went back down the corridor and asked for

Miss March to thank her also and let her know that his quest had been successful. He then took the lift down to the ground floor and left the building.

Paul stepped out into the warm Canadian fall full of optimism. He hailed a taxi and gave the driver the address that he had extracted from the records. The driver drove him to a pleasant area known as The Glebe and pulled up outside a three storey detached house. Paul climbed out and thanked him. It was a nice house in a good neighbourhood and it reassured him. His search had been fairly straightforward up until now, but he felt his luck couldn't last. He walked up onto the front deck of the house and rang the bell. A young woman eventually answered the door. She was extremely helpful, but said she couldn't give him very much information as she hadn't lived there very long. She had never heard of a family called the Baileys, but she directed him to a house further down the street on the opposite side. She said a Mrs. Young lived there. She was in her eighties and had lived in her house since it had been built. As a consequence she knew everyone who had lived in the neighbourhood for the past fifty years. The young mother felt sure that she would be able to help. Paul thanked her and walked over the road to the house she had pointed out.

His heart was pounding with anticipation as he rang the door bell. It was opened by a large, elderly, lady. He explained his quest and she beamed. She knew exactly who he was talking about; she had known the Bailey's very well. Unfortunately she told him that they had passed on and their son, Andrew, had sold the house. His heart sank, but she carried on chatting and told him that Andrew had been an only child and a credit to them. Paul asked if she knew where Andrew was. She said no she was sorry she had no idea, but she knew that he had done well and qualified as a doctor. Paul couldn't believe his ears; this was a real piece of luck. He could look up Andrew Bailey in the medical register and it would be relatively easy to find him, or to find out what had become of him. Paul smiled to himself at the thought of Florence's son becoming a doctor, like his father, it must have been in the blood. Mrs. Young was still talking and Paul heard her say that the last time she had heard from him he was working at the City Hospital. She thought that he had qualified in orthopaedics, but she couldn't be sure. So Florence's son was a doctor and was working at the same hospital as himself, it was quite a coincidence.

As he left the house, Paul felt a sense of achievement. 'Tom' at last had an identity. He was Dr. Andrew Bailey. It was quite uncanny, Dr. Bailey, Paul could have met him in the course of his work at City Hospital and been totally unaware of the significant part that he was going to play in his life. As he worked in the emergency outpatients' clinic he referred patients to every department in the hospital including orthopaedics. He knew most of the consultants there, but the name Bailey was not familiar to him. Still it was a huge hospital and the fact that Paul didn't know him did not mean that he was no longer working there. As soon as he got back to the hospital he intended to find out whether Andrew Bailey was still employed in orthopaedics. He now felt fairly confident of finding him. If he had transferred to another hospital, personnel would have a record of where he'd gone and would forward a letter from Paul. But even if that failed, he could surely be located through the medical register. Paul was very satisfied with his day's work, but it was not over yet. He was determined to return to the hospital even though he was still off duty, because he couldn't wait to discover whether Andrew Bailey was still in Ottawa. He went straight to his office to search the medical register. He looked in the index and there was his name, Dr. Andrew Bailey, Orthopaedics, City Hospital. He snapped the book shut as a gesture of triumph. According to this year's register he was still practising in orthopaedics.

He wasn't sure what to do next. He really needed to speak to Katy and Emmie before he took any action. However, his curiosity got the better of him and as he was in the hospital he decided to see if he could at least get a glimpse of this Dr. Bailey. It was crucially important that he didn't resemble Dr. Pickard facially, as that would complicate matters terribly. Emmie had given him a fairly detailed description, so he knew what to look for. He went up to the orthopaedic department and asked for Dr. Bailey. The receptionist paged him and he came to the reception desk. Paul had prepared some make believe story about a non-existent patient of his who had been referred from the accident and emergency department. Eventually a tall, dark haired, rather pleasant looking man appeared at reception. He introduced himself as Dr. Bailey. Paul began to tell his prepared story, but he couldn't take his eyes off the man. He was so like Florence and Emmie. He had their large dark eyes and tawny skin. He also bore an uncanny likeness to Freddie. Dr. Bailey began to look a little uncomfortable under Paul's scrutiny and Paul realised that he was being rude, so he stopped staring. Dr. Bailey listened patiently to Paul's story, but quite obviously couldn't recall the non-existent patient. However, he promised that he would check with his secretary. Paul apologised and mumbled some excuse about having used a different doctor. He felt rather guilty that he had asked a busy colleague to look for a patient who didn't even exist, but it had been worth it to see what Andrew Bailey looked like. This man was obviously Florence's son, there was such a strong physical resemblance. Paul was very relieved to have discovered that he did not resemble his father, well facially he didn't anyway. He also seemed a really nice chap, though obviously you couldn't tell a lot from one brief meeting.

Paul decided to ring Emmie that evening. When he did get through she was very cool, in fact it was rather more than cool, she was quite hostile. She was very annoyed and quite upset. He had been back in Canada for two weeks and she hadn't heard a word from him. It had seemed like an eternity and she thought that once he had returned to his old life he had quite forgotten about her and her grandmother. Of course, it had never occurred to him to telephone just to reassure her and see how she was. He thought that Emmie wouldn't want to hear from him until he had something definite to tell her. She was really put out that he had taken so long to let her know what was going on. However, once she heard his extraordinary news, she forgot to be cross and became very curious. Firstly she asked for a physical description of Andrew Bailey and was very relieved to hear that he didn't seem to resemble his father. She asked Paul if he could perhaps obtain a photograph for her to look at and he said he would try. After some consideration, they both felt that

Paul should speak to Andrew and explain what was going on. It was going to be quite a task. Paul, relieved that Emmie's coolness had passed, would have agreed to anything so as not to upset her again. As he rang off he made a mental note to ring regularly.

The following day, on his return to the hospital, Paul once again went up to the orthopaedic department to ask for Dr. Bailey. He looked a little puzzled to see Paul again so soon. He thought he had made it clear to him that he had no knowledge of his patient. Paul immediately explained that he needed to see him alone. He confessed that the patient was a simply a device to enable him to contact Dr. Bailey. He explained that there was a private and sensitive matter that he needed to discuss with him. Dr. Bailey looked quite surprised. He asked what it concerned, the private matter, but Paul declined to say. Something in Paul's manner made Andrew Bailey realise that he was desperate to talk to him so he agreed to Paul's suggestion that they should meet for lunch the following day. Neither of them had the time to meet before then. They agreed to meet at a pleasant little restaurant round the corner from the hospital, away from prying eyes.

Paul had no idea really how he was going to approach the subject of Andrew Bailey's adoption. He came to the conclusion that the direct approach was the only way. Andrew was already waiting at their table when Paul arrived. He was so curious to find out what Paul wanted to discuss that he had turned up early. Paul joined him and they ordered a soft drink and a steak and salad each. Paul then took a deep breath and started to explain why he had wanted to speak to him so urgently.

'I'm sorry I barged in yesterday. I had to see you

without raising your suspicions. I have something to tell you that is of the utmost importance to you and I feel totally ill equipped for the job. I think the only thing for me to do is to come straight out and tell you what has happened. I have a sister who is a social worker at a psychiatric hospital near Liverpool, it is called Granthall Hospital.' Paul wasn't sure but he thought Andrew Bailey flinched slightly at the name of the hospital, however he carried on, 'She has a dear friend called Emmie Clayton who has just discovered that her grandmother, Florence Clayton, was committed to the hospital during the First World War. She was committed as a lunatic. I mean no disrespect; I'm simply using the terminology that was used then. She spent over two years in the asylum, although she had no psychiatric problems. Her crime was that she was pregnant and had no husband. Her family were told that she had died of an infectious disease and had no idea that she had been admitted to the asylum. Her father had her committed under a false name so that no one would be able to trace her. Florence was known in the asylum as Mary Davies.'

At his point Andrew Bailey interrupted Paul, 'I know something of this, but please carry on.'

'Well, as I said, Florence was heavily pregnant when she was admitted to the asylum. Almost immediately she gave birth in the asylum infirmary. It was a difficult birth and she was told that the child, a boy, had been still born. Emmie and Katy, my sister, decided that it would be interesting to examine Florence's in-patient file. It was still kept in the archives even after all this time. They both thought that there may be some information in the file that may be useful to them. There most certainly was. When Katy went to the archives to read the notes she was handed two files. One was the report from the infirmary detailing Florence's confinement and one was her in patient file. It was the first file that caused the surprise. It documented that Florence had been expecting twins. Even Florence herself was unaware of that fact. They were both boys and indeed one was still born, but the other, about whom she was told nothing, lived and was adopted by a Canadian family. I have reason to believe that you are that surviving twin.'

Andrew Bailey looked at him in silence for a moment and then reached into his pocket and pulled out an old yellowed form. He handed it to Paul without saying a word. Paul took it from him and opened it up. It was a birth certificate and it was identical to the one that Katy had removed from Florence's file. She had given it to Paul to take with him to Canada. She thought it would help his search. Andrew's form registered the birth of a male child born in the asylum. Paul spread out Andrew's birth certificate and the one Katy had given to him, side by side on the table cloth. They were the duplicate birth certificates of a male child born to Mary Davies in Granthall Asylum on the same day. Paul looked up at Andrew Bailey and slowly turned them both around so that he too could examine them side by side. He looked at them and then closed his eyes. He was so full of emotion that he didn't trust himself to speak. The waiter arrived at that moment with the water and the steaks. Paul ordered two whiskies to accompany them. He felt they would be needed.

Eventually Andrew Bailey, after a struggle, gained control of his emotions sufficiently to speak, 'I was always told that I was adopted, but I loved my parents and had no desire to find my real mother. That is until I found this birth certificate with my date of birth on it. It was with my adopted mother's private papers, which were given to me after she died. I felt if I made enquiries about my real mother at that point, it would be alright. I wouldn't be hurting anyone. My mother and father were both dead, I have no brothers or sisters. My wife died two years ago, suddenly of a heart attack and we had no children, so there was no one who would be affected by the discovery, other than myself. Armed with the information on the birth certificate, I decided to go to England for a vacation and see if I could discover more about my real parents. I travelled around and finally landed in Liverpool. Whilst I was there I tried to learn something about my mother. I realised, as I am nearly sixty myself, that there was always a possibility that she may be dead. In fact I was prepared for anything. But suddenly I needed to know who she was, even if it upset me. However, I am rather confused.

When I arrived in Liverpool I took the birth certificate to a records department in a general hospital. They had copies of the asylum records on micro fiche and they found a Mary Davies, who had a baby on the date stated on my birth certificate, but it said that her child had been still born. There was a copy of the death certificate and no mention of a live birth. I began to wonder if this birth certificate had nothing to do with me and it was simply a coincidence that it was in my mother's possession. I mean the records stated categorically that the child was dead and there was no mention of a twin, although the records clerk did make a joke about me being a twin. What was I to think? I didn't even know if this birth certificate belonged to me. Although instinctively I knew it did, it was too much of a coincidence that my mother should have it. Anyway I then decided to go directly to the asylum, which is now a psychiatric hospital, and make enquiries there. I saw a social worker, an elderly woman. She was the chief social worker. I asked her if she could make some further enquiries for me, but she was most unhelpful. She said that records of patients who had died or left the hospital were private and could not be accessed by the general public. I felt pretty much that I had drawn a blank and I returned to Canada the next day. Then you turn up out of the blue with this bombshell. It seems it is my birth certificate and Mary Davies is my mother.'

Paul was very annoyed on Andrew's behalf. It sounded as if the social worker was the one that Katy disliked so much, Mrs. McKendrick. Anyway, that was a problem he would address later.

'That social worker had no right to tell you that they are private. All the files are open to the general public now, as long as they can prove they have a valid reason for wanting to read them. By the way, strictly speaking Mary Davies is not your mother; your mother's name is Florence Clayton, or Florence Kingsley, which is her married name.'

'This becomes more of a mystery all the time. I think you better tell me all about my mother and her family. Do you think that she will want to see me? Would it be too much of a shock?'

'I think there is one thing I have to tell you. You haven't enquired about your father at all.'

'No well I kind of thought he was unknown.'

'No, he was known. There is no easy way to tell you this, he actually raped your mother when she was a fifteen year old girl and she became pregnant as a result.'

Andrew Bailey looked stricken and it was some moments before he could speak, 'Hell, that's kind of hard to take in. So that's how she came to be pregnant? Why did her father allow her to be put in an asylum, I mean it wasn't her fault.'

'The man who raped her was an elder of the church. He said she was lying, that she had been playing up to the village boys. Her father had always somehow distrusted her, she was extremely beautiful and his warped form of Puritanism placed beauty and sin in the same box. She was beautiful therefore she was promiscuous. He believed the rapist. He had her certified as morally insane and committed to Granthall as a punishment. As I have already explained, he told her mother that she was dead. That's the main reason that he had her committed under an assumed name, Mary Davies, so that she could never be traced.'

'Gee, that's rough. I don't know what to say. This presents the whole problem in a new light. I'm not sure she would want to see me, a child conceived under those circumstances, what if I resemble my father? What a mess, nevertheless I will do whatever you want me to do. I won't pretend that this latest development hasn't been upsetting, but it hasn't diminished my desire to see my mother, I sure as hell want to meet her.'

'There is one more thing I haven't told you, Florence is now seventy six and she has been diagnosed with lung cancer. She is still fairly well in herself, I believe, but she hasn't got long to live.'

'So I haven't got time to mess about.'

'Not really. Look can I make a suggestion? What if we sent Emmie a set of photographs of you? She knows someone who actually knew your father and could confirm whether or not you resemble him. This is a terrible thing to do to you. I mean you must be devastated by this news already without us making you run some kind of eligibility test.'

'Yea it has been quite a shock, but I quite understand the sensitivity of the issue. This poor lady is at the moment unaware that she even has a son, let alone one who may remind her of a terrible time in her life. Let's do it. Send the photos, even arrange for me to meet this lady if necessary and if she feels that meeting me won't upset my mother too much, then hell I can finally meet her. How fantastic would that be?

'Very fantastic,' smiled Paul, who was beginning to like this man very much indeed.

After the meal, Andrew and Paul went back to Andrew's home and selected some photos taken at various times during his life and gave them to Paul. He immediately went downtown and posted them to Emmie. He had already spoken to her on the telephone to explain what he was doing. Emmie realised that the only person who was still alive who knew Dr. Pickard was Sarah. She would be able to tell them whether Andrew resembled his father. She was going to have to contact her anyway, because up to now she had no idea that Florence's illegitimate child had lived. Emmie also realised that Sarah was the only person who could really decide whether meeting Andrew would upset Florence or not.

Paul had told Emmie how much he liked Andrew, he

had seen quite a lot of him since their original meeting and they got on very well. He felt that Florence, Andrew and Emmie would all benefit from meeting and getting to know one another. Instinctively she knew that Paul was right. She listened carefully to him her heart full of love for this very special man who had gone to the enormous trouble of finding Andrew. He had done so much for her. If he liked Andrew then Emmie trusted his judgement. She also liked the way that Andrew was willing to step aside if he thought that meeting him may upset Florence. However, she felt that she must talk to Sarah first and ask her advice. After all she had actually been there and had a better insight than any of them about what Florence's reaction would be.

After his initial blunder, Paul kept in close touch with Emmie and informed her of all developments concerning Andrew. He also rang Katy after he spoke to Emmie. He felt that she should know about Andrew's abortive visit to Granthall in search of his mother. He was sure that the social worker he spoke to, from the description he had given Paul, was Katy's manager, Mrs. McKendrick. He told an outraged Katy what had happened to Andrew. He also advised her to tread carefully in whatever she decided to do. She must remember that Mrs. McKendrick was her senior. However, he agreed with Katy that that did not excuse her from blocking Andrew's access to his mother's file. Her behaviour was extremely unprofessional and very worrying. Katy assured Paul that she would not do anything stupid. She intended to follow the correct procedure and make a formal complaint to the right people. She had no intention of dealing with the woman herself, but she was very annoyed.

Chapter Twenty Six

Once Paul had returned to Ottawa, Emmie felt very flat. From meeting him when she was out with Katy to enlisting his help in finding Florence's son, her feelings had developed from a strong teenage crush into a mature love. Suddenly, within days, he had become an essential part of her life. It had happened so quickly she could hardly believe her own feelings and the intensity of those feelings frightened her; she was afraid that he may not return her feelings and she was afraid of being hurt. She felt that once he settled back in Ottawa he would probably make some cursory enquiries about her grandmother's lost son and then forget Emmie even existed. It didn't help her mood when he failed to ring during the first few weeks. Since then, however, he had somehow miraculously found Andrew Bailey, he had kept in close contact with her, he seemed to be concerned about her and was taking a serious interest in her affairs. She began to relax a little and to enjoy the wonderful feeling of elation that she felt whenever she heard his voice. She had had a very difficult time and she was also very tense about having to tell her father everything that she had discovered about her grandmother's past. She wasn't looking forward to it at all.

She knew how she was going to approach the subject. She had planned it as well as she could, rather like a military campaign or a courtroom battle. She had in her possession the document that Florence had written all those years ago to Sarah in Devon explaining to her how she had been raped. She also had the letters that Martha had written to Sarah informing her of

Florence's death and she had the committal forms that Martha found in Josiah's desk. This was so that she had written proof that would corroborate what she was telling him. She knew how Freddie's mind worked and the papers would prove that what she was telling him was the truth. As well as all this written evidence she had compiled a small collection of carefully chosen photographs to show Freddie. The photographs would make the people concerned more real to him. If they remained vague, elderly, rather shadowy figures who he couldn't picture as real people, then he would find it hard to connect with them. In turn that would make it more difficult for him to relate to Florence's past and the terrible tragedy that had befallen her.

She had arranged for Freddie to call round to Chestnut Lodge on the Friday evening after Paul left for Canada. She carefully set the scene by placing a decanter full of whisky, a glass and an ashtray next to his favourite chair. She felt sure that he would need a drink. Eventually she felt ready to meet him and sat calmly while she waited for him to arrive. Freddie as usual was prompt and arrived, as arranged, at seven o'clock. Emmie felt really sorry for him as he had absolutely no idea what he was about to hear. He entered the house in his usual blustering manner, still complaining that he hadn't heard from his mother. She took him through to the little sitting room, poured him a large whisky and sat him down. He caught her determined mood almost immediately. As he took a drink from his glass he cast her a questioning glance. He realised almost at once that he was here for a serious purpose. Emmie had something to tell him and he instinctively knew that it was not something pleasant.

'What's the matter Emmie? There's something wrong I know there is. I can see it in your face.'

'I've got something to tell you, Dad, and I think it is going to shock you.'

'My God you're not pregnant are you?'

Emmie wondered why men, particularly fathers, always thought if young women had 'something to tell' them, they must be pregnant! If it hadn't been such a serious occasion Emmie would have laughed and teased her father, but she didn't she just shook her head.

'No Dad, I'm not pregnant, but I have got something to tell you, which is going to take some time and I'm afraid will give you a bit of a jolt. Just listen and bear with me while I tell you the full story'

By now Freddie was more than a little apprehensive and threw her a very concerned look. In his experience problems usually concerned sex or money. Well they'd dealt with sex. So was it money? Emmie was never extravagant so he wasn't too concerned that it might be about money. Suddenly he had a momentary flash of insight. Death, of course, his mother, yes it must be something to do with his mother.

'Is mother dead? Has she died suddenly abroad, alone? I knew this would happen. I just knew it would. I told you she shouldn't just go off on her own like that.'

'No Dad, calm yourself I haven't heard from Gran, although this does concern her. Now listen to me carefully and hear me out before you say anything else. When Gran asked me to look after the house, in her absence, she asked me to sort out some papers for her. They were kept in an old tin deed box in the boot room. What she was actually doing, without me realising it, was starting me on a quest, which led me to find out the truth about her past life. What happened to her then was so traumatic that I don't think that she could ever talk about it, except to grandfather. However, I don't think she wanted to die without us all knowing the full story. I think she particularly wanted you to know, but you were the one person that she found difficulty in talking to. I think she was afraid that you wouldn't believe her and she couldn't have stood that.

Basically Dad, when Gran was fifteen years old she was raped by one of the elders of her father's church. It happened after Sunday School when she was in his care and under his protection and it was an appalling breach of trust. She was so young and so innocent that she didn't even know exactly what had taken place, only that this awful man had hurt her. As a result of this rape she became pregnant. Martha, her mother, thought that she was just ill and sent her to stay with Sarah, Grandpa Edward's sister, in Devon and it was there that Sarah discovered the truth.'

Freddie had been very quiet up to this point, but he couldn't contain himself any longer and interrupted, as Emmie knew he would. 'What is this nonsense Emmie? Where did you get all this from? You know it can't be true, someone would have told me or your Aunt Elizabeth before now if it were.'

Emmie didn't reply, she simply handed him the piece of paper, written in Florence's hand that described the rape. She knew her father would recognise his mother's writing, even if it was an immature hand. She also knew that there was no point in arguing with him. He would not believe anything without proof. He took the piece of paper from Emmie and searched in his top pocket for his spectacles. With them perched on the end of his nose he started to examine the document. It took him some time, so Emmie went into the kitchen to pour herself a glass of wine. When she returned he had finished and was just looking pensively into the fire. He waved the piece of paper at Emmie as she entered.

'I suppose that this is genuine?' Emmie nodded. 'It looks like mother's writing, but it's quite immature, but then it would be. I don't know. What a dreadful thing to happen, appalling. I can hardly believe it. I hope he was punished. She was telling the truth, wasn't she? I mean it wasn't just a young girl's imagination. You know what they can be like.'

Emmie was beginning to realise why Florence had left her the task of telling her father. Whilst his reaction might exasperate her, it would have emotionally wounded Florence. 'Dad, of course it's true. She was too sexually naive to make up such a story. Sarah gave it to me. It was Sarah who told me the whole story when I went to stay with her in London.'

She was amused to see her father look uncomfortable when she used the phrase 'sexually naïve'.

'I didn't know you'd seen Sarah, when did that happen?'

'I went to London last weekend to see her. I had some questions that I needed answering. When I started to investigate the contents of the box I read Martha's journals. Martha was Gran's mother, as you probably know. Her journals came to an abrupt and rather disturbing end and I was really curious to find out why. Sarah was the only person who could tell me. I think that Gran actually intended me to go to Sarah. She was the only person left who knew the full story you see.'

'Didn't mother tell her parents what had happened?'

'No Dad, she didn't fully understand the consequences of what had happened to her. She was also afraid of not being believed. It made her ill. No one understood what was wrong with her. In desperation Martha, your Grandmother, sent her to stay with Sarah, who was living in Devon. Don't forget in 1916 we were in the middle of a world war. Anyway to cut a very long story short, Sarah discovered Florence had been raped and was pregnant and she told her husband, Charles, obviously. He insisted that Josiah, your grandfather, be informed, as he was Florence's legal guardian. Charles arranged to meet him in London and told him the whole story. He and Sarah felt that Gran should stay in Devon, have the child and then come home and no one would be the wiser. Josiah would not agree. He wanted Gran to come back to Liverpool. As he was Florence's legal guardian and next of kin they couldn't argue. By informing Josiah, Charles did what he thought was right. He couldn't really have hidden Florence's condition from Josiah and he had no idea what a warped character he really was. However, once he had told Josiah about Florence's pregnancy, he had lost control of the situation and had to agree to whatever Josiah planned.'

Freddie sat quietly listening, forcing himself not to interrupt and Emmie continued, 'Josiah took Florence home and he told Martha that Florence was seriously ill with an infectious disease. When she returned home he would not allow Martha to see her. After a few days had passed, he lied again to Martha and told her that Florence's condition had deteriorated to such an extent that she had to go to the infirmary. He then told Martha that she had died in there.'

'What! Why on earth did he lie? What had happened

to Mother?'

Emmie handed her father two of the letters from Martha to Sarah telling her of Florence's death. He read them in silence. 'I don't understand.'

'No Dad neither did I. Sarah thought that Gran must have died in childbirth not of an infectious disease. She thought Josiah had lied to spare Martha's feelings and she played along with the deception; she didn't have the heart to tell Martha that Gran was pregnant. Martha would have been devastated if she'd known about the rape. Anyway, Sarah felt it didn't matter why Gran had died; she was too upset really to care. Everyone believed Josiah and accepted that Gran was dead. They never suspected what he had really done and until Josiah died some two and a half years later it remained his secret. After he died, whilst sorting through the papers in his desk, Martha accidentally triggered a switch hidden in one of the pigeon holes. It opened a secret drawer, which contained some papers. When she read them she realised, with a mixture of horror and relief that Gran was not dead. Josiah had had her committed to an asylum. Apparently, she had her baby in the infirmary there, but it was still born. He had craftily had her committed under a false name, Mary Davies, which was illegal, but he was an influential man. He had no trouble getting the necessary signatures. Without the papers, even if the family had suspected what had happened to her, they would never have found her.'

Emmie paused to sip her wine and Freddie just stared at her. He was obviously very shocked. 'Go on,' he said quietly, 'What happened next?'

'Well, when she discovered the papers, Martha could only assume that Gran was still an inmate in the asylum, but she had to find out for sure. As you can imagine she was devastated that her husband had deceived her in such a monstrous way. Grandfather Edward was her solicitor. He was marvellous, a real hero. He managed to confirm that Gran was fit and well physically and still an inmate in the asylum. However, he also discovered that she was totally traumatised and had not uttered a single word for over two years. She was completely dumb. After a very difficult legal tussle to prove her true identity, he finally got her discharged. He and Martha took Gran home, to Chestnut Lodge, and slowly they nursed her back to health. Edward had a deep understanding of trauma, after his war experiences, and he spent hours with Gran. He also managed to find a psychiatrist with experience of, what they called shell shock, which was really just trauma. Together the three of them nursed her back to health. Here, these are the committal papers that Martha found.'

She handed Freddie the committal papers, he took them from her and slowly started to look through them. He was devastated, she could tell. She had decided that she had to blurt out the story as quickly as she could and give him the backup evidence and she had been right. It was the only way to tell him. Although he was a typical barrister and it took him time to absorb facts and make decisions, she could see that he fully accepted her version of events. He was just having difficulty absorbing the full implication of what had happened to his mother and he was very upset.

He kept reading the different papers and sipping his whisky, taking time to refresh his drink. He kept shaking his head in disbelief. He did express doubt just one more time, but it was without conviction. 'There is no doubt

I suppose that it really happened, the rape I mean? Yes of course it did.'

Emmie couldn't believe her ears, what was it with men and rape? Perhaps most men were so inherently decent that they couldn't conceive of anyone committing such an odious crime. That being the case, they felt that women must make it up. She didn't know, but they always, in her admittedly limited experience, doubted the word of the woman until they had proof to the contrary. Again she realised, with startling clarity that Florence could not have coped with that question, 'Yes Dad it did, I've explained all that. Her father didn't believe her either, that was the problem. He thought that she was promiscuous and had made the story up. He believed Dr. Pickard, the rapist, was innocent. That's why she has never told her story since. That's why she couldn't tell you. If you'd doubted her or her story... well that was something she could never risk.'

'And true to form, I did doubt it didn't I? You are quite right. It's just so difficult to believe that anyone would do that to an innocent young girl. He must have known that it would ruin her life.'

'I don't think he cared.'

'Let me have a look at those photographs, you've shown them to me before haven't you? The other day when I visited, before you took off for London, I commented then that I looked like Josiah. My God, she must have seen him every time she looked at me. Did she hate me do you think, because I looked like him?'

Emmie's heart went out to her father; he looked like a hurt little boy, 'No love, I most certainly don't. I think that at certain times the past overwhelmed her and she had to escape into herself again. I think she loved you deeply and that love was complicated by the fact that you looked like her father. It made her feel guilty that she could confuse the two things. She also knew that her withdrawals distressed you and that upset her, but she couldn't control them. I think she suffered from guilt and was worried that she may have passed her damage onto you in some way. It hurt her to think that.'

'I did find it difficult sometimes. I never felt that she loved me completely, you know? I felt I must be doing something wrong. In a way it's a relief to know that the problem had nothing to do with me at all. She did love me didn't she?'

'Of course she did,' Emmie went over to her father and gathered him up in her arms. She just wanted to heal his hurt and confusion, 'She loved you very much, she still does.'

Emmie and Freddie talked long into the night. He was terribly upset by her revelations, but Emmie felt that it had been a therapeutic experience for him as well and that it explained many contradictions in his relationship with his mother. They talked about the various occasions when Freddie had considered Florence's behaviour hurtful and odd. Emmie had never felt so close to her father and she had never realised how vulnerable he was where his relationship with his mother was concerned. She loved him more that night than she had ever loved him before and she felt a closeness between them that was new. At two fifteen in the morning the telephone rang. It was Susan. She was frantic. She had woken up and found Freddie was still out. She thought he'd had a road traffic accident or something. He was genuinely sorry to have upset her and Emmie called for a taxi to take him home. He could collect his car in the morning.

She kissed him good night and gave him a big hug goodbye, but as he left she was very aware that there was still more he had to know. She hadn't told him of the existence of a half brother. She felt that it was too much for him to cope with. He had just discovered a new dimension to his relationship with his mother and she didn't feel he was quite ready for a contender for Florence's affection.

Chapter Twenty Seven

The morning after Emmie had told Freddie what she had discovered, she felt emotionally ready to face Sarah and tell her about Katy and Paul's discovery. She steeled herself and then picked up the phone and dialled. Once she heard Sarah's warm voice at the other end she relaxed, 'Sarah, hello, it's Emmie.'

'Emmie, my dear, how are you? How lovely it is to hear from you!'

'I was ringing to see if you have recovered from my traumatic flying visit and feel ready to come up and see us.'

Sarah laughed her lovely tinkling laugh, 'Well it took me a while, but I am fully recovered now. Are you alright? I have worried about everything that I told you. I felt that it might be too much for you to absorb all at once, but when I started to worry, I remembered that you were Florence's granddaughter and would have inherited her resilience.'

Emmie smiled to herself, 'Thank you for your faith

in me. I have to admit it was quite a shock, but I am so pleased now that I know. I feel that I only knew half a grandmother, a lovely half I admit, but only half. I now know a whole grandmother and love her all the more for it.'

'I'm so glad Emmie, so very pleased that you have reacted in that positive way and I think that you are right. We need to know all about someone before we can fully appreciate them.'

Emmie took a deep breath, she couldn't decide whether to tell Sarah over the phone or wait for her to come up to Liverpool before she broke the news about Florence's surviving son. She had agonised over her decision and finally decided to tell Sarah over the telephone. It would give her time to absorb this latest development on her own. She could think it over and decide what should be done, 'Sarah, I have something to tell you.'

'Oh no, has something happened to Florence, has she deteriorated?'

Emmie felt terrible, 'Oh no, no, nothing like that, I'm so sorry I didn't mean to alarm you I never thought... No Sarah, Gran is still away, but there have been further developments in her story. As ever in this saga there is no easy way to tell you gently so here goes. Are you ready?'

'As I'll ever be, what on earth has happened now?'

Emmie took a deep breath, 'When Florence was pregnant, she was expecting twins.'

'What!?'

'I'm afraid so, obviously she didn't know. It seems that one of the twins was still born, but the other twin lived. Florence was never told of his existence. She was never given the opportunity to see him or to hold him. The hospital authorities arranged for him to be adopted almost immediately after his birth. A Canadian adoption agency found a home for him over in Canada. Apparently there was a big move to populate the colonies after the First World War and he was sent to Ottawa.'

There was a long silence on the other end of the phone; it was some time before Sarah spoke. 'I can't believe it, how could they do that to a young mother? I am appalled. Canada you say? I vaguely remember something about a move to 'populate the colonies', as they called them then. It was after the war. Oh my dear, how did you find all this out? Are you sure that it's correct information? I mean after all this time.'

'Oh yes, it is correct. Do you remember me telling you that my friend Katy worked at Granthall Hospital as a social worker? Well as a kindness to me she went down into the archives to locate Florence's, rather Mary Davies's, records. She thought that she may find something that would comfort me; you know some information about her time in the hospital. Well what she did find was the medical report from the infirmary, detailing Florence's confinement. In it she found two birth certificates and a death certificate. There was also some information about the Canadian adoption society, but no details of the adoptive parents.'

'I honestly don't know what to say. I'm quite literally speechless. What do you think we should do? Do you think we ought to try to find this young man well he won't be so young now will he? By my calculations he'll be nearly sixty.'

'We've found him Sarah.'

'Oh Emmie, how have you managed that in so short a time? Dear me, I've got to stop saying 'oh' I'm stood here with my mouth open looking like a goldfish. How did you find him? Have you met him?'

'No I haven't met him, but a dear friend of mine has. Paul, the friend, is a doctor and works in Canada. He managed to find him. His name is Andrew Bailey. Quite coincidentally he is an orthopaedic consultant in the same hospital that Paul works in. Paul likes him very much. The strange thing is that he has been over to England to look for his real mother. He found what he thought was his birth certificate with his adoptive mother's things when she died. He had been over to England to try to find her, but the hospital were most unhelpful, so he went home empty handed. Paul had to explain the circumstances of his birth; you know the fact that Gran was raped. It was very difficult, but he took it well. His main consideration is that he doesn't want to cause Gran any distress by suddenly turning up. I suppose we are all concerned that it may remind her of what happened and none of us want to upset her. It's so difficult Sarah. Obviously, Andrew wants to meet his mother. We thought that you may be able to help us.'

'Me dear? How can I help?'

'Well we may be naive, but we thought if you could look at his photograph, even meet him, well you knew Dr. Pickard. We thought if he didn't resemble his father too much it wouldn't be such a problem for Gran. Are we being stupid?'

'On the contrary, I think you are very wise. This is a very sensitive issue and has to be dealt with very carefully. What a thing to happen. To find out that dear Florence has a son. Of course I will do anything that I can to help.

Would you like me to travel up to Liverpool?'

'Would you Sarah? I would be so grateful. I really need some help and support. There are serious decisions to be made and I can't make them alone. I am going to speak to Paul tonight and he and Andrew are going to try to get compassionate leave and fly over to England. When they arrive, perhaps you could meet him?'

'My dear, of course, I shall catch the lunch time train tomorrow. I can't leave any earlier than that; it takes me a little while to get going in the morning. I will let you know what time I arrive in Liverpool. Is that alright? I can't believe that this has happened. Emmie, you know, as the significance of your find dawns on me, I feel very optimistic. Something good has come out of that terrible episode. If your friend Paul has taken to Andrew, then maybe he's taken after his mother. We must not forget that he is the son of our wonderful Florence. I'll need a bit of time to think it through Emmie, but I think Florence would want to meet him.'

With that the two women said goodbye and Sarah went upstairs to prepare for her journey.

After speaking to Paul, Katy was beside herself with rage, she was absolutely furious. How dare that bloody woman interfere and withhold information from someone trying to trace their real mother? How dare she? Paul told her when he phoned. He purposely told her while she was at home in the evening, so she could calm down before going into work. He had cautioned her to be careful and to speak to the appropriated authorities and not take matters into her own hands. She realised that Philip's 'American' was in fact a Canadian. It was Andrew Bailey, Florence's son. What untold damage she could have done. She could have kept a mother and son apart for ever. He told her that he had no time to waste; she knew that he had to return to Canada and still she prevented Andrew from seeing his mother's files. What she had done was inexcusable.

The following day when she went into work, she avoided Mrs. McKendrick. She asked for an appointment to see the Superintendent, Mr. Evans. She was told she could see him later that morning at eleven o'clock. She did her ward rounds first then when the time came she went to Mr. Evans's office. She had to wait for a while then was ushered in by his secretary. She told him that she had come to make an official complaint, mainly about the business concerning Andrew Bailey.

Mr Evans listened very carefully to what she had to say. He then told her, in the strictest confidence that he had received several complaints of a similar nature. He told her that he was taking her complaint very seriously and would be considering further action. He asked if she could supply him with written evidence, which she agreed to do and then he thanked her and said goodbye.

She was pleased when she left the office, but also felt slightly disloyal. McKendrick was old and she may not get another job. She was confused and decided to go over and see Sister Parkinson and tell her what she had done. She needed someone to reassure her; she needed to know that she had done the right thing. She also wanted to let Sister Parkinson know what Paul had discovered in Ottawa. She was in her office when Katy arrived and as usual headed straight for the kettle with a welcoming smile. Katy told her all about Paul's successful quest in Canada and she was delighted. She also told her about Mrs. McKendrick's part in the saga and she was less pleased, 'I told you that woman was a menace ages ago. How many other people has she lied to or withheld the truth from?'

'I don't know, but I feel guilty, what if she gets the sack because of me and has no means of supporting herself?'

She smiled knowingly at Katy, 'They won't put her out on the street without a reference. Mrs. McKendrick is fifty nine years old. She is due to retire next year and in my opinion should have gone long ago. She was a passably efficient social worker, but she has no management skills and it was a mistake to promote her beyond her capabilities. They will simply 'ask' her to take early retirement and she will leave quietly. That would be my reading of the situation. They can't allow her to keep making fundamentally flawed decisions the way she has been doing. You did the right thing and you mustn't worry. She will be well cared for, the hospital will have a new social work manager and everything will turn out for the best. Now, tea, and I want to hear all about this long lost son.'

<hr/>

That evening after Emmie had spoken to Sarah she rang Paul in Canada and explained that she had contacted her. In turn he told her that both he and Andrew had applied for compassionate leave. In fact, Andrew had gone one step further and made enquiries about taking long term leave of six months or so. He felt that if all went well and he met Florence and it was a successful meeting then he would like to enjoy those last few months with her and his new found family. He didn't want to be too optimistic, but he felt that he had to make some preparations. Paul told Emmie that hopefully he would be home with Andrew in the next few days. He arranged to send her details of times and flight numbers. However, the one thing that he didn't tell her was that he had, in fact, terminated his contract in Canada.

Emmie suggested to Paul that Andrew stayed in her flat, whilst he was in England. It was empty as she was still living at Chestnut Lodge. She felt that it would give him a measure of independence and would not be as impersonal as a hotel. It would make him feel more a part of the family. The only blight to mar Andrew's visit was the dreadful concern that Sarah may feel that he looked too much like Pickard. They would have to make a serious decision about the effect that it might have on Florence if he did. Paul had assured Emmie that no matter how much Andrew wanted to meet his real mother; he was an intelligent and sensitive man who would not want to destroy the peace of an elderly woman's final months. He put her feelings first, even if it meant that he may never actually meet her. In confidence he had told Paul that the delight in finding his real family would lessen the blow of not being able to meet his mother and would be a huge bonus in itself. Naturally he ached to meet his mother and Emmie felt that he must be an exceptional man if he would forgo the experience of meeting her, in order to avoid any possibility of upsetting her. It really was a complex situation. However, as Emmie put the phone down she felt cautiously optimistic. She also felt a little glow of pleasure at the thought of seeing Paul again. She realised that it must have been difficult for him to get leave again so soon after having visited his family. She also appreciated the fact that he would be around for a while to support her during this family crisis. It was going to be a difficult few days and she still had no idea when her grandmother intended to return. Emmie calculated that she had been away for nearly four weeks and she had originally reckoned on her being away for about a month. If that was so, then her return was imminent and time was running out. However, she was sure that her grandmother would ring and warn her that she was coming home. She wouldn't just arrive unannounced.

Chapter Twenty Eight

Emmie drove to Lime Street Station to meet the London train. Sarah had telephoned from Euston to say that her train would be arriving on time at five thirty. Emmie then intended to take her to Chestnut Lodge and give her something to eat and settle her down for the night. She was very concerned that all this excitement should not be too much for an eighty two year old woman to cope with. The last thing she wanted was to be responsible for anything happening to Sarah. In the short time that she had got to know her she had become very dear to Emmie.

She parked the car and walked to the platform where the London train was expected. It drew in on time and

Sarah stepped down followed by a very handsome young man who was carrying her suitcase. He insisted on helping Sarah with it all the way to the bay where Emmie's car was parked. He then put it into the boot for them and said goodbye.

'Did you get his phone number?' Emmie joked.

'I knew you'd say something like that!' Sarah laughed, 'He was just a charming young man helping a very old lady.' Emmie smiled raising her eyebrows at Sarah.

'Sarah he was gorgeous!'

'No doubt, but the only reason he was with me was because he was kind and I was safe!! You are naughty and you're making me blush. Do you know since you arrived on my door step two weeks ago I've had nothing but excitement and adventures and do you know I find I like it!'

Emmie leant over and planted a kiss on her velvety cheek before putting the car into gear and pulling out of the station and into the oncoming traffic.

On the way to Chestnut Lodge, Sarah and Emmie discussed the new development in Florence's story. They both concluded that they couldn't decide whether it was a good thing or not. Sarah said that they really had to assess whether Florence could cope with meeting Andrew and she wouldn't be able to gauge that until she had met him. She felt it was a huge responsibility and she was taking it very seriously. Sarah was the only person left alive who remembered Pickard and as far as Emmie had been able to discover, there were no photographs of him, so any decision that they made was reliant on Sarah's memory.

It was quite dark when they arrived at Chestnut Lodge, but Emmie had left the light on in the hallway together with the porch light and they provided enough light for the two women to see what they were doing. Sarah hadn't visited her childhood home for some twenty years and she felt very nostalgic as she entered the house. After Emmie had taken her coat and suitcase, she asked if she could just wander around for a while on her own. She wanted to look in each of the rooms and revisit her memories alone. Emmie fully understood and once she had taken Sarah's things up to her bedroom she tactfully retired to the kitchen, where she started to prepare their dinner. This gave Sarah time to reclaim the house and reacquaint herself with the scenes of her youth. She slowly strolled around each of the downstairs rooms in turn, lighting the lamps as she went. So many memories came flooding back to her. In the blue drawing room she could almost envisage her parents reading in front of the fire after dinner on a Sunday evening. She almost expected them to look up and ask her if she had had a pleasant journey. It was in the far corner of the drawing room that a very nervous Charles had quite suddenly and unexpectedly dropped to one knee and asked her to marry him. He gave her quite a fright and for one awful moment she thought he had collapsed. She was so shocked when he proposed that she couldn't answer him for several minutes. However, she soon pulled herself together and accepted him, there was no danger that she was going to let that lovely man escape her and how happy they had been. She did regret the fact that they had never had a child, but it had been a wonderful marriage. She turned back into the hallway and looked towards the staircase, in her mind's eye she could see her darling brother, Edward, walking down the stairs in his brand new, rather stiff, khaki uniform. He looked uncomfortable and self conscious as though he were playing someone else's part. He was still only a child really, but he was prepared to do his duty for King and country. If she or her mother or father had known then what that duty would involve, they would have kidnapped him and imprisoned him in the cellar until the hurricane of slaughter had spent itself and the world had returned to sanity. But they were amongst the fortunate few. Edward had returned. Exhausted and quite changed, but he had come back to them.

She sat down on the hall chair and looked around. When did it happen? When did you stop being young and become old? She hadn't noticed it happening, but time had ruthlessly moved on. All those people she had loved were now dead, she was the last one, well she and Florence, but soon it would just be her. She suddenly felt very lonely. She thought about the people that she had loved in this lovely old house and came to the conclusion that you never really died until there was no one left alive who remembered you and then you slipped into oblivion. She sat for a few moments savouring her memories and then stood and went into the kitchen to join Emmie.

Before she left for the station Emmie had prepared a chicken casserole and put it into the Aga to cook slowly. As she approached the kitchen the delicious smells reminded Sarah of how hungry she was. Emmie was busy preparing the vegetables and she looked up and smiled when Sarah entered. Whilst Emmie was busy she wandered into the little pink sitting room where Florence had sat in complete silence for all those months. She could see her now, silently rocking backwards and forwards, whilst she, Edward and Martha tried to find a way to break through to her. And now this son had turned up. What should she advise Emmie to do? Her instinct was that Florence should meet her son. She felt it would be a crime against both of them to deny them knowledge of each other. Yet she was so afraid of hurting Florence in any way. Lost in her thoughts she hadn't noticed that supper was ready and Emmie had started to lay the table. She called to Sarah to come and sit down and then produced a bottle of crisply chilled Chardonnay and poured two glasses. They sat at the kitchen table both wrapped in their own thoughts whilst they ate. After the meal, Emmie brought out the photograph album that she had put together and Sarah had a wonderful time looking through it. She recognised one or two people who Emmie couldn't place and gave them a name and identity.

'Photographs,' Sarah told Emmie, 'Were a wonderful record, once the subjects had been identified and named, they would stay alive for generations.' She supposed that her generation was the first to have photographic records of dead relatives. How technology had changed the way people lived during the eight decades of her life, trains, motor cars, aeroplanes, telephones, photography, the list was endless. She supposed that the next generation would have films of their families. Sometimes she felt that she had outlived her time.

They talked endlessly about Florence and her family and most particularly of Florence's living son. Neither of them had quite adjusted to the idea that they had a living relative who had been unknown to them for their respective lifetimes. They were both nervous about the impending introduction and discussed at length what they thought they should do. Emmie had only that morning received the photographs of Andrew that Paul had sent over from Canada. When Sarah had finished looking at the album, she handed them to her. Sarah gazed at them silently for some time before she spoke.

'Emmie, it's quite amazing, quite amazing. This man, Andrew, is the image of Martha's brothers and well, obviously Martha herself, but a male version. I find it quite uncanny. I knew them all very well you know. He doesn't seem to resemble his father facially in the photographs; however he may look completely different in the flesh. You know I do feel we are wrong to make any judgement about whether he should meet his mother. It's so unfair on him. It seems so, well, cosmetic somehow, making such an important decision and basing it on the way he looks. Yet how could we present Florence with a son she didn't even know existed who is the image of a man who raped her? It really is an impossible situation. Does this dear man fully understand the delicacy of the situation?'

'Well, Paul seems to think he does and I would trust his judgement completely.' Sarah cast a sharp glance at Emmie, but made no comment. She had noticed that Emmie seemed to hold this Paul in high regard and she had wondered if her feelings ran deeper than that, but she had enough to cope with at present and that could wait until later. She returned to the subject of Andrew Bailey.

'You know, Florence loved her uncles. If Mr. Bailey, Andrew, resembles them as closely as he appears to in the photograph then I feel somehow that this man is a gift sent from God. When Florence was raped it destroyed something good in her life. If she finds a son that she can love, well it would be a positive thing, something to give her peace, a gift of goodness born of evil, a balance to outweigh the injustice, who knows? Am I making any sense?'

Emmie nodded and smiled, she had been thinking along similar lines herself.

'I think what I am trying to say Emmie is that we have no right to play judge and jury. We now know that Florence has a son and she is entitled to know of that son's existence and meet him. She must be the one to make up her own mind. We must risk upsetting her, because we cannot keep the truth from her. That would be too cruel.'

Emmie agreed with Sarah and they continued to talk about Andrew until Sarah decided that she must go to bed and rest.

———⟨⟡⟩———

Paul and Andrew had flown in from Ottawa on the same evening that Sarah arrived from London. Emmie had arranged for Paul to take Andrew straight to her flat and settle him in, then the four of them, together with Katy, would meet and have lunch at Chestnut Lodge the following day, Tuesday, when they had all had time to rest and prepare themselves.

Tuesday dawned to find both Emmie and Sarah in a highly agitated state. Things were no better at Emmie's flat. Andrew had suddenly had an attack of nerves and was seriously wondering if he really was sane to go through with this meeting. He began to think that he was going to cause more harm and disruption to his real family, particularly his mother, than was morally acceptable. Paul quietly calmed him down and told him not to be so ridiculous. He couldn't come this far just to back out at the last minute. He kept quietly reassuring him, until it was time to leave.

As they approached Chestnut Lodge, Andrew asked Paul to stop for a moment while he absorbed the scene. The beautiful Georgian house set in its own grounds would, he supposed, in different circumstances, have been his family home. He would have lived in this elegant house and played in this lovely garden with his brother and sister. He thought it was so strange the way life tossed you around like a helpless cork bobbing on the sea. You were pulled this way and that by the currents until eventually you reached dry land. It was all so fragile and completely out of your control. However, he had no regrets, he had been lucky; his adopted Canadian parents had given him a wonderful childhood and he was grateful to them, but it could have been so different. He felt quite choked and had to struggle to control his emotions. It took him a few moments to collect himself and before he could talk to Paul, he was so moved. Eventually he asked, 'So is this the family home where my mother lived with her family?'

'Yes,' Paul answered, 'As far as I am aware this is where she spent the rest of her time after she was discharged from hospital.'

Andrew just gazed, 'I had good parents, I loved them dearly and they gave me a wonderful start in life, but when I look at this house I feel the strangest feeling of belonging. Something I have never truly felt before. I'm very grateful to you Paul for taking the time to find me and for giving me the opportunity to discover my roots. Forgive me for being over-emotional, but this is quite a difficult time for me. Come on, let's go in or we'll be late and I must create a good first impression!'

Sarah and Emmie had seen the car turn into the drive and stop. They thought for one horrible moment that Andrew had changed his mind, but then the car moved forward again and pulled up outside the front door where Emmie and Sarah were, by now, waiting to greet them. Katy as usual was late.

After the anxiety and drama it was all so easy. Sarah and Andrew greeted each other like the long lost relatives that they actually were. Their relationship was that of aunt and nephew and it was immediately obvious that they liked each other. Emmie felt an immediate rapport with this quiet, confident man, her new uncle. It was a pleasantly unique experience as he was the only uncle that she had ever known. Paul just quietly observed the happy scene, content in the knowledge that he had played a major part in making it happen. Andrew was such a likeable man; he was so straightforward and honest that he fitted into the family circle immediately, without causing so much as a ripple.

They all retired to the pale blue drawing room for drinks before lunch. Andrew seemed to absorb his surroundings like a thirsty man drinking his fill. Throughout the introductions, Sarah observed him very carefully, but she could see no obvious physical likeness to his father. She had to admit to herself that it was a terrific relief. It made her task so much easier. She felt that he must have inherited the very best of both parents. She had warmed to him immediately and she accepted him without question as Florence's son. Physically he resembled Martha and her family, but he also had an easy manner and great charm that reminded her of Florence herself

It was Sarah who brought up the delicate subject of whether or not it was wise for Andrew to meet Florence. Before they went into lunch she asked Emmie to bring in the photograph album that they had looked at the night before. It contained a family photograph of Martha, her parents and her brothers that she wanted Andrew to see. She found the photograph and then handed it to Andrew. He was visibly shocked.

'It's unbelievable, myself, me they all look like me. It's a very old photograph, but they are obviously relatives, but how are we related?' He looked to Sarah for an explanation. She told him they were his grandmother, Martha, Florence's mother, and her parents and most importantly Martha's brothers. Andrew was so like them it was uncanny; at times Sarah had to remind herself that he was not one of Martha's brothers.

Andrew looked up from the album and in spite of himself, spoke in a rather choked voice, 'You have no idea what this means to me, to find my family, but I promised Paul here that if you felt at any time, in any way that my very existence, or my meeting your mother would, in your opinion, bring back unhappy memories or disturb her peace, then I would be satisfied in simply finding and meeting my family. I would forgo any meeting with my mother if you felt it would upset her. I gave my word and I will abide by any decision that you make.'

It was Sarah who spoke first; she made it clear that she felt that Florence must know her son. He bore little or no resemblance to his father and she felt that meeting him would not upset Florence. She also apologised to Andrew for what she termed their gross insensitivity. She felt that they had been unjustly putting him through a vetting process. Emmie agreed with her. She stressed it was for the protection of Florence and they did not mean to insult him. He, in turn, admitted that it had been rather a shock to learn the circumstances of his conception and it took him some time to come to terms with it, in fact, he probably never would. But he fully understood their worries and their touching determination to protect Florence. At this highly charged moment the front doorbell rang, Katy had arrived, late as usual.

Lunch was a great success, everyone got along so well. Andrew was an intelligent and witty man and they were all drawn to him in their different ways. Sarah noticed that Paul and Emmie kept stealing surreptitious glances at one another and was rather pleased. She liked Paul immediately and hoped her instincts were correct. There was just one more hurdle to overcome and that was Freddie, he had to be told before Florence returned. Emmie was genuinely worried. He had already had a terrible shock accepting his mother's past. Their relationship was delicate and she was afraid he might be jealous of Andrew's very existence. Just as lunch was ending, the telephone rang. Its shrill ring cut the atmosphere like a knife. Emmie leapt from the table and ran into the hall to answer it. Everyone looked one to another. They all instinctively knew that it was Florence announcing her return.

Chapter Twenty Nine

Emmie, as soon as she heard her Grandmother's voice, transferred to the phone in the sitting room so she could talk privately with her. She knew her lunch guests would be able to cater for themselves and she could rely on Katy to serve coffee. She needed time and space to talk to her grandmother, 'Just one moment Gran, I'm going to change to the telephone in the sitting room then we can talk privately.'

'Alright sweetheart, have you got guests?'

'A house full Gran, I won't be a tick.'

Emmie moved into the sitting room and once she was settled she picked up the receiver and shouted for Katy to put the receiver down in the hall, 'Oh Gran, how lovely to hear from you, we've been a little worried about you, well Dad has anyway.

She heard her grandmother laugh, 'I knew he'd make a fuss, I hope he didn't think that we'd colluded against him.'

'No Gran, he realised that I was just as much in the dark as to your whereabouts as he was. Anyway where have you been?'

Her grandmother took a moment to answer and a gale of laughter came out of the dining room, 'Who've you got there Emmie, some of your friends?' Emmie felt a moment of panic, but just said calmly, 'Yes just Katy, a friend from school and her brother and some friends. I hope you don't mind.'

'Mind? Certainly not, I'm very grateful to you for minding the house. Emmie, you're not annoyed with me for taking off suddenly are you?'

'No Gran, not at all. I realised you needed time to yourself. Are you alright?

'I knew you'd understand Emmie, and yes, I'm absolutely fine. I'm at Elizabeth's; you know she's involved in an important project in the Orkney Islands? Well I knew it would be difficult for her to come and see me and I felt I ought to spend some time with her. I needed to explain properly to her just how little time I've got left. We've had a few lovely weeks together and I've been able to say my goodbyes. I tell you what though Emmie, it's pretty bleak up here. I have to be honest, I never really understood Elizabeth's interest in birds, but she loves her work and seems very happy.'

Emmie laughed, Gran and her daughter were so different. She often wondered just who Elizabeth was like. She loved her study of birds more than anything else and had never had any ambition to marry or have a family. She was a complete mystery to Gran and their relationship had always amused Emmie. She decided that she had to let her grandmother know that Sarah was in Liverpool.

'Sarah thought that's where you would be.'

'Sarah, you've seen Sarah?'

'Yes Gran, don't sound so surprised. I think you knew that I would. I've sorted out your box like you asked me to and I have to admit to doing a bit of detective work.' There was a slightly awkward pause.

'Gran I know everything. Oh love why didn't you tell me? Didn't you think I'd understand? You had a terrible time.'

'You know everything Emmie?'

'Yes Gran, everything, I wish you had told me years ago, but truly, I understand why you couldn't.'

'Does your father know?'

'Yes, I told him everything.'

'What did he say?'

'He was as upset as I was. We all love you and we can't bear to think of anything hurting you. We could hardly believe that you had survived such a traumatic time.'

There was another pause, 'I can't talk about it on the phone.'

'I know, love, I know, but you don't have to now do you? It's all accepted. It's all over.'

'Did your father blame me?'

'No, no, of course not love how could he? Who would? Only bigoted Victorians thought in that ridiculous way. When are you coming home? Sarah's here and we all want to see you; we have so much to tell you.'

'Tell me? Tell me what?'

'It'll keep Gran, just come home.'

'Oh I will, I've missed you all so much and I felt so guilty, leaving you to do my dirty work for me, but I couldn't do it Emmie.'

'Gran, I know, I understand and I really didn't mind. It's just made me love you all the more. Now come home!'

'Oh Emmie, I knew you'd understand. I'll catch the train down tomorrow afternoon. Can you meet me about three o'clock at Lime Street Station?'

'Yes of course. Love you, take care, and see you tomorrow.'

Then there was a loud click and her Grandmother was gone.

Emmie walked back into the dining room to face five expectant faces gazing in her direction, 'She's coming home tomorrow. She's been with Aunt Elizabeth in the Orkney Islands. She's researching some birds or something up there and Gran wanted to spend some time with her and explain about her illness…' Emmie's voice trailed off.

'I said that was where she'd gone.' said Sarah. 'Oh I can't wait to see her again.'

Then there was an awkward silence as everybody digested the fact that Florence was finally coming home. Seeing her again and explaining the existence of Andrew was not going to be easy. Everyone, for their own individual reasons, felt anxious about her return. Emmie, particularly, realised that she had to have another meeting with her father and it had to be that night. He had to be told about Andrew and if possible meet him, before her grandmother returned.

Freddie opened the door and peered out suspiciously. As Emmie stepped out of the gloom into the glow of the two coach lamps that lit either side of the front door, his face relaxed into a smile, 'Well this is a pleasant surprise you'd better come in. What are you doing here at this time of night? Why didn't you ring?'

'Hello to you too Dad,' said Emmie as she pecked him on his proffered cheek as she stepped into the hall, 'Is Mum in?'

'Yes, she's just got back from her bridge club.'

Freddie led the way through to the lounge, as he called it. His house was completely different from that of his mother's. It was very modern, architect designed and all plate glass and open spaces. Emmie always felt as though she were staying in a hotel on the rare occasions when she returned home for the night. It wasn't remotely like a home, but it was very chic and tasteful, in its way. It was typically Susan.

Her mother was sitting in one of a pair of white leather swivel chairs in front of a large colour television, which was all white and chrome and perched precariously on four spindly legs. Her father had obviously been sitting in the other one and they were having a night cap before retiring. Susan rose when Emmie entered the room and came over to greet her and give her a kiss, 'Well this is a pleasant surprise, but what brings you here so late?'

'I think we better all sit down, I've got something to tell you both and it's going to come as a shock, another shock I should say.'

Freddie and Susan looked at each other as they lowered themselves back into their seats and Freddie complained, 'What? No more Emmie, I don't think I could take any more shocks.'

'Sorry Dad, just one more, but it's important.'

To ease the tension, Freddie leapt up and offered Emmie a drink. She refused so he settled down in his seat again and he and Susan both concentrated their gaze on Emmie like expectant children.

'I don't really know where to begin, has Dad told you Mum, about Gran's experiences as a young woman?'

Susan nodded somewhat warily. 'Yes he has and it explains quite a lot don't you think? I can't criticise your grandmother, but, well it would have made her odd moods easier to understand if we had known.'

'I know, but she just couldn't talk about it. Anyway there's more to tell. Whilst investigating Gran's past I, or rather Katy, made a rather startling discovery.'

'What discovery?' questioned Freddie.

'We discovered that Gran had a son.'

'Yes, you told me, but you said he was still born.'

'I thought he was, but unknown to everyone, including Gran herself, she was expecting twin boys. One was still born, but the other one survived and was adopted. He was sent out to Canada.'

Freddie and Susan just stared at Emmie, barely comprehending what she had just said. Eventually Susan spoke, 'Is he still alive? I mean do we know anything about him?'

'Oh yes,' Emmie replied, 'Paul, Katy's brother traced him through the adoption agency in Ottawa, his name is Andrew Bailey, he's an orthopaedic surgeon and awfully nice and he is staying at my house now.'

Emmie barely stopped for breath as she blurted out the full story. Freddie and Susan sat with their whisky glasses suspended in mid air obviously wondering if they had heard correctly, 'What?' exclaimed Freddie, 'I have a half brother. Is that what you are telling me? I have a half brother who is Canadian and staying at your, well your grandmother's house, now, at the moment? Is that what you are saying?'

'Er yes, and Aunt Sarah is there too.'

'Oh good, well that makes it alright then. What do you expect me to say Emmie? How did you think I would react after all you told me the other day?'

'I'm sorry Dad; I know this must be a terrible shock. I didn't know how to tell you.'

'Does your Grandmother know anything about this?'

'No not yet.'

'Good God, this goes from bad to worse. What do you think she is going to say when she finds out? I need another drink.' He stood up and ambled towards the drinks cabinet, 'Will you get me one as well darling?' asked Susan with a slight note of hysteria in her voice.

'Is there anything else you haven't told me Emmie?' asked Freddie as he returned to his seat.

'No Dad, nothing'

'Are you sure?' Emmie nodded, 'I can't believe it, first the story of my poor mother's past and now an unknown, unheard of, unsuspected half brother. What's he like?'

'Really nice.'

'Is he…?'

'No, no, nothing like his father, he looks like Martha's brothers apparently, according to Sarah, that is. This is hard for him as well you know, Dad. Anyway we'd really like you to meet him tomorrow.'

'Oh would you indeed, well I suppose I will have to meet him before Mother does. Really Emmie what are you going to come up with next?'

'Nothing Dad, that's it, I promise. No more.'

Freddie looked at Susan for reassurance, but didn't receive any, 'I don't know why you're looking at me like that.' she retorted, sighing loudly, 'I'm as shocked as you are. Well I suppose we'll have to meet him. What time do you want us Emmie?'

'We thought about ten o'clock, at Chestnut Lodge.'

'You keep saying 'we', who are 'we' exactly? Susan asked.

'Oh, well me, obviously and Sarah and Andrew, your half brother, Katy Molyneux, from school and Paul, her brother.'

'Right,' said Susan, not understanding why these people were involved, but too tired and shocked to enquire any further.

'I am sorry this is such a flying visit I'm really sorry to

upset you like this, but what could I do?'

'Nothing love, it isn't your fault. In fact, all this must have been a strain on you. You get home and we'll see you tomorrow. Have you heard from Mother?'

'Yes, she's arriving home tomorrow afternoon. She's been with Aunt Elizabeth and her birds in the Orkney Islands.'

'I suppose I should have guessed that's where she went. I still don't know why she had to make such a mystery out of it. Come on dear, I'll see you out.' said Freddie rising from his chair ready to escort Emmie to the door. He helped her to her car, gave her a kiss goodbye and reassured her that they would be at Chestnut Lodge the following day. Looking bemused and shocked he turned and ambled back to the house and Susan. Emmie drove away in turmoil. She felt so guilty that she had rather thrown this news at them and then fled. Yet perhaps it was for the best. It would prevent Freddie from dwelling on it. And he had a tendency to dwell and expect the worst.

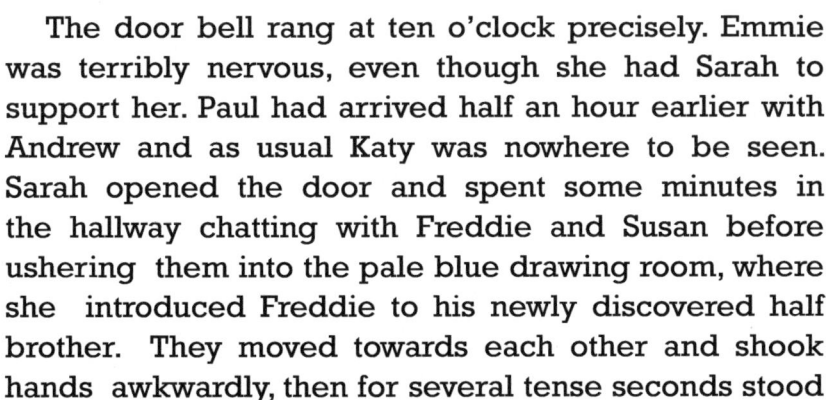

The door bell rang at ten o'clock precisely. Emmie was terribly nervous, even though she had Sarah to support her. Paul had arrived half an hour earlier with Andrew and as usual Katy was nowhere to be seen. Sarah opened the door and spent some minutes in the hallway chatting with Freddie and Susan before ushering them into the pale blue drawing room, where she introduced Freddie to his newly discovered half brother. They moved towards each other and shook hands awkwardly, then for several tense seconds stood looking at one another, not quite knowing what to do. Impulsively Andrew did a very Canadian thing and flung his arms around Freddie. They stood for some minutes in an emotional embrace, whilst everyone looked on in silence, rather taken aback. Eventually they pulled apart and examined each other. Physically they were of a similar build; both were tall and broad, but facially Freddie resembled Josiah and Andrew resembled Martha. However there was no mistaking that they were brothers.

It was Andrew, who eventually took the initiative. Freddie was completely paralysed by British reserve. He suggested that Freddie and he took a stroll around the garden together alone to catch up and get to know one another. A rather bemused Freddie agreed and they left by the French windows.

The remaining group busied themselves with pouring coffee and talking about anything but the relationship between Andrew and Freddie. Then the door bell rang, it heralded the arrival of Katy. She rushed in eager to know how the meeting between the two brothers had progressed, but everyone was waiting for them to reappear from the garden and couldn't really tell Katy anything. The atmosphere in the drawing room was quite tense as Sarah, Susan, Emmie, Paul and Katy waited for Andrew and Freddie to come back into the house. As Emmie knew from experience her father could be very judgemental and once he had taken a dislike to someone it was almost impossible to change his mind. It was crucial that he and Andrew liked each other. If there was any hint of animosity it would make it so difficult to integrate Andrew into the family.

Eventually the French windows opened and the

brothers stepped back into the drawing room. Emmie quietly sighed with relief. They were laughing and smiling and were still deep in conversation. It was quite obvious that they liked each other. Emmie thought it was uncanny that they seemed to have bonded immediately, especially as she knew how difficult Freddie could be to get to know. She felt that this bonding had a lot to do with Andrew's approach to Freddie. He was the older brother and was quite at ease with himself, Andrew seemed to supply the missing piece to the jigsaw that was Freddie's insecurity and it happened immediately. Sarah glanced over at Emmie and they exchanged a conspiratorial smile. They were both overwhelmingly relieved. If they had disliked each other it would have been a logistical nightmare and Freddie was unpredictable and insecure so both women had been worried about the outcome of the meeting.

What was even more amazing was that Andrew had charmed Susan. He instinctively knew that he needed her as an ally if he were to enjoy a close relationship with his brother, so he made a huge effort to flatter her and he paid her a great deal of attention. As everyone in the family knew, this was the direct route to Susan's heart, and she and Andrew became firm friends almost immediately.

Emmie had prepared a light buffet lunch in the kitchen and Freddie and Susan stayed to eat with them. Sarah had suggested that everyone left before Florence arrived, so that she wasn't overwhelmed. Emmie wanted her to be rested and calm before she confronted her with the news about her son. No one could predict how she would react and everyone was anxious. It would take time for her to absorb the fact that she had a son who she presumed had died sixty years ago. Everyone agreed that Emmie and Sarah should tell her when they were alone. About two o'clock everyone left. Andrew was going back to Freddie and Susan's for dinner and Paul and Katy were going home. Emmie saw her mother and father to the door with Andrew and then returned to the kitchen where Paul was just retrieving his coat. Katy had disappeared into the garden with Sarah. She was pleased to have a few moments alone with Paul. She wanted to thank him for all that he had done in finding Andrew and bringing him home. She started to tell him how grateful she was, but she didn't get the chance as soon as she started to speak he simply gathered her up in his arms and held her tight. She was momentarily stunned, but also delighted. Then he kissed her and said, 'Emmie, this is not the time or the place to discuss our future together, but when this difficult time has passed I want you and I to have a serious talk. I wanted to tell you that I have terminated my contract in Canada and I want you think carefully about our future together. I want to include you in my plans and I need to know if you feel the same about me as I do about you; quite simply and unexpectedly I have fallen in love with you.'

Emmie could hardly speak, 'I also love you Paul, I really do,' was all she could say and he smiled down at her before kissing her again. He released her as they heard Katy and Sarah returning from the garden, where Sarah had been picking some late autumn flowers for Katy's mother. As they entered the kitchen, they both noted Emmie's flushed cheeks and Paul's wide smile and they both drew their own happy conclusions. Katy and Paul left together, although they were in separate cars and Sarah and Emmie set about clearing the kitchen until it was time for Emmie to go and collect Florence from the station. Sarah was dying to find out what Paul had said to Emmie, but the latter was lost in her own thoughts and didn't seem to want to talk about him. However, Sarah could tell that something wonderful had occurred between them as Emmie was almost floating round the kitchen. She had to be satisfied with the evidence of her own eyes for the present. It had been decided that Emmie should collect Florence alone and meet Sarah back at the house. As the time to leave approached, Emmie dried her hands, took off her pinafore, collected her coat and handbag and kissed Sarah goodbye. She was terribly nervous, but knew she must not betray her nerves for her grandmother's sake.

Chapter Thirty

Florence knew that something was the matter as soon as she saw Emmie at the station. She was unnaturally tense. She went through the motions of greeting her grandmother and she listened politely on the journey home while Florence told her all about her visit, but she was distracted somehow. She wasn't really paying attention. Florence was a little distressed, and wondered if Emmie had been affected by what she had learned about her time in the asylum. Had it affected her relationship with her granddaughter? She hoped not.

She was pleased to see Sarah waiting at Chestnut Lodge, but it only served to heighten her anxiety. There was something the matter, but she couldn't think what it was. Now, sitting in the pale blue drawing room with Sarah and Emmie, she had found out. As soon as she had had something to eat and was rested, they told her as gently and as kindly as they could that she had a son who she had never met. She looked from Emmie to Sarah and back again hardly comprehending what she had been told yet somehow deep inside, she wasn't really surprised. She had always felt that something was missing, that something had been taken from her in the asylum and never been returned. Obviously she couldn't have known that her son had lived, it was more an intuitive feeling. She put it down to the fact that she was traumatised by her experience, but now that she had learned of Andrew's existence it made sense somehow. She was very pale, but quite controlled. Emmie didn't know what to do. She made a move to leave the sofa where she was sitting beside Sarah, and go to comfort Florence. However, Sarah caught her sleeve and gently prevented her from doing so. Sarah could see that Florence was having an immense struggle with her emotions and felt that it was best if she was left to work through them in her own way. It must have been a terrible shock to learn that she had given birth to a live son almost sixty years ago and had been completely unaware of his existence during the intervening years. It must have been an even greater shock to learn that people existed who were so immoral that they deliberately kept that knowledge from her. Florence closed her eyes and leaned back in her armchair. She stayed motionless, in that position, for some time, whilst Sarah and Emmie watched her anxiously.

Eventually Florence tried to speak, but her voice was strangled and unnatural. She asked Emmie to get her a glass of water, which she sipped at thoughtfully before speaking again, 'In all the years since I was discharged from the hospital I have never spoken about my confinement. Never. Not even to that wonderful psychiatrist, Dr. Cripps that Edward found to help me. I couldn't talk about it, I just couldn't. It was so harrowing, so distressing an experience that I think it actually scarred my mind.' Her voice was so quiet and choked with emotion that Emmie and Sarah had difficulty hearing her, but they kept very still and strained to hear. As Florence told of her experience tears started to flow down her cheeks, but she made no attempt to wipe them away. She almost seemed unaware of them as she struggled to give voice to the experiences of that painful time. The disclosure of the existence of her son seemed to trigger a release. It made it possible for her to revisit her confinement in the infirmary and to talk about it for the first time, 'My waters broke on the ward so they took me down to the infirmary for the confinement. It was a cold, dark, comfortless place and I was the only patient on the ward. I was absolutely terrified. They cleaned me up a little, gave me a fresh hospital nightgown and told me to get into bed and then they left me alone. I was so frightened. I did as I was told and lay silently in the icy, comfortless, hospital bed whilst trying to control the pain. I watched the shadows from the gas lights flicker across the ceiling, they seemed to be mocking me and I just lay there with tears streaming down my face. The pain was terrible, but I was afraid of crying out.

There was one elderly nurse in charge and she was assisted by a patient, who acted as an orderly. I lay there alone in the gloom for what seemed like hours. The pain was just bearable at first, but it soon increased to a level where I couldn't help but scream out. I knew nothing whatsoever about childbirth, other than a few very basic facts.' Florence paused for a moment and closed her eyes. 'It was very frightening; all I wanted was my mother. I felt an overwhelming need for her comforting voice and reassuring touch. I was already living in a nightmare, but this was unbearable. I was also confused; I couldn't understand why she had abandoned me. I thought that she may have been disgusted with me, like my father. It never occurred to me that she had no idea where I was, that she had been told that I was dead. I was in mental torture and physical agony all at the same time. The contractions kept tearing across my body, but I didn't get any assistance or pain relief, not even a kind word. The nurse came in from time to time to check on my progress, but she just told me to be quiet. She kept saying that girls like me got what they deserved and the least I could do was bear my suffering in silence. Like me! What sin did she think that I was guilty of? And who did she think she was, how dare she presume to judge me? She made me angry and the pain just sharpened my anger and removed all my fear and inhibitions. Just as during my nightmares, my voice returned with the pain and I screamed and swore at her in a way that shocked me. I didn't think I even knew such words. Anyway it shut her up and she left me alone, still in agony and still screaming, but feeling slightly vindicated.

The patient orderly came in occasionally and laid a damp cloth on my head. She tried to be kind, but she was afraid of the nurse. Any kindness that she showed me had to be hidden from her, but she did try to comfort me and I blessed her for it. She held my hand for a while, but then she had to go. I was in a blur of agony. I think that I passed out once or twice. I certainly thought that I would die. The nurse came back periodically to examine me. During one of these routine examinations I thought I heard her laugh and say, 'Well I never,' but everything was just a blur of pain.

Towards the end as the contractions became really strong, she stayed with me and tried to give me some help. She told me when to push. I screamed for some pain relief, but she wouldn't give me anything. I don't think that they did in those days and I'm not sure that she had anything to give me anyway. She continued to tell me to push and by now the contractions really were strong. The nurse called for the patient orderly to come back onto the ward and then she gave her a hurried list of instructions. She rushed off and came back with a trolley. It was cream and I remember that the wheels squeaked. It contained a couple of enamel bowls, together with some towels and medical instruments. Suddenly I felt a kind ripping followed by a feeling of release. It was as though something had left me and the contractions eased off for a while. It was such a relief. I felt as though I was going to die of exhaustion, then suddenly after a brief interval they started again. This time they were worse than ever. The patient and the nurse were messing about on the trolley with a bowl. I couldn't see clearly what they were doing, but there was something white on the trolley and there was a lot of blood. But then the pain of the contractions took over and I passed into a world of agony again. It seemed to go on for hours then I felt another dreadful ripping sensation and suddenly it was all over. The pain finally stopped. I was exhausted, but I heard my baby cry. It was quite wonderful, that cry, it made it all seem worthwhile.

When I had recovered a little I gestured to the nurse that I wanted to hold my baby. I was, you remember, completely dumb. The only time my voice returned was during the labour and apparently when I had nightmares.

The nurse just looked at me and said, 'It's still born; it's dead.' I didn't believe her, I shook my head, I'd heard the baby cry, I knew that it was alive. I was too weak to do anything, but I gestured frantically. Suddenly the nurse seemed to lose patience with me and thrust an enamel basin under my nose. There was a dead baby in it, I reached out to touch it and it was still warm. There was the undeniable proof, the baby was dead. It was a cruel, brutal way to convince me, but I realised it must be my baby. They couldn't have produced the body of a new born baby at will. They told me he was a boy and all I wanted to do was to hold his little body, but they wouldn't let me. Then I just wanted to die with him. Even in my distress I caught the patient looking at the nurse as if she hated her, a vicious look as though she could kill her, but she soon resumed her subservient expression when the nurse turned round.

I broke my heart after the confinement, I just cried for days. Apart from the ordeal of the birth, I now realise that my hormones were completely out of balance. I'm sure that I was suffering from post-natal depression on top of the natural grief of losing my son and the trauma of being confined to the asylum. I was in the depths of despair and I felt terribly ill. I was also running a high temperature so they kept me in the infirmary instead of sending me back to the ward.

The infirmary was cold and bleak, but it was hygienic. The nurse cleaned me up after the birth and I think she stitched me as well, but I was left in a terrible mess and suffered for years afterwards. Eventually I had to have an operation, later on in life, before I had my other children. Whilst I was in there, I was left entirely alone. Occasionally the patient orderly, who they left to nurse me, checked on me, but she never spoke to me. As I had lost my ability to speak on entering the asylum we communicated with smiles and nods. She was kind and gentle and I was grateful to her, as I was very ill for a long time. I don't really know how long. She even managed to find me some aspirin, which helped a little with the pain. But oh! What would I have given for my mother or you Sarah,' she nodded at Sarah and it was the first time Florence had acknowledged her or Emmie's presence. While she was telling her story she seemed to have gone back in time and completely re entered the world of the asylum.

She was silent for a while and then began to speak again, 'I can't really describe the pain I felt lying in that bed. I don't mean my body, although I was in a great deal of physical pain after the birth. It was my heart, it hurt physically; I was in such anguish. I had lost everything and everyone that I had ever loved. My father, who I had mistakenly considered cared for me, turned out to be a vicious sadist, my mother and all my friends had abandoned me, or so it seemed. But it would have been bearable if I could have had my baby, just for a few days. I knew that even if he had lived they would have taken him after a few weeks. You couldn't keep babies in there; they always took them from you and put them up for adoption. You had no say in the matter. But I would have known he was alive. I could have looked for him, maybe found him later, when I left the asylum. He's always been the missing link.'

She sat in silence again, reflecting that awful time as the tears poured down her face, unchecked and unnoticed. Sarah and Emmie just sat quietly; they didn't know what to do or say. Sarah was horrified that they had unleashed this torrent of emotion and reminded Florence of the hell of her confinement, yet something told her that it was necessary, that it was somehow cathartic, the last milestone on a long and painful journey. Eventually she looked up at them, 'I knew, inside I mean, I always knew that my baby had lived, I felt its life force, I heard its cry. I just knew it had been born alive, but then they showed me this dead baby. It was still warm. It must have been mine, where would they have got it from? It was dead, but I always knew something was wrong. I never thought about twins. It never occurred to me that there had been two babies; it never crossed my mind. How could they do that to me? Let me think that my baby had died? Why were they so cruel? Why did they lie? It is that that I can't understand. I had done nothing wrong, but they punished me. I had been attacked, abused and raped, I was an innocent girl, but still they blamed and punished me.' Again she went into herself. Sarah and Emmie were really beginning to feel terribly guilty that they had revived Florence's nightmare memories.

After a lengthy silence she suddenly started talking again, 'When I had Freddie and later Elizabeth, it bore no resemblance to my confinement in the asylum hospital. It was so different. I had them in a private nursing home.

I was loved and cared for; I was well looked after, kept warm, given pain relief and kindness. But I couldn't help looking back to that previous birth and thinking about my poor dead son. It was so strange, the feeling of joy I had when Freddie was born, the life force that I felt was the same as when I had my first child in the infirmary, exactly the same. I was sure, in a totally illogical way, that my son had lived, that somehow they had tricked me. However, I never spoke those thoughts out loud or they would have put me away again.'

It hurt Emmie to hear her Grandmother talk about being 'put away' again and she realised that it must have always been a subconscious fear of hers that she would do or say the wrong thing and find herself in the lunatic asylum again, but this time for ever. She felt Sarah gently nudge her and she finally went over to comfort her grandmother. Emmie knelt at the foot of Florence's chair, put her head in her lap and placed her arms gently around her waist. Florence, almost abstractedly, tenderly stroked her hair. Emmie felt such an overwhelming love for her grandmother that she just wanted to make her safe and happy and banish all those terrible memories, 'No one would ever have put you away again Gran, no one. Grandpa Edward wouldn't have allowed it. You have been quite safe since the death of your terrible father because everyone loves you. We were so afraid of telling you about Andrew. We were afraid it would make you ill again, because it would remind you of the attack.'

'Rape,' Florence corrected her as she placed her hands on Emmie's shoulders and gently pushed her away so that she could look straight into her eyes. Her face was still wet with her tears, but she was calmer as if she had purged some inner torment and both Emmie and Sarah felt relieved, 'My child was just that, Emmie, my child. Once I had accepted that I was pregnant I forgot about that man who raped me. The child was mine. I grew to love it as my pregnancy progressed and I was devastated when it died.' She looked over the top of Emmie's head at Sarah, 'Can you both understand that? Do you understand what a wonderful gift you have both given me? You have returned my lost child to me. I always new, somehow, that he wasn't dead.

Florence was slowly recovering from the effects of the turbulence of the emotions that had engulfed her as she recalled and described the terrible weeks of her confinement. She looked first at Emmie and then at Sarah, 'I knew, I absolutely knew in my heart that he was alive, but the evidence against that fact was overwhelming. Then I come home to this fantastic, extraordinary, unbelievable news that you Emmie, have discovered that I was right, my feelings were true, my instincts sound. My son was alive at birth, but not only have you confirmed that, you have actually found him. I cannot believe that you have found him. I wish you could share my deep feeling of joy; my feeling of completion, yet those feelings are still tinged with fear. It's a fear that Andrew will disappear before I have time to meet him, or that he will reject me. But I have found him, I know he is alive and through that knowledge, I have gained my revenge on them all.' Emmie hugged her harder.

Florence was much calmer now and she reached to the side table for a tissue, 'I'm sorry to have been so dramatic,' she pulled a wry face, 'Not very British, but I had to tell the story of my confinement and obliterate that memory, because I don't need it any more, not now that I have found my son. I can't believe I am really going to meet him, my son, I am finally going to meet my son.' She shook her head in wonderment then kissed the top of Emmie's head.

'When can I meet him? What's he like?' she asked tentatively, 'Is he like Freddie?' She looked down at Emmie and over at Sarah, who was the first to reply, 'Yes and no, you can tell that they are brothers, but Andrew resembles Martha's side of the family. He looks like your mother's brothers. He is a lovely man, just as they were.'

Florence smiled gently and asked again, 'When can I meet him?' This time Emmie replied, 'Tomorrow Gran, if you feel well enough to cope with the stress. We didn't know what to do for the best.'

'I suppose after nearly sixty years I can wait for a few more hours. Also I want to be composed, to look my best and I am afraid. What if he rejects me? What if he blames me for abandoning him?'

This was such an absurd idea that Emmie and Sarah nearly laughed, but they could see that Florence was genuinely afraid of rejection. Sarah spoke for both of them, 'Florence, I have only met him briefly, but I am sure that there is no likelihood that he would reject you. He is as anxious to meet you, as you are to meet him!'

The three women talked for some time longer. Then eventually, quite exhausted, they reluctantly collected their belongings and went to bed.

Chapter Thirty One

It had been decided that Florence would meet Andrew the following morning at Chestnut Lodge. The hours before the meeting between them were charged with emotion. Florence wanted to look her best and she and Sarah went through every outfit in her wardrobe. Sarah was touched by Florence's excitement and anticipation. She was like a young girl planning her first date. Finally she decided on a pale blue suit and matched it with a cream blouse. Emmie did her hair and finally she was ready to meet Andrew.

Emmie had arranged for Paul to bring Andrew over to Chestnut Lodge at ten o'clock. They both felt that it would be easier for Florence to meet Andrew on home ground. She had decided that she would like to greet him in the pale blue drawing room. It was a room where all the major dramas of her life had been played out, Edward had proposed in there, she had celebrated her anniversaries and the children's birthdays in that room and it seemed appropriate that she should meet her son, Andrew, in the family drawing room. It had been decided that Sarah and Emmie would stay with Florence and together with Paul they were the only people who would witness the reconciliation. Freddie and the rest of the family had been invited for lunch. Florence sat tensely with Sarah and Emmie and at ten o'clock precisely the door bell rang. Everyone jumped and then they smiled at themselves. Emmie answered the door and ushered Paul and Andrew into the room. Andrew, with his normal Canadian informality just walked straight over to Florence and she held out her hands to him, neither of them could speak, they were both so emotional. He took her hands and gently raised her to her feet. They just gazed at one another. Sarah, Paul and Emmie silently and tactfully withdrew to the kitchen.

Florence and Andrew stayed together in the pale blue drawing room for some time. Later Florence told Emmie it was just so easy to talk to him. There was no awkwardness between them. She felt as though she had always known him and that he had been away for a long time and had come back. They just talked and talked as if they were catching up on each other's news after a long absence. Occasionally they were overcome with emotion and hugged and cried then they started talking again. Florence confided in Emmie that she felt, because she hadn't voluntarily given Andrew away and was actually unaware of his existence that there were no feelings of guilt or recrimination to spoil the meeting. There was no underlying resentment on Andrew's part or regret on Florence's part that might have marred their discovery of each other. She said it was a joyous meeting and he was exactly as she would have imagined him to be.

Eventually, Florence and Andrew emerged from the pale blue drawing room glowing with happiness and joined the others in the kitchen. They all felt rather foolish that they imagined that Florence might have been upset at the discovery that she had a son she knew nothing about. She was so ecstatic at having found him that Emmie actually experienced a slight pang of jealousy, but it soon passed.

Freddie and Susan joined the party at twelve and Florence dispatched Emmie to the boot room. There were two bottles of vintage champagne in there that Florence had been saving for the right occasion. She imagined that it might be Emmie's engagement or a christening, but this was the most apt occasion that she could imagine. Whilst Emmie was gone, Sarah laid the champagne flutes out on the kitchen table. In the boot room Emmie switched on the 60 watt bulb, in order to find the bottles and her eye caught sight of the tin box nestling under the bench. How its secrets once released had changed the fortunes of her family. It was quite amazing, like Pandora's box, the tin box had initially revealed to Emmie all the sins, crimes and heartbreak of the past, but she was left with hope and hope was what was found at the bottom of Pandora's box and it saved the world. Hope is also what had sustained Florence for sixty years and she too had been rewarded. Emmie smiled to herself, she was delighted at the outcome and could never have guessed that tidying out an old will box would have led to the discovery of a lost son. She turned off the light, making a mental note to replace the sixty watt bulb and carefully cradling the precious bottles, made her way back to the kitchen. On her return Freddie opened them and poured the sparkling liquid before he proposed a toast to his newly discovered brother and his wonderful mother.

Emmie had been slightly concerned that her father might feel excluded once Florence and Andrew had been reconciled, but his earlier rapport with him was as strong as ever and rather than being excluded it seemed that Andrew had bound the three of them together. Freddie's relationship with his mother was stronger that it had ever been. So happy did the three of them seem that it was Susan who felt quite excluded and Freddie had to fuss her back into the family circle. However, Andrew continued to work his charm on Susan and she was soon joining in the general happiness. Florence, in spite of her illness, looked wonderful and simply glowed with happiness. When they had drunk their champagne they went into the dining room and Emmie served a casserole that she had prepared earlier. It was a wonderful, informal lunch. Florence had Freddie on one side and Andrew on the other and she just looked from one to the other with a wondering smile throughout the meal. Emmie sat and watched her grandmother with a deep feeling of contentment. She had never seen her look so relaxed and so obviously happy. In the past she a ways seemed to have been haunted by a feeling of sadness. Obviously, Emmie had never understood what caused that sadness; she was just aware of it. But it had gone. Andrew was the missing link that completed the chain. She felt Paul's eyes on her and she looked up to meet his gaze. He smiled and quietly lifted his wine glass to toast her; she smiled and responded to his toast. Both Florence and Sarah noticed and they exchanged a conspiratorial look. Today was Florence and Andrew's day, so Emmie and Paul had to wait before they seriously considered their own position, but she thought that she really couldn't be happier.

During lunch Freddie suggested that Andrew should move into Chestnut Lodge and stay with Florence. Both Andrew and Florence thought it was a wonderful idea. Emmie was relieved. She would be returning to her flat now that Florence was back and she felt that she couldn't suggest that Andrew take her place in case the idea upset Freddie. She was always aware that she had to consider her father's feelings. However, she needn't have worried and was amazed when Freddie suggested the move. He was thrilled to have found a brother. Elizabeth and he had never been close, they were so different. He had been a sensitive child whereas she had been completely self sufficient. In contrast, he felt he could relate to Andrew, who was also sensitive and they had a great deal in common.

Emmie studied Andrew closely through lunch. She thought he was a delightful man; it was almost as though God were compensating Florence and the family for having been cheated of his presence during the intervening years. He was almost too good to be true and he reminded her of the Martha that she had come to know through her journals. She, like Andrew, spread happiness and put everyone at their ease. Her great misfortune was to have met Josiah, who never appreciated her goodness. Andrew's delight at having found his family was obvious. He joked and laughed all through lunch and kept patting Florence's hand, just to reassure himself that she was still there. Whilst she was watching Andrew interact with Freddie and Florence, she was fully aware of Paul's presence. She still couldn't believe that he had told her that he loved her. Things had moved at such a frantic pace over the last few weeks that her head was whirling. They would have time to talk now that the problem of introducing Florence to Andrew had been overcome. It was like a fairy tale, false imprisonment, lost loves and missing sons, but hopefully they would, if only for a while, live happily ever after. There was a cloud on the horizon, Florence's imminent death, but at least she would die happy, completely reconciled with her family.

Even in the midst of her own happiness, Florence saw what was developing between Paul and Emmie.

Both she and Sarah had noticed the furtive glances and shy smiles that passed between them and they were delighted. He was the sort of man that she had hoped Emmie would meet. Florence had not felt this light hearted joy since she was a teenager. The happy, carefree years of her youth were obliterated by the assault in the Sunday School hall. Since then she had known happiness, but there had always been a feeling of sadness and loss deep inside her and it had overwhelmed her at times. She had always thought it was as a result of her experience in the asylum, but now she recognised it as a feeling of loss, the loss of her child. She looked over at Andrew. He was all that she could have hoped for. He was kind, sensitive and intelligent. In the pale blue drawing room that morning they had discussed his upbringing in Canada. He had good adoptive parents and she was relieved to hear that he had been well cared for. He had only had time to give her a brief outline of his life, but they had weeks, maybe months, to remedy that. She looked at Freddie, he seemed so relaxed and at ease with Andrew. The only two things that marred her happiness were that Edward was not there to share it with her and the guilt she felt about her dead son, but today was a day for happiness and resolution. She had grieved for her dead son for sixty years. It was time to put him to rest.

Sarah sat and surveyed the joyous scene. She felt the loss of Charles quite keenly in this happy group. Also it would have been lovely if her brother Edward could have been there, but she thought that it may have been difficult for him to accept Andrew. Florence was radiant. How could she and Emmie have ever doubted that they should tell her about her lost son? Paul and Emmie's happiness hadn't escaped her either. Their's was a blossoming romance, but Sarah felt confident that it would endure. She would miss Florence, but she felt that she could let her go now. Florence's harrowing story finally had a resolution. Her much loved son, Freddie, now knew the whole truth about her past and had not only accepted it, but seemed to embrace it. Freddie and Andrew had bonded in a wonderful way, she had said her goodbyes to Elizabeth, she had been reconciled with her lost son and now it looked as though she would live to see Emmie settled, maybe even married. Suddenly her thoughts were interrupted by the peal of the doorbell. It was Katy. She was full of apologies for being late; she had been called into the hospital on an emergency. Once she was settled at the lunch table she was the hero of the hour. If she hadn't gone delving into the archives in order to help Emmie, no one would have known of Andrew's existence. Katy basked in their praise, whilst making self deprecating noises. She was secretly delighted at the outcome. The reason that she enjoyed her work as a social worker, was because sometimes she could make a real difference to people's lives and bring them happiness.

Florence suddenly started, as if she'd remembered something.

'Emmie?'

'Yes Gran?'

'When you sorted out the tin box did you find a little leather pouch in it?'

'Oh yes Gran, I'd quite forgotten!'

'Go and get it will you?'

Emmie went to her grandmother's bureau, unlocked it, retrieved the little parcel of jewellery and brought it back to the dining room. She handed the parcel to Florence, who carefully unfolded the soft cloth and laid out all the pieces on the table cloth. There were two pairs of gold earrings, a locket, a cameo brooch, a diamond pendant and matching ring and a wedding ring, just as Emmie had found them. She looked round the table.

'These were my mother's things. I couldn't bear to wear them when she died so I put them in the deed box. I had forgotten all about them, but now I have a use for them.'

She picked up a pair of gold earrings and passed them to Katy, she then passed the other pair to Susan, the cameo she handed to Sarah and the rest she wrapped up in the cloth and passed to Emmie. The four women sat holding the various pieces of jewellery not quite sure what to do.

'I want you all to accept these pieces as my gift, my thank you for all you have done to reconcile Andrew and me. It is a small expression of my gratitude and can't repay what I really owe, but I'm sure Martha, my mother, would have wished her jewellery to have been used in this way.'

All the women mumbled that it wasn't necessary, (including Susan, who Florence had tactfully included, but who had actually taken no part in the quest) but they were all clearly touched and voiced their thanks. Emmie stood up and walked round the table to give her grandmother a kiss and hug on everyone's behalf. As she walked back to her place at the table she thought, 'What a fitting finale to my quest, now everything in the box has been neatly sorted, identified and allocated and the past has finally been laid to rest.'

As Freddie suggested, Andrew moved into Chestnut Lodge. He and his newly found mother got to know each other very well during those last months of her life. She lived for another twelve months. Emmie and Paul got engaged and married during that time. They brought the wedding forward because Emmie desperately wanted her grandmother at the service. Florence's joy at witnessing Emmie's happiness, together with her delight at exploring her new relationship with Andrew seemed to give her a new lease of life and she was quite well until the last few weeks before she died. As her condition deteriorated her family took turns in nursing her. They kept her at home and engaged the services of a specialist nurse. Florence was well looked after and her pain was tightly controlled. She died peacefully one late autumn morning in the little pink drawing room surrounded by all her family.

Andrew sold his property in Canada, retaining only a simple cottage on one of the lakes in the Gatineau Park for holidays. He bought a small Georgian lodge near to his brother, Freddie, and settled into a life with his new family. Susan was in her element trying to match make and find him a new wife and he happily went along with all her plans. However, he was quite content just to be close to his newly discovered family. He would thank God for the rest of his life that he found his mother and had sufficient time to get to know her properly. Whilst he had loved his adopted mother and father and was thankful to them for giving him a loving and secure childhood, his love for his real mother was overwhelming. He enjoyed his final months with her and it made him feel somehow complete. As long as he lived, he never forgot the words with which she greeted him on the morning of their first meeting, 'Hello Andrew, welcome home, I've been waiting for you all my life.'

blurb.com